JETHRO WADED OUT OF THE POOL AND INTO shallower water. He lifted his arms and raised his face to the sky. With his eyes closed, he began to chant a prayer. He did not notice the sudden calm, nor did he see the oddly swirling, greenish blotches that tinted the clouds just above him.

He had just finished his prayer when the twister touched down just behind him. He felt himself tumbling over, a wall of water crushing him down into the mud and sand of the streambed. His breath escaped, pounded from his lungs. He rolled and flipped; all was a rumbling blur. He saw his own body suspended in air, with swirling walls of mist and spray all around him, turning him over and over again. He suddenly descended, the ground rising to meet him, roaring toward him through sheets of water . . .

ALSO BY EARL MURRAY
Available from Tor Books:

HIGH FREEDOM

EARL MURRAY

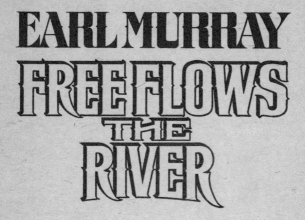

FREE FLOWS THE RIVER

TOR

A TOM DOHERTY ASSOCIATES BOOK
NEW YORK

This is a work of fiction. All the characters and events portrayed in this book are fictitious, and any resemblance to real people or events is purely coincidental.

FREE FLOWS THE RIVER

Copyright © 1991 by Earl Murray

A Tor Book
Published by Tom Doherty Associates, Inc.
49 West 24th Street
New York, N.Y. 10010

ISBN: 0-812-51102-6

First edition: May 1991

Printed in the United States of America

0 9 8 7 6 5 4 3 2 1

Again, to my mother, Viola L. Murray,
and to my father, Ray A. Murray.
Thanks for your love and support.

PART ONE

Spring–Summer
1849

ONE

THE SUN DESCENDED THROUGH A DARKENING afternoon sky. The deep blue suddenly filled with thick clouds, and water splattered heavily in big droplets against the Crow lodges nestled in the early summer grass along the valley of the Elk River, now called Yellowstone by Long Knife traders. Camp fires hissed and drove fearful villagers into their lodges. Small boys scurried back from the hills above camp, clutching their first bows and arrows. Women digging roots closed the flaps on their elkfoot bags, frowning at the specter of dark sky.

The rain came in gusts, highlighted by streaks of jagged light. The boiling clouds scared the very old, for they saw in them the portent of change. They pointed bony fingers and held their hands over their mouths, for just a short distance from

3

the village, a thin black spout dropped from the sky and touched the earth, then jerked back up into the swirling mass overhead.

A giant spirit danced a black song of death.

At the mouth of a small stream upriver from camp, Jethro Thompson emerged from a sweat lodge and felt the cool rush of moisture against his heated, naked body. He had not seen the funnel, nor could he hear the shouting villagers in the distance. He heard nothing but the slapping of leaves and the groaning of tree limbs overhead.

It was a good sign to Jethro, the strength of the storm. It would aid him on his journey. He filled his lungs with deep breaths as he approached the stream's bank. An entire day drenched in sacred smoke and steam had prepared him for his first quest for power. Although half white, Jethro would be looked up to and considered great in the Crow nation, a leader within the band called Kicked-in-Their-Bellies.

Jethro Thompson, like his father before him, was to become a special warrior. Thane Thompson had been one of William Ashley's men who came upriver in the summer of 1824 to trap beaver. Thane and a few others had settled among the Crow people and been accepted by them as their own. He had lived through a savage encounter with a grizzly and had been given the name of Bear Man. After leading the Crow into battle several times, Thane Thompson had become one of the most honored of warriors.

4

Now a living legend, his name had spread throughout the mountains.

The journey to gain honor and power was something Jethro wanted to do for his father as much as for himself. With his twenty-second winter just behind him, Jethro knew that he must carry his father's tradition forward and bring honor to his family. In the custom of his mother's people, he would seek power from Mother Earth and Father Sky, and the strong animals that knew the ways of the land. He hoped to have a medicine dream, within which he would receive a message and be given the strength of one or more of these animals. He would know their spirits and learn from them; they would become his protectors and his source of power throughout his life.

He would seek his vision among the high peaks of the Beartooth, the mountains to the south and west. He would take no food or water with him, and he would wear only a breechclout. Although winter's breath would still blast the high plateau, he would gain his warmth from within—warmth from those whom the old people had told him would be his protectors, if he really believed his mission to be sacred.

Jethro carried a long-stemmed pipe in the crook of his right arm: the Sacred Pipe of the Kicked-in-Their-Bellies, loaned to him for his journey by a village medicine man named Bull Comes Ahead, one of the strongest spiritual leaders of the entire Crow nation. Bull Comes Ahead was the present Father and keeper of the pipe.

The offering of the Sacred Pipe to Jethro for

his journey was an omen to the people. It meant that Bull Comes Ahead thought Jethro to have strong connections to the Powers, to be special enough to possibly become a great spiritual leader as well as a warrior. "The pipe spoke to me in a dream," Jethro remembered Bull Comes Ahead telling him. "The pipe told me there would some day be another Father to pass the pipe on to, and that this man's son would be a special person among the people. That man is Thane, your father, and that special person is you."

Jethro had prepared diligently for his journey. His time spent in the sweat lodge had cleansed him, had brought his mind into the world where dreams are made and where the Powers live and speak. He could not know when his vision would come, or even if it would come. He could only journey to the top of the mountains with the pipe and do that which he was directed to do from within. He must then wait for what might happen.

Heavy thunder rolled overhead, and the rain fell harder. Jethro laid the pipe upon a tuft of grass at the water's edge, and with his eyes closed, raised his face to the sky as he entered the stream. He did not see the formation of eerie clouds surging and swirling in the sky just overhead. He thought of nothing but his mission.

He immersed himself in a large pool at the base of the bank and gasped. The current ran deep enough to come to the shoulders of his six-foot frame. Refreshed, he wiped water from his face and breathed deeply. He noticed a change in the air, the strong odor that came with lightning and thunder, the odor of power from above. His skin tingled.

From his left Jethro heard the gravelly cawing of ravens as they appeared just overhead, borne on the wind. Four of them banked from the flock and swooped down toward him as if to land, but rose away at the last moment and were carried over the treetops by the storm.

Jethro stared after them. He forgot about his tingling skin and the heavy ozone in the air, for the birds were an omen. He knew without question that they had come to usher him into the world of the unknown, the unseen. As a boy, he had raised more than one pet raven and had come to know their place within the Great Mystery of life. It was the raven that brought the magic of change, be it for good or for bad.

This event also told him that he would certainly be honored as a member of the Raven Society before another winter passed. As one of the more prominent of the warriors' clubs, the Ravens had sent many into battle who had brought honor to the people. The club competed with the Kit-Foxes and the Lumpwoods for the most honors, and Jethro anticipated with anxiety his becoming a warrior. Since the time he was a small boy, he had wanted to be a member of this exclusive group. The appearance of the birds now told him that he would soon learn what it meant to be tried as a man and as a warrior.

Jethro turned back toward the sweat lodge and waded out of the pool and into shallower water. He lifted his arms and again raised his face to the sky. With his eyes closed, he began to chant a prayer. He did not notice the sudden calm, nor did he see the oddly swirling, greenish blotches that tinted the clouds just above him.

He had finished his prayer and was looking at the Sacred Pipe when the funnel touched down directly behind him. He felt himself tumbling over, a wall of water crushing him down into the mud and sand of the streambed. His breath escaped, pounded from his lungs. He rolled and flipped; all was a rumbling blur. He felt as if the water were pouring through him, as if his body were porous, like the nets of vine that the Indians of the rivers to the west used for catching fish.

He was totally helpless; his mind and body seemed separate units. He saw himself suspended in air, with swirling walls of mist and spray enveloping him, turning him over and over. Then he suddenly descended, the ground rising to meet him, roaring toward him through sheets of water. He felt the grit of soil against his flesh and the harsh scraping of wood and stone, agony from head to foot.

Although it took but a moment in time, to Jethro it seemed an eternity. Suddenly it was over. The roaring was gone.

Coughing and spitting, Jethro discovered himself in a tangle of brush at the edge of the water. With no idea of what had struck him, he lay with his back arched, his lungs heaving, rain pouring from the sky into his open mouth. He turned on his side and coughed, breathing heavily once again. Pain coursed through his entire body. He waited, not wanting to move until he knew for certain whether or not he would cross over to be with the ancestors.

The pain subsided and his mind grew clearer, convincing him that he was not dying. He moved his aching arms and legs slowly. He realized that he had no broken bones or serious internal injuries, but his right knee hurt badly; it was already beginning to swell. He could move the joint, but not without considerable pain.

Still dazed, he finally struggled to his feet. He put weight on the knee and found that he could barely support himself. He could manage, though, for he knew the code of a Crow warrior: if a man could walk and could mount a horse, he could carry on his life in a normal fashion. Jethro felt lucky that he had not crossed over.

He looked to the sky. The sun was lowering over the horizon and the clouds were beginning to part overhead. Intermittent sheets of rain poured over him, thinning the coating of mud that covered his body, soothing the tingles and scratches left by wild rose and plum. Here and there, lines of blood trailed with the water.

He realized that he had been attacked by a huge dark spirit of the kind that roamed the clouds to the east, in the land of their enemies, the Lakota Sioux. Smaller whirlwinds—little dust spirits—were common near the mountains during the warm moons, but the long and twisting monsters rarely descended here.

As his mind grew steadily clearer, Jethro realized with sudden anxiety that the Sacred Pipe was missing. It was not on the bank where he had placed it, nor was it anywhere nearby. Limping, he combed the riverbank, pushing his way through tangles of brush, separating the thick growth, probing the ground underneath for the feel of the pipe. He pushed away the pain in his knee as best he could, as well as the now continuous sting of his numerous cuts and bruises; this was much more important. With the sun going down, he had little time left in which to find the pipe.

He limped back to the sweat lodge—untouched by the storm—and got his breechclout. Then, out from the trees a way, he turned in a slow circle, hoping to glimpse the pipe lying somewhere in the open. He saw nothing but shadowed sage and drenched grass. The pipe had seemingly disappeared. Had the giant spirit snatched it up and taken it away forever?

Jethro returned to the streambank and once again searched frantically. Losing the pipe, storm or not, worried him a great deal. The pipe belonged to the people; it was their life's blood. Sacred ceremonies for the renewal of life centered around the Sacred Pipe and the smoke it sent upward, calling First Maker to hear the prayers of the people. If he did not find it, bad fortune would descend not only upon himself, but upon the entire Crow nation. And it would certainly mean that his quest for a power animal would be difficult, if not impossible, to fulfill.

This journey held the key to his becoming a man. He could not hope to become a warrior unless he had a spirit helper. Going into battle would be suicide without the aid of the unseen. He could not hope for glory or honor, or for special induction into the Raven Society. The life forces surrounding an honored warrior would never come to him without a successful vision quest.

Jethro finally realized that he would not find the pipe. The giant spirit had it. He thought about returning to the village and telling Bull Comes Ahead what had happened. Surely the medicine man would understand and would know what to do. He sat down on a fallen log near the stream, his head in his hands. Was this the end of his journey? No, he must not let this stop him. He must go ahead with his plans, with or without the pipe. If he let the giant spirit win, other spirits would come whenever they wanted to, just to keep him from gaining power.

Jethro had been preparing for his mission from the very day the river had opened up and the ice had cracked and popped under the warming winds and the strain of the current. He had been off by himself often and had said many prayers. He could not wait any longer now; he would go into the mountains.

Jethro rose, limped into the stream and washed the rest of the mud and grit from his body. The current numbed his knee and he tried not to think of the injury. He stepped out again to examine his other wounds, including the many scratches caused by the wild rose and plum he had tumbled through. Although some of them were long and ugly, they were not deep enough to require sinew stitches.

As he turned toward the mountains, his eyes caught movement just to one side of him. The

11

figure of a boy emerged from the brush, his arms raised to present him with the Sacred Pipe.

Jethro felt a surge of relief flood through him.

"I found this," the boy said. "As I came out to see you, it was lying in my path."

It was Little Bow, Jethro's only nephew. His hair soaked and matted against his head, he stared up at Jethro through large black eyes.

Jethro accepted the pipe. It had not been damaged. "I thank you a great deal, Little Bow," he said. "I was worried. You have helped me greatly."

"I don't know if I should be here," the boy said. "I saw the giant black spirit come down. I came because I was worried. Will my coming bring other bad things to you?"

"Nothing more will happen," Jethro assured him. "You have nothing to fear."

Jethro was not surprised to see his nephew. In fact, he would have been disappointed if Little Bow had not shown up. The boy had been talking to him for days about the upcoming journey to find the medicine animal and had hoped to see him before he left. Jethro thanked the Powers that Little Bow had become worried enough to come out from the village.

Little Bow, who had just seen his eighth winter, had already surpassed the other boys his age in learning the ways of a warrior. The people held no doubt that Little Bow would some day become a great leader among them. Early he had learned to read the signs of the land and to know when game or danger were near. He had a keen ear for animal sounds and signals, especially for those of birds, and had learned to imitate many of them.

"Did you tell your mother you were coming out here to see me?" Jethro asked.

"I did not have time to tell her where I was going," Little Bow confessed. "When I go back, I will tell her I was with you. She will understand."

Jethro was not certain of that. Little Bow's mother was his older sister, Rosebud. She had lost her husband, Turtle, in battle with the Lakota Sioux. Shortly after that she had lost her firstborn, a boy named Eli after an old fur trapper, in a drowning accident. Still without a husband, Rosebud had been overprotective of her only remaining child. Rivers, and water in general, made her tremble. There was no doubt in Jethro's mind that she would be very worried if Little Bow did not return soon.

"I see that the giant spirit hurt your leg," Little Bow said. "And you are scratched and bruised. Will the spirit come back after you?"

"The spirit has traveled far away into the sky," Jethro said. "You don't have to worry."

"Are you afraid?"

Jethro considered the question, knowing that he must give his nephew the most honest answer he could. Gaining personal power was not something to be taken lightly.

"It is true, I do have fears to face," he told the boy. "As a person grows from childhood into an adult, there are changes in his life that come about. There is no one who doesn't have something deep within that he does not wish to see.

13

Since I am seeking personal power to guide me through life, I must now face those things I do not feel comfortable with. I must get to know them as a part of myself, so I can learn to accept who I am and where I am going."

"I know who you are," Little Bow said quickly. "You are a strong and brave man. I know this. You are the best teacher and protector anyone could ask for."

"I am glad you feel this way," Jethro said, appreciating the boy's sincerity. "Now I must leave on my journey, and you should return to the village."

"Please, can I talk with you first?" Little Bow pleaded. "There is something you must know."

"I told you, the giant angry spirit is gone."

"It is not the spirit, I don't think. I don't know what I saw."

"What you saw?" Jethro asked.

Little Bow's large eyes suddenly filled with tears.

"You really are afraid for me, aren't you?" Jethro observed. "What is troubling you so?"

Little Bow buried his face in his hands. "I don't want you to go."

Jethro sat down on the bank, groaning as he extended his injured knee and folded the other leg beneath him. He drew Little Bow down beside him, concerned with the urgency in his nephew's voice.

"What is this you speak of having seen?"

"I don't want to be afraid for you, but I am," Little Bow said.

"I am protected," Jethro assured him. "I am

going on my journey with a good heart, and I am seeking truth. I am open to the good that will come to me. You need not worry about me. I will return."

"I know you will return," Little Bow said, gripping Jethro's hand. "I just don't want you to be hurt."

"Hurt? Why do you fear so much for me?"

"I saw something in a dream, something that I didn't like," Little Bow explained. "It was coming for you. It wasn't the big spirit, either. It was something else."

Jethro knew from stories told by the elders that the strongest warriors always received difficult tests during their quest for power. Often these tests brought them into death and back. Jethro felt that he had been as close to death as he could be without crossing over. But maybe he would have to come even closer before his journey was ended.

He took a deep breath and looked into his nephew's eyes. "Tell me about your dream," he prompted.

Little Bow frowned in concentration. "I saw a man on a hill carrying a pipe, a great big pipe. It looked so big in his hands." He spanned his own hands out. "I know that the pipe was special and that the man I saw was you. There were horses running around you in a circle, white ones and black ones, and they were shaking their heads. Then two of them fell, one white and one black, and something that looked bad came into the circle where they had fallen. This bad thing changed the whole dream."

"What did this bad thing look like?" Jethro asked.

Little Bow was frowning even harder now. "It looked like a very big and tall badger. But it had horns and red eyes, and there were jagged stripes across its front. It made me very afraid. It was going toward you, but not very fast. And it would stop and jump around. There were other strange-looking animals that came through the circle where the horses used to be, but I couldn't see them very well. They all stayed back away from you and the scary horned badger."

Jethro watched Little Bow squint again and toy nervously with the grass beside him. There was obviously more to the dream, but the boy was having difficulty in telling it. Jethro was not certain of the symbolism, but it was possible that Little Bow might have seen what was to become his uncle's medicine animal—a badger.

But that did not seem likely. The image would not have been so strange-looking, with horns and red eyes, and it would not have frightened Little Bow if it had been a good image. It was a dream hard to understand.

"Then there was someone else who came into the circle and kept trying to stand in front of the horned badger," Little Bow continued. "I think it was a woman, but I couldn't see her face, just long black hair and a deep red light for her body. Red like the color of the flowers that come on top of the mountains in the middle of the warm moons—the flowers that look like the paint-brushes warriors use for their medicine drums. Do you know the color?"

Jethro nodded, picturing the dense clusters of scarlet flowers that bloomed in the warm seasons across open, sage-covered hills and meadows. It seemed an odd color to represent a person, but Little Bow obviously remembered clearly what he had seen in his dream. And it was something that had frightened him more than anything he had ever seen before.

TWO

"I KNOW IT WAS A WOMAN," LITTLE BOW continued. "She looked very strange with all that red around her. It was like she had deep red light for a body and was covered on top with long black hair. She had her arms up as if she was trying to stop the horned badger. And it was looking at her, and its eyes were pulling the red from all around her. The light was going into the badger as it went for you."

Jethro became even more puzzled. The dream must have had something to do with his journey for power; there could be no other reason that Little Bow would have seen him with the Sacred Pipe in the center of all this.

He thought that the horses circling around him were probably symbols of the journey and of the power that came from knowledge and understanding; that was what the old people always said to those who spoke of having had horse visions in their dreams. Horses running and tossing their heads came in dreams often, especially to warriors or to men who knew power. But the significance of the horned badger and the deepred woman was not so easy to understand.

"Do you remember what happened at the end of your dream?" Jethro asked.

"I just remember seeing the woman, with her hands up, and the horned badger," Little Bow replied. "I don't know where they went or what happened, because my mother woke me up to eat."

Darkness was fast approaching. Only a thin streak of crimson remained over the mountains to the west. Jethro stared into the darkening clouds above the horizon, thin and trailing wisps that strung out lengthwise, like a woman's hair. He struggled to his feet.

"Your leg is getting worse," Little Bow said.

"Not so bad that I can't go ahead with my journey," Jethro told him. He put a hand on his nephew's shoulder. "Now hurry back to your lodge so your mother won't blame me for keeping you out after dark. I will see you first thing when I come back and tell you if I learned anything about your dream."

"Think of me when you pray to the spirits," Little Bow said. "Tell them that I want them to be good to you and to take care of your knee. Tell them you have taught me how to hunt and how to search for food. You are deserving of all they can give you. Tell them that."

Jethro smiled. "I'm sure they know your thoughts."

Little Bow smiled back. "I'll be waiting." He turned and ran toward the village through the wet and slippery grass, a bobbing shadow soon lost in the approaching night.

Jethro took a deep breath and turned toward the mountains. He must once again prepare himself mentally for his journey to the Beartooth Plateau. His injuries could not be even a small part of his thinking; he knew that he was being tested, for the injuries were very painful. Yet they were not severe enough to hold him back. He must go with what strength he had already acquired.

Jethro looked once more toward the sweat lodge to ask the spirits for additional guidance. As he peered through the shadows, he noticed that Bull Comes Ahead was standing near the lodge, his white hair gleaming in the waning light. This was a surprise, for Jethro had been told the day before by the old medicine man that they would not meet again until after Jethro's return from the Beartooth.

Jethro approached, holding the Sacred Pipe across his heart. Bull Comes Ahead was wearing his most sacred ceremonial garments. A large buffalo headdress covered his white hair, the right horn painted white, the left painted red. He wore his special ceremonial shirt made of otter and lined along the sleeves with the bodies of chickadees stuffed with sweet grass. Around his neck there hung a medicine necklace of stones, the claw of a large hawk suspended from its center.

"I saw the giant black spirit come down from the sky to attack you," he said as Jethro greeted him. "It must have been sent by our enemies to the east, the Lakota, or the Cheyenne. I see that you can walk, but how badly are you hurt?"

"Nothing can stop me from my journey," Jethro said firmly.

Bull Comes Ahead nodded, his facial muscles twitching slightly under the sagging, ancient skin. Dark blue paint covered the left half of his face; the right half, painted white, was dotted with red and black.

"You are certainly chosen," he said. "You could have been killed."

Although Bull Comes Ahead never spoke of his age, there were those who said he had seen over eighty winters. He appeared younger, as though he could see many more winters ahead. He had had a dozen wives, all of whom had preceded him in natural death. His thirteenth had been with him for six winters and was not yet thirty years old.

"You have come to me for a reason," Jethro said. "Is there something you wish to tell me about about my journey?"

Bull Comes Ahead stared into Jethro's eyes. "I don't know what to tell you," he finally replied. "I cannot understand fully what I feel, but I know it is not good. You have survived the giant spirit, yet something equally as dangerous awaits you."

"Equally as dangerous?"

21

"Maybe more so."

"Should I not go?"

"That is for you to decide." He handed Jethro a large leather pouch. "I have no other medicine articles for you. Just this tobacco leaf. I should have other things, I know, but for some reason, the spirits will no longer direct my thoughts to medicine for your journey. I cannot understand what is happening. It seems to me that the spirits are keeping me from helping. I don't know what to do."

"I do not understand what you are saying."

Bull Comes Ahead was noticeably uncomfortable. "It is as if a shadow has passed between what you are to do and what I am to know about it. I can only say that if you decide to go, you must be very careful. Something is wrong."

Jethro then related Little Bow's dream to him and waited for the medicine man's response. But Bull Comes Ahead could not seem to get the images of the dream to make themselves clear in his mind. He shook his head.

"I cannot say what is happening here between us," he told Jethro. "I know only that I must let you decide for yourself what to do. I cannot say to you what I do not know or understand."

"Do you feel that if I go, my life might end?" Jethro asked.

"I can only tell you again that you have to make up your own mind," Bull Comes Ahead said flatly. "I spoke to your parents, who said that they also want you to make your own decision. They do not want to have anything happen because they spoke to you. It is all your decision. I will go now; I have no more to say."

Bull Comes Ahead turned quickly and began shuffling through the wet grass toward the lodges. Jethro frowned. Deep turmoil worked within him. As he watched the old medicine man melt into dark shadow, he pushed himself hard to know what to do. He realized that he could not turn back, that he could only go ahead.

He looked to the mountains, now jagged shadows against a sky strewn with glittering specks of light. High above, the Other Side camp fires were many and bright, an omen that made him wonder if his journey was to end with his joining the spirit world.

Jethro watched the distant outline of the mountains disappear into darkness. The storm had cooled the night air and made the sounds of frogs and crickets seem louder than normal. He opened his mind to nearby insect voices and listened for anything else he might hear. Nothing harsh or of warning came to him. With the water gurgling in the stream and the subtle sounds of the settling camp, it was as peaceful an evening as he could remember.

Jethro slipped the Sacred Pipe into its otterskin sheath and placed it in the crook of his arm. He began to walk through the darkness toward the mountains. Now that his journey had begun, it was no longer up to him as to where his footsteps led him; he would allow the spirits to guide him and direct his course, for they knew the way far better than he. He would gladly face whatever he might find, for he was determined to gain the power he needed in order to know the true meaning of a strong warrior.

The moon emerged through a trailing film of cloud, a white ball cut neatly in half. In the far distant shadows, the high foothills rose to meet the mountains. By daylight tomorrow, Jethro would be nearing the timber, and another full day of climbing would bring him to the rocky peaks of the high country.

Jethro followed the main trail along the stream toward the mountains, his mind empty of thought. He tried to disregard the pain in his knee and the stinging welts left by the wild rose and plum. He must not think of what had happened; no influences from the past could be allowed to interfere with what was to come, not even the giant whirling spirit.

It was time for feeling, for learning. No questions could be asked about what might take place and what he might see. He could not dwell on anything he had heard from either Little Bow or Bull Comes Ahead. It must be as if he had never been warned of danger.

He came into a grove of aspen at the base of a small draw. Its sweet smell gave him a renewed sense of purpose and peace. Everything lay behind him; only that which he hoped to accomplish entered his thoughts. He sat down and leaned back against a tree. He rubbed his sore knee for a time and felt himself relax. He inhaled deeply and released his breath slowly, then closed his eyes for a moment to rest. He was immediately asleep.

In his dream, the four ravens returned, almost close enough to touch. The black medicine birds floated lazily, their large wings outspread, only the tips moving gently. Gliding. They moved so effortlessly. The sun played against them from somewhere ahead, bringing out lines of color—blue, and deep, almost imperceptible green—hidden within the layers of black feathers.

He rose with them and followed on the wind, heading into a realm of strange medicine and change. They were strong teachers. If they accepted him as a student, great powers of perception could be his.

Jethro gave himself fully to his dream, soaring upward toward the ravens. This was how the old people taught the dreamer to behave: to rise with the birds and become one of them, if they would allow it.

As Jethro neared the ravens, each bird in turn spread its wings into the current and rose higher into the sky. The harder he tried to reach them, the higher the birds soared. As he was about to give up, the ravens slowed their soaring, as if waiting for him, as if telling him not to stop now that he was so high. He felt a surge of elation and turned up toward them again.

When he had nearly reached them, things began to change. Each bird grew large and its feathers puffed out as the dream sky became dark. The ravens held themselves immobile in flight, their heads turned behind them, to the north. With a series of raucous calls, the birds arced upward into a strong current of wind that carried them far beyond him. As he lost sight of them, he awakened, disturbed.

The sky on the eastern horizon was scarlet, a band of light blue spreading out above it. Jethro came to his feet, gripping the pipe tightly. Small birds sang morning songs, and five bull elk that had been grazing next to the aspens turned to watch him, then arched their velvet-covered antlers over their backs and trotted into the shelter of nearby pines.

Jethro left the aspen grove, the remnants of his dream flight still with him and giving him a suspended feeling. He studied the dawn sky and watched the stars fade. He searched from horizon to horizon and found no movement of any kind above him. The ravens of his dream and their world of power had evaporated with the approaching day.

The dream bothered him, particularly the end of it, when the birds had turned and looked behind them, then quickly soared away. How was he to interpret that? Perhaps it would not be the ravens that showed him the Other Side. Perhaps they were only toying with him; he knew that they were mischievous and forever playing tricks.

Again he began his walk toward the mountains, the ravens still on his mind. He grew ever more discouraged that he had not been able to reach them. There had been other dreams, similar in nature, wherein he had launched himself into the sky to soar with these black birds of knowledge. Never in any of his dreams had he been able to reach them to learn the strange medicine of their kind.

Jethro began to see why his dreams had always ended without fulfillment. He realized that he lacked patience, that he was working too hard at attaining his powers too quickly. Whatever he was to learn would come at the right time and not before. That was something he could not change.

He realized also that attaining his powers would be much harder than he had envisioned. His body grew steadily weaker from fasting and the time spent in the sweat lodge, as well as from the battle with the giant spirit. He had had nothing to drink before going into the sweat lodge, and he would take no water at all until he had learned what he must.

Any nourishment his body might obtain would come, as the old people said, from that which the spirits allowed to enter him through Mother Earth and Father Sky: from what his feet and body touched, from what came on the wind to his lips, and from whatever his lungs brought in through breathing. The spirits would feed him and give his body water.

As the sun rose fully above the eastern horizon, Jethro took time to give thanks for another day of life and to ask that his journey give him a new direction, a new pathway that would help his people. He prayed for the power to accept what came to him and to do what he was asked without question or complaint.

As he looked across the foothills toward the mountains, Jethro felt his strength and determination being tested. The streaks of snow remaining on the summits seemed a great distance away. He wondered if his hunger and thirst would overcome him before he reached the high plateau where he would seek his vision. He knew that he could not allow himself that kind of doubt. Although he did not yet feel the weakness and exhaustion that would come in the next few days, he realized fully what would be required of him and how he would have to draw upon a greater strength than he had ever known if he were to make this journey a success.

Holding the Sacred Pipe securely, Jethro continued toward the heavy timber, crossing out of the valley bottom and entering upon a trail along a small stream that would take him to the base of the forest. The morning sun spilled light gold from the east across hills thick with grass and flowers, layers of heavy green topped with dark reds and yellows and blues, mixed with gray patches of sage and low shrubs, rolling on forever toward the mountains.

To the west, a morning thunderstorm mushroomed over the Beartooth. The clouds were thick and dark, drifting in his direction. He did not know what to think. They reminded him of the storm the night before, when the angry spirit had funneled down upon him. Power was coming once again, either to be with him or to be against him.

He climbed up from the small stream to the top of a rocky bluff that pointed toward the storm. There he stretched out his arms and made his offerings, asking that his journey be blessed with a vision and that he might learn his pathway. As he chanted his prayers, his dream of the ravens suddenly invaded his consciousness, as vivid as if it were happening again.

With his eyes closed, he saw the large black birds soaring above him as he struggled in vain to reach them. As before, the birds were turning their heads behind them; but this time he could see their eyes plainly, large and startled. Just before the birds disappeared, they stared into the north.

Jethro opened his eyes and turned toward the north. Although both land and sky were empty, the message was suddenly clear: the ravens had returned to warn him of danger. He recalled Bull Comes Ahead's prophecy of danger lying ahead, and now the ravens were telling him that he could expect it from the north. He realized that whatever it was that Little Bow and Bull Comes Ahead had tried to warn him of, it was almost upon him.

The sun had topped the horizon and the river was lined with women drawing water in bladderskin bags. Conversation was centered around the upcoming Tobacco Society dance and planting ceremony that would take place with two other bands at the changing of the moon.

Among those at the river was a young woman who listened to the talk while filling her two water bags. Cuts Buffalo had just passed her sixteenth winter. She was the only surviving girl-child of Many Leaves and Strikes-the-Heart; twin girls born three winters ahead of Cuts Buffalo

29

had died as infants, in a drowning accident on
the Yellowstone.

Now, as the sole daughter in a lodge with two
older brothers, Cuts Buffalo was very busy helping her mother with the chores of preparing food
and maintaining the lodge. Enemy Seeker and
Fox Caller were twins, born five winters ahead
of Cuts Buffalo. They knew many of the skills
required to become warriors but they had not
yet sought a vision or been on a raid.

Cuts Buffalo's father had gained much honor
among the Crow people. He had led many raids
for horses against both the Lakota and the Blackfeet, and once against the Striped-Arrow people,
the Cheyenne. A lance had pierced his lower leg,
and two long scars, knife wounds across his
chest, signified that he had achieved high honor
in warfare.

Cuts Buffalo herself was becoming well known
throughout the village, especially among the
young warriors, all of whom kept watch for her
as she went about her daily chores. Many of the
women, young and old alike, envied her her combination of beauty and graciousness. Even with
her numerous responsibilities, she maintained a
smile and took a moment to laugh with friends
and relatives. She was industrious and planned
her work effectively, thus allowing for time to
herself.

Although Cuts Buffalo could now easily marry,
she planned to remain in the family lodge until
her brothers became warriors and took wives of
their own. This would ease the burden placed on
her mother and make it possible for Cuts Buffalo

to be given to a strong warrior whose parents had good property to exchange on behalf of their son.

Cuts Buffalo was slim and subtle of movement and had already gained the attention of two of the most worthy suitors within the band; both of them had seen twenty-five winters and had gained a number of war honors. Each was ready and eager to give fine horses and weapons to Strikes-the-Heart. Each was learning to play love songs on his flute. Cuts Buffalo's friends had asked her often which of the two men she preferred. Either of them would certainly make a fine husband, but she had no desire to choose between them.

Although both warriors had called to her on their flute, Cuts Buffalo had never answered by finding them. Neither had met her in the evening shadows, nor had either of them pressed her to see him, for they were aware of her father's wishes to hold her until her brothers were married.

Cuts Buffalo viewed this as a blessing, for she was not ready to give herself to anyone for whom she had no desire. She held but one man in special esteem, and he could not marry her for some time. He must first make his vision quest to seek power and learn from the spirits. She thought of Jethro often, wondering if he had reached the high Beartooth. She worried about him, for the giant black spirit had nearly killed him. The story had increased her concern for his welfare.

Cuts Buffalo thought of him now as she filled her second water bag. She overheard one woman asking another if she was afraid for her son, who, it was said, would have to face grave danger on his journey for power. Cuts Buffalo looked around. One of the most honored women among the Crow people, Morning Swan, was telling the woman who had asked the question that she was not afraid for her son.

"He has honor in his heart," Cuts Buffalo heard Morning Swan say. "He has no reason to fear, nor do I."

"But there is word that Bull Comes Ahead has warned him about a grave danger that lies in his path," the woman continued. "Can't you give presents to Bull Comes Ahead and ask him to talk to the Powers on Jethro's behalf?"

Cuts Buffalo watched Morning Swan. She might have taken offense, but she did not.

"I have told you," Morning Swan said, "that Jethro's journey is his own. No one can interfere."

The woman nodded to Morning Swan and went back to her work. Enough had been said. All of the women understood that the private matter of personal power, sacred in its bestowal upon an individual, should not be discussed openly.

But Cuts Buffalo remained worried. She wanted to learn what she could about Jethro and knew that she could glean little here. Perhaps Bull Comes Ahead could help her, if he only would. Bull Comes Ahead had prayed and conducted a ceremony on Jethro's behalf. There seemed no doubt that the old medicine man would have some insight that would ease her mind.

Cuts Buffalo picked up her water bags, eased her way through the women, and quickly departed. She worked her way onto the well-worn trail leading back to the village through the willows and cottonwoods. Women were coming and going, for it was the busiest time of day in the village.

She hurried along the trail, thinking of Morning Swan. Although she knew that deep within Morning Swan's heart there had to be concern, she had to admire the woman for dealing so well with her fears. It could not be easy to have a strong and brave son who, as the whole village now knew, was facing trials so dangerous that even the most powerful of medicine men was unable to foresee them.

It was well known among the people that Morning Swan held special powers of her own. The people knew her as an independent thinker, one not afraid to speak her mind. She had alienated herself from many of them because of her strong convictions about the coming of the fur traders, who had allied with the Crow against their enemies. Morning Swan had predicted that the liaison would not last.

From the very beginning, Morning Swan had been adamant against the trapping of beaver in the streams and rivers that crossed Crow lands. She had argued that taking all the beaver would forever alter the bottomlands and turn them into dry and dusty flats. She had lost a favorite aspen meadow where she went as a child. The trees had died out, and the meadow of bog flowers was

33

gone, victims of flooding and then drought after the beaver were exterminated.

After the loss of most of the beaver, many among the people now listened to Morning Swan's words when she spoke. Morning Swan was once again angry and afraid. Now that the beaver trade was over, the trappers were not going back where they had come from. Instead, they were building more fort lodges along the rivers and calling the people in to trade for buffalo robes. Many argued that the trade items brought by the Long Knives, such as tools and cooking utensils, had made life much better for the people. But Morning Swan insisted that they would pay in the end.

Soon there would be many more white people coming, Morning Swan said. They would want more and more buffalo robes. They would build more fort lodges, and their horses would eat more grass from the river bottoms. The buffalo would move elsewhere. In time, the main food source for the Crow people would be thinned out and scattered across the vast lands below the mountains.

Cuts Buffalo did not want to dwell on Morning Swan's tragic prophecies. Instead, she dared to dream of a happy life with Morning Swan's son. Jethro was a unique combination of his mother and father: a strong-willed thinker and a fearless adventurer, set on finding his own pathways. He could communicate with anyone in the mountains, and he could read from the books his father had brought into Crow lands when Jethro was young. He possessed the unusual medicine

34

to look into these books and tell what they meant. Cuts Buffalo knew no other young men who could do that. Jethro was truly special.

Cuts Buffalo now wanted to prove to Jethro and his family that she was worthy of him. She would learn to read from the books if he so wished, and she would do whatever else, beyond the usual chores of a wife, to please him like no other woman could. She wanted him to notice her and to reciprocate her feelings. To her, that meant everything—most of all, it meant her future.

THREE

CUTS BUFFALO ENTERED THE VILLAGE AND HURried to her lodge. Upon seeing her mother engaged in conversation with a group of women near a neighboring lodge, she left the filled water bags next to four bags that needed filling and headed for the center of the village, where the important men lived.

She stopped at the door flap of Bull Comes Ahead's lodge and called in to him. After a short silence, she was asked to enter.

"Ah, it is Cuts Buffalo, daughter of Many Leaves and Strikes-the-Heart," the old medicine man said. "Please, sit down and talk."

Cuts Buffalo took a deep breath and seated herself on a buffalo robe reserved for guests. She could see that he was still dressed in his best ceremonial clothes and still wore his sacred cer-

36

emonial headdress, his attire the same as that of the previous night.

"Did I interrupt you?" she asked.

"No, you did not," he answered. "I have said all the prayers that I will say."

Cuts Buffalo studied Bull Comes Ahead's stern features. The night before, when Jethro had left for his vision, Bull Comes Ahead had performed a ceremony on a hill outside of the village. Because he had been wearing the same paint and the same medicine shirt then as now, the people had come to know for certain that Jethro was going to face something bad on his journey.

Cuts Buffalo fumbled with the fringe on her elkskin dress. She wished now that she had not come, but it was too late.

"I am concerned about Jethro, the son of Morning Swan and Bear Man," she said finally. "I overheard some of the women at the river saying that he would have a hard time during his journey for power. Is this true?"

Bull Comes Ahead nodded. "That is what is being said. Talk has a way of gaining its own power, but Jethro will not have an easy time of his journey, that is true."

Cuts Buffalo continued to toy with the fringe on her dress. "I know you think a great deal of him," she said. "Are there any prayers you could say to bring him protection?"

His eyebrows raised. "Do you have an interest in his welfare?"

Cuts Buffalo kept her eyes down. "I am in no way tied to his family, yet I am concerned. Do you understand?"

Bull Comes Ahead nodded slowly. "You have a brave heart to come and tell me this. How can I help you?"

"Is there some way you can send one of the spirits you know to help Jethro?" Cuts Buffalo suggested. "Maybe he needs protection."

Bull Comes Ahead studied her for a time. "There is nothing I can do for him," he said then. "He must face his dangers alone. He must make his own decisions about what he will do. I have been warned not to interfere in any way. I *cannot* interfere, as I have no power to see into this matter. I can only ask the Powers for his safe return. Nothing more."

"He will return safely, though, won't he?" Cuts Buffalo asked.

Bull Comes Ahead studied her further. She cared enough about Jethro to reveal her deepest concerns. "I believe he will," he finally said. "I don't know what he will have learned or what he will have faced, but I feel that he will not cross permanently into the spirit world."

For the first time since entering the lodge, Cuts Buffalo smiled. It was not a broad or happy smile, but it was nonetheless a smile.

"I didn't know that you and Jethro were close," Bull Comes Ahead remarked. "In fact, I didn't know that you two even knew one another well."

"We don't," Cuts Buffalo said. "We don't know one another at all—at least, Jethro doesn't know *me* at all. Maybe in time he will come to know me well and want me for his wife."

"He is not yet of age, even should he have a

vision," Bull Comes Ahead pointed out. "He must also gain war honors, or wait until he is older."

"It will be some time before my father allows me to marry," Cuts Buffalo said. "My two older brothers have yet to become honored warriors. Perhaps they will gain their honors close to the time that Jethro does. When he is ready to take a wife, I will be ready for a husband."

Bull Comes Ahead nodded slowly and smiled. Then he looked up as his wife, Calling Bird, entered the lodge with a skin bag bulging with water. Her dark hair was neatly braided. She had smooth skin and a quick step, almost as quick as her dark eyes. If there was any news worth learning in the village, Calling Bird was among the first to hear of it.

Now she looked at Cuts Buffalo and her eyes widened. "Oh! So here you are. Your mother has been to the river twice and all over the village looking for you. I think she wants you right away."

Cuts Buffalo knew that she would get a stern lecture on responsibility from her mother as soon as she returned to the lodge. She would hear that she should have at least finished filling the water bags before she went to visit Bull Comes Ahead. But had she done that, her mother would have found something else for her to do, and there would have been no time left for visiting.

Although she knew that facing her mother was not going to be pleasant, Cuts Buffalo felt a great deal better. It had been worth the visit for her peace of mind. She rose and bowed slightly.

"Thank you for letting me know, Calling Bird," she said with a smile. She turned to Bull Comes Ahead. "Thank you for making me feel better."

Bull Comes Ahead nodded and smiled again. "I'm glad if I helped in some way."

Calling Bird looked at Cuts Buffalo. "Did he make you feel better?" she winked and a smile spread across her face. She turned to Bull Comes Ahead.

"I know better than that," she said. "You are far too old to make young girls feel much better. Probably they don't feel anything."

"I'm glad that's what you think," Bull Comes Ahead told her. "That way I can get away with a lot."

Cuts Buffalo left the two bantering and hurried back to her lodge. She had two empty water bags in her hands and was leaving again for the river when her mother came up behind her.

"Where have you been?"

"I went to Bull Comes Ahead's lodge to talk to him about Jethro," she replied. "I did not intend to be gone so long."

"There is lots to do around here. You should get ahead with your chores first, then talk to the people you want to visit."

"I don't see how I could ever get ahead on my chores," Cuts Buffalo pointed out. "There is so much to do. I felt I needed to learn what I could about Jethro from Bull Comes Ahead. He believes that Jethro will return safely."

Many Leaves nodded. "I know how you feel about Jethro. You have been good enough to tell me of your dreaming thoughts during each day.

But you know the custom: he has a few winters yet before he can take a wife, and honors to gain."

"He will gain honors soon," Cuts Buffalo said with conviction. "And when Fox Caller and Enemy Seeker have taken wives, Jethro will come to our lodge and call for me."

"I hope you are not only dreaming."

Cuts Buffalo picked up the skin bags and turned for the river. "No, Mother," she said. "I am not only dreaming. It will happen."

Little Bow sat in the cover of a thick growth of willows along the river. It was a secret place, one of his favorites. The only entrance was a small hole next to a fallen cottonwood log. Inside, Little Bow could see out through a few places, but no one could see in.

Little Bow's best friend, a boy named Jumps Ahead, sat with him. Jumps Ahead had been born just one moon after Little Bow. The two boys had proven themselves adept in making things happen that were fun, and often dangerous.

Jumps Ahead stood a few inches taller than Little Bow, with a slimmer build. He had the gift of stamina and, like Little Bow, was not afraid to test himself. He was already known for his prowess at swimming and could outdistance older boys in long races across the mountain lakes.

Little Bow and Jumps Ahead had shared a number of adventures that had led them into trouble, as well as a number they had not been caught at. It evened out pretty well and kept them planning continuously. They came to the willows often to outline various activities, including stealing meat from drying racks and hitching rides on certain buffalo ponies belonging to important warriors and therefore off limits to small boys.

Today the two friends were making an important decision, as important as any they had considered in their entire lives.

"I don't think it's a good idea," Jumps Ahead was saying. "I'm not afraid, but we could get into an awful lot of trouble. I don't want to have to stay near my mother's lodge for the rest of the warm moons."

"This is important," Little Bow argued. "I know that we are warned never to go far from the village. But we have to do this. I feel that the spirits want us to go."

"Maybe the spirits want *you* to go," Jumps Ahead countered, "but I don't have that feeling."

Little Bow brooded for a time. Jumps Ahead seemed to know what he was thinking right away.

"You shouldn't think of leaving by yourself, either," he told Little Bow. "That would be even worse for you. And if you didn't come back, I wouldn't have anybody to do things with. Stay here. You know Jethro will return. He told you he would."

"I just don't feel good about him," Little Bow said. Although he had made the comment before, he could not help emphasizing the fact that he was worried. "I know something has happened. I just want to help if I can."

"There's nothing we can do, Little Bow," Jumps Ahead said. "It would be better if you simply forgot about it. Jethro will return."

Little Bow thought some more. He twisted the end of a willow branch until it was frayed.

"I wish there was some easy way I could get a fast horse and go to look for him," he said. "I could do it once it turns dark, but I don't want to wait that long. Maybe I'll just try now and see what happens."

"The horse tenders are watching," Jumps Ahead pointed out. "They will see you and stop you."

"Not if I have a fast horse."

Jumps Ahead blew out his breath. "It sounds like you are going to go no matter what," he said. "If you are, then I'm going with you."

Little Bow smiled. "I knew that you would come with me. Let's go get a couple of horses. They have to be fast enough to outrun the horse tenders."

"Maybe if we do it right, we won't have to outrun anybody," Jumps Ahead suggested. "I know that my cousin, Weasel Shirt, is watching the horses over near the rocks at the far end of the herd. And I know that he likes to look at the girls when they are swimming. Especially that one named Grass-in-the-Morning. He would do anything to see her."

"How do you know the girls are swimming?" Little Bow asked.

"I don't know that they are," Jumps Ahead replied. "I *hope* they are. He won't like it if I tell him to go see her and nobody is swimming."

43

Little Bow laughed. "You're just going to say she's swimming so he'll go look?"

"Yes."

Little Bow laughed again, certain of their plan. "When he goes to look for Grass-in-the-Morning, we take two horses and ride to find Jethro."

"It will work," Jumps Ahead said. "Weasel Shirt has a buckskin that he lets me ride sometimes. He knows I can ride and watch the horses while he is gone for a short time. I have done it before while he watched Grass-in-the-Morning swim."

"Do you think he will believe you?" Little Bow asked.

Jumps Ahead nodded confidently. "You don't know my cousin and how he likes to watch Grass-in-the-Morning at the swimming holes."

"Good," Little Bow said. "Then let's do it. We have to go now. It is already late in the morning."

"What about taking food?" Jumps Ahead asked.

"We haven't got time," Little Bow told him. "We have our bows. We can get some rabbits, or maybe some of those fat ground squirrels up by the buffalo wallows."

Little Bow and Jumps Ahead crawled out of the willows and hurried along the river toward the far end of the horse herd, taking care to stay well under cover. Anyone seeing two young boys headed away from the village would certainly stop them to ask where they were going.

Little Bow hid in a clump of dogwood and watched while Jumps Ahead hurried out to the edge of the herd. Weasel Shirt was sitting on the buckskin, making certain that the herd was contained. Little Bow viewed the herd, noting a lot of good buffalo ponies. Boys of all ages made it a point to keep track of the best horses for war and hunting, and who owned them.

Finally, Little Bow gathered a handful of grass from a wet area nearby and slipped out toward the herd. He had picked out a fleet black stallion called Night Runner, whose owner was a good friend of Jethro's, a young man named High Elk.

Little Bow stayed low to the ground and watched Jumps Ahead talking to his cousin. Jumps Ahead kept pointing to a spot downriver, closer to the village, and Weasel Shirt finally slid down off the buckskin and caught another pony.

Little Bow almost whooped. He waited until Weasel Shirt was out of sight, then ran out with his handful of lush grass to where Jumps Ahead was catching him a horse by the mane.

"That isn't the one I want," Little Bow said.

"What's wrong with it?" Jumps Ahead demanded.

"I want that one." Little Bow pointed to the black.

"That is not a wise choice, Little Bow," Jumps Ahead said quickly. "That is Night Runner, High Elk's best buffalo pony."

"That is exactly why he is a good choice," Little Bow said. "Night Runner is one of the finest ponies in all the herd."

"You will make High Elk very angry."

"No, we'll get back before High Elk misses him," Little Bow said. "If you won't catch him, I will."

45

"Hurry up then," Jumps Ahead said angrily. "If Weasel Shirt finds out I was lying about Grass-in-the-Morning and comes back before we're gone, we're both going to be in a lot of trouble."

"It won't take long," Little Bow assured Jumps Ahead. "Just be ready to ride fast if we have to."

Little Bow eased through the herd to the black buffalo pony. He had seen High Elk ride the horse proudly on many occasions. High Elk had captured the pony in the Black Hills during a raid against the Lakota, and the warrior always displayed it during camp parades and summer trade fairs for all to see. Little Bow had often watched High Elk give demonstrations of the horse's ability to run and turn by knee and hand contact.

Little Bow held out the grass for the sleek black stallion. When the horse had a mouthful, Little Bow grabbed a handful of mane and swung himself up.

Jumps Ahead rode over to him on the pony he had caught for himself, frowning. "I think you'll get in trouble," he told Little Bow again.

"And you won't?"

"Not as bad as you. That is one of the finest horses in the entire herd."

"Do you think I would take a poor one for rescuing Jethro from enemies?"

"Maybe just a little poorer," Jumps Ahead told him. "High Elk will never forgive you."

"I think he would rather I borrowed his best horse for helping Jethro than to see Jethro die,"

Little Bow stated. "Now, bend low over your pony and let's ride toward the mountains."

Jethro stood on the bluff and continued to look north into the rolling hills as far as his eyes would bring vision. After a short time he realized that he should be looking closer in; the danger was nearly upon him.

A column of four riders eased their horses along the stream below. Two warriors rode in front, followed by a woman and another warrior in the rear, who turned on his horse often to view their back trail. Jethro could see clearly by their dress and adornments that they were Blackfeet, age-old enemies of the Crow. Ever since the Crow people had broken off from the Hidatsa along the Missouri and journeyed west to make their new home at the foot of the mountains, there had been continuous warfare with the Blackfeet.

Jethro studied them closely as they continued to ride along the stream toward him. They were taking a chance, just three warriors and a woman traveling through the heart of Crow hunting grounds. Jethro considered the possibility that perhaps more followed. Little Bow's fears and Bull Comes Ahead's prophecy of trouble were coming to pass; his meeting enemies dressed for war while he himself had no weapons could be the greatest challenge to survival that he would meet on his journey.

He could not escape them now. They had already noticed him standing atop the rocky bluff and were pointing at him and talking. There did not appear to be others following, and Jethro felt

some relief in that. But without any weapons
with which to defend himself, four might as well
be forty.

The riders drew closer to the base of the hill.
This was a time for strength and courage. He
would stand tall and still and meet their advance
with a stern gaze. He would make them believe
that they should not fight him or harm him in
any way. This day belonged to him.

Jethro realized that the Sacred Pipe and the
pouch given him by Bull Comes Ahead were his
protection. The old medicine man had told him
he would know when to use them; there was no
doubt in Jethro's mind that this was the time.

He untied the flap and carefully removed the
large tobacco leaf, rolled tightly. The rumbling
of the thunderstorm grew louder as the clouds
thickened along the base of the mountains.

Jethro looked to the storm and then back to
the tobacco leaf. Carefully he unfolded the leaf.
Its veins were painted a bright blue that gave off
a strong glow in the early light.

Jethro held up the leaf, offering it to the sun.
In his mind, a song formed. He began to chant:

> I hold the Sacred Leaf,
> the power that is Great Spirit.
> My enemies are cast away.
> I hold the Sacred Leaf,
> the strength that is Great Spirit.
> My enemies scatter in fear.

Then Jethro turned toward the invaders, holding up the leaf in one hand and the Sacred Pipe

in the other. He switched the pipe to the hand holding the tobacco leaf and held his free hand up in the sign of peace so the warriors might see that his mission was not one of war. Still they advanced, kicking their horses into a gallop toward the base of the bluff. The one nearest the woman rode quickly to the front; he was a large warrior, mounted on a black pinto covered with jagged lines of red paint.

Jethro stood his ground, waiting. He remembered what Little Bow had told him about the dream, about having seen the horned badger and how the dream had scared him. The lead warrior on the black pinto was wearing a large badger headdress, with attached buffalo horns.

The sight held Jethro fast, every muscle rigid. Then he heard the song in his head once again and began to chant it aloud. He held both the pipe and the tobacco leaf over his heart and felt strength coming into his body—a subtle, yet powerful, surge of energy that coursed through him. Over the mountains, the storm boomed through the otherwise silent morning, bringing the charge of the Powers to the air.

The four Blackfeet pulled their horses up at the base of the hill and studied him. They talked and pointed, all but the woman, who just watched and listened, her eyes fixed on Jethro.

Gusts of wind moved the feathers that adorned the warriors' hair and war shields. Although the sky was clear overhead, rain flew in large, cold drops that stung like shards of ice. Jethro rejoiced in the omen, the sign that the strength of the storm had come to him. The dark clouds were still a distance away, but the force of the winds high overhead was bringing the rain. He knew that no giant spirit would be descending on him today. The forces would be fighting on his behalf.

The strong charge in the air increased and the woman looked to the sky, her eyes wide, her fingers tracing the moisture along her cheeks. She shouted something to the warrior with the horned badger headdress and backed her horse around to leave. The warrior quickly pulled his pony in front of hers. She shook her head no to everything he told her, pointing toward the storm while she spoke.

The badger warrior waved his war lance violently at the woman and yelled in her face. The other two warriors joined the argument, all of them talking at once. Jethro watched the woman shout at each of them, especially at the badger warrior. She continued to jab her finger toward the thunderheads and then toward Jethro, tossing her head vigorously. None of the men wanted to listen, and the woman finally fell silent. Then she began singing to the head warrior, a song of mourning, a song that held the words of his coming death.

The warrior, now enraged, yelled at her again and struck her across the back with the blunt side of his war lance. She stopped singing and lurched sideways, clutching a handful of her horse's mane to keep from falling to the ground. The warrior turned his pinto toward Jethro and threw his head back, screaming to the sky.

He pulled a war ax from a sheath on his saddle and waved it in the air. The woman kicked her pony ahead and reached out to grab his arm, but he had ridden too far in front of her. She could only stare helplessly with wide eyes as he started up the hill toward Jethro.

Jethro curled the tobacco leaf and held it, together with the pipe, in his right hand. He raised his left hand straight out toward the oncoming warrior. The man advanced, riding with his head thrown back, waving the ax in a large arc, driving his heels ever harder into his pony's ribs. The rise up the bluff was steep, and the pinto churned through loose dirt and rock, the warrior yelling louder the closer he came to Jethro.

As the warrior neared, Jethro could see paint lines of jagged red and white across his bare chest, and a heavy black line from temple to temple across his forehead. The red lines on his pony, coated now with sweat, flashed in the early sunlight. Three eagle feathers adorned the forelock of the horse's mane; one of them bounced out and drifted to the ground.

The warrior had his ax raised and was nearly to the top of the hill when Jethro suddenly swung the Sacred Pipe out from his chest and raised his head to the sky, yelling in a high-pitched voice; it was a long, loud wailing sound that rose above the Blackfoot warrior's war cries. The pinto reared, its eyes rolling in fright, its back legs slipping in the loose rock. The warrior slid quickly from the pony's back but lost his footing and fell heavily on his side, jerking the pinto's reins.

The squealing horse, its head twisted sideways, flipped onto its side, slamming a front

51

shoulder hard into the warrior's ribs. The woman screamed and started her pony up the hill, but one of the other warriors took hold of the reins, stopping her horse. The woman jumped to the ground, wailing, and began to run up the hill.

The fallen warrior's black pinto struggled to its feet in the loose rock and galloped down the hill. The two other warriors turned their horses and kicked them into a dead run, leaving the woman by herself, her head raised to the sky in grief. Jethro looked from her to the fallen warrior. He was certain that what had just happened would change his journey for power in a way he could not yet understand.

FOUR

JETHRO LIMPED DOWN THE HILL TO THE FALLEN warrior lying twisted on his side. The man appeared to be dead, but when Jethro leaned down, he heard hoarse breathing and a low gurgling in the warrior's throat and lungs. He quickly turned him over and faced his head downhill. The unconscious warrior coughed and a thin spray of pinkish red blew from his open mouth out onto the rocks.

The woman had stopped wailing. She began climbing the hill again, no hint of caution in her stride. She was small and slim, with dark eyes that shone with intensity. She wore a dress of elkskin trimmed with red beads. She made a sign, indicating to Jethro that the warrior was soon to become her husband. Jethro motioned her forward.

As she bent over the fallen warrior, she touched his face lightly. "I told you not to be foolish, Big Owl," she whispered in Blackfeet. "You have never learned to listen to me. Now you will die and leave me to mourn you." She turned to Jethro. "You have much power. I don't know what you will do with me."

"I wish this had not happened," Jethro addressed her in her own tongue, "but he did it to himself. The signs were there, and he paid no attention."

The woman was surprised to hear Jethro speak her language fluently. There were many among the tribes who spoke many languages, but it was unusual to come across an enemy who could speak her language this well.

"You look to be Absaroka," the woman said, "but you speak the language of the Pikuni."

"Yes," Jethro replied, "I am Absaroka, one of the Crow people. My mother learned your language as a young woman. She lived among your people. I, in turn, learned it from her. I know many languages."

"Your mother lived among my people?"

"A war party stole her as a young girl, and she was raised among the Small Robes. Her name is Morning Swan. She left your people and was pursued by a warrior named Rising Hawk."

The woman's eyes widened. "Your mother is Morning Swan?"

Jethro nodded.

"I know the story well," she said. "To this day, Rising Hawk speaks of the Crow woman whom he wished to be his wife, the strong woman who escaped with her girl-child and married a Long Knife. So you are their son?"

"I am," Jethro acknowledged.

"That explains your power," she said with a nod.

The wounded warrior began to moan and jerk his arms. The woman leaned over him and tried to speak to him, but he faded back out of consciousness.

"It seems certain he will die," she said. She clenched her fists in frustration and looked up at Jethro. "I tried to stop him. I saw the signs. I knew the spirits were with you this day. But he would not listen. He wanted to gain honors and revenge. His brother was killed two moons ago by your people."

"Perhaps warriors from another band," Jethro told her. "The Kicked-in-Their-Bellies have not fought the Piegans since before the last cold moons."

"It does not matter which band fights," she said angrily. "You are all Absaroka, and enemies of my people."

"I did not want to meet an enemy," Jethro told her. "See, I carry a Sacred Pipe and sacred tobacco. I am not painted, nor am I decorated for war. Take him back to your people, so he will not die."

The Piegan woman looked at Jethro for a time. She noticed his badly swollen knee and his many cuts and scratches, indicating to her that he had already survived fighting and was held special in the eyes of the spirits.

"You have the right to count coup," she finally

said. "There is great honor in what you did to Big Owl. We planned to marry. He was a strong fighter among my people. I do not believe you would not take the coup and become honored among your own people."

"I am not on a journey of war, as I just told you," Jethro explained. "It was not of my wishes to have blood flow this day. But it has happened, and that cannot be changed. Were you born into the Small Robes band?"

"Yes," she replied. "I am Many Berries." Her tension eased, but she seemed unable to believe that Jethro would decline to take honors on an enemy.

"I will help you cut poles to build a drag for him," Jethro said. "You can find the other two warriors who rode away in fear and with their aid, leave for your own lands. Then I will continue on my journey."

"Why would you do this?" she asked, her eyes softening. "Why not leave me to do it alone?"

"I want the spirits to understand that I do not mean harm to your husband," Jethro told her. "I nearly lost my life to a giant angry spirit just last night. That is why I walk with a limp and have so many cuts and bruises. Now I feel that the spirits want this warrior with you to live. If he dies, I do not feel that I can go ahead with my journey."

"Do you believe the spirits are testing you?" she asked.

"I am certain of it," Jethro replied. "I must do what I can to save him."

"If Big Owl lives," she said, "he will not understand."

"That does not matter. I know what I feel."

Jethro helped her ease Big Owl down the hill and settle him near the stream. Using the ax the warrior dropped in his fall, Jethro began to chop down a young cottonwood near the river. Many Berries stood and stared at him for a time. Finally, she began stripping leafy branches to serve as a cushion.

While they built the drag, Jethro grew concerned that the other two warriors might return and that he would have to fight them.

"They are gone for good," Many Berries told him. "They were to travel with us for only a short while. Then Big Owl and I were to be on our own."

Jethro studied her for a moment. It had not seemed logical that they should have been so few in number, but for the other two warriors to abandon Many Berries and Big Owl made no sense at all. He wondered what she was leaving out of her story.

"I don't understand," Jethro said. "Were you being sent out of Blackfeet lands for some reason?"

Many Berries bowed her head. "Big Owl thought I had lain with the son of a powerful warrior. The young man's name was Spotted Horse. Big Owl attacked him and nearly killed him. Big Owl then turned on me, but Spotted Horse's brother and others stopped him and made him understand that he was wrong."

"You are lucky that Big Owl wasn't killed there in the village," Jethro told her.

Many Berries looked down at the unconscious warrior. "Yes, but it now seems likely that he is to meet with death anyway. He rode at you in direct defiance of all the omens. I do not know what to do that will keep him from crossing to the Other Side."

"I told you, he must not cross over."

Many Berries looked hard at Jethro. "There is nothing I can do for him. You have the power. It is all up to you."

Jethro realized the truth in her words. She and Big Owl had been banned from their people and had no place to go. Without the help of a medicine man, Big Owl would certainly die. Jethro's decision to help them, however he could, might mean the difference between Big Owl living or dying. And the spirits were certainly watching his decision. He knew that if he truly wished to keep the warrior alive and not put his journey for power in further jeopardy, he would think of something to do. He realized that he could make but one choice in the matter.

"I will take you and Big Owl back to my village," Jethro finally said. "We have a good medicine man; I know he can bring Big Owl back to health. He has much power. It may take the passing of an entire moon before Big Owl will fully recover, but then he will be able to hunt and both of you can go where you will."

"Your people will not want that," Many Berries said. "They will want both of us to die."

"No. I will tell them that the spirits have told me what to do, so that I can finish my journey. You have nothing to fear."

Many Berries remained skeptical. Although she knew that Big Owl would die if he did not receive care soon, she also realized that without a doubt the Crow people would surely kill him if they could. Frustrated, she helped Jethro lay Big Owl across the drag. The warrior opened his eyes and began to moan. She tried to talk to him, but he did not recognize her and had no idea of what had happened to him. His breath was ragged, and he coughed blood continuously.

"We had better hurry," Jethro said.

"I have changed my mind," Many Berries told him. "I will go away with Big Owl on my own. I don't want to go to your village."

Jethro stared at her. "Where will you go?"

"I don't know. I will help him in some way."

"He needs more help than you can give him."

"You don't know that!" Many Berries argued. "You don't know what I can do."

"It doesn't matter. I am taking you to my village."

"No!" Many Berries yelled. "You cannot take me, or Big Owl either, any place I don't want to go."

"Which are you more afraid of?" Jethro asked. "Is it my people, or seeing Big Owl cross to the Other Side?"

Many Berries turned toward the mountains, thinking her decision through. Was she afraid for herself, or did she have enough strength to allow a medicine man to help Big Owl? She did

not want Jethro to think she would not do what
was best for the man she had decided to marry.

"You are right," she said finally. "I have no
choice but to let you take us to your people. I
do not have the power to keep him from death,
and if I wait any longer, he will surely cross
over."

"We will go now, and we will hurry," Jethro
said. "I have as much stake in this as you."

As he traveled back to the village with Many
Berries and the injured warrior, Jethro knew
that now his journey to gain power would have
to begin again at another time. What he had set
out to do had been interrupted, and he felt there
was no putting it back together. He was certain
there would be even more obstacles to face if he
continued, perhaps tests that could bring him
death.

In addition, he felt that he could not abandon
Many Berries and Big Owl once they reached
the village. Even though he had told Many Berries he would convince the villagers that the
spirits had directed him, he knew that her worries were well founded. Any number of angry
villagers would be unhappy about the presence
of an enemy among them; they bore too much
bitterness. Many would certainly want the two
out of the village immediately, especially those
who had lost relatives to the Blackfeet in battle.

Despite this, Jethro knew that he had to take
Many Berries and Big Owl to the village. He had
to fulfill his promise to the spirits. It was clear
to him now: preserving life, even if it belonged

to a mortal enemy, was most important at this time. Nothing else mattered.

The sun crossed overhead and a breeze rustled the grasses. The sky spread clear blue from horizon to horizon, with only a faint wisp of white over the Beartooth to remind Jethro of the early storm.

Many Berries walked beside Big Owl's black pinto pony. She said nothing except in response to occasional conversation that Jethro initiated. He walked with noticeable pain but never slowed his pace. He had told her the entire story of the giant spirit the night before and how he had nearly met death, making her ever more satisfied that this man had connections to the Powers.

It was still difficult for her to accept that she must soon enter an enemy camp. Yet she seemed resigned to the fact that her life had taken a strange twist and that she could do nothing about it. Her anger came and went, but she said no more to Jethro about going off on her own with Big Owl.

Just after midday they stopped for a rest along the river. Jethro fashioned a digging stick from the fork of a young willow branch and worked a number of wild carrots from the damp soil.

"You have decided to eat?" Many Berries asked, surprised. "I knew to look at you that you were fasting. Why aren't you going to continue on your journey?"

"That will have to begin again at another

time," Jethro replied. "I don't feel right about going ahead now."

Many Berries untied a small parfleche from the back of Big Owl's pinto. She held it out to Jethro. He thanked her, then quickly opened it and took out a handful of pemmican. He sat down on a log and ate the pemmican and roots together, looking up at the mountains frequently.

"I don't have a good feeling about going up there now," he repeated. "I don't know how I'll begin again, but I must."

Many Berries watched him eat while she knelt over Big Owl. The warrior remained unconscious, and there was no way of knowing if his condition was worsening or not. She could only hope that he held on until the medicine man saw him.

Then her thoughts turned to Jethro again, to this powerful young man who so curiously wished to save Big Owl. She left the warrior's side and took a seat beside Jethro on the log.

"I would like to ask what you were seeking on your special journey," she said.

Jethro ate without speaking.

"I know you really should not tell me. I shouldn't have asked."

Jethro finally answered, "I was in search of a spirit helper. I had hoped to gain power and to learn what lies before me. But it seems that it is not meant to be, at least not for a time."

Surprised, Many Berries stared at him. "You mean that you are not yet a warrior?"

"Do you see coup feathers in my hair?"

"Many times coup feathers are removed on journeys for special medicine."

"That is true," Jethro agreed. "But I am seeking my first vision."

"You showed no fear as Big Owl charged you," Many Berries said. "I thought you were already a seasoned warrior and were out alone to gain even more power."

"No, I've had a lot of dreams, but I haven't gone out as a warrior does and seen things to learn what they mean."

"Dreams are visions, too," Many Berries pointed out. "There is much to be learned from dreams. I'm not telling you something you don't already know, but three different elders among my people have learned a lot about themselves and their lives by reliving their dreams. My people look to them for answers to many things."

"I am aware that dreams can give a person insight into himself, and also foretell things," Jethro said. "But a journey for power must be made in a different way. At least for me it must be different. I cannot become a respected warrior just by learning things through dreams." He bent down to dig another root from the ground.

Many Berries shrugged and looked out toward the mountains.

"Is there more you wish to say?" Jethro asked.

"Only if you want to hear me."

"I want to hear you," Jethro said. "Tell me what you know."

Many Berries turned from the mountains. "It

is the same among my people," she told Jethro. "You must gain a vision to become a true warrior. But maybe dreams can help you learn how to gain that vision. Are you certain you were going to the right place to gain your power? Maybe you are supposed to go to another place."

Jethro thought for a moment. He had taken for granted that the Beartooth would be the place for his journey; he had considered no other. The Beartooth was a site of power, and there were many stories that could not be explained of what existed up there. The Powers made it their abode, and they had helped his father, whose power animal was the grizzly bear. Jethro had just assumed that he should journey to the home of his father's power. But Many Berries had made an interesting comment.

"Why would you think that your place of power shouldn't be chosen by the ones who are to give you the power, and not by yourself?" Many Berries continued.

"The Beartooth is a place of power," Jethro pointed out. "It is vast, and very strong."

"Are there no others?" she asked. "Do not the peoples of other tribes go to other places of power? Why would you decide where power lies, when it does not come from you? Why wouldn't you let those who give it show you where you are to receive it?"

Jethro knew that Many Berries was right. There were many places within the Crow hunting grounds that the people went to seeking power. The Beartooth happened to be a favorite.

But there was another, smaller range of mountains they called the Crazy Mountains, upriver from the main camping areas, that held a very unusual power. The talk among the elders made everyone believe that those mountains were for special people.

Upon thinking about it, Jethro knew that he should remain more open to considering another place where he might seek his vision. It was something to consider seriously.

"Maybe you're right," he told Many Berries. "Maybe I should be more receptive to learning of where I might go for power. Why would you tell me this? I am your enemy."

"You are not treating me as an enemy," she said. "I do not see why I should treat you as one."

Jethro finished the last of the pemmican. He helped Many Berries give Big Owl some water, and they started again for the village. As they traveled, Jethro began to see that Many Berries was probably right: his stubborness could very well be impeding his progress toward a vision. He, who did not have the power of the spirits, certainly could not make the decision as to where his power would come from. He must remain open to what might come to him. Many Berries had a lot of insight.

The sun had now reached halfway to the western horizon. They had made good time, considering his wounded knee, and Jethro knew they would reach the village well before nightfall. Many Berries asked if they could stop again so that she could give Big Owl more water. He now cried out for it often.

"He is so hot," Many Berries commented. "He will soon burn himself up."

"We'll go as fast as we can," Jethro told her. "We haven't far to travel now."

As they started again, Jethro saw two riders coming out of the trees just ahead. He recognized High Elk's black buffalo pony, Night Runner, and saw that Little Bow was atop its back. Jumps Ahead rode with him on a buckskin.

When they approached and reined the horses, Jethro was just getting over his shock. "What are you two doing this far out from the village?" he asked Little Bow.

"I was certain that you were in danger," Little Bow said, glancing quickly at Many Berries and the injured warrior. "I see you have fought well. Tell us what happened."

"I'll tell you the whole story back in the village," Jethro told him. "The danger is now for you and Jumps Ahead. Do my sister and Jumps Ahead's mother know where you two are?" He knew the answer even before he asked.

"We forgot to tell them," Little Bow replied.

"I was certain of that," Jethro said. "And how did you get the horses?"

"That's a funny story," Little Bow told him. "You must hear it."

"It won't be so funny to High Elk," Jethro remarked. "How are you going to tell him you stole Night Runner?"

Little Bow frowned. "Not stole, *borrowed*."

"You borrow something when you ask for it first," Jethro pointed out. "Are you going to tell me he gave his permission for you to ride his pony so far from the village? Or even to ride the pony at all? What if you were thrown and hurt?"

Little Bow hung his head. "We just wanted to help you."

"I am grateful for that," Jethro acknowledged. "But what could you have done?" It was hard for him to have anger, for he knew that Little Bow's intentions had been good. "How do you think two small boys could save me from something very powerful?"

Little Bow shrugged. "We might have saved you, if you had needed to be saved. But there is no need to worry about that now, so we won't."

Jethro could not help grinning, but he did his best to hide it. There would be those back in the village who would not find it quite so amusing, however.

"The best thing you two boys can do now is to save yourselves any more problems," Jethro suggested. "Stay down by the river under cover and go right back to the village. Tell them where you found me. And tell High Elk not to be too angry. Send him back with two of my horses. Now hurry. Maybe they haven't come looking for you yet."

The boys turned the ponies and kicked them into a run toward the village. Jethro knew they were in deep trouble; taking two good horses and going off without telling anyone was inexcusable.

Still, it was a courageous act for two small boys, and underneath their mothers' anger there would be admiration and pride. The entire village would know that the two possessed the fortitude to attempt dangerous missions.

But small boys were by no means expendable. They were needed to grow into warriors, sorely needed by the people. Unexpected things could happen to them on their way to manhood. Foolish chances made everyone nervous. There were so many ways to die that counting them only brought bad luck. Accidental death took a great toll, as did bad winters without food. And anyone who traveled in small groups was asking for trouble, especially young boys with adventure on their minds.

"I hope Little Bow and Jumps Ahead don't get into too much trouble," Jethro said. "They have good hearts."

"They are very brave," Many Berries commented. "They will make fine warriors."

"If they get to be that old," Jethro said. "I'll bet you did things like that."

"Maybe occasionally. But I usually got caught and had to stay around the village and watch the women work."

"You must not have stayed around for long," Many Berries said. "You know more for your age than anyone I know. In fact, you are the most special person I have ever met."

"Those are nice words," Jethro said.

"You have said nice words to me, also."

"We had better get going now, and you had better be ready," Jethro said. "There will be no nice words from my people when we reach the village."

FIVE

A
S THEY DREW CLOSER TO THE VILLAGE, HIGH
Elk appeared on Night Runner, together
with two warriors and two of Jethro's
best horses. His finest, a dashing young stallion
named Flame, had been given to him by his father after a successful buffalo hunt in which
Jethro had killed four cows with only five arrows.

The warriors with High Elk were armed and
dressed for battle. Jethro was not surprised:
when two young boys ride into a village after
being absent without permission and announce
that enemies are near, no one fails to heed the
news.

High Elk was nearly as tall as Jethro, with a
slightly slimmer build and a jawline that stood
out prominently. He wore his hair waxed high in

front with bear grease and had the tails of two squirrels attached to the belt that held up his breechclout. He, like Jethro, had yet to become a warrior and lacked the adornments of the other two. And also like Jethro, High Elk yearned for the day when he could place a coup feather in his hair.

Originally of the Sore-Lips clan, High Elk had come to the Kicked-in-Their-Bellies with his mother when he was twelve years old. Lodge Builder had married into the band not long after High Elk's father had been killed in battle against the Piegans; she had also lost her three older brothers. High Elk and his mother had lost a lot of relatives to the Blackfeet.

Nearly the same age, Jethro had become instant friends with High Elk after a long and tiring spring morning when the two of them had chased a fledgling raven across the expanses of the upper Yellowstone valley. The young raven had been able to use its newfound soaring abilities more easily than Jethro and High Elk had predicted. Still, they had finally caught the young bird when a down draft off the face of a cliff had brought it to the river's edge.

Since that time, Jethro and High Elk had shared a lot of experiences, including dangerous horse and warrior games. Now that they were past those first carefree days, they hoped to be bound together soon as war brothers.

It usually pleased High Elk to be in Jethro's company, but today he pinched his face tight and set his jaw. He and the others held their horses back a way from where Jethro stood near

71

Many Berries, who was once again tending to Big Owl.

At first Jethro had thought High Elk was angry about Little Bow and Jumps Ahead, but now he knew different. Many Berries' prediction was accurate: it was going to be very hard to make the villagers understand why he had spared Big Owl's life.

"Little Bow found you, I see," Jethro said to High Elk. "I'm glad you've come."

High Elk nodded stoically, eyeing Many Berries and the injured warrior. "I have come, as you asked, to help you back to the village. After tonight I don't want to talk to you for a full day. Your father is out hunting or he would have come with us, I am sure."

"I knew that he was to leave on a hunting trip," Jethro said. "I will see him in the village. I thank you again for coming, but you shouldn't have if you didn't want to."

"You are my closest friend," High Elk said solemnly. "I didn't want you to have more trouble."

"Maybe you haven't looked too closely," Jethro said, "but the trouble is over."

"I can see only enemies that are still alive," High Elk said, glaring at Many Berries. "To me, that means the trouble *isn't* over."

Jethro could see that the other two warriors concurred, but he would not allow his own opinions to be swayed. He told High Elk and the others his story. They listened without expression, even though they could see the fear on Many Berries' face as Jethro described the storm. Then High Elk rode forward with the two ponies, Flame dancing in eagerness to be on the move.

"You must understand," Jethro said to High Elk, "that I have been directed by the spirits. I do not want this warrior to die if I can help it."

"They couldn't have been Crow spirits," High Elk said, holding the reins out. "Not of our people. You were directed by *bad* spirits, I would say."

"Who are you to say where the spirits come from, or how they give messages?" Jethro asked angrily, grabbing the reins from High Elk. "Do you profess to know all there is to know about the Other Side?"

High Elk's face remained rigid. "I only know that my father has crossed over and that I no longer have any uncles on my mother's side of the family, all because of their people." He pointed angrily to Many Berries and Big Owl.

Jethro held Flame's reins and helped Many Berries onto the other pony. "I know you have mourned their loss," Jethro told High Elk. "But that has nothing to do with what happened today. It is all different. I have tried to explain it to you."

One of the other warriors spoke up, his voice angry. "It is not good to bring them to our people. It is foolish!" The other one agreed and the two grumbled further.

Jethro jumped up onto Flame. "Stop this!" he said, his voice vibrating with anger. "Who among you would go against what the signs tell him?

73

Which of you would wish to sleep with angry spirits nearby?"

"The spirits we know do not get angry at the death of an enemy!" one of the warriors shouted. "All of our people know that."

"Did you ever think that maybe the rest of the villagers think the same way?" High Elk asked Jethro. "Don't you know that the rest of our people will not have any more understanding than we here do?"

Jethro steadied his pony. His face was hard. "I must take this warrior to Bull Comes Ahead. I must do what I can to save him. I feel this very strongly. If all of you agree that you want nothing to do with this, I can take the woman and her husband back to the village on my own."

The two warriors with High Elk jerked their horses around and left immediately. High Elk remained. He did not look back to watch them become lost in the dust cloud they had created, but instead kept his eyes on Jethro.

"You are the one who spoke the loudest," Jethro said, "yet you are still here."

"Even though you are foolish," High Elk told him, "you are still my friend. You will always be my friend."

They rode in silence and soon came in sight of the village. Many Berries grew nervous as she watched the people gathering. Jethro tried to calm her, but nothing he could say lessened her anxiety.

The entire village gathered while Jethro and High Elk led Many Berries and Big Owl into camp. High Elk rode far enough away from the other two so that no one would miss his disdain for Many Berries and Big Owl. Everyone in the village knew that Jethro and High Elk were close friends, but they saw no reason why they should share the same feelings about wounded enemies.

The people pointed and talked as Jethro led Many Berries toward the center of the village. Some showed visible outrage, while most looked as if they were seething inside. Their deep respect for Jethro kept anyone from coming forward to insult the two Piegans.

High Elk rode off to join a group of young braves and warriors who were watching with interest. Jethro noticed Little Bow at the front of the crowd, held fast by his mother. He knew that Little Bow was lucky not to be sitting by himself in the lodge.

The more he observed the people, the more apparent it became to Jethro that his decision to return with Many Berries and Big Owl had turned the village upside down. As he dismounted, everyone held back but his father and mother. Both of them had had many difficulties in the past resulting from encounters with Blackfeet people, but neither displayed any hatred toward the two Piegans.

"It looks like you had some serious trouble," Thane said to Jethro. "You didn't get up into the mountains, then?" The years had woven little threads of gray into Thane's red-brown hair and had carved a series of thin lines into his face, yet he stood as tall and straight as ever in his buckskins and broad-brimmed hat. The tail feather of a snowy owl had never been taken from the hat-band, and he still wore the grizzly-claw necklace on special occasions.

Jethro shook his head. "I wasn't meant to go this time. I will have to try again."

"Little Bow told me about your knee. Any wounds more serious than that?"

"No," Jethro answered. "I was lucky."

"You can tell me the whole story later," Thane said. "I can see that you have other problems right now. Your mother and I are glad you came back safely."

Bull Comes Ahead then joined them and looked hard at Jethro. "Things are already beginning to happen to you," he said.

"I'm lucky to be alive," Jethro told him, holding out the pouch with the tobacco leaf in it. "The medicine was very strong."

Bull Comes Ahead waved the pouch back to Jethro. "It is yours to keep. That is why I gave it to you. If your heart is always good, the medicine will stay strong."

"I told this woman that maybe you could help this man. She is supposed to marry him," Jethro said. "I feel that the spirits want me to try to save him."

Bull Comes Ahead bent over the wounded warrior. He shook his head. "I don't know if I can do anything or not. He is hurt very badly."

"I have nothing with which to pay you," Many Berries told him. "I can work for your wife, if that is what you wish."

"I will do what I can and I will not worry about

any payment from you," Bull Comes Ahead told her. "It would be better if you did not live in my lodge, as my wife has lost two brothers to your people in battle."

Many Berries stared at Bull Comes Ahead. "Why would you try to help Big Owl then, if it will mean causing trouble between you and your wife?"

"My wife must learn to understand," Bull Comes Ahead said. "What is past is done and cannot be changed. She and I have talked about this before. What can be changed is what we are doing now, and what comes with each changing moon. It does not matter that you are enemies of the Crow people. He is an injured man, and if I were in his place, I would wish for someone to help me. So I will do it."

Bull Comes Ahead called for some of the village men to help carry the warrior to his lodge. A number of warriors came forward willingly, for what Bull Comes Ahead had just said made perfect sense to them. But others of the people, those who had lost brothers and husbands to the Piegans at one time or another, were angered by the thought that some of their own were helping a sworn enemy. Bull Comes Ahead's wife was among them.

"What are you doing?" Calling Bird asked as the medicine man was about to enter their lodge.

"You can see what I am doing," he replied. "I was asked to try to save this warrior's life, and that's what I am going to do."

"But he is of the Blackfeet, an enemy of our people. Surely you can see that."

Bull Comes Ahead moved to one side with his wife. Behind them, villagers had begun to shout their opinions about what was going on.

"If I were wounded and in an enemy village, would you not want someone to try to help me?" he asked Calling Bird.

"I would not expect it," she told him. "They would not do it."

"How can you be so certain?"

"Our people are enemies!" Calling Bird said again. "What if he lives to kill more of our people? Why are you such a fool?"

"One who offers help to another is no fool," Bull Comes Ahead pointed out. "A fool is one who holds back and allows fear and hatred to make important decisions."

"Can't you see that this will set the people against you?" Calling Bird persisted. "Jethro would have been better advised to have killed them both and brought their scalps for us to dance over. As it is now, you and he are making a lot of people very angry. Perhaps they will never forgive either of you, whether the Piegan lives or dies. Their anger will never die."

"They were angry before the warrior was brought to me," Bull Comes Ahead pointed out. "I cannot be responsible for that. When their brothers and husbands went to war, they knew there was a chance they would not return. That had nothing to do with me. So don't blame me for everyone's anger."

"But you know that the Blackfeet have been our enemies since we came to these lands," Calling Bird said, her tone turned to pleading. "We have always fought them. Now you intend to save one who may fight against us once again."

"Maybe it would be better if we weren't fighting all the time," Bull Comes Ahead told her. "Did you ever think of that?"

"It's too late to make peace!" Calling Bird said, spitting out the words. "There have been too many killed on both sides. There will always be war."

"Tell that to the war chiefs," Bull Comes Ahead remarked. "I am a medicine man, a healer, and it is up to me to keep the other side of war in balance. You knew that when you came as my wife into my lodge. It is up to me to work for peace, and that is what I am going to do today."

Bull Comes Ahead turned and strode into the lodge. There he found Jethro and Many Berries preparing a bed for Big Owl. He instructed Many Berries to gather five medicinal plants—the roots, stems, and leaves of each—and place them separately into buffalo-foot handbags. When she had been given the handbags and told where to locate the plants, Jethro set out with her toward his mother's lodge.

"Are you certain your mother will want to help in this?" Many Berries asked.

"I have no doubt."

As they hurried past angry villagers, Many Berries again wondered at Jethro's determination to save Big Owl. The spirits must have made his course of action very plain to him. But he could not think that everyone else would do as he wanted just because of what the spirits had told him.

"Perhaps your mother feels the same anger as those who are shouting," Many Berries suggested. "After all, she was taken as a child and has lost relatives in battle. How can you insist that she help me?"

"I know my mother quite well," Jethro replied. "I am not going to insist that she help you, but I am certain that she will."

Many Berries soon learned that Jethro knew his mother every bit as well as he had boasted of. Morning Swan did her best to make Many Berries as comfortable as possible. She had spent considerable time nursing a wounded lover herself—in fact, two of them. One had been Jethro's father. She knew what Many Berries was feeling.

Although her raven hair was now tinged lightly with gray, Morning Swan still retained the lithe figure of youth. She still worked hard at women's duties but maintained her abilities on horseback as much as she ever had. After her abduction and as a young woman among the Piegans, she had become wife to a warrior named Long Hand. He had died slowly from a terrible hip wound received in battle and she had mourned him. Upon his death, Morning Swan fought the tradition that said she must become wife to Long Hand's tyrant brother, Rising Hawk. Rather than suffer that, Morning Swan had fled with her little daughter, Rosebud, and had soon met Jethro's father.

"We should hurry and collect the plants,"

Morning Swan told Many Berries. "I will see if
Rosebud will help us. That way we can work
much faster and get them to Bull Comes Ahead
much sooner."

Jethro left them then and returned to Bull
Comes Ahead's lodge. The ancient medicine man
was already taking the first steps of his healing
ceremony. He was painting his face white on one
side and black on the other. A crimson stripe ran
down the middle of his forehead, along the
bridge of his nose and down under his chin, ending at the base of his throat.

While Jethro watched Bull Comes Ahead paint
himself and sing songs, Little Bow came into the
lodge. He said nothing for a time, but took Jethro's hand and stared at the wounded Blackfoot
warrior.

"Will he die?" Little Bow asked.

"It is hard to say," Jethro replied. "But he is
far closer to crossing over than he is to coming
back to this life."

"What happened to him?"

"I was praying on a small hill when he and the
woman and two warriors came. He charged up
the hill at me to count coup. When I raised the
Sacred Pipe, his pony reared over backward and
fell on him."

Little Bow looked up at Jethro. "He is the
horned badger of my dream, is he not?"

Jethro nodded. "I believe that he is, and Many
Berries is the woman you saw trying to stand in
front of him."

Little Bow smiled. "He doesn't scare me as
much as he did in the dream."

Bull Comes Ahead finished his singing and turned to Little Bow. "I want you to go and find your friend, Jumps Ahead, and bring him back to this lodge with you. You and he are strong boys. I want both of you to help me talk to the spirits on behalf of this warrior."

Little Bow's eyes grew large. "You wish to use *me*?"

"Yes," Bull Comes Ahead said. "You and Jumps Ahead. Now hurry and find him. I want to get you ready and begin the ceremony."

Little Bow was still staring at Bull Comes Ahead in disbelief. This honor was enormous. It meant that Bull Comes Ahead thought a great deal of him and Jumps Ahead, and respected their bravery and their commitment to Jethro's welfare.

"Hurry!" Bull Comes Ahead told Little Bow. "There is not much time."

As Little Bow scurried out of the lodge, Jethro knelt down beside Big Owl and noted the extremely shallow rising of his chest and the tightly drawn skin along his facial bones. He turned to Bull Comes Ahead.

"Do you think you can save him?"

"I cannot say. I will try, as you and the Black-foot woman have asked me to do. Tell me, what happened out there?"

"It is difficult to explain," Jethro said. "I kept seeing the ravens and they looked back, warning me of an enemy approach from the north." He looked down at Big Owl. "This man was crazy. He charged at me, even though the storm came.

82

He just kept coming, and the Sacred Pipe saved me."

Bull Comes Ahead sat stoically, thinking. "The Sacred Pipe has always fed us and been good to us. But now there is something happening. I don't know what it is."

"Do you feel you shouldn't have given me the pipe to take on my journey?"

"Oh, no! I *had* to give you the pipe. I told you, I dreamed about that. But the pipe won't let me see what is to happen. It is for you to see and to do whatever must be done."

Jethro took a deep breath. "Do you even know why this is happening?"

"It is part of the bad times that are coming," Bull Comes Ahead replied. "I am certain of this. Perhaps it is some kind of test. I don't know. I don't think it will matter anyway. There are many bad times ahead."

Jethro knew what Bull Comes Ahead was saying; all of the people were aware of the prophetic stories the elders were telling. Bull Comes Ahead and many of the elders in the other clans and bands talked openly about the anger of First Maker toward the Crow people. In the past, a terrible spotted sickness had decimated the Crow. More of them had died and now rested on burial scaffolds than now lived within the entire Crow nation. In one village, it was told, many warriors had ridden their best ponies off of a high cliff in sacrifice. Although the sickness finally departed, grief and sadness persisted.

"First Maker is very angry," Bull Comes Ahead

now said to Jethro, who had heard this many times before. "There is no way we can appease Him. I thought that maybe by giving you the Sacred Pipe to take with you, something might come to you. I guess something did come to you, and it seems to have been bad."

"Then why do you want to help me save Big Owl's life?" Jethro asked.

Bull Comes Ahead looked at Jethro solemnly. "I am going by your feelings. I am doing this for you. This is what *you* want. I must trust what you want. Don't you trust yourself now?"

Jethro felt confused. The Blackfoot warrior had wanted to kill him, yet he was asking Bull Comes Ahead to save the man's life. Although this went against the traditional way of thinking about warfare, it was what he had felt—and still felt—he must do.

"Do you think you can save him?" he asked again.

Bull Comes Ahead gave the faintest of smiles. "I will do what I can. He is very close to the spirit world now, very close to crossing over. If he lives, it will be through the strength of the young boys and the desires of the Powers that will it. I have no way of knowing at this time."

"I will know that I did what I could, whether this man lives or not," Jethro said. "But do you think that Little Bow and Jumps Ahead will blame themselves if he dies?"

"It will be a good lesson for both of them," Bull Comes Ahead said. "Whether this man lives or dies, they must know that to try to do what can be done for the sake of life is very important. It may be that this warrior will be called to cross over. From your description of how he charged you and did not care about the omens, it would seem that way. But either way, the boys will learn something in their hearts and will think more highly of life. That is for certain.''

SIX

LITTLE BOW RAN THROUGH THE VILLAGE TO-
ward Jumps Ahead's lodge, dodging pup-
pies and small children along the way. He
wanted to shout for joy. Healing ceremonies
were very sacred, and no one who performed
them, especially a medicine man of Bull Comes
Ahead's greatness, chose just anyone to assist in
them.

Jumps Ahead's mother was sitting in front of
the lodge, beading a new elkskin dress for herself. Only four winters older than his own
mother, Crane had already suffered greatly in her
life. She had lost three husbands in battle and
another during a buffalo hunt. Now no one
wanted to marry her.

In addition, everyone believed that the spirits
did not want her to bring forth life. Despite her

marriages to four different men, Jumps Ahead was her only child.

Crane was as pretty as nearly any woman among the people, but the warriors believed her possessed by bad spirits who had caused her husbands' deaths. No warrior went near her, and she took part in few of the people's ceremonies. She was not asked to join any women's organizations, and was left alone most of the time. In effect, she was an outcast, allowed to stay with the band only for her safety.

Crane was resigned to her life as a loner and seemed to care little about what others thought of her. She was a Crow and a member of an influential medicine clan, so no one spoke out against her publicly. Meat, and hides for clothes and lodging, came from her brothers. They helped her but also feared her, since a man could not have her as a wife and remain alive.

Little Bow had always gotten along well with Crane. He cared only—in the way of boys his age—that Crane allow Jumps Ahead to play games with him and share his young life. He realized that Crane remained alone whenever he took Jumps Ahead off with him. Yet he knew that she was not concerned about her own welfare. Instead, she worried about Jumps Ahead incessantly.

Little Bow could recognize many traits in Crane that were clearly present in his own mother. Each woman herded her son like a prairie hen herding its chicks and wanted to know her son's every move and where he was at all times. Little Bow had not spoken with Jumps Ahead since returning from their search for Jethro; he had, in fact, not seen Jumps Ahead at all.

Little Bow knew that Jumps Ahead had found himself in very deep trouble, and he felt himself responsible. He hoped to make amends to Crane. He was sure that she would feel better when he told her they were to be honored by helping Bull Comes Ahead in a healing ceremony.

Little Bow approached Crane with a beaming face. She was intent on her beading and did not look up at first, sewing feverishly with a thin thread of sinew and a porcupine quill. He noticed that the muscles in her face were as knotted as those in her arms. She spoke before he could utter even a single word.

"So, it's the mischievous boy who wanders far from the village, taking others with him, bringing worry to each mother's heart."

Little Bow's eyebrows raised. "I just—"

"It would have been better had you gone alone," Crane continued. "Jumps Ahead knows how frightened I was when I couldn't find him. It will be a long time before he goes very far from my sight."

"It was for a good reason," Little Bow said defensively. "I was worried about Jethro. I wish you wouldn't be so angry."

"Did you come to try to talk me out of my anger?" She looked up, her face twisted. "Did you come to try to take away the pain I remember, the pain of having someone whom you love very much go and never come back?"

Little Bow looked into her eyes. Sadness had replaced the anger. He realized now that Crane had prepared herself for her son's death, that she had believed he would not return alive.

"I came to tell you some good news," Little Bow said. "Some news about honor for Jumps Ahead and me."

"Honor?"

"Yes. Bull Comes Ahead has asked us to help him with a healing ceremony. Can Jumps Ahead go back to his lodge with me?"

"What healing ceremony?"

"To help the wounded Blackfoot warrior."

Crane's jaw muscles tightened again. "You must be joking."

"It's no joke. Bull Comes Ahead has asked Jumps Ahead and me to take part."

"No, I mean you must be joking to come here and ask permission for Jumps Ahead to take part."

Crane was now angrier than before, angrier than Little Bow had ever seen her. She jabbed her sewing quill into the material and stifled a scream when it broke.

"I didn't come to anger you," Little Bow said, backing up a step. "This is something that should make you very proud of Jumps Ahead."

Crane rummaged through a deerfoot bag to locate another needle, her breath tight.

"Don't you want to be proud of Jumps Ahead?" Little Bow persisted.

"A son makes his mother proud only when he learns to respect her feelings," Crane said. "Jumps Ahead certainly has no regard for my feelings. I don't believe you could possibly care that much about your mother's feelings, either."

Desperate now, Little Bow appealed one last time to her sense of pride. "This ceremony is something very special. Jumps Ahead is being given great honor."

Crane respected Little Bow's persistence, but she would never allow him to change her mind. She found another needle and began to thread it.

"I don't want my son doing anything for a while," she said. Her voice began to rise again. "And certainly not to help those two Piegans. I cannot understand what has happened to Jethro." She looked up at Little Bow, her eyes filled with anger. "To bring an enemy into the village and expect everyone to understand! That is impossible."

"He has a sacred mission," Little Bow pointed out. "Don't you know the spirits have asked him to do this?"

"I don't care what you say, Little Bow, I can see no reason to save the life of an enemy." She got the quill threaded and started back to work. "You might as well return to Bull Comes Ahead now and leave me alone. I won't change my mind."

"May I talk to Jumps Ahead?"

"I said go!"

Little Bow turned away from her, but his hurt quickly changed to anger. He turned again, faced Crane, and stuck out his jaw. "No wonder nobody likes you. No wonder. You *are* bad medicine!"

Then he ran, churning through the dust of the village toward Bull Comes Ahead's lodge. He worried that the old medicine man would be angry and that Jethro would be disappointed in him. He did not know how he would explain this to either of them. Maybe Bull Comes Ahead would no longer want him to help with the ceremony.

When Little Bow entered the lodge, he was fighting tears. He sat down beside Jethro and bit his lip.

"Did you talk to Jumps Ahead?" Jethro asked.

Bull Comes Ahead answered for him. "Jumps Ahead is not allowed to participate in the ceremony, is he?"

"Crane won't let him," Little Bow said. "She is a mean woman."

"Now, you should try to understand how she feels," Jethro said. "If you had only a single son in your life and he was gone long enough to cause you worry, wouldn't you want to make him understand that life must be held sacred?"

"Yes, but not for so long," Little Bow said. "She has kept him in the lodge ever since we got back."

"She was deeply concerned about him," Bull Comes Ahead said. "What if you two had met death?"

Little Bow looked up into the medicine man's eyes. "I would meet death any time for Jethro."

Bull Comes Ahead nodded. "I know that. It is because of your understanding of virtue, even at such a young age, that I have asked you to help me in this healing ceremony. Perhaps it is not proper for Jumps Ahead to participate."

The door flap moved and Jumps Ahead burst into the lodge. He was out of breath. "I did not want you to start without me!"

Little Bow jumped to his feet. "How did you get here? Your mother told me she would never let you come."

"It was *your* mother who made this happen," Jumps Ahead told him. "She heard you shouting and told my mother that you shouldn't have gotten angry. She hugged my mother and said you didn't mean it. Then my mother said you were right and told me to come over here."

"I'm glad it has turned out this way," Bull Comes Ahead said with a smile. "This is a good sign. Now we must go to the sweat lodge for a time. The women will be back with the plants before long."

Jethro prepared to leave as Bull Comes Ahead instructed the boys on their part in the ceremony, but the old medicine man stopped him at the door flap.

"What has happened today has brought change among our people," he said. "I told you before, I feel that there is more change to come. Just continue to listen to yourself."

"I'm glad you are helping me to get through this," Jethro said.

"I am trying to tell you that this is only the beginning."

Jethro felt himself growing concerned.

"You have always done what was right for you,

even as a small boy," Bull Comes Ahead continued, "and you can be certain that you have
pleased the spirits once again. You must realize,
though, that your pathway from here on will
become even harder. Much harder than you expect."

"My quest for power will meet further trouble?" Jethro asked.

"You can be certain of it," Bull Comes Ahead
replied. "Anyone who is destined to carry the Sacred Pipe must face great adversity. It is in how
you accept this adversity that you will be judged
by First Maker."

As he left the lodge, Jethro realized that Bull
Comes Ahead was warning him. Whether Big Owl
lived or died, his journey to manhood would become more difficult. Just because he was working to save Big Owl's life, it did not mean that he
would receive special favors from the Powers.
Any greatness he acquired would be long and
hard in coming.

Cuts Buffalo had watched Jethro enter the village with the two Blackfeet and had heard of
what had happened. The story had spread like
fire before a hot wind. Many of the people continued in their outrage, while others contended
that Jethro was right. If Jethro felt that he must
help an enemy, the feeling must be honored. Even
some who had lost relatives in battle stood up
for Jethro and Bull Comes Ahead.

Now Cuts Buffalo stood among the women and
watched Morning Swan and Rosebud accompany
the Blackfoot woman into a meadow beyond the

village to dig medicine plants. Everyone knew about the healing ceremony to try to save Big Owl's life. Cuts Buffalo thought about this young woman: she had to be terribly worried about the wounded warrior, and concerned about the hostility of the people as well. The pressure she felt must be tremendous.

In a way, it did not seem fair. The young Blackfoot woman was powerless. She had been thrust into a circumstance over which she had no control. Although Cuts Buffalo realized that she would be placing herself right in the middle of the conflict, she wanted to help the woman. She decided to follow after the three and offer her assistance.

Cuts Buffalo knew Morning Swan and Rosebud only casually. She felt that this would be a good opportunity to get better acquainted with them and to hasten the plant collection at the same time.

Once she caught up with the women, Cuts Buffalo volunteered her help. She was welcomed gladly. Many Berries studied her and then turned her attention back to Morning Swan, who was leading them to the site where the medicine plants grew in profusion.

They began their work in silence, concentrating first on yarrow and prairie sage. Many Berries turned to stare at Cuts Buffalo occasionally, but never spoke. Rosebud finally asked Cuts Buffalo what had made her decide to help.

"I wanted to get to know you and your mother better," Cuts Buffalo said honestly. "I realized you could use help in gathering the plants, although you didn't really need it. Three is enough to do it quickly. But I decided to come along anyway, if you would let me. You see, I have always liked Jethro . . ."

Rosebud and Many Berries looked up from their work. Morning Swan strolled to a nearby juniper tree, acting as if the news did not surprise her.

". . . and I want to be Sits-First-Beside-Him wife to Jethro," she continued. "Just as soon as I can."

Rosebud raised her eyebrows. Many Berries said nothing, but studied Cuts Buffalo from the corner of her eye.

"Jethro isn't yet a warrior," Rosebud pointed out.

"I am aware of that," Cuts Buffalo said. "I am also aware that he will likely be so before the winter moons come. He is that strong."

"I am wondering, then . . . has Jethro already approached you?" Rosebud asked. "Has he played the flute or held out the blanket for you?"

"No," Cuts Buffalo admitted, stuffing yarrow stems and leaves into an elkfoot handbag. "I'm not certain he even knows I exist."

"He knows you exist," Morning Swan assured her, smiling as she put a number of juniper cuttings into a large skin bag. "I'm not going to tell you what he thinks of you, for I can't be certain. But I've seen him look at you from a distance."

"You have?" Cuts Buffalo exclaimed. She felt herself bursting from within. She was so grateful to Morning Swan for sharing the information that she wanted to hug her.

"It could be that he looks at a lot of the young women," Many Berries said. She looked down at her work, speaking matter-of-factly. "Maybe there are other women he looks at for a longer period of time."

Many Berries' comments shocked Cuts Buffalo. She could see that both Morning Swan and Rosebud were also taken aback. After a long silence, Morning Swan asked Many Berries, "Does my son suddenly interest you more than the man we are trying to save?"

Many Berries continued to look down at her work. "Your son is a powerful man. He will be even more powerful once he becomes a warrior. Any woman with eyes and feelings can see that. Any woman would want that man for a husband."

"What you see in my son is obvious," Morning Swan told Many Berries. "I asked you if he has overwhelmed you enough to come between you and this wounded man you say you want to marry."

Many Berries finally looked up at Morning Swan. "The man who becomes my husband will be strong and proud. Big Owl is strong, or he would have crossed over already. Perhaps he will live to become my husband. That I cannot tell yet. But if he does not, I will have someone like your son to provide for me. I want someone like Jethro to bring me the finest skins for dressmaking, to seat me on his best horses and parade me in front of all the other women. Yes, I want someone like your son. And there may be no one else like your son."

Many Berries went back to digging matter-of-factly. Morning Swan and Rosebud exchanged glances and continued cutting juniper. They realized that they were doing a sacred thing for Bull Comes Ahead and were violating ethics by their conversation. Nothing should be said, except in discussion of the plants.

They trained their thoughts back on their work, although Many Berries' words still echoed like sudden thunder in their heads.

Cuts Buffalo stared at Many Berries for a long time before she continued working. Anger welled up within her, an emotion she knew she must not entertain at this time. But it appalled her to think that Many Berries—a total stranger—had the nerve to come into her life and claim the right to Jethro should her own man die.

Cuts Buffalo thought about confronting Many Berries. The Blackfoot woman needed a lesson in manners. But she held her tongue and began to collect the last of the medicine plants.

On their way back to the village, Cuts Buffalo walked beside Morning Swan, a distance behind Rosebud and Many Berries. "Many Berries seems to think that she has free run of our village," she said to Morning Swan. "I can't imagine that. What kind of woman is she?"

"Take heart," Morning Swan told her. "She is only proving to you that my son is worth your desire."

"I don't need her to convince me of that," Cuts

Buffalo said impatiently. "I just wonder what makes her think she can have anything she wants."

"That is her nature," Morning Swan said with a smile. "You would be wise to understand that woman as best you can. I have a feeling that she will be your strongest competitor for my son's affections."

"You can't mean that."

"Isn't it obvious to you?" Morning Swan said. "Can't you see that Many Berries has one of the strongest men among the Piegans? She no doubt picked him out and managed to get him for herself because she thought—and rightfully so—that the man was powerful and would do well by her. For some reason, that warrior made a big mistake in confronting Jethro. He may pay for it with his life. But even if he lives, Many Berries will always think Jethro the stronger of the two. She may decide to leave Big Owl and go after Jethro."

"It is not fair that she should stand in my way," Cuts Buffalo said angrily. "She is not even of our people. Why should she want to make it hard for me?"

Morning Swan stopped and turned to face Cuts Buffalo. "What makes you think that anything worth having should be easy to get? It takes a lot of hard work to find and hold that which is the best. Only the best attain that which is the best."

"Why should I have to compete with an enemy?" Cuts Buffalo asked.

"For that matter, don't you consider other

young women among our own people enemies when it comes to wanting my son for a husband?"

"That is not the same."

"It is the very same. You may not think of our people in the way you would a tribal enemy, but you are certainly competing for what you want. You must work hard to get it."

"Many Berries has no right to Jethro," Cuts Buffalo argued. "He is one of our people. She can stay with her own tribe. She can pick men from within her own people."

"You can't keep someone like Many Berries contained within boundaries," Morning Swan pointed out, starting again for the village. "She is too strong. Her destiny takes her where she can strive to win."

"I want your son more than she does," Cuts Buffalo said. "You know that."

"It's not for me to decide who has my son in marriage," Morning Swan told her. "He must make that choice himself. He must make it on his own, without influence from anyone."

Cuts Buffalo clenched her teeth. "I will show Many Berries that she can't have just any man she wants. At least she can't have the man *I* want."

Morning Swan smiled. "Now you are talking like the kind of woman who would make Jethro a very good wife."

As they entered the village and made their way to Bull Comes Ahead's lodge, Cuts Buffalo realized the truth in Morning Swan's words: Jethro was certainly destined to become one of the most sought-after warriors among the Crow people, and gaining him for a husband would be a difficult task. Love by itself would not be enough; it would take more determination than affection.

SEVEN

AS NIGHT FELL AND THE HEALING CEREMONY
got underway, the village remained divided over the issue of Many Berries and
Big Owl. High Elk, even though he was Jethro's
closest friend, joined with a number of people to
demand that Many Berries take Big Owl—
whether he lived or not—and leave the village.
High Elk insisted to those who asked him that
"he was doing it for Jethro's sake."

Jethro paced in front of his family's lodge, his
arms crossed, his mind whirling. His mother and
father were visiting at another lodge; they had
told him often that they would have no part in
his decisions. They had said that becoming a man
and a warrior meant allowing your innermost
self the freedom to make choices without bias

from anyone else. He could not even speak to them about his feelings.

There was no point in approaching High Elk again. Jethro had already done that several times, and each time High Elk had hurried off in the other direction. Jethro had felt foolish calling after him and had finally given up. All that remained was to await the outcome of the healing ceremony.

While Jethro paced, one of the warriors who had accompanied High Elk earlier that day approached cautiously. Seven Deer—four winters older—stood nearly as tall as Jethro, but he was not as well built. Strong and clear-headed, he had saved more than one fellow warrior from death during a raid against the Lakota Sioux the summer before. He had already gained high respect among the people.

"I know that you are angry," Seven Deer began, "but High Elk's feelings, as well as my own and others', are just as strong as yours."

"It is not anger that flows through me," Jethro told the warrior. "It is sadness that my best friend would work to destroy what the spirits have asked me to do."

"High Elk says that the two Piegans are very bad medicine," Seven Deer said quickly. "He says that they remind our people of grief and will bring only more grief."

"How can he know this?" Jethro questioned. "How many dreams has he had regarding these two people?"

"He has not spoken of any dreams," Seven

Deer responded. "But that does not mean he is wrong."

"I just want to know what makes him so sure he is right," Jethro said. "I have never seen him like this."

"It is as I told you," Seven Deer repeated. "There are those of us, especially High Elk, whose feelings on this matter are as strong as yours. We believe that only bad can come of this. It is a sensing we have."

"Why don't I have this sensing then?" Jethro insisted.

Seven Deer shook his head. "The spirits are telling you something different. That is not to say that either of us is wrong. It is only to say that something unusual is bound to happen."

Jethro agreed. In fact, the very beginning of his quest for power had been witness to unusual happenings. Large, dark spirits such as the one that had descended on him with the storm appeared rarely in Crow lands. There were legends of huge, twisting spirits that descended upon the grasslands far to the east. Such a spirit would certainly have killed him. As it was, he had been lucky. Although he had been injured, his pain for some reason had not overpowered him.

His knee was still sore and would remain tender for some time to come, but it was going to be less of a problem than he had at first envisioned. And the cuts and bruises would not burden him or slow him down. He only hoped that the situation with Many Berries and Big Owl would favor him as well.

Jethro found himself agreeing with Seven Deer

on a few points, but he still did not think that talking against the healing ceremony was warranted.

"There is no way to stop High Elk from what he is doing," Jethro said, "but I don't think it's right for him to protest the healing ceremony. It does not show much respect for anyone, especially for Bull Comes Ahead."

Seven Deer shrugged. "It is possible that even Bull Comes Ahead can make a mistake."

Jethro watched Seven Deer turn and walk away to join the men of the village, who were gathering and talking. Jethro saw his father among the elders. All of the important men were there, and a council meeting would be held during the healing ceremony. The issue of Many Berries and Big Owl was urgent enough to be discussed as soon as possible.

Jethro watched the men for a while longer and then turned as his mother approached. "Stop worrying so much and have something to eat," she said. "You have had nothing for four days, and you stand around waiting for something over which you have no control."

"I've had something to eat," he said as he walked with her back to the lodge.

"Oh?"

"Yes. Many Berries gave me some pemmican. And I dug some yampa to eat with it."

Morning Swan smiled. "She wanted you to get some strength so you could speak to everyone on her behalf."

Jethro sat down next to the fire and watched

his mother fill a tin trade cup with stew. "She's not so bad," he said. "I believe her heart is good."

"Then why does she want to marry a man like Big Owl, a man who goes against the signs given by the spirits?"

Jethro thought back to earlier in the day, when the thunderstorm had come in over the bluff. He could again see Big Owl's wild eyes as he kicked his pinto into a run up the hill at him.

"She tried to warn him," Jethro defended her. "He wouldn't listen."

"How well does she listen and look?" Morning Swan asked. "Does she do things she shouldn't?"

Jethro swallowed a mouthful of stew. "I don't know, Mother. I hardly know her."

"But you like her."

"I told you, she seems to be very nice. I think she just wants to be a friend."

Morning Swan chuckled. "A very good friend."

Jethro looked up from his stew. "What are you saying?"

"I should tell you now of the feelings about you shared by two women," Morning Swan replied. "They almost began to fight over you."

"What two women?"

"Many Berries and one who is near marrying age in the village. Her name is Cuts Buffalo. You know of her. I've seen you watching her."

"I know who she is," Jethro said. "Why would these two women be quarreling over me?"

"Maybe if you thought for a moment, you could understand," Morning Swan said. "Cuts Buffalo has told me that she would like to become your wife. And Many Berries wants to marry a man of

power. A man such as you will become very powerful—if he doesn't meet his fate first."

"Are you telling me that both women want me
for a husband?"

"That is what it sounds like to me."

"I thought Many Berries loved Big Owl."

"For different people there might be a different
meaning of love."

"Why are you telling me this?"

"There are many tests that lie before you,
Jethro," Morning Swan replied. "I am just saying that you are being called upon by the spirits
to be wise, even though you have not yet reached
the age of an elder."

Jethro thought for a moment. He realized that
Cuts Buffalo was already old enough to become
a wife and that even now there were two warriors in particular eager to take her into a lodge.
He knew these young warriors and knew that the
only reason they were not pressing her father
was that her brothers had not yet become warriors, with families of their own. Until that time,
she would be required to continue helping her
mother in their lodge, because that was the way
her father wanted it.

Jethro had not been aware, though, that Many
Berries would show that kind of interest in him,
especially in front of strangers. Even though he
was highly thought of, his vision quest and sub-
sequent raids against enemies for honors would
be the only measure of his real worth as a warrior.

Jethro caught his mother staring at him, looking right into the very depths of his being. He

knew that she had caught him trying to hide from the truth. She knew full well that he was trying to hide even from himself, and that he had grown attached to Many Berries during the short time he had known her.

"Do you know my heart, Mother?" he asked.

"It is not for me to decide your destiny," Morning Swan replied. "Just be certain that you look to the Powers before you decide what to do."

"It is hard to know what to do," he said. "I don't know why I have these feelings for Many Berries."

"There is nothing wrong with the way she looks," Morning Swan said, "but a lovely appearance doesn't always mean a lovely heart. Just remember that."

Both the council and the healing ceremony were underway when one of the warriors who had been on watch in the hills above the village rode in with five traders. Jethro had a messenger summon his father and the other elders from the council. Jethro and High Elk, along with some of the warriors and a few elders, watched while the traders began unloading packs from the backs of six mules, passing out gifts to everyone.

Thane asked Jethro, "Did they say who they are?"

"No," Jethro replied. "They just rode in and acted like they wanted to take over."

"Do they have whiskey with them?"

"I don't know."

"We had better stop this before they have our

people all excited over what they've brought," Thane said.

When they reached the visitors, they found that many of the villagers were already examining gifts—small-caliber trade rifles for the men and cloth dresses and trinket jewelry for the women. Jethro stood back and listened while his father joined the village elders in questioning the newcomers.

Their leader was dressed in ragged and greasy furs and wore a faded red French *voyageur*'s cap. He spat a stream of tobacco juice as he studied Jethro's father.

"I don't know any of you," Thane Thompson told him. "Who do you work for?"

"American Fur," the trader replied with a grunt, dismounting and looking around the village. "Who else would a man work for?"

Stoutly built and light-complected, near Jethro's age, he held an air of contempt for everyone, including the men who rode with him. He squinted as he surveyed the village and began scratching his hair under the worn cap. He studied the grit he had collected under his nails and spat again before he spoke.

"I been looking for my uncle for quite a spell since coming west. He used to work for the company, but they don't know where he's at." He looked squarely at Jethro's father. "I heard there's a big-medicine white man named Thompson who's a chief among the Crow and that he might know something about my uncle. Would you be Thompson?"

Thane nodded. "Who's your uncle?"

"His name's Jack Cutter. Ever hear of him?"

Thane looked hard at the man. "You're not looking for Jack Cutter."

The trader smiled crookedly. "You don't believe me? I'm his nephew, Harlan Cutter. Why wouldn't I want to find my uncle?"

"The American Fur Company knows what happened to Wild Jack Cutter," Jethro's father continued. "If you work for the company, you also know. He was killed by Blackfeet over ten years ago."

"Well, I reckon I did know that for a fact," Harlan Cutter admitted with a raw laugh. "I just wanted to see if you felt bad about him dying the way he did."

"I didn't have anything to do with the way he died," Thane told Cutter. "Your uncle was a man who got himself into a lot of trouble. That time he got himself in too deep."

Harlan Cutter squinted hard. "All I know is that my uncle wrote me when I was a kid. He promised to bring me out and let me live out here with him. I never got to come when I wanted, and I don't think he should have died."

"What do you know about the way he died?" Thane asked.

"Enough to know that if it hadn't been for you, he would likely be alive today."

"He was in that Blackfoot village before I got there. Or didn't the company tell you that?"

"I got my news from those who know," Cutter contended. "I believe what I want."

Thane nodded. "Now that we've discussed your uncle, what other business do you have?"

"I just come to do some friendly trading," Cutter replied. "No hard feelings." He pointed to the women with their cloth and the men with the trade rifles, all of them admiring the wares. "See anything wrong with that?"

"Is it buffalo robes you want?" Thane asked.

"Could be," Cutter said. "I want to be as good a trader as Uncle Jack was. I figure I can do good out here for the company, just like he did."

He went on talking about how his uncle had been a good man and had always been generous to everyone. Jethro had been a boy when Jack Cutter roamed the mountains with a small, sick man named Toots, killing and stealing. Those who knew the man stayed a great distance from him. It was obvious to Jethro that Jack Cutter's nephew was the same kind of man.

Harlan Cutter turned his head slightly to scratch again under his cap. Jethro moved closer and to one side to get a better view of something that looked like a growth on Cutter's right cheek. He continued to move around until the light of the fire showed Cutter's disfigured face in more detail. A mass of scar tissue, partially hidden within his patchy beard, welled up from skin coated with dirt. The remnants of a tattoo trailed in black lines around the edge of the scar, which appeared to be from a burn. Jethro stared until Cutter stopped talking and looked at him.

"You would have liked it," he told Jethro. His eyes showed no trace of emotion—no humor, no anger, nothing. "It was a fine piece of work, a lady at that. But I ain't going to say what she looked like. Got it in St. Louis from a breed Ki-

owa. He put it in with a needle and charcoal."
He patted his cheek. "The Sioux tried to burn it
off with a hot knife, but I spat in their faces."

The traders with him nodded and voiced their
approval. He stopped patting his cheek and spat
at Jethro's feet. "You're half Injun and half white
yourself, ain't you? Half and half."

"Is there something wrong with that?" Jethro
asked.

The trader raised his eyebrows. "Who taught
you to talk?"

Jethro smiled slightly. "Why haven't you
learned yet?"

Cutter frowned. He turned away from Jethro
to look for Jethro's father and saw him standing
beside the farthest two mules.

"I see you'd rather trade in whiskey than in
buffalo robes," Thane Thompson said, pointing
to the kegs loaded on the backs of the animals.

Cutter ambled back with his men and spoke
without concern. "I figured a man like you could
appreciate good quality. It ain't like the other
stuff you'll get, I'll guarantee that."

Jethro watched while his father untied one of
the kegs and hauled it over in front of the fire.

"Check it out if'n you don't believe me," Cutter
said. "The best you'll find, I'll guarantee."

Thane hoisted the keg and tossed it into the
flames, where it exploded into a fireball. "It
seems to be pretty good stuff," he said. "Let's see
about the other kegs."

"Hey, what do you think you're doing?" Cutter
demanded.

Jethro stepped in front of him. "You ought to

know that this band of Crow does not trade for whiskey. In fact, we don't trade with anybody who brings whiskey in here."

"Are you crazy?" Cutter said. He started to raise his fist against Jethro, then thought better of it. He and his men watched while Thane Thompson hurled the rest of the kegs into the fire.

Harlan Cutter turned and ordered his men back on their horses. He began hissing vulgarities at both Thane and Jethro. "You got no right to do that to company property. Wait till they hear about it."

"You can trade with somebody else, Cutter," Thane told him. "We don't need your kind around here."

Cutter spat as he climbed onto his horse. "Thompson, you and that half-breed son of yours had best stay out of my way from now on. I know some Blackfeet who'd pay good robes for your hair."

"Maybe you'd better leave while you still have yours," Thane warned.

Cutter's eyes glistened with hatred. "It ain't over." He spurred his horse, and his men led the mules behind. The five were soon lost in the darkness at the edge of the village.

Jethro watched them go and turned to his father. "What kind of man is that?"

"There's not much that's human to him," Thane replied. "He's just like his uncle was, mostly rabid wolf."

"Will he come back?"

"It's not likely, but my guts tell me we'll see

112

him again, some day. And I'd say we'd better be ready to shoot first."

Bull Comes Ahead's lodge was totally dark and filled with smoke from the burning of sweet grass and sage. The medicine man was singing to the rhythm of a drummer seated at the back of the lodge, as he had been doing since the beginning of the ceremony.

Little Bow knelt next to the prostrate form of the injured Blackfoot warrior, with Jumps Ahead across from him, their arms outstretched, their hands joined over the warrior's chest in the darkness. Little Bow felt as if his arms were made of rock, and his knees and back were beginning to cramp. The aching had come and gone many times, and now he thought he would collapse if Bull Comes Ahead did not finish soon.

Jumps Ahead felt the same way. Although the idea of the ceremony had been exciting at first, the boys now realized what hard work praying could be.

During the initial stages of the ceremony, Little Bow had concentrated on what was taking place. The drumming and the singing had brought him into a state of calmness and peace. It had not been hard to hold his hands up. As the ceremony had progressed, his mind had begun to wander to things that he enjoyed doing, to make the time go by faster.

Now Little Bow had run out of thoughts and was coming ever closer to collapse. But he could not let Bull Comes Ahead down. He worked to summon more strength once again.

While trying to ease his torture, it occurred to him that his thoughts should be on viewing the wounded warrior as healed, as well and active. That was the reason for the ceremony in the first place. He wanted to speak to Jumps Ahead, to tell him what he had discovered, but he knew that it would not be appropriate. He realized that Jumps Ahead had no doubt realized that by now himself, as Jumps Ahead squeezed his hands tightly.

Little Bow began to concentrate on the warrior's health. In his mind he saw the warrior up and walking around, his arms raised to the sky in thanks and devotion. He saw Big Owl with the woman, Many Berries, at his side, both of them smiling. The sky above them was blue, and they were looking up into it.

As he concentrated, Little Bow became aware that Bull Comes Ahead was singing a different song. Also, the medicine man had begun to shake a large rattle in time to the drummer's beat. The sounds filled the entire space, as if the drum and rattle were circling around the top of the lodge. Little Bow wanted to look up but kept his eyes closed and his concentration on the warrior.

Suddenly Little Bow was aware of something beside him, something small. He felt a little being next to him, occasionaly brushing against his back and arms. Then he was aware of more than one—in fact, many of them were moving through the lodge. Little Bow knew that they were not visible, not even in daylight; they were just small forms of humanlike energy, moving everywhere throughout the lodge.

Little Bow realized that Jumps Ahead felt them also, for he was tense and his hands were sweating. Little Bow sensed them moving over the warrior, causing the wounded man to jerk and gasp, bringing groans from him. When the warrior's hands and legs moved, it was all that Little Bow and Jumps Ahead could do to remain kneeling over him.

Then suddenly the warrior was still. The little beings were gone. Bull Comes Ahead had stopped singing, and there was no sound of drum or rattle. A heavy stillness filled the lodge, a deep feeling of change. Little Bow stared at Jumps Ahead through the darkness, and both boys jumped to their feet and scooted back as the warrior raised himself to a sitting position and asked, "Where am I?"

EIGHT

JETHRO HAD HAD LITTLE SLEEP. HIS KNEE WAS still swollen and sore, affording him no movement without extreme pain.

When light broke in the east, he sought the river so as to revive himself. The main bathing place was already filled with village men discussing Big Owl and the ceremony that had saved his life. Jethro decided not to try to mingle among them. Besides, their stares would make him uncomfortable.

He limped out of the village, toward a secluded spot where lovers often met. There the river broke into several small islands, isolated and of easy access from the main bank. A light breeze rustled the treetops. Bird song flowed in a dense chorus from every branch.

The grass along the benchlands above the river,

now shooting seed heads, was damp with moisture from a late-night shower. Near the secluded site, four doe bounced from the water into the sage and grass of an upper terrace, their spotted fawns beside them.

Jethro removed his breechclout and stepped into a deep water hole near the bank. The chilly current slapped him and brought renewed vigor to every fiber of his being. He recalled the day before, when the cold stream had revived him from his sweat and the giant black spirit had descended upon him.

Somehow that seemed far in the past, as if the sun had crossed the sky many times since then and now it was only a vague memory. He felt that he had grown older in a short time and would soon grow even older. He realized that impending events would enable him to see the Crow world through more mature eyes. He felt that everything around him was changing rapidly. Perhaps he was dreaming. He splashed water on himself and blinked, but the scene was still there—the trees and grass and sky; the deer, now staring at him from a hill above the river.

He emerged from the water and had begun to replace his breechclout when he heard a gasp. Cuts Buffalo stopped at the water's edge with a start.

"I did not mean to disturb you," she said, turning away. "I will go elsewhere for water."

"No, you don't have to go," Jethro told her. "I have finished bathing. I will go so you can fill your water bags."

"Are you sure? I don't want to drive you away."

"You aren't driving me away," Jethro told her.

"Then don't go," Cuts Buffalo said. "Not yet. Please." She sat down at the river's edge. "Would you stay and talk to me for a while?"

"I guess I don't have to go right now." He sat down next to her. "What do you want to say to me?"

"I want to tell you that you did the right thing when you saved the warrior's life. Now you can continue your quest for power with honor."

"I hope so," Jethro said. "You know, Big Owl was healed by the Little People. I hope they are happy with me."

"I heard that," Cuts Buffalo said, her head bowed. "They are very strong medicine. Something must be going to happen."

Jethro picked up a stone and tossed it into the current. "I am afraid that many of our people are angry with me now. I can feel it."

"Do not worry about it," Cuts Buffalo told him. "The Blackfeet are enemies of our people, it is true, but I admire you for doing what you felt was right. It took a lot of strength to make the decision you did."

"Thank you," Jethro said. "It is good to know there are a few others who believe as I do."

"There are more than you think," Cuts Buffalo said, "but they are afraid to speak up."

"Why can't they say what they want?" Jethro asked, his voice strained with irritation. "Look at my mother, she's always saying things that others don't agree with, or don't want to hear."

"Your mother is a very strong woman, and esteemed among the people," Cuts Buffalo pointed out. "She can say what she wants. She has position."

"She got her position by saying what she felt was truth," Jethro said. "Others can do the same."

"Don't be so hard on our people," Cuts Buffalo said. "Many of them have lost relatives in battle with the Blackfeet. There is much bitterness in some hearts."

"That has nothing to do with one warrior and a small woman."

"To the people it does. Big Owl and Many Berries could have many children. It is possible some of them could come back to kill our people."

"So, are you changing your mind now?"

"No," Cuts Buffalo said quickly, "of course not. You should know that saving an enemy's life is a hard thing for many to accept. It means a change in thinking, and most of us cannot believe that the tribes throughout these lands will ever see one another as friends, not after all that has happened."

"Do you think that it could ever be?" Jethro asked.

"I don't know. It would be wonderful if such a thing could come to pass."

"Change for the good can come only when people want it badly enough," Jethro said. "Bad change is something that can be forced upon you when you turn your back on good change."

Cuts Buffalo sat in silence for a moment. "Do you think our people will see bad change?"

"I am almost certain of it," Jethro said. "If you

listen to the elders, you can hear it coming. They don't simply say, 'Things are going to be bad.' They comment on how there is always talk of fighting and killing, and not just going for horses. In the old days, honor was earned in raiding for horses and taking an enemy's weapon without killing him. Today everyone wants to kill off his enemies. That brings angry thoughts all the time. The elders say that constantly thinking bad thoughts brings bad to the thinker."

"Do you think that all of the tribes have been doing this?"

"Of course. War has become too important. We spend far too much time harassing one another and far too little time in contemplation, as the elders say. In this way, we have brought more bad upon the bad we have created. I'm not certain that the people who live and hunt across these lands really know that change is coming because of this. The elders know, but they are powerless to stop it."

"Your mother has talked a lot about it," Cuts Buffalo said. "It makes many of the women nervous, for the things your mother says often come to pass."

"My mother has a lot of wisdom, as does my father," Jethro said. "My mother is afraid that the way of life we have known—the way that has been handed down from the ancestors—will soon be in the past and that we will have to change. My father's people are coming into our lands in large numbers. Some of them are good, but most of them think only of war. They want to own and control. They want everything for themselves."

"It must be hard for your father to see this happening among his own people."

"He came out here to get away from that," Jethro explained. "An uncle wrongly accused him of killing his own father. His uncle wanted everything for himself and would have killed my father had he stayed. All because of power. Now others just like his uncle are spreading out everywhere in these lands."

"Is there no way to stop them?"

"Our people are welcoming them," Jethro said, "so that they might fight with us against the Blackfeet and the Lakota. That is what the elders are talking about; everything is based on war."

"Your father has had to fight a great deal," Cuts Buffalo said. "I can see that he is tired of it."

"My father has learned a lot since he was my age," Jethro said. "War is what changed the lands he came from. The stories he tells of those lands are hard to believe. He says that there were once many tribes who hunted, but now all of them are gone. White men now have the land. Lands that were once filled with trees and grass are now filled with tobacco. But they do not honor the sacred tobacco, he says. They smoke it only because it keeps them from seeing the truth."

"In our way, tobacco makes you see the truth," Cuts Buffalo said. "How could it be used in any other way?"

"Anything used for good can be used for bad just as easily. It is all in how the user thinks."

"If I think good, then good will follow. Is that right?" Cuts Buffalo asked.

"Yes, that is how it works."

"Then if I think about you often, will I see you often?"

Jethro grinned sheepishly. "That is difficult to say."

"I suppose it also depends on how often you think of me."

Jethro looked into her eyes. "I can tell that you are one who can easily see the truth."

Cuts Buffalo smiled. "That is why I wanted to talk to you. I wanted to hear truth, and you are a man of truth."

"You should wait to call me a man," Jethro said, rising. "I have not yet become a warrior."

"In my heart you are already a man," Cuts Buffalo said. "You are a true warrior. It is so, there are things you must do to prove this, and you might have to face yet more bad things, but there is no doubt that you are one of the strongest men our people have ever seen."

Big Owl's recovery was slow. Although he had sat upright momentarily during the healing ceremony in Bull Comes Ahead's lodge, he remained prostrate for nearly a week afterward. His sudden reaction during the rites was due only to the great power in the lodge.

No one could predict how long it would be before Big Owl was strong enough to leave the lodge. Even though Bull Comes Ahead administered herbs to him often, he lapsed in and out of consciousness, enduring continual pain—a condition, Bull Comes Ahead told Jethro, brought on by the spirits to teach the warrior not to go against the signs in the future.

Anticipating the time when Big Owl could be moved, Many Berries erected a lodge at the far edge of the village, away from the others. Since the lodge would be only temporary, she built it from four main poles and overlapping tree branches. She saw no need to go to all the work of tanning hides and sewing them, not when she and Big Owl would be leaving as soon as possible.

Since he had brought them to the village, it was up to Jethro to provide meat for Big Owl and Many Berries. He killed two elk, and Many Berries skinned and butchered for three days, drying meat on racks for another four days.

Calling Bird, still angry, remained in her sister's lodge the entire time, not even speaking to her husband. She had sworn not to speak to him until Big Owl was gone from the village. She became increasingly withdrawn, and she scowled as she watched Many Berries work, wondering how the woman could be so nonchalant in an enemy village.

Despite her anger, Calling Bird continued with her daily chores; but she acted as if Bull Comes Ahead were no longer alive. He was often gone from the village anyway, praying in the hills, asking for direction in this unusual matter. She would place a pot of food for him in front of the lodge, just enough for him and nothing extra for Many Berries and Big Owl. Then she would leave

immediately, to avoid any contact whatsoever
with Bull Comes Ahead.

Calling Bird felt sure that she would never
approve of what her husband had done for Big
Owl. It was unthinkable, especially in the wake
of the atrocities the Blackfeet had committed
against the Kicked-in-Their-Bellies. She had lived
through a lot of anguish and knew physical as
well as mental pain very well: the last joints of
three fingers on her left hand were missing, the
result of her removing them in mourning for
loves ones killed in battle. She wanted nothing
to do with any of the Blackfeet people.

The only ones to show any interest in Big Owl
besides Bull Comes Ahead and Many Berries
were Jethro and Little Bow. The boy came to the
lodge only in Jethro's company, and his curiosity
overwhelmed him. Even though he remained lying down most of the time, Big Owl was an im-
posing figure. Little Bow became fascinated with
him. If Jethro had wanted to save him, he must
be special.

Little Bow and Jumps Ahead had discussed
what had occurred on the night of Big Owl's recovery; they realized that a powerful medicine
had answered Bull Comes Ahead's prayers.
Among the Crow people there was no stronger
medicine than the tiny people of the high rocks
and caves, who came to answer only the greatest
among medicine men. Little Bow and Jumps
Ahead realized that they had met the Little People.

Both of the boys had heard stories about the
Little People and what they could do. They were

rarely spoken of, though everyone knew they existed and could feel them where they lived, up among the high rocks of the mountains. It was said that there were only two reasons that you might encounter the Little People and be allowed to see them: either you were a chosen one and would be given power in return for favors done for the Little People, or your life was nearly over.

Either reason meant that there would be tests and great difficulties in a person's life. Understandably, there were parts of the mountains—especially the Beartooth, the Wind River, the Crazy Mountains, the Big Horn, and the small and powerful mountains that held the Medicine Rock—where the people did not go unless seeking power, or for some sacred reason. Thus, the Little People were rarely discussed openly.

Jethro realized increasingly that unusual powers were watching over his destiny, powers that could bring tremendous changes to him and his people. At times the realization brought him fear and anxiety, and dreams that were filled with swirling clouds and rows of trees buffeted by strong winds, reminding him of the day the giant black spirit had swirled down upon him. One thing was clear in his mind: if the Little People had come to save Big Owl, the outcome could be wonderfully good or terribly bad.

For this reason, most of the people did not even discuss the healing ceremony. Big Owl had lived, an incredible thing in itself, and the Little People would no doubt show more influence over things that happened in the future. No one wanted to displease them. The people just wanted their enemies to leave camp and allow life to return to normal.

During this time, Big Owl remained nearly helpless as his crushed chest continued to heal. Many Berries took the opportunity to go off by herself often, roaming the hills away from the village, as if indifferent to Big Owl's condition. Often she would seek Jethro while he was out on some bluff waiting for a sign to begin his vision quest again. He found himself enjoying her company, although he knew that this could only bring more bad luck. And those in the village who were against the enemy visitors, including High Elk, took the opportunity to point their fingers.

It would not have bothered them had Jethro been looking at Cuts Buffalo instead of at Many Berries. At times Jethro wanted to seek out Cuts Buffalo and have conversation with her again. For talking, she had been good. He did not seek her, though, because of the way he knew she felt about him. He could think of her only as a true friend, as close as a sister would be. But in her eyes, he stood taller than any brother; he was the one she wanted to marry.

Jethro had thought about marriage often. It would be expected of him once he gained his personal power and held the status of a warrior. It bothered him now that he did not want to marry from among the women of his own people, that another seemed more suited to him.

With each passing day, Jethro grew more attached to Many Berries. She would come to him whenever Big Owl was resting and find things to discuss with him, even small things, just to make conversation. He found himself looking forward to these meetings, although he knew they could not continue once Big Owl was well enough to travel.

As much as he tried, Jethro could not keep himself from desiring her. She was bright and courteous, and seemed to know his every inner thought. The feeling distracted him, and he wished that Big Owl would recover quickly so that the two Piegans could resume their lives together, away from the Kicked-in-Their-Bellies.

That way, life would become much easier for him and for his people. There would again be harmony between those who had sided with his cause and those who had not. Besides, it would allow him to concentrate on the matters that he had considered important before meeting Many Berries and Big Owl.

Big Owl finally regained enough strength to care for himself. He moved from Bull Comes Ahead's lodge into the lodge kept by Many Berries, saying nothing to Jethro, not even a thank-you for sparing him, or to Bull Comes Ahead for the healing ceremony. He never once suggested that he would find a way to offer gifts to the medicine man for having prayed on his behalf.

Big Owl constantly wore the same hateful look that Jethro had seen on his face on the day the warrior had attacked him. It made Jethro wonder if he had really done the right thing. He thought about the night of the healing ceremony, when Bull Comes Ahead had tested his confi-

127

dence in himself. No matter what was to happen, he could not let himself doubt his decision.

And he thought often of what Cuts Buffalo had said to him at the river, assuring him that she and others supported him, although silently for the most part. Her words—as if coming from an adoring sister—had made him feel very good at the time, but now he was facing a test.

The beginning of this test came early one morning when Little Bow rushed up to Jethro and handed him a knife. "I found this tied in Flame's mane," he said, breathless. "I think it is Big Owl's."

"It does look like Big Owl's," Jethro agreed. "You go find someone to play with."

Jethro started for Big Owl and Many Berries' lodge. Many Berries was out picking Juneberries, and Big Owl was lounging in front of the door flap, eating from a bowl of stew. He did not bother to rise at Jethro's approach.

"Why haven't you brought us more meat?" Big Owl asked, his mouth full. "Do I have to go out and show you how a *man* hunts?"

Jethro ignored the remark. The issue at hand was far more pressing than the warrior's impertinent statement. He held up the knife. "Does this belong to you?"

"Yes, it is mine. Just toss it down to me."

"Before I give it back, I want to ask you some questions," Jethro said. "First of all, what was this knife doing tied in my horse's mane?"

"I'm laying claim to the horse," Big Owl replied matter-of-factly. "When I leave, I'm going to be riding him."

Jethro was dumbfounded. "That is a poor joke."

"No joke. Truth."

Jethro tossed the knife past the door flap and into the lodge. "You don't know what truth is, Big Owl. You couldn't see it the day you attacked me on the hill, and you can't see it now. You will certainly never leave this village with Flame."

"You will not stop me," Big Owl said boldly. "That is why I tied the knife to the horse's mane. I will use the knife on you and then take the horse with me."

"Why are you such trouble?" Jethro asked. "I saved your life."

Big Owl grunted. "I would have lived had you just left me alone with Many Berries. As it is now, you have complicated things very badly."

Jethro could not believe what he was hearing. How could Big Owl even begin to think he could have survived without help? The man was definitely not in his right mind, but he was serious.

"Maybe it would be better if I put you back on the drag and had a pony haul you to where you fell?" Jethro suggested. "You wouldn't be able to survive even now."

Big Owl glared at Jethro. "I would survive!" He rose to his feet. "It is you who will not survive. I do not even believe it was you on the hill that day. You are not strong enough to have been that person."

Jethro bristled with anger. "I believe that all your strength lies in your talk, Big Owl, and nowhere else," he said. "You make poor decisions.

You need someone to watch over you, just as a child does."

Big Owl's eyes grew enormous. "I will show you who the child is, you Crow dog!"

Before Jethro could react, Big Owl kicked him squarely in his sore knee. Jethro went down, grimacing, clutching his leg. He curled up to protect his stomach and groin as Big Owl began a series of kicks, slamming him repeatedly in the ribs and the back of the head.

Big Owl finally came around to attempt a kick at Jethro's face. Awaiting the blow, Jethro grabbed Big Owl's foot and wrenched it sideways. Big Owl landed heavily on his damaged side. He groaned with the pain that welled from within, then cursed and clawed his way to his feet, his right arm bracing his ribs.

Jethro pushed himself up, his knife drawn. Although the pain in his knee was extreme, he would not allow Big Owl to get away with anything more.

"I see you have changed your mind about wanting me alive," the warrior said with a smirk.

"You have changed it for me," Jethro retorted.

"I would kill you now," Big Owl said, "but I would have to go out and find Many Berries before I could get your horse and leave. That would be difficult."

"If I see or hear of you coming anywhere near my horse again," Jethro warned, "I will tie you to a rope and have you dragged."

"You won't have that horse long enough for that," Big Owl said with contempt.

"I have heard enough from you," Jethro said.

"I have given you every privilege, but now you are no different to me than any other enemy. You had better be ready to leave this village very soon. Otherwise, you may never leave."

Big Owl laughed. "I will leave here. I will have your horse. And I will have your hair as well."

Jethro gritted his teeth against his anger and the pain in his knee. This man was more than a match for his patience. He felt like killing him. But he could not walk, much less fight. He knew that he should stay away from Big Owl now; otherwise, he would likely be provoked to go against the spirits and kill the warrior.

His knee throbbing, Jethro turned away from Big Owl. He did his best to walk normally, but he had to stop frequently to keep from collapsing, while behind him, Big Owl laughed and laughed.

NINE

JETHRO THOUGHT OF BIG OWL EACH TIME HE TRIED to walk. After a few days the pain lessened, but he still had the urge to rebreak Big Owl's ribs for him, just so that the warrior might learn a lesson.

But Big Owl would never learn anything, Jethro concluded. He realized that all of this was a test of his patience. Things could certainly be running a lot smoother than they were, but the spirits wanted to see how well he would bear up under the stress. He knew this, and because he knew it, the spirits were making it that much harder: if you think you have gotten through the rough spots, think again.

Cuts Buffalo kept her distance, watching events as they developed. She never approached Jethro openly, as she had at the river, but reverted to the traditional method of sending a go-between once in a while, just to inform Jethro that she was asking the spirits to help him. It bothered her that Many Berries was always pressuring him and that he seemed to be falling in love with her. But in her heart she knew that Many Berries was not the kind of woman he really wanted.

Jethro admired Cuts Buffalo for her sense of self-worth. He realized her attraction to him, although he could not understand why she felt the way she did. He realized also that Cuts Buffalo would certainly make a wonderful wife, but he wanted to be certain of his feelings toward her before he made a decision to marry.

His thoughts at this time, he knew, could not center around marriage. He had to first prove himself worthy of that responsibility. His quest for power had to be foremost, together with plans to raid an enemy camp and gain honors as a warrior. Thoughts of maintaining a wife and family could come in the future, likely not before the passing of the next season of cold moons.

In the meantime, Jethro had many obstacles to face, not the least of which had been placed before him by his own doing. Big Owl had become a far greater challenge than he had imagined possible. There had been times when he wondered what could possibly be worse than splitting the clan down the middle, but his father and mother had told him often that he should never let the bias of others change his mind about anything.

Despite his struggle, Jethro kept a positive attitude. Unless he literally chased Big Owl and Many Berries from the village, he would have to wait for Big Owl's injuries to heal. If he pushed Big Owl and Many Berries away and something happened to them, he felt that he would find himself in the same situation he had created in the beginning. He had to ensure, as much as possible, Big Owl's safe journey out of Crow lands. He hoped the spirits would relinquish their unending demands on him once the warrior was gone.

In the meanwhile, he continued to prepare for another vision guest. His knee would be sore for some time to come, but he could walk, and he could climb steep inclines if he did not hurry. He would have plenty of strength; now he just needed a sign from the spirits that he might begin again.

Jethro ascended the hills often, looking for the sign, watching and waiting. But nothing came. He spent a lot of time off by himself, trying to decide whether or not he was leading his life in the right manner. High Elk had left the village on his own vision quest, and Cuts Buffalo's twin brothers would prepare themselves at the changing of the moon. Those once behind him were now passing him.

Jethro considered that his feelings for Many Berries might be holding him back. Although still drawn to her, he tried to avoid her as much as possible. But he could not keep his mind off of her. If he allowed himself to dwell on her, he fantasized that the two of them could be happy together. That would not be possible, not without his having to leave his people.

So he spent every moment he could by himself, roaming the hills, listening to the sounds of the land—the flow of midsummer water, the lowing of drinking buffalo, the screeching of hawks and eagles, the high howl of wolves in the darkness. All of them were a part of his learning, of his knowing what he must do.

Despite Jethro's efforts to remain by himself, Many Berries found him one afternoon near a bubbling spring in an open meadow above the village. The water gurgled, filling a hole that overflowed and fed a nearby stream. The sun shone through hazy clouds, and the bees droned, searching the deep blues and yellows and reds of wild flowers for nectar.

As Many Berries approached, Jethro felt happy despite himself. She sat down next to him and smiled. "At last we are alone together."

"I don't know if that is good," Jethro said.

Many Berries pulled a fuzzy-topped daisy from the ground beside her. The dainty blue petals had shriveled and fallen, and the seeds awaited flight, tiny plumes ready to carry them on the wind.

With a sudden puff of breath, Many Berries sent the seeds hurtling out into the breeze and watched them rise higher and higher, until they became lost in the distance.

"They were born to travel very high, to be carried into the blue," she told Jethro. "That is what you were born to do, if you will only spread your arms and allow the wind to carry you."

Many Berries still had her eyes on the floating seeds; she smiled as they spread in all directions and finally out of sight. He could not find words to say to her.

"This is nothing you don't already know," Many Berries said, pulling another daisy and blowing the seeds out. "You can feel it within you. You know the rules of power. You were born with that knowledge. That is why you will live for a very long time."

"How can you see all of this when even Bull Comes Ahead has not told me words of this nature?" Jethro asked.

Many Berries shrugged. "Maybe he can see it, or maybe he can't. Either way, he is a holy man and is not supposed to talk to people about what will come for them. You know this. He can work with you to show you how to prepare yourself, but the journey is yours alone. And you will make that journey, if you decide you want to."

Jethro studied her. "What do you mean, 'if I want to'?"

"It is like a question you put to yourself: what do I want and how do I find it? It is like the time you wanted to go into the Beartooth to find your power but learned that your power might not come from the Beartooth. You must release yourself to the wind, like the prairie seeds, and go where you must go, without thinking that the wind will tell you. You must trust the wind."

"Are you saying that I have been sitting around and not going out to find what I must?"

"Haven't you?"

"I wanted to wait until you and Big Owl had left the village."

"Am I that big a distraction?" she asked, smiling again.

Jethro frowned. "No, you are not a distraction." He broke a small twig between nervous fingers. "Yes, you are," he finally said. "I have to tell you how it is in my heart. I've been thinking about you a lot. That is why I wanted to wait until you and Big Owl were gone . . . I thought it would be better for gaining my medicine."

"There you are, 'thinking' what is best for you again," Many Berries chided him. "Why don't you just go ahead and learn what you must do from feeling it?" She leaned over, her shoulder next to his, almost touching him. "Don't you think that on your journey through life there will be many distractions that will work to take you from your purpose? If you 'think' about all of them, you will never feel what you must in order to gain power."

Jethro felt desire for her welling up in him. He wanted her to continue to tempt him, to lean closer. She wanted him, he knew that. He also knew that she was right about his quest for power, that her and Big Owl's presence in the village was no excuse for delaying his journey. Maybe waiting for the right sign had been foolish. He should be high in the mountains right now.

"Why are you telling me all this?" Jethro asked.

"No one else can tell you like I can, not in the same way." Her voice was almost a whisper. "Maybe you don't want to hear my words, but with me, you would become a warrior like no other."

"A warrior who would kill your people. Do you want that?"

"I have no people now," Many Berries said. "You know my story. All my family are dead. I have no future with the Small Robes."

"What about Big Owl?"

"I do not think he desires me any longer."

"Doesn't desire you?"

"He no longer wants to lie with me."

Jethro could not understand Big Owl not having any desire for Many Berries, unless the warrior had been hurt in the fall under his horse and was no longer capable of sexual activity. If that were the case, it could be the explanation for Big Owl's intense anger.

"Have you tried to talk to him?" Jethro asked.

"He will not talk about it. He just becomes angry."

"Maybe in time," Jethro said. "Maybe he is injured and will heal in time."

"Time will not help Big Owl or me," Many Berries said. "It is you I want, Jethro. You know that. Don't you want me? I have thought all along that you did."

"You know that my feelings are mixed," Jethro said. "I have grown to care for you a great deal, but I cannot be certain that our lives are to be lived with one another."

Many Berries leaned back in the grass, resting on her elbows, and raised her knee, her dress sliding to expose her thighs, her breasts pressing tightly against the fabric.

"You belong to Big Owl," he said, his desire for her growing. "No matter what you have said about me, about us, you are promised to him."

"I don't belong to anyone, not yet," Many Berries corrected him.

Jethro's eyebrows raised. "You told him you would marry him," he reminded her. "That is your promise."

"If I am to keep my promise, isn't he obligated to want me and to care for me? Isn't that his promise?"

"Yes, I would think so."

Many Berries gave the smallest of smiles. "He has already told me he doesn't want me."

"Even if we were destined to be together, we would have to leave this village," Jethro said. "My people are upset as it is. It would not be good for either of us."

"What makes you think we have to stay here?" Many Berries asked. She raised up from her elbows and pulled off her dress. Then she stood up, free in her nakedness. "I am going to refresh myself in the spring. You coming?"

She leaped into the water, laughing. She immersed herself and came up dripping, her small, sleek body glistening in the afternoon light. Jethro's eyes feasted on her. She giggled and splashed him.

"What are you waiting for?"

Jethro stood up. Many Berries clambered over and took him by the hand, dragging him into the water. She reached down for his breechclout.

"You don't need this," she said. "Let me see if I can help you."

She put an arm around his neck and forced his lips to hers, searching with her other hand. He pulled her closer, his breath quickening, as she stroked him to further excitement.

"You feel so good to me," she whispered. "So strong!"

Jethro kissed her neck, her breasts, his mouth lingering on her nipples; then he lifted her from the water and onto the grass, where she pulled him down on top of her.

"You are so powerful," she murmured, running her hands over his muscular frame. "So very powerful."

She wrapped her legs around him, and Jethro unleashed his passion. Her cries drove him ever higher, until finally he spent himself totally.

Jethro lay on his back in the grass, Many Berries' head resting on his chest. But Many Berries could not settle down; she laughed and ran her hands over him continuously. Jethro tried to talk to her about his journey for power, but she wanted to talk only about what would happen upon his return, what would happen to them.

"A great deal lies ahead of me before I can consider anything else," Jethro said. "But I feel good about you."

"That is what I wanted to hear," she said. "Now, kiss me again. I'm not through with you yet."

Just after sundown, Bull Comes Ahead descended the hill toward the village. He had been out praying. He watched Jethro and Many Berries enter the village from another direction. The two displayed a boldness that would cause trouble if it continued, adding to the already complicated problems that now existed. Bull Comes Ahead had watched Jethro's growing attraction to Many Berries with worry. He wondered about her intentions and knew that Jethro's display of affection for her would eventually tear him away from his own people.

Besides becoming alienated from the band, Jethro would certainly find himself fighting Big Owl for Many Berries. Bull Comes Ahead knew that Big Owl did not need additional reasons for bitterness. Since his going up into the hills each evening to pray, Bull Comes Ahead had become increasingly aware of Big Owl's discontent. Although Many Berries certainly contributed a great deal to his attitude, she likely had not caused it in the beginning. Big Owl had brought it with him from Blackfeet lands.

Bull Comes Ahead could not understand Big Owl's deep hatred. The warrior seemed uncaring of the sacrifices that were made to keep him alive. Enemy or not, reason would dictate that Big Owl should show respect for others.

And now that Many Berries was enticing Jethro to fall in love with her, matters would only become worse.

Bull Comes Ahead decided not to approach Jethro on the matter. Jethro now faced an important time in his life, and the spirits were no doubt testing him to see what kinds of honor he was worthy of. Bull Comes Ahead decided that the best thing he could do was to return to his lodge and worry about his own problems there.

He would have to build a fire and warm up the food Calling Bird had left for him while he was in the hills. There were a lot of things he now did for himself that made him appreciate how much Calling Bird meant in his life. He had not seen or talked to her for a considerable time.

Although he now spent most of his time walking the hills in prayer, he thought about his wife often. He wondered if she still held her deep anger, and if she had tried to understand his decision to perform the healing ceremony for Big Owl.

He realized that he could never allow himself to be sorry for having performed the ceremony, lest the Little People become angry with him. He had made his decision, and there could be no thought that he had made a mistake. The powerful medicine of the Little People had nothing to do with error. The only error existed in the minds of those who would make the mistake of judging and trying to change what had already happened.

As with Jethro, nothing for Bull Comes Ahead had been the same since the coming of the two Piegans, a circumstance that led Bull Comes Ahead to conclude that the spirits were testing him as well. Besides the matters of Big Owl's attitude and his own loneliness without Calling Bird, there were many troubling questions concerning the future of the Crow people.

Bull Comes Ahead had never before faced such churning within himself. He thought he had learned all about his emotions long ago. He had been tested in many ways—including ordeals of near death, through which he had learned a great deal—but he had never felt the strong and tearing concern that now surged within him each time he laid eyes on Big Owl.

As he drew closer to his lodge, Bull Comes Ahead reflected on his observation of Jethro's return to the village. There was something about the manner in which Jethro had been walking— with the light, yet strong steps of decision—that told Bull Comes Ahead that the youth had reached a conclusion. The old medicine man feared the worst; was it possible that Jethro and Many Berries were going to be spending even more time together, no matter the consequences?

As Bull Comes Ahead, still thinking about Jethro, approached his lodge, he smelled the aroma of a fresh buffalo tongue from within, and he stopped in amazement. He eased himself though the door flap.

Calling Bird sat near a fire, stirring the contents of a large pot. "Thane Thompson brought you three buffalo tongues," she said matter-of-factly. "I thought you might like to eat them tonight."

"I would like that very much," Bull Comes Ahead told her. "It smells as if you have indeed prepared them well."

Bull Comes Ahead could not hide his astonishment that his wife had returned. Calling Bird tried to act as if she had never been gone. She fidgeted in her seat near the fire.

"Maybe he should have brought more tongues," she said. "You look like you haven't eaten well for a time."

Bull Comes Ahead grinned. "I am a good medicine man, but I'm not good at eating alone."

"Come over here and sit down," Calling Bird urged. "I've been stirring this meat since you came in the door. I can't stir much longer."

Bull Comes Ahead took a seat beside his wife. She ladled meat and vegetables into a clay dish painted with Hidatsa designs and handed the vessel to him.

He set the dish of food down. "I've missed you a great deal," he told her, taking her hand in his. "I'm glad you are back."

Calling Bird blinked away tears. "I was foolish to stay away. I now realize it is not good to carry anger for so long. It is very bad for the spirit." She leaned over and put an arm around him. "I am sorry."

They held one another for a long while, rocking in each other's embrace, renewing the tenderness they had built together over time. Although this had been the most serious of their arguments, their love would not allow disagreement to hold them apart any longer.

"I have watched you climb into the hills each night," Calling Bird said, wiping her eyes. "And each night I wanted to be waiting for you when you returned. I have been so foolish. I just want us to be as before, and our people to live as before."

"The Piegans will be gone soon," Bull Comes Ahead told her. In his mind he saw Jethro and Many Berries together, and he pushed the thought away. "When they have departed, we can put all of this behind us."

Calling Bird took a deep breath and turned her eyes to him. They were filled with concern. She gripped Bull Comes Ahead's hand. "Can you feel anything else? Like certain danger?"

"Yes, my heart is heavy for our people," he replied. "There are many feelings in the air, and it is hard to know from where they are coming. Is there something you want to tell me?"

"I am afraid for us," Calling Bird said. "I feel that something bad will happen. What about the Sacred Pipe? Why haven't you yet performed the sacred ceremony to give it to Jethro's father?"

"I want to wait until after the Piegans are gone," Bull Comes Ahead told her. "And I wanted Jethro to take the pipe into the mountains for his vision."

"But the bad spirit came down from the sky when he took the pipe," Calling Bird pointed out.

"I do not believe that had anything to do with the pipe," Bull Comes Ahead said. "I believe that

Jethro must face many hardships. I do not know why, but I feel this."

"Maybe he is not to become a warrior, but a medicine man," Calling Bird suggested.

Bull Comes Ahead looked at her and his eyebrows raised. "I have wondered about that. He has always believed he was meant to follow in his father's footsteps. But maybe, because of his dreams, he is more like his mother."

"What has he told you about going back to find his power?" Calling Bird asked.

"Nothing. I haven't asked, and he hasn't offered to tell me anything."

"The cold moons will be here before long. Surely he will want to go up to the mountains before the snows are too deep."

"You are right. Soon the nights will bring cold and snow to the high country. He had better decide what he wants to do."

"Certainly the pipe ceremony will take place before then," Calling Bird said. She looked over to where the Sacred Pipe, secured by otter fur and wrapped with sweet grass, hung on the side of the lodge, just off the ground. "I feel we must give the pipe to Thane Thompson soon. It does not belong here any longer."

Bull Comes Ahead sat in silence, the wrinkles in his ancient face pinched with worry. "There are things that must happen," he said finally. "I believe that the coming of the two Piegans has brought change to us, and will bring even more change. It was Jethro's decision to bring them to the village, and the spirits will certainly reward him—if he can pass the tests."

"What tests?" Calling Bird asked.

Bull Comes Ahead turned and stared at the Sacred Pipe. "No one can say. But I am positive that they will be as difficult as any ever faced by a young man of the Crow nation."

PART TWO

Summer–Fall
1849

TEN

THE MOON CHANGED WITH NO SENSE OF PEACE returning to the Kicked-in-Their-Bellies. The village moved to find new grass for the horses. Its next move would be to the plateau at the base of the Medicine Rock Mountains. There the people would join with other bands and clans in the summer medicine ceremonies.

Usually the middle of the warm moons brought a festive mood. This year it brought only fear and unhappiness. A number of the Kicked-in-Their-Bellies who belonged to the Tobacco Society did not even take part in the sacred planting ceremony, so great was their concern that Big Owl's presence would bring bad luck. And no one from the Kicked-in-Their-Bellies planned to participate in the Sun Dance ceremony. The people felt ill at ease with the two Blackfeet in their midst, and the dissension continued to grow.

Big Owl learned of Jethro's secret meetings with Many Berries. He beat her nearly senseless late one evening while Jethro was off hunting. Upon his return, Jethro had to be restrained by his father.

"Don't be foolish," Thane advised. "Think hard before you risk your honor for such a woman."

"How can you say that?" Jethro asked. "You don't know her."

"I've known others like her," Thane said. "I believe you will see in time."

Jethro now wanted Many Berries more than he had before. But she had taken to avoiding him, and he could do nothing about it. Seeing her would only provoke Big Owl further. He tried not to think of her, but her image invaded his mind everywhere he went.

High Elk had returned from his vision quest eager to take the trail to war. He wondered out loud in front of the villagers what was keeping Jethro from returning to the quest for his own power. Cuts Buffalo's brothers had climbed into the Beartooth, each seeking his own vision in a different place. They had returned with renewed vigor, ready to become warriors.

The people began to look toward the two brothers and High Elk as their future leaders. Jethro was all but forgotten. Because of his liaison with Many Berries, many of the villagers now shunned him. Some even began to discuss a move to live separately until Big Owl and Many Berries were gone.

Jethro did not know whether to try to stop them or to show indifference. He had long ago quit trying to explain to them that he knew he was doing the right thing and that his decision had not been his, but that of the spirits. His father advised him to ignore the bitterness and to prepare for another vision quest. Nothing else would provide him with the answers he sought.

Little Bow, as always, offered Jethro as much support as he could. He realized his limitations when it came to adult problems, but he felt that his concern was as deep as anyone's. He wished to return the love and caring he had received from Jethro over the passing of the seasons. Jethro had taught him to hunt and how to live as a warrior, in harmony with the land. Survival was foremost, and there was no better teacher of that than Jethro.

After a long council session, Bull Comes Ahead succeeded in holding the band together. Big Owl had announced that he and Many Berries would leave after the passing of two suns.

The next afternoon, Little Bow came running to Jethro as he returned from a walk outside of the village. "Jethro, there has been trouble!" he exclaimed. "You must come quick!"

"What has happened?" Jethro asked.

"Big Owl tried to steal Flame. High Elk stopped him. They would have fought, but Big Owl fell from the horse and hurt his ribs. He is lucky that High Elk didn't kill him."

"Where is Big Owl?"

"He went back to his lodge," Little Bow re-

153

plied. "Now High Elk and some of the other warriors are preparing to kill Big Owl."

"I am glad you found me," Jethro told the boy. "Go back to your lodge and stay with your mother."

"I would like to go with you."

"We have talked many times about your wanting to put yourself in dangerous situations," Jethro reminded him.

Little Bow nodded. "I understand. Be careful."

"Don't worry. Just stay with your mother."

Jethro found High Elk, along with Cuts Buffalo's brothers and some of the other young warriors; they were painting themselves for war.

"What are you doing?" Jethro asked.

High Elk turned from a small trade mirror. His face was lined with heavy smears of black and red.

"Big Owl has gone too far. We will play the hands game, and the winner will challenge him to meet his death."

"Little Bow said that he tried to steal Flame."

"I would have killed him then if some of the others hadn't stopped me."

"Did he tell you why he wanted my horse?" Jethro asked.

"He wouldn't say. He just yelled insults. When I came toward him and offered him a knife to defend himself with, he began to cough. I didn't think he had fallen that hard or that his cough was real, but the others cautioned me against slaying a wounded person, someone who couldn't die an honorable death."

"But you still intend to kill him," Jethro pointed out. "Isn't that what you just told me?"

"He said that when he became strong again, he would return to kill every Crow dog he could find," High Elk replied, his war paint twisting with his angry expression. "We watched him shout at Many Berries and throw her to the ground. We intend to see how well he fights against a Crow warrior."

"Let me talk to him first," Jethro said. "If I can persuade him to come here and promise in front of you to leave the horses alone, will you and the others drop the idea of killing him?"

High Elk shook his head slowly. "I cannot understand why you keep defending this Piegan. He would kill all of our people if he could, yet you stop anyone from ending his life."

"I don't want anyone to die," Jethro said. "Do you agree to what I just asked, that you and the others will not attempt to kill him if he promises to leave the horses alone?"

"I don't think you can make him say that," High Elk told Jethro.

"I will make him wish he hadn't even thought of stealing my horse," Jethro promised.

"And if you can't make him listen to you, then what?"

"It is my horse he tried to steal," Jethro explained. "If anyone is to kill him, it should be me."

High Elk looked down at Jethro's knife. "You had better not turn your back on him."

With the village watching from a distance, Jethro strode to where Big Owl and Many Berries were talking loudly to each other outside their lodge. Big Owl held his ribs tightly, obviously in great pain. He turned to Jethro with a scowl.

"Have you come to take my woman?"

"You know why I'm here," Jethro said. "Why did you try to steal my horse?"

Big Owl twisted his mouth into a small smile. "No one in your village can care properly for horses. If I hadn't been so eager and alerted the horse tenders, I would be gone with your best buffalo pony. I told you I would take that horse. I will."

"You will die trying," Jethro said. "I know now that my obligation to save you is past. I brought you here and you were healed. If you die by your own hand, the spirits will not hold me responsible."

"There is no one in this village who can kill me!" Big Owl's eyes widened in an angry glare.

Jethro stepped toward him and met his hard eyes. "Did you ever think that the people here might have wanted to trust you? Can't you understand that you don't spit in the face of the man who helps you? At one time there were many among us who wanted you to live, more than you think. So maybe they would like to believe that you would do honor to yourself and this village. After all, you were brought back to life here."

"I owe this village nothing!" Big Owl spat. "I told you that. I owe no Crow dog anything!"

"It sounds to me as if you prefer to live with anger," Jethro said. "That is not very wise in an enemy camp. You might find that you *will* die. And you will not have my horse or Many Berries. Maybe she will die as well."

"He is right," Many Berries told Big Owl, siding with Jethro. "I have told you many times that you put us both in a great deal of danger."

"Why should I fear these enemies?" he asked her. He turned to Jethro. "Even a small boy knows how to take care of his horses. When the time comes, I will laugh when I hold up your scalps for my people to see."

"How are you going to show your people anything?" Jethro asked. "Aren't you banned from Blackfeet lands forever?"

Big Owl frowned. He turned to Many Berries and back. "Did this woman tell you what happened?"

Jethro nodded. "Otherwise I wouldn't have brought you back here to help you."

Big Owl turned to Many Berries and raised his hand. Jethro started to step forward.

"Stay back," Many Berries told him. "Let him strike me if he wishes. It is the only power he has now in his life—hitting a woman."

Big Owl's eyes blazed. He lowered his hand, listening with increasing anger while Many Berries continued to ridicule him.

"This man has lost all of his power. He can no longer even ride a horse. So now he must find other ways to convince himself he is still a warrior. I will no longer have anything to do with him. I wish to be with a warrior who has strength and courage, one who will not worry if his wife is strong and has her own opinions."

"You are not stronger than I!" Big Owl yelled.

Many Berries raised her eyebrows. "Why would a man of strength have to raise his voice so loud to make himself heard?"

"You need to learn to listen when I tell you who you are," Big Owl said angrily. "You are always wanting to be in front, where everyone can see you. You don't even know that, do you?"

Many Berries looked to Jethro. "I can no longer tell you he talks from sickness. He is well enough to want to steal a horse, so his words are not filled with fever. He suffers only the fever of his angry heart."

"Anger is what keeps you alive," Big Owl told her. "An angry man feeds you even better than a bowl of the finest cuts of buffalo meat."

Big Owl's words seemed to have no effect on Many Berries. She did not so much as blink.

"So am I not the kind of man you want?" Big Owl snarled. "Isn't that why you followed me into the hills? Isn't that why you kept after me?"

"You are not as strong as you were then," Many Berries told him. "And you believe that you have more power than the spirits do, or you would not have challenged this man when he was on a sacred mission." She pointed to Jethro. "The day you show me you are more powerful than he, I will believe that we are truly meant to be together."

Jethro was stunned. Many Berries' comments made him realize that Big Owl was right: Many Berries could not love anyone who did not meet her need for power and authority. Initially she had wanted to be associated with the most successful of warriors within her own people, and had chosen Big Owl. Then she had thought Jethro would become powerful within the Kicked-in-Their-Bellies. It appeared that she would take up with anyone whom she thought could fulfill her desires.

Jethro saw clearly now that in the beginning, Many Berries had been certain that Big Owl would die. She had presented herself to him because she had been impressed by the manner in which he had turned Big Owl's horse on the bluff. As long as Big Owl seemed to have lost power, Many Berries had no use for him. But what if the warrior again became powerful? She would likely want him back. But in the meantime, she would use Jethro to aggravate him.

Big Owl pointed at Jethro while he glared at Many Berries. "This man has yet to gain even a single coup. He has no war honors, yet you think of him as a mighty leader?"

"I know what he will be some day, and what you will never be," Many Berries said defiantly. "This man has shown me power, and he cares about me more than you do. He wants me for his wife."

Big Owl turned his glare upon Jethro. "Is what she is saying true? Have you told her you care a great deal for her and want to make her your wife?"

"I didn't come to argue with you about Many Berries, or anything else," Jethro said. "I came to tell you that there are warriors among my people who caught you with my horse today and that they will come later and challenge you."

159

Big Owl grunted. "I could handle any three Crow warriors at the same time."

"That is not what I heard," Jethro said. "I was told you were challenged by a single warrior and you began coughing. How can you stand up to your words if you are not healed enough to fight?"

Big Owl was silent, glaring, his fists clenched.

"I don't know what has caused your anger," Jethro continued, "but it is foolish to display it so openly. There are many warriors who would gladly take your scalp and leave the rest of you for the wolves. Can you understand that?"

"It would be an honor to have the wolves, my brothers, scatter my bones," Big Owl said, lifting his head. "But there will never be a day when a Crow warrior can end *my* life."

"There are many Crow warriors, Big Owl," Jethro pointed out. "Maybe you had better sing your death song."

"If you are so certain they wish to fight me, why did you come here and tell me?"

"I came to give you a choice," Jethro said. "These can be my last words to you, and I will leave you to your enemies' mercy; or you can come with me and assure them that you will not try to steal any more horses."

"You want me to bow down to them?"

"You have no other choice. Either that or your death song."

Big Owl knew that Jethro was right. If Jethro left him, he would fall prey to the angry young warriors, and no one in the village, not even the medicine man who had saved him, would interfere. He had no choice other than to do as Jethro suggested or prepare to die in an enemy camp and see the woman he had intended to marry become wife to a Crow.

There would be another time, Big Owl convinced himself; he would have another opportunity to show Many Berries that he had not lost his power. He took a deep breath and looked past Jethro, his head up.

"I will go with you," he said. "I will tell the warriors that I do not intend to steal your horse. I will be content with just my black pinto. Will that keep them from wanting to kill me?"

"It won't keep them from *wanting* to kill you," Jethro said honestly, "but it will keep them from *actually* killing you. In addition, you must tell them that you intend to leave the village soon. When you are gone, there will be no more danger to you from them."

Many Berries remained at the lodge while Jethro and Big Owl went to High Elk and the other warriors, who were still painting themselves and singing war songs. Big Owl walked with difficulty. He had reinjured himself badly, and this would add further days to his stay in the village.

When Jethro approached with Big Owl, High Elk stepped forward with the others. "You did manage to make him come to us, I see," he said. He looked at Big Owl and motioned to Jethro, then spoke to Big Owl in sign.

"This is a good day for you. Every day is a good day for you as long as you have this man looking out for your life."

161

Big Owl bristled with anger. But he knew better than to respond in a negative way. "I have come to say that you have no reason to fear for your horses," he said to High Elk in sign. "I will be gone soon, with Many Berries, and you will see no more of me."

"How soon will that be?" High Elk asked.

"My ribs will need the passing of maybe three or four suns. Then I can ride far from here."

High Elk grunted. "When you were stealing Jethro's horse today, how far did you intend to ride?"

"Why don't we forget about today?" Jethro suggested. "Big Owl has given his word against further aggression. He has told you when he plans to leave with Many Berries. All is well now."

"All is not well," High Elk contradicted him, "but we will leave things as they are." He turned and looked hard at Big Owl. "I do not need any more excuses to kill you."

Big Owl's jaws tightened, but he remained still. Jethro turned and led him away, back to where Many Berries was waiting.

"I hope you are true to your word, Big Owl," Jethro said. "If you are not, there is no way I can interfere again. I know that the spirits will no longer hold me responsible."

"This will be the last time you will speak on my behalf," Big Owl told him. "If we ever speak again, I will hold the upper hand."

When Jethro was gone, Big Owl struggled to get comfortable in the lodge. Many Berries had built a low fire, and now she poured water into a skin pot.

"Why do you say you want that mixed-blood Crow more than you want me?" Big Owl asked.

"It will do you no good to remain angry with me," Many Berries replied, stirring in venison and roots. "I have made up my mind and you cannot change it. I am going to stay behind when you leave."

"I should run my knife through you," Big Owl said. "That would make things final."

"Go ahead, if you wish," Many Berries told him. "I do not fear death. You have struck me enough times. And besides, it would do you no good. You would still not have me."

Big Owl glared over at her. She did not even bother to look at him. He took hold of the knife handle at his waist, then released it. She was right, it would do no good to kill her. It would cause a great stir in the village and give cause for some of the hotheaded young warriors to kill him. Besides, she would certainly not become his in death.

"What makes you think he even wants you?" Big Owl finally asked. "I think he knows you by now."

Many Berries grinned. "You can think what you want, Big Owl," she said, "but I know Jethro better than he knows me. I can make him want me, even if he thinks he doesn't."

Big Owl grunted. He could not dispute her threat. He had wondered often enough himself whether he had taken Many Berries because of love or because of her beauty and the attention

163

she attracted. A woman of her style and grace made other warriors regard the man with her as very lucky.

It did not matter now. She had pledged to become his, and she would be his. He would see to it that she wanted this marriage as badly as he.

Big Owl thought further for a time. Jethro had certainly caused his relationship with Many Berries to suffer, but getting rid of Jethro right now was out of the question. And even if he could somehow force Many Berries onto a horse, she would eventually find a means of escape from him and return to the village. He would have to devise a way to gain back her approval, through her desire for power.

As he thought, his eyes lit up. He knew exactly what would recapture Many Berries' admiration—and bring himself great honor among the Small Robes as well. They would tell him they were sorry they had ever sent him away and make him an important warrior among them.

Big Owl watched Many Berries dish herself a bowl of stew. She nudged the pot toward him, but he ignored it. Instead, he painfully moved over next to her.

"I still want the Crow man, Jethro," Many Berries said quickly. "Nothing you can say will change my mind, if that's what you're going to try to do."

"Go ahead and stay here with Jethro," Big Owl said. He smiled. "You will be sorry, for I know of a way to keep him from ever gaining power."

Many Berries turned from her meal. "What are you saying?"

"I am saying that I am going to prove to you and to all of the Blackfeet people that I am the strongest warrior that has ever lived. I am going to bring back to my people very powerful Crow medicine. I will make it *my* medicine. Then I will be honored as no warrior before me has ever been honored. You don't have to be my wife, though. You can stay here with a man who will soon be broken."

Many Berries thought at first that Big Owl was just blustering again. But his conviction made her curious. She hoped he had not gotten some crazy idea.

"Are you going to try to kill him?" she asked. "I have told you before how foolish that would be. You couldn't even steal his horse, so why think of killing him?"

"Did I say I was going to kill him?"

"What else could you be talking about?"

"I will do something that will bring me a lot more honor than just a scalp."

Big Owl left Many Berries hanging. He continued to smile, watching her curiosity peak. He would not tell her any more than he absolutely had to, in order to keep her wondering.

Many Berries could stand the tension no longer. "Tell me more about this honor you are going to gain," she said.

"I will *show* you rather than tell you," Big Owl promised. "When the time is right. It has to be when I am strong, when I can ride fast and my insides do not hurt so badly."

"It sounds like you have a plan to do something that will take a lot of bravery."

"I do."

"Are you serious? Or is this a joke?"

"This is no joke," Big Owl contended, his eyes hard. "I will do what no other Piegan warrior has ever done, and we will ride back to our people in triumph."

"What could you possibly do that would allow us back among the Small Robes?"

"I said that I will tell you when the time is right," Big Owl told her. "I will see how much you really care for this Crow dog. Mark my word, if you stay with me, you will be wife to the strongest warrior the Blackfeet nation has ever seen."

ELEVEN

ALTHOUGH MANY BERRIES CONTINUED TO BE curious about Big Owl's plan, he ignored her, smiling, and looked to the north, the home of the Blackfeet. Many Berries wondered if he might have a good plan after all. He seemed to be waiting to act until the right moment presented itself. He kept saying that when the grass became yellow, his rise to power would begin.

Jethro announced to the village that he had dreamed for four nights in a row and had received visions that told him he must become a medicine man. He must journey to the Crazy Mountains for fulfillment of his vision quest. The Beartooth gave power to many, but the small range of jagged, mysterious peaks that stood alone just across the valley from the Beartooth were meant to be his sacred mountains.

167

Jethro knew that his powers would differ from those of most other warriors, and be far stronger. He would follow in the way of Bull Comes Ahead and lead his people as a peace chief. When Many Berries heard this, she was disappointed in Jethro; she did not desire a peace chief for a husband. She soon became convinced that Big Owl would eventually have more power than Jethro. Medicine men were special in the eyes of the people, but strong warriors were the ones who paraded their wives.

She planned to tell Jethro that there would be no more meetings between them, and to thank him for sparing Big Owl's life. Big Owl should be happy now; there would be no warriors for Many Berries other than himself.

Late one afternoon, Many Berries found Jethro away from the village, sitting along the river. The sun neared the horizon and the air was calm. She watched him sit in contemplation of his new quest.

"You will soon be a very different man," she said as she sat down near him. "Do you feel that you will disappoint your father?"

Jethro shook his head. "Of course not. Whether I am a warrior or a peace chief, it makes no difference to him. He will be just as proud."

"You would have become a great warrior, Jethro."

"Wasn't it you, Many Berries, who told me to follow what I feel?"

Many Berries nodded sheepishly. "That is true, I did tell you that."

"So, that is what I'm going to do."

"I will miss you," she said. "I want to thank you for what you've done. I will talk to you no more after this."

"Is Big Owl ready to ride now?" Jethro asked, trying to ignore the emotion he was feeling.

"Big Owl will be able to ride as well as he ever could before long," Many Berries said. "At least, that is what he tells me."

Jethro nodded. "He ought to be strong enough then to keep you happy. Maybe he'll gain more power than you think. Enough to make you who you want to be."

Many Berries was silent. She watched the late-summer water flow lazily though the channel, while killdeers and various small birds pecked among the rocks and gravel for food.

"I know what you must think of me," she said finally, "and I can understand. But you must believe me when I tell you that the first day I met you, I began to care a great deal for you. And the day we made love near the spring . . . that was very special to me. I still feel that you are special. But you have chosen a pathway that does not appeal to me."

Jethro nodded again, his eyes trailing a kingfisher that darted down from a cottonwood limb to skim a small fish from the water. "Why is it you think more of a warrior than you do of a peace chief? Does having a powerful warrior for a husband mean more to you than happiness with a man you could love deeply?"

She did not hesitate. "Power in war is most important. Yes, of course. You know that a woman whose husband has horses and war honors is bound to be thought of more highly than someone who cannot ride with fine dresses in the parades. I insist on having everyone think of me as a woman who can have what she wants, because I *am* that kind of woman. I believe now that Big Owl can give me all that."

"What has made you change your mind?"

"It is a feeling I have."

Jethro turned again to the river. "It seems to me that you and Big Owl belong together," he said. "Each of you is so obsessed with the wrong kind of power that you do not watch and listen for the signs that tell when to go ahead and when to go back. That will lead to destruction, for both of you."

"Do you wish me death?" she asked.

"No, of course not," Jethro replied. "I am only saying that you will find trouble if you want power for the sake of power."

Many Berries rose quickly. "It sounds like you want to place bad luck upon me. I would never have thought that of you." She turned and hurried away.

Jethro wanted to call out to her, but held himself back. He thought for a moment and concluded that Many Berries had distorted the truth. Deep within, she knew that he spoke the truth, but she did not want to face it. For some reason, she again thought that Big Owl could provide her with everything she wanted. Maybe High Elk had been right when he said the bad spirits were very strong within Many Berries and Big Owl.

Jethro continued to watch the birds forage along the rippling shoreline, bobbing and probing and chattering among themselves in their high-pitched voices. They seemed to have so little to be concerned with, such an easy time of their lives. Like the seeds, they seemed to be content to just hurtle up into the breeze and float along above the river's winding course.

Although they were small and light, they possessed a power and dignity of their own. Each species knew its limitations and exactly how it fit into the chain of life. Good and bad seemed obvious to them: finding food was good, and falling victim to a food-seeking predator was bad. Nothing could be simpler.

But the warrior must face a more complicated scheme, one that made the quest for power essential. Every bit of knowledge the warrior gained from the birds and animals increased his superiority over his adversary. Each of the animals lived to the fullest, and none could be considered good or bad in themselves. Bull Comes Ahead would often say that to have power is to recognize the bad as well as the good and to learn to handle each with authority. Jethro knew that these words meant to remind him that even though good was sought, bad had its place in the balance of the chain of life.

Jethro considered Bull Comes Ahead's words as true knowledge. He saw that a warrior must not think that evil can be obliterated; instead, a warrior must recognize that evil can only be defended against and sent away. The test comes in recognizing it and in making certain that it never gains influence over that which is good.

Jethro now knew why he had felt compelled to

save Big Owl's life. The spirits had been telling
him that there is no way to combat evil except
by right decisions. To fight evil with evil, as Bull
Comes Ahead had pointed out, only brings that
which is most evil to the fore. To have left Many
Berries to care for the dying Big Owl would have
been just as destructive as intentionally killing
the warrior out of anger.

Now that Big Owl had nearly recovered and
Many Berries had decided to go with him, Jethro
hoped that the bad spirits would leave as well.
He could see that deep inside Many Berries there
existed a woman whom he could love for the rest
of his life; but there was somebody else there as
well, somebody evil.

Jethro realized that Many Berries was someone he should take no more interest in, someone
he could not *afford* to take any more interest in.
If he allowed his thoughts to settle on her as they
had in the past, he would not be able to concentrate on his goals. He found it odd to think that
she had given him so much direction, yet in the
end was not good for him. It would not be possible for him to live with her and at the same
time grow in a spiritual manner; the part of her
that cared only about power did not care for him,
just for his strength. And she wanted to be
around that kind of strength, no matter who the
man might be who possessed it.

Jethro noticed a slight movement in the willows next to the shore. He watched as a bobcat
pounced from the shrubs to grab one of the killdeers at the water's edge. The remaining birds
cried out in unison and flew noisily downriver.

The trapped killdeer flapped momentarily in a cloud of its own feathers before resigning itself to death, while the bobcat glanced up quickly at Jethro before slinking into cover.

Jethro began to prepare once again for his journey, fasting and praying by himself for long periods of time, looking off into the direction of the Crazy Mountains. His knee felt sound again, and his stamina was back to normal. Knowing where he would go and what he must do made him confident that this time he would gain considerable knowledge.

He paused in his endeavors only to participate in the fall buffalo hunt, which proved as successful as any the people could remember. The Kicked-in-Their-Bellies killed and butchered over a thousand animals: plenty of meat and robes for the winter. There would be no need to hunt any more, although the leaves were yet to begin falling from the trees.

Big Owl and Many Berries were still in the village, avoiding the main lodges most of the time. Big Owl caused no more trouble, but remained silent and seemingly contemplative. Many of the warriors, High Elk especially, could not understand this dramatic change of character and spoke of it often. Jethro felt it best to simply accept the about-face and not try to draw any conclusions. If Big Owl was not causing trouble, that was good.

Jethro began to feel that everything had turned again to his favor, and to the favor of his people. With the success of the hunt and the uplifted

173

spirits of the villagers, it seemed that the recent strife and turmoil might now be in the past.

One morning Jethro arose before dawn to pray and seek more answers. He walked through a draw just north of the river the people called Little Canyon waters and then went a good distance farther, across open grassland. The late-season heat and absence of rain had made the grass brittle, but a cool night's coating of dew sparkled on the dried leaves as the sun rose over his shoulder.

Jethro began to sense that something powerful was about to happen. He realized that his life would again be in danger, and he began to look in all directions as he walked. A powerful thunderstorm, unusual in intensity for the time of year, broke over the peaks of the Crazy Mountains to the west. It moved toward him, out across the broad and open flats, sending heavy, jagged lines of crackling white energy to the earth.

The clouds grew darker and the thunder heavier. With each streak of lightning, the air exploded. An enormous cloud of dust was beginning to rise from the ground beneath the storm. At first Jethro worried that there might be another huge, dark spirit lurking in the clouds, but no funnel was visible. He finally concluded that the area of dust was too wide and too high for such a spirit.

As he felt the wind whip his face, Jethro suddenly realized that the earth was trembling beneath him. In the distance, near the ground at the bottom of the dust cloud, he saw a sea of dark brown. Buffalo!

He froze for an instant, his eyes fixed on the stampeding herd. With no place to go, he would be trampled in a short time. He tried to think of where he might run, but it was futile. The Little Canyon waters lay too far south for him to reach them in time; nothing but rolling, open grassland surrounded him on all sides.

He turned toward the east and started to run. This would surely test his knee, and he could only hope that it would hold up. As he churned his way through the grass and sage, he knew that he had no logical chance of survival. He could not stop, though, and continued to run blindly. He left his fate to the spirits, opening himself up past the terrible fear that swept through him. He resigned himself to die a dignified death, facing the oncoming herd, if he could not find sanctuary.

The herd gained continuously, yet Jethro poured out his energy. His lungs burned from the depths of his chest. The oncoming torrent, pounding ever closer, grew louder than the thunder overhead. Sweat poured from his brow and stung his eyes, blurring his vision.

His knee grew numb and his legs began to lock up. He nearly fell as he topped a small hill and looked down into an isolated gully where a spring broke from the lower lip of the opposite hillside. Against the near side of the hill and fed by the spring, there grew a long cottonwood tree, spreading huge arms toward the clouds. A pair of ducks burst from a small pond created by the spring, their singing wings pulling them upward and over the top of the hill behind him.

Jethro could not remember this place being here. He concluded that he had just never noticed it, hidden as it was in the vast open.

He stumbled down the hill, falling twice in his frantic effort to reach the tree. The herd pounded every closer toward the crest behind him. Soon a huge mass of buffalo would be pouring over the top, racing from the lightning and thunder pursuing it.

Just before reaching the tree, Jethro fell again. He scrambled on his hands and knees to the base of the cottonwood and pulled himself to his feet, grasping lower branches to raise himself. Splatters of rain broke against his face, and he hauled himself up the trunk just as the buffalo topped the hill. He could hear them bawling and rushing toward him as he scrambled higher into the tree, his arms numb from exhaustion.

The cottonwood, though large, shook under the tremendous power surging around it. Golden leaves came loose and showered down past him, while the rain came harder and a relentless wind whipped the dust into thick, swirling clouds.

The cottonwood was jolted several times, and once Jethro slipped through the branches, catching himself just before falling out of the tree. He stared down in horror, his feet dangling close to the surging mass of buffalo. He regained a measure of balance and clutched the main trunk with his arms and legs, holding on with all the strength he could muster.

Below, the herd plowed though the draw, one

huge wave after another of dust and dark brown and thundering sound, plunging down upon itself, rolling through its own momentum. The leaders of the herd had stumbled through the bottom, some of them falling and trampled by those behind. Others had piled up atop the leaders until the draw had filled, allowing the remainder of the herd to stampede over their backs to the other side.

Rain poured for a time while the herd continued past the tree, lightning popped over their backs to make the buffalos' terror ever greater. Gradually the sound diminished and the rain lessened, until finally only scattered gusts of wind remained.

The herd had passed, leaving behind the pitiable bawls and gasps of the wounded and dying. Jethro rubbed layers of sweat mixed with dust from his face and brow. He lowered himself slowly, shaking uncontrollably, watching flailing buffalo struggle to free themselves from the pileup.

He reached the bottom and looked around at the desperate animals, many of them with broken legs, unable to pull free, yet lunging helplessly, their mouths frothing and their eyes rolling wildly. The sun was breaking through. The two ducks sailed in from the opening of blue sky, then veered off; their pothole of water had been obscured by the mass of dying buffalo.

Jethro was still shaking when he turned to see, just beneath the cottonwood, something large and white among the brown and black of the broken bodies. He stumbled around the tree and stared. An immense white bull, free but for one hind leg, stood trapped by the carcass of a dead cow.

The bull did not lunge or otherwise struggle for freedom, but stood silently, gazing ahead. Looking closer, Jethro saw that the animal was very old and likely had no intention of wasting itself in a fruitless effort at escape. It seemed content to wait for death.

The cow trapping the white bull had fallen so that its neck was twisted back, one horn caught in the roots of the cottonwood. The bull's hind leg had slipped down between the bank and the cow's neck.

It was impossible to tell whether the white bull had broken its leg or not. Jethro knelt down, careful not to excite the creature, and began working on the cottonwood root with his knife. The bull turned to look at him, staring with large black eyes, panting from exhaustion, yet unafraid. Its ancient mouth hung open, and Jethro could see that what teeth were left had been worn down to the gums.

He worked for the remainder of the afternoon to free the bull, carving at the root and resting intermittently. Around him, wolves and coyotes appeared in great numbers to scavenge the dead and eat the wounded alive. Magpies and crows gathered, floating in from all directions, jabbering and cawing and pecking, hopping from back to furry back, jerking strips of flesh from torn and gaping wounds.

Only once did the white bull become nervous, when a black wolf ventured toward a fallen buffalo nearby. The wolf stood still and watched Jethro, its tongue hanging and yellow eyes glowing, its pure black coat shining in the sunlight. Jethro stood up and the wolf growled deep and low, then retreated to find another victim.

Finally, as the sun began to descend over the Crazy Mountains, Jethro carved the last chunk from the root and pulled the dead cow's horn free. By jerking and twisting the cow's head, he was able to free the bull's leg. Yet the old bull did not move.

Jethro sheathed his knife and after catching his breath, leaned forward and placed both hands against the bull's hip. He felt a tremendous flow of power through his entire being that made him close his eyes. When he opened his eyes, the bull was moving. Discovering that its leg was free, it lunged forward and stumbled out of the pileup.

Jethro watched the white buffalo move past the tree. Its leg had not been broken. The bull made its way slowly up the torn slope of the far hill, ignoring the scavengers that went about their feasting, tearing at limbs and intestines in the growing evening shadows. At the top of the hill, the bull turned to look down at Jethro.

Jethro stared, his mind dazed by the creature's incredible medicine; his whole body felt uplifted to a degree of lightness. He turned away and looked up into the cottonwood, through branches now nearly leafless, and into the darkening sky overhead. He felt the tree speaking and stepped over to the trunk, where he placed both hands just under a limb above his head, feeling the surge of strength that flowed down from the sky and through him, into the deep roots below.

The tree had been his salvation—the Tree of Life—and it was fitting that he honor every tree he passed from that time on, until the spirits came to take him to the Other Side.

When Jethro turned to look up the hill again, the white bull had vanished. Its power remained, though, and Jethro realized that if he lived his life in a just manner, the power would be on every hilltop where he looked, available to him whenever he needed it. It was a gift of life, for life.

As the sun fell behind the Crazy Mountains, Jethro began his walk back to the village, feeling the strength within him, knowing that his journey to the mountains for his vision quest would attain great success. His life might be filled with grave trial, but he had confidence that he would some day have the power to overcome anything the spirits thought fit to send him.

TWELVE

BIG OWL SURVEYED THE VILLAGE. ALL WAS PRO-
gressing as he had planned. A wisp of
wind, just enough, blew softly from the
southwest. As the sun neared the western horizon, the camp was peaceful, with women going
for water or picking berries outside of camp to
the tunes of flutes held by young warriors. The
elders smoked and talked around small fires,
content with the outcome of the fall hunt and
their world as they now saw it.

Best of all, Big Owl noted with satisfaction,
Jethro still had not returned from his walk, and
Bull Comes Ahead was also away from the village, praying as the sun was falling. It was necessary that these two be gone for his plan to
work. Big Owl looked out to the shadows falling
against the hills north of the camp, watching

carefully as the young horse tenders began changing shifts. He could now move the two ponies he wanted and secure them in hiding until the time was right.

With attention to every detail, Big Owl slipped out of the village and into the herd. While the horse tenders were distracted by conversation, he located Jethro and High Elk's prize buffalo ponies and hobbled them in the first small draw upriver from the village. The draw was steep and clogged with brush, an excellent place in which to keep horses out of sight temporarily. Flame and Night Runner would be added bounty for him to take to the Piegan village.

Big Owl clapped his hands with anticipation and slipped back into the village. With quick steps he neared the lodge he and Many Berries shared. He slipped past the door flap and found Many Berries inside, beading a pair of moccasins for herself. He knelt beside her, his eyes excited.

"Gather everything you want to take with you and wait for me in that first brushy draw along the river at the north edge of the village."

"What are you talking about?" she asked.

"The time has come for me to prove to you that I will be the strongest Piegan warrior to ever live."

"What are you going to do?"

"There is no time to discuss it. I must act quickly. Now do as I say and go out to the draw. Stay to the shadows. There are two horses hobbled there. Do not leave until I come to meet you. Then we will ride to great honors among our people."

"Now is the time for you to tell me what you're going to do," Many Berries insisted.

Big Owl's face tightened. "It doesn't matter to me if you come or stay. There will be plenty of women who will throw themselves at me when I go to the Small Robes. I only thought it would be you who would most like to be married to me, a man who has something no Piegan has ever been able to get before. Suit yourself. I have no more time for you."

Big Owl picked up a small stick of flame from the fire and left before Many Berries could comment or ask any more questions. He moved quickly into the trees along the river and waited. The form of Many Berries, carrying a small skin bag of belongings, emerged from the lodge and hastened into the shadows.

With a grunt of satisfaction, Big Owl blew on the small flame to keep it alive and began to traverse the tree line along the streambed. He watched in all directions, brushing lightly through snowberry and chokecherry, until he reached his destination.

Darkness was approaching fast, allowing him to slink from the brush and under the brow of a hill to the place where he had piled dried grass in several clumps. He hurried from clump to clump, igniting the dry tinder with the small stick of live coal, enjoying the streaks of crimson—fanned by the southerly breeze—that quickly spread into the surrounding grassland.

Then, back in the trees along the riverbank, he laughed as he crouched in the shadows and watched the men of the village hurry toward the thickening smoke at the perimeter of the lodges. Women and children screamed and ran toward the river, crossing in front of his hiding place so close that he could have reached out and grabbed one of them had he so desired.

The flames spread from the grassland into the south side of the village. Some of the women rushed ahead of the fire to take down lodges and salvage belongings. Warriors ran from the river with pouches and bags of water, dousing what they could, trying to save the village, shouting for their loved ones. The smoke was so thick in the twilight that it was impossible to determine in which direction the fire was spreading.

Unnoticed, Big Owl moved with ease to Bull Comes Ahead's lodge, located near the center of the village. He pushed past the door flap just as Calling Bird was emerging with the Sacred Pipe. She was knocked backward and the pipe fell from her grasp.

Big Owl grabbed the pipe and turned. Calling Bird lunged forward, grasping an ankle, crying for help. Big owl pulled out his knife. She held on desperately as she felt the sharp blade enter her shoulder two, three, then four times before she was finally forced to release him. She continued to cry out. As Big Owl brought the knife down once more, she raised her hand in front of her face. He sliced through the palm of her hand.

With her free hand, Calling Bird grabbed his wrist and jammed his thumb back. Big Owl grunted and the knife slipped from his grasp. He had turned to leave when Calling Bird, having snatched up the knife, reached with the blade and sliced a line across the calf of his leg. He yelled but did not stop, clutching the Sacred Pipe as he twisted past the door flap and fled into the blinding smoke.

Big Owl rushed through the confusion, knocking down villagers in his frenzy to get away. He ignored the burning line that traced across the back of his leg as he scrambled through the darkness to the small draw. There he found Many Berries waiting with the horses.

She met him with wide eyes. "What have you done?"

Big Owl held up the pipe. "Now do you believe me when I tell you about gaining great honor?"

The flames behind Big Owl outlined the pipe in its otterskin pouch. Many Berries knew immediately what he was showing her.

"How did you get it?"

"I have planned for this day very well," he replied. "But I was almost too late. The woman was taking it out of the lodge, and I got there just in time. The fire spread faster than I had thought."

Many Berries shook her head in disbelief. "You have spoken truth," she said finally. "That will bring us more honor than anything else you could have done."

Big Owl nodded. "Cut the hobbles on the horses and get on one of them. We must be back in Blackfeet lands before the sun rises."

Jethro ran through the darkness. The flames had been visible from a long distance, the smoke dancing up into the night on the gusting wind.

He had not thought the lightning had reached that far south, but it appeared that the storm had passed through without rain. He learned the truth soon after he entered the village.

His mother and Rosebud were with a group of women caring for the frightened children. He noticed the deep frowns on the women's faces.

"Was the storm that bad?" he asked.

"It was not the kind of storm you speak of," Morning Swan told him. "Find your father. It is he who should tell you what has happened."

Thane Thompson had rushed to gather the various warrior societies, organizing cleanup procedures and determining who had suffered the greatest losses. Although few of the lodges had been actually burned, the entire village would participate in the ceremonies needed before the displaced families could gather poles and begin reconstruction. Losing lodges to other than natural means was the sign of a great problem. Praying in the right manner was the only insurance that no more harm would befall the families.

"What happened?" Jethro asked his father.

"Big Owl and Many Berries have offered their thanks for our hospitality," Thane answered. "They took our buffalo pony, and High Elk's as well. They even went so far as to steal the Sacred Pipe."

Jethro felt his stomach fall. "The Sacred Pipe is gone?"

"And Calling Bird was nearly killed. It is only by her strength that she escaped death."

"What of Bull Comes Ahead?"

"He was in the hills praying. He is tending to her now."

Jethro felt strong anger well up from deep within. His mind flashed back to all of the warnings that had been given him about Big Owl and Many Berries. Now he regretted having ever brought them to the village.

He found Bull Comes Ahead brewing herbs in his lodge for Calling Bird. She was lying on her side, her hand wrapped, her swollen arm and shoulder covered with poultices. Despite her injuries, she maintained her sense of humor.

"I'm always sewing things for him," she told Jethro. "It's about time he sewed something for me, although I wish it didn't have to be for the stitching of knife wounds."

Jethro had trouble forming a smile. "I'm sorry this had to happen," he told her. "I am to blame."

"Was it you who did this?" Calling Bird asked. "There was a lot of smoke, but I was certain the person looked just like Big Owl."

"He wouldn't have done this if I hadn't brought him back to the village," Jethro said. "I wish now I had just gone ahead into the mountains to seek my vision."

Bull Comes Ahead reached over and placed a hand on Jethro's shoulder. "You should not talk that way. Have you stopped believing in what the spirits told you to do? Do you now believe you should have allowed Big Owl to die?"

"I had no idea that he would do something like this."

"You know Big Owl," Bull Comes Ahead corrected him. "You had every idea that he would

187

do something like this. That is the kind of man he is. But it does not mean that you shouldn't have done what you were supposed to do."

Jethro took a deep breath. "What if he had killed Calling Bird?"

"He didn't. There is no use in talking that way."

"It was only by the choice of the spirits that he did not kill her," Jethro argued.

"Don't forget what you are supposed to learn about this," Bull Comes Ahead told him, his voice deep with emphasis. "You cannot turn back from what you have started. You must go ahead and not think about what might have happened. It is finished."

"What he is trying to say," Calling Bird put in, "is that more bad luck will come if you don't believe in yourself."

"You must be very certain of yourself," Bull Comes Ahead said, "no matter what follows."

Jethro left the lodge full of anger. He could hardly contain his eagerness to go after Big Owl and Many Berries. He gathered High Elk and Cuts Buffalo's brothers, along with some of the other young warriors, to discuss the matter. They grouped in a circle around a small fire.

"It has happened," High Elk told him. "I told you so many, many times to be careful. It has finally happened."

Jethro glared at his friend. "You don't have to remind me of it. I am not going to dwell on it. Right now I want the Sacred Pipe back, along with the scalps of Big Owl and Many Berries."

High Elk and the other warriors voiced their

approval. There was not a single person in the village now who would not gladly perform the scalp dance, considering what had just taken place.

"There is one problem," High Elk said. "You are not yet a warrior. No one will follow you."

"I will change that soon enough," Jethro told him with conviction. "I will journey into the Crazy Mountains and I will receive my power. Then I will be ready. I have to make things right by my people, and I know the spirits will help me."

High Elk took Jethro's hand and clasped it in the handshake of power, the handshake of warriors, while everyone else whooped war cries.

"Now you are beginning to sound like the Jethro I really know, the old Jethro, the one who is destined to become a strong leader," High Elk said. "Begin to prepare yourself again. Do this. I want you to go to war with me; I want you for a war brother. No one else could be the same."

Jethro returned the firm grip. "That is what I will do," he said. "I will prepare for the journey I know I am supposed to make. And when I am finished, we will become war brothers against the Piegans."

The sun burned the morning chill from the high foothills as Big Owl and Many Berries neared the Piegan village. The colors of the late warm moons had come to the lower Two Medicine country, and the trees and shrubs were clothed in scarlet and gold.

As Big Owl and Many Berries had expected, a

contingent of warriors rode out from the village to meet them. The village had known of their presence for some time, for the Wolves—the scouts on watch over the village—had reported seeing them when they were still a long distance out.

The warriors reined in their horses, all of them expressing amazement that Big Owl had survived. But why would he have the nerve to come back? At first some thought he was a spirit, returning to take revenge against the two warriors who had left him on the day he had fallen under his horse. But then he screamed a war cry and held the Sacred Pipe high over his head. No spirit would ever touch a sacred object.

"I have counted the most honorable coup of any Piegan warrior against an enemy," Big Owl declared. "I now deserve to dwell among my own people again. I have done something that none of you has ever done. Can any one of you tell me this is not so?"

A warrior named Red Calf, who rode a large roan stallion, studied Big Owl intently. He wondered why Big Owl had been blessed by the spirits; it was not every day that a warrior brought home a trophy of this stature.

Red Calf hated Big Owl. It was he who had been accused by Big Owl of indiscretions with Many Berries. Ordinarily the accusation would have been thought of as a joke, but Big Owl had come at Red Calf with a knife, not even trying to learn what had truly taken place. Many felt that Red Calf would have prevailed against Big Owl— even though he was unarmed. Red Calf had been in one battle, with the Lakota Sioux, and had already proven himself a brave and formidable fighter. It would not be long until he was a strong leader.

Red Calf's side of the story had finally been heard in council. It had been obvious to all of the elders that Many Berries had been playing games. She was known for that. After Big Owl had tried to kill him, Red Calf had stopped the other warriors from killing Big Owl and had insisted instead that he be banished from the village.

Under the circumstances, Red Calf would have been perfectly within his right to have killed Big Owl, and Many Berries as well. She had approached Red Calf and had subtly attempted to seduce him. Then she had lied about what had happened, just so she could see what Big Owl would do on her behalf. She had certainly seen Big Owl's obsession for her, and it had made her feel powerful. She had not thought that it could cost her the right to further life in this world. But Red Calf had told the council that he saw no sense in ending their lives over a matter so trivial.

Another warrior, on a brown-spotted stallion, sat next to Red Calf and studied Big Owl and Many Berries closely. Takes Many Horses was not as large as Red Calf, but he was every bit as ferocious in battle. He had been one of the two warriors with Big Owl and Many Berries on the day they had come upon Jethro, having been one of the two selected to make sure that Big Owl and Many Berries left Blackfeet lands.

Takes Many Horses had been afraid to ride out and meet Big Owl and Many Berries; he had been the one to suggest that they were spirits. But now he realized that Big Owl was flesh and blood.

He studied Big Owl as hard as Red Calf did, concluding that something amazing had happened that the warrior was yet in this world. He had witnessed Big Owl's attempt to reach the Crow atop the hill and had watched while Big Owl's pony had caved his ribs in. And he recognized the pipe in Big Owl's hand as the same that had brought the thunder and lightning down upon them.

"Did you take the pipe from the strong one who was on the hill that day?" Takes Many Horses asked Big Owl.

"The same one," Big Owl lied. "He did not stand a chance against me."

Many Berries frowned. She felt that Big Owl had indeed been blessed by the spirits to have somehow obtained the Sacred Pipe, but its power would work against them if he lied about how it had come into his hands. She knew that he had not fought Jethro for the pipe, for Jethro had been out of the village. She knew that he had not even had to fight Bull Comes Ahead for it, for he had also been gone at the time.

Many Berries still wondered how he *had* managed to get the pipe and escape the village without a fight. During the journey back north, she had asked Big Owl. She knew it was he who had set the fire, but the pipe would certainly have been among the first things the people would have attempted to save.

Big Owl had told her that it had been very trying and very difficult getting the pipe, that a number of warriors had fallen to him, but that he had not had the time to scalp them. He told her that he had even lost his knife in the hard fighting.

Many Berries had wondered at the time about his story. He had only the gash across the back of his leg to show for his battle against many in the village. She had wondered how he would explain this to everyone else.

"This is a most powerful pipe among the Crow people," Big Owl continued. "Without it, they are nothing. I now have the power to destroy them."

"How were you saved from death?" Takes Plenty Horses asked. "On the day I last saw you, your horse had fallen upon you and you were near to crossing over. Why did this not happen?"

Big Owl looked first at Takes Plenty Horses and then at each warrior, reading their curiosity, knowing that he was now the envy of every one of them. His feat had been incredible; even the bravest among them could not top it.

"I was not meant to die on that day," he finally replied. "I am here among you, which shows that I was meant to have this pipe and to lead my people to victory against the Crow nation. Is there any among you who can dispute this?"

The warriors began to nod. They had heard from Red Calf and Takes Plenty Horses of how the spirits had descended against them on that day. They had heard the story of the tremendous storm that had come to the aid of the lone Crow man standing atop the hill. They knew that Big

Owl had fallen under his own pony and been crushed. They realized that Big Owl must now be telling the truth in claiming that his medicine was the greater. He had the pipe to prove it.

Red Calf then spoke up. "It is fitting that you be welcomed back among our people. You have indeed accomplished much and are worthy of honors. We will look to you for leadership from this day forward. We will look to you when we talk of war against the Crow people."

The warriors nodded and voiced their agreement, then turned their horses and parted so that Big Owl and Many Berries could lead them into the village. Big Owl looked at Many Berries and smiled, and his eyes said to her, "Now is there any doubt of who has the most power?"

THIRTEEN

JETHRO WATCHED THE SUN FALL FROM THE TOP OF Crazy Peak, the highest peak in the Crazy Mountains. He stood on snow that was crusted to ice by cold wind, his arms raised to the sky, his face and body coated with bear grease against frostbite. He had come to where he was supposed to be and had watched the sun disappear into deep red, as he had seen in his dream. Now he awaited the depth of this night, which would bring him his future.

He once more turned the backs of his arms to the western horizon, allowing the cooler streams of his blood to mix with the sun's last light. Along each forearm there were four deep gashes, made by the talons of an eagle's foot from Bull Comes Ahead's lodge. He had cut the gashes at the same angle as the streaks of red paint along the top of the Sacred Pipe, which was now in Big Owl's possession. He would offer his injured arms to the sun in prayer that the Sacred Pipe come back to the Crow people.

This night would carry over into his fourth day of fasting, his fourth day since leaving the sweat lodge and beginning his journey for power once again. The walk to the mountains had been smooth and uneventful, but his effort to reach the summit had been exhausting. Although he had been weak earlier in the day, he had regained his strength almost to its entirety when he had met a single raven, which had floated from the sky onto a branch of a pine tree nearby.

"As soon as the sun is gone, you will see into the great darkness," the bird had told him. "Look for me when you leave the top of the rocks. Bring a handful of snow with you until the vision is finished and then, stand strong under the tree I have selected for you. Those that you should listen to will come to you either in the air or on the ground. If anything comes from below, out of a hole, stretch out your arms and you will be lifted. Do not be fooled. Listen only when you are off the ground."

Jethro continued to hold his arms to the sun, waiting until the crimson sphere slid below the horizon. In the twilight, he sang a short song of asking:

> *I come to you a humble child,*
> *and ask that you see my tears.*
> *The Sacred Pipe lives no more*
> *among the people.*

*I ask that you send light
and show me where to find it.*

Jethro stepped down carefully from the rocks, into the darkness of the east slope. He scooped up a handful of crusted snow and cautiously picked his way down the hillside and into the forest. He progressed through the shadows, the tops of the trees swaying with a sudden strong breeze, their trunks creaking and groaning as if in torture. A full moon rose. It was deep orange in color and moved quickly skyward into sweeping clouds split into long, ragged streaks by the wind.

Jethro looked for the raven, the black bird's words buried deep in his mind. He was certain that he would be tested by dwellers from below. He had heard little about them, for the people were afraid to speak of their existence lest it bring the beings up from their world to cause tragedy. Although he did not care to meet them, Jethro knew that tonight he had no choice.

He heard the wind whisper in his ears, like voices calling to him from every direction. He stopped to stare at the moon, feeling himself drawn closer to it, as if moving forward until close enough that he could touch the glowing sphere.

Then across the face of the moon there appeared a winged shadow, a large bird that circled from far out in the sky and finally settled, cawing, into the lower branches of a nearby pine tree. The bird peered at him briefly, its eyes glowing a brilliant white, and then flew back out into the face of the moon, swerved, and was lost in the night.

Jethro neared the tree, seeing a small circle of glowing white on the ground. This was the place where he must face the night. He stepped into the circle, and the light grew brighter. Although he tried to relax, he could not, but stood firmly under the tree while the wind sang its tormented songs. The moon rolled farther up into the sky, growing misty and distorted as the clouds thickened around it and closed off its glow.

Jethro had felt light all day. The lack of food and water for four days had weakened him. Now he felt his body gradually become even lighter, as if his weight were disappearing altogether. The hunger pangs, gone since the previous day, returned briefly to his stomach, then spread through his entire body, as if he hungered for something other than common, solid food. His body quivered. He realized that he would not have long to wait until the darkness brought him visitors.

As the wind whipped along his back, Jethro felt the heavy black night settling in around him. Despite his knowing what to expect, he began to experience a fear that reached deeper into him than anything he had ever known. It made him aware of that which cannot be described, only felt and then registered deep within. Something in the very depths of his being told him that he would soon face that for which he had been longing, that for which he had worked so hard to find.

It began with movement just behind him and

to his right. Although he was aware that it was night, Jethro could see as clearly as if early morning daylight had dawned around the tree. He turned. A rabbit, as white as the snow atop the summit, was skirting its way through the grass toward him. It was screaming, the shrieks high-pitched, so that Jethro's ears filled with the sound.

"Take me quickly!" the rabbit called out to him. "I am nearly killed!"

Jethro tried to speak but could not.

"It is above us!" the rabbit shouted, climbing into Jethro's arms.

Jethro looked up to see huge broad wings descending from the summit of the mountain, a massive shadow that filled the sky and blanked out the twinkling lights. The Thunderbird! He realized that he could not give up the medicine of the giant eagle, but he did not want to see the rabbit's last moments, either.

"Throw out the snow!" the rabbit instructed.

Jethro quickly tossed his chunk of snow out into the grass. It thumped and bounced and rose into a white rabbit, larger than the one in his arms. The Thunderbird, its wings folded, then plummeted down, the rush of wind from its flight sounding a deafening roar.

Jethro closed his eyes as the Thunderbird's wings bowled him over and over. His arms flew open and the rabbit disappeared. The roar lessened and Jethro sat up. The moment his eyes opened, the roar was gone. He found himself still inside the circle, but the Thunderbird had disappeared, as had the large rabbit risen from the chunk of snow. The light around the tree once more grew bright.

Just up the hill, a huge bighorn ram stood broadside to him, its immense horns curled fully around and then halfway curled again. The ends of the horns were tapered, not broomed from fighting. Jethro realized that no other ram could stand against this one in battle for long.

The ram stared at him with large, bulging eyes, dark and simmering, eyes that held a consciousness far surpassing any Jethro had ever before experienced.

"Who are you?" Jethro asked.

"You know who I am," the ram said in a clear, even voice.

Jethro knew the ancient story of the twin boys. The weaker envied the medicine and gifts of the stronger one so much that he plotted to kill his brother. But his brother survived the attempt on his life, and from a ledge onto which he had been pushed, looked out into a vast canyon below. A bighorn ram came to him and carried him back to the summit, giving him divine wisdom. It was revealed that the bighorn ram was the medicine sought by the evil twin, but granted only to the good twin.

Many said now that a lone bighorn ram represented the spirit of the good brother. For this reason, all bighorn sheep were held sacred.

"You have finally come to seek your power," the ram said. "I have been waiting for you. I have traveled from the Bighorn Mountains, to the south, to be with you. I was not certain that you were ever coming."

Jethro became nervous. "Are you angry with me? I have never sought to hunt you or your kind."

"I have come to bring you strength, not to destroy you," the ram said. "Walk up here to where I stand."

Jethro, trembling, placed one foot ahead of the other.

"Don't be afraid of me!" the ram boomed. "Don't you trust me?"

Jethro stared at the powerful creature. Its large eyes were growing ever larger.

"I don't know."

"Of course you don't," the ram said. "You don't trust yourself! You cannot hope to trust anyone or anything if you don't first trust who you are."

"I have made bad decisions," Jethro said.

"You speak of saving the life of the Piegan warrior," the ram said knowingly. "That is what I mean when I say you do not trust yourself. How do you know that your decision was bad?"

"Big Owl stole the Sacred Pipe," Jethro said. "That is certainly reason to think that I shouldn't have saved him."

"If you hadn't saved him, you would not be alive this day," the ram informed him. "You should realize that."

Jethro understood that Big Owl was supposed to live for a reason he himself could not understand. But what of the Sacred Pipe?

"It is a real test to know what to do about the Sacred Pipe," the ram said, again knowing Jethro's thoughts. "Your decisions will determine many things. Nothing will be easy."

Jethro stared at the ram, wondering whether he would meet with death before he retrieved the pipe, wondering what would happen to his people should that happen.

"Do you still fear death?" the ram asked.

"I will accept death at any time," Jethro replied. "I want only to get the Sacred Pipe back for my people first."

"The sun will rise and fall and the grass will be nourished whether you find the Sacred Pipe or not," the ram said.

"But we live in fear without the pipe," Jethro said. "And I am responsible. Even if I do not live a day afterward, I would like to bring the Sacred Pipe back to my people."

"Come all the way up to me," the ram instructed.

Jethro placed himself in front of the ram. The ram's hair suddenly turned pure white, and its facial features turned gnarled and wrinkled before Jethro's eyes.

"Put your fingers into my mouth," the ram said.

Jethro did as he was instructed. The ram had no teeth, and Jethro's fingers ran over smooth gums. When he pulled his hand back, he saw that his fingers were crooked with age. He shook his hand and his youth returned.

"Do you remember the white buffalo you helped?" the ram asked.

Jethro nodded.

"Do you remember that the bull had no teeth?"

Jethro's eyes widened. "Is what I am feeling

true? Am I destined to live a long life, to become ancient, like Bull Comes Ahead?"

"Do you believe your feelings?"

"They are very strong."

"As strong as the feelings you had when you decided to save Big Owl's life?"

"Stronger. I *know* what you are telling me. But what have I done that is so wrong? Why can't I die as a strong warrior, on the battlefield, and go into the spirit world with honors?"

"There are many ways of gaining honors," the ram replied. "You know this already, for you have taken chances. But no chance that you will take will cause you to cross over before your time."

Jethro felt tears brimming in his eyes. "Why am I being punished? What have I done that is so terrible that I am destined to become old and wrinkled?"

"There must be those with wisdom as well as those with war honors," the ram said. "You already know that you are to become a medicine man. But to be warrior *and* medicine man is a difficult thing."

"Why should I need to become both?" Jethro asked.

"You are not ready for knowledge of that kind," the ram said. "Just remember to keep your dignity. You are to be one who will be known even after you have passed on. The Crow people will always remember you as a sincere elder among them, one who taught and guided them, as Bull Comes Ahead has done. You must accept this as your destiny."

Jethro took a deep breath. He would witness the death of many friends and family members as the winters passed, and he would not join them on the Other Side for a long time after. He knew there could be no alternative; if he was not to die until he grew very old, there was no way that he could cross over sooner, no matter how hard he might try. Not even an attempt to take his own mortal life would send him over; there were many lost, wandering spirits who had done this, and unless someone among the living made special sacrifices for them, they were forever doomed to live as dust devils sweeping across the plains during the hot moons.

"When you go from this mountain," the ram continued, "remember what you have seen and felt. Your life will be much more fulfilling if you think of yourself as chosen and fully able to withstand the tests you will face. The rabbit will show you how to find those who will help you, as you helped the rabbit. Your abilities to rise above the everyday will come from the eagle, and your sight into the future of others from the raven. But your strength will come from me, and it will be me whom you will seek most often."

"Is it here that I will always find you?" Jethro asked.

"You will know when and where to seek me," the ram replied. "I hope you have learned now that it is important to believe your feelings, no matter what others might think of your actions."

"I have learned this," Jethro said with conviction. "From this night forward, I will never question what I truly feel is right action."

The ram blew loudly and shook its massive head of horns. "There will be times when you must lower your head and not be stopped. Remember, you rule the mountain."

"I will remember."

"And do not be fooled by those who would try to make your journey and your decisions easier," the ram continued. "You will be sorely tested."

"I will remember," Jethro repeated. "What must I do to find the Sacred Pipe?"

"Your lesson is patience," the ram answered. "Your lesson will teach you to know when right action is required. Do not believe that the Sacred Pipe will be easy to recover. Now return to the circle."

"But I will get the pipe back in time, won't I?"

"Return to the circle," the ram repeated.

Jethro turned, stepped down the hill and into the circle. When he looked back, the ram had vanished. In its place was something small and man-shaped, something powerful standing alone in the shadows, watching him.

Although he could not clearly see the small, man-shaped being, Jethro was certain that it was a main chief among the Little People. Had the ram been this Little People chief in disguise, or had it truly been a bighorn sheep? It did not matter, for the power was there.

Suddenly Jethro could see nothing, not even the shadow of the Little People chief, as once again darkness returned to the circle. The wind slowed to a murmur and the blackness grew dense, bringing with it an eerie calm. Overhead,

205

the moon continued to hang low. The stringy clouds parted briefly, but long enough for Jethro to detect movement once again. This time it came from his left.

Just down the hill, a dead pine tree stood off by itself, its wizened branches jagged in the night. Something was emerging from a hole in the ground between two of its gnarled roots. There was a flash and the sudden appearance of a form near the tree. The form began to take shape as a hazy white shadow, flowing and shifting. Then it became a woman with long, trailing hair.

"Jethro! I have finally found you. I have been lost, so lost! Comfort me."

The woman drifted toward him. His eyes grew wide. The being had taken the form of Many Berries. He shook his head, hoping to dislodge the image from his eyesight, but the being remained, using Many Berries' voice, drawing closer, arms outstretched.

"Jethro, oh, Jethro! I did not want to leave you. Big Owl made me go with him, but I have returned to you."

Jethro began to speak, but then he remembered the raven's words. What stood before him could not be real, for it had come from a hole in the ground. And the raven had warned him not to listen until he had spread his arms and allowed the black bird's powers to work for him.

The image of Many Berries drew closer, reaching out for him. Jethro quickly spread his arms. He felt his body grow lighter, his arms extend outward even farther. Although he could not see in the darkness, he was certain that he was clothed in black, glossy feathers; he felt himself covered with them. Then he rose from the ground and hovered on the night wind over the image of Many Berries.

"Why have you come?" he asked. "If you are truly Many Berries, why did you emerge from a hole under the dead tree?"

"I can't hear you," the image said, "not from way up there."

"I can hear you just fine," Jethro told her. "Who are you, and why have you come?"

"I can't tell you while you're up there."

"I won't come back down," he said. "If you can't speak to me while I'm up here, you cannot be real."

"I am real!" the image said, its voice now sounding different. Instead of Many Berries' sweet voice, Jethro heard tones that were gruff and irritated. "I want you down here so I can talk to you. Come down here now!"

"Go back into the ground," Jethro ordered the image. "There is no place for you with me on this night. Or on any other night."

"Are you telling me to leave?" The voice sounded like Many Berries' once again. The words cracked with emotion, and tears flowed down the face.

Unimpressed, Jethro stated firmly, "I am telling you to go. Do it now!"

The image suddenly transformed itself into what Jethro took to be a wolf with an owl's head. The being's large, round eyes glowed yellow, its pupils a burning red, and it hissed at Jethro from

207

a huge beak that frothed a thick fluid that smelled like vomit.

"Be gone!" Jethro yelled again. "I want nothing to do with you!"

The owl's head turned in a full circle, then swung upside down on its neck. Its red and yellow eyes bulged like tiny skin bags filling with water. While Jethro watched, the eyes burst open, releasing small flying creatures resembling bats, only incredibly hairy and with heads like crested woodpeckers.

The creatures flew straight at Jethro, but he did not move or flinch. Before reaching him, they dissolved into balls of blue mist, like smoke, and trailed off into the night.

"You have no power over me," Jethro told the being. "You cannot scare or harm me."

The being, now headless, wailed from the open hole where the owl's head had rested and turned over onto its back. In a moment it was a round ball, emitting a foul odor, like the stink boiling up from the ground at the headwaters of the Yellowstone. The ball turned into flame and rolled in a pulpy mass down the hill and into the ground beneath the dead tree, pulling the patches of blue mist with it.

When the flame and mist were gone, Jethro settled down to the ground. As he touched the earth with his feet, radiant light broke the eastern skyline, blinding him. He closed his eyes and opened them. Then he did it again. His eyesight had changed. Suddenly he could see as well as an eagle.

Jethro looked toward the horizon, his eyes focusing a great distance out, clear into the Medicine Rock Mountains down river. Then, only for an instant, just long enough for him to know what he had seen, the Little People chief appeared to him, standing on the highest peak of the Medicine Rock Mountains.

Jethro stared, then blinked. He felt himself falling forward. He put his arms out to catch himself, but they plunged into the earth, clear up to his shoulders. As his chest hit the ground, he felt a jolt within his body; it was sharp, like a bolt of lightning. He worked to pull his arms free, but they were held fast, his struggles were to no avail. Again he felt a sudden jolt, and his arms were released. He tried to rise, but fell and rolled over onto his back.

He lay stunned for a time, not certain whether he had crossed over or not. His lungs burned. He gasped and arched his back, his lungs expanding to bring oxygen into his body. He blinked and sat up, his heart pounding. When finally he could see again, there was a raven sitting above him in the tree.

"Take a small piece of bark from this tree and keep it with you, in your medicine bag," the raven instructed. "And take some of the grass from within the circle. Braid it as the center strand in a short length of sweet grass."

"What else must I put into my medicine bundle?"

"You will know, or you will be told," the raven replied.

Jethro felt himself becoming dizzy. His eyesight grew fuzzy, then returned to normal. He shook his head repeatedly. Finally, his mind seemed to clear. The raven still sat on the branch above him.

"Who was that who came out of the ground?" Jethro asked. "I have never before seen a creature so terrible."

The raven turned its head sideways to look at him and cawed before flying off into the rising sun, its broad wings churning the air slowly and deliberately. Jethro struggled to his feet. He glanced at the small hole at the base of the dead pine tree and shuddered. Would he ever know?

He started down the mountain. In the far distance, the gravelly call of the raven echoed throughout the stillness of the morning forest.

FOURTEEN

LITTLE BOW AND JUMPS AHEAD WERE JUST leaving their special meeting place along the river, a new secret spot they had discovered and now made use of frequently. Each time the village moved camp they had to find a new hideout; but the river, with its thick tangles of trees and brush, always afforded such places.

The boys discussed their upcoming meeting with a select group of friends. Their club was organizing an event that would bring all of them glory. Just as the men had their warrior societies and the younger horse tenders had their social orders, it was only fitting that the boys had their own clubs, too; membership taught them the ways of men at an early age. The Magpies were ready to strike.

Today the Magpies were planning a raid on the

meat racks. These raids, most frequent just after the spring and fall hunts, led to many an honor for small boys who secured choice pieces of drying meat before they were caught. Tongues were especially important and worth taking great risk for, although any large cut from the hump or the back would allow a boy to wear a long tail feather from the noisy black-and-white birds from which they took their namesake.

Little Bow told Jumps Ahead of his idea for the big day. He had made the plans, as it had been his turn to do. He already possessed four magpie tail feathers from previous raids and did not feel compelled to gather any more for a while. One of their members, however, had yet to achieve even a single feather through no real fault of his own. He was named Running Hawk.

Little Bow thought this would be a good day to surprise Running Hawk with a chance to achieve a feather. Running Hawk had been blinded from a fall into a camp fire as a toddler. But his handicap did not bother him, nor did it bother any others in the village. This was a boy whom people wanted to be around and to learn from.

Running Hawk was considered special. Although his eyes had been burned out and his face terribly scarred by the fire, courage and diligence were his trademarks. He never complained about his condition, but only worked harder to stay abreast of his friends.

It was not from the kindness of the other boys that Running Hawk belonged to the Magpies. He had earned his right. More than once he had retrieved cookware and beads from various lodges, and he had easily passed the initiation into the club, all of this proving that his lack of sight had greatly heightened his other senses.

In addition, he had taught Little Bow and Jumps Ahead—as well as the other members of the Magpies—the ways of the night: what to listen for and how to move with the flow of darkness. The boys had learned a great deal from one who had been pressed to discover things that those with eyesight had not reason even to think of.

But stealing meat in the middle of the day was a different matter. Camp dogs were alert, and there were scores of watchers to make sure that the meat was not disturbed. The older men and women took pride in spotting boys who were planning meat raids, blind or not, and in thwarting their success.

Little Bow and Jumps Ahead, with their plan fully in mind, arrived at the prescribed meeting place and discussed their day's work with the others.

"Calling Bird has some of the best parts of the buffalo out drying in the open," Little Bow told them after asking for quiet. "Since she was stabbed by that Blackfeet warrior, Big Owl, everybody has been nice to her. I have a plan to get some tongues and back fat."

"That won't be easy," one of the boys said. "I heard her telling my mother last night that she was going to be watching for 'little pests' around the meat. And she told my mother that she didn't mean flies, either."

"And Cuts Buffalo and her mother are helping Calling Bird with her meat, since her shoulder and back are still sore," another boy pointed out. "Cuts Buffalo watches things closely, even more closely than Calling Bird does."

"Yes, but since Jethro is up in the mountains seeking his vision, Cuts Buffalo will be dreaming of him and not watching too closely," Little Bow said. "She always thinks about him, even when he is around the village."

The boys snickered. Little Bow was right; Cuts Buffalo was in love. She dreamed too much to be a very good watcher.

"What about Cuts Buffalo's mother?" the boy persisted. "She's too crabby to be in love. If she is, she doesn't show it."

"She won't be any trouble," Little Bow said. "You know her—she can't remain in one place for very long. Jabber, jabber. She is always going off somewhere to gossip and leaving the work to Cuts Buffalo. She will be wandering around before we even get ready to attack."

"I hope you're right," the boy said. "We haven't had much luck lately."

"We'll do well this time," Little Bow assured him. "We'll get a tongue or two from them."

"I don't care what you say, whoever takes meat from *those* racks deserves *two* feathers," another boy remarked. "Since it is your plan, are you going to try first?"

Little Bow shook his head. He looked at Running Hawk, who had been listening in silence. "It is time for Running Hawk to get some good meat. He hasn't won a feather yet."

The boys cheered their approval. Running Hawk was both embarrassed and elated. He appreciated Little Bow's thoughtfulness. He knew that without some kind of special help, his chances of ever getting away with a piece of meat were slim.

Little Bow explained how they would help Running Hawk into hiding near the meat racks, then momentarily divert Cuts Buffalo and Calling Bird's attention so that Running Hawk had a chance at the meat racks.

"We each have to do our best for Running Hawk," he said. "I know we haven't tried anything like this before, but it will work."

With the plan understood by all, they set out for the village. They broke into groups of two and three, some pretending to play with bladder balls and others discussing horses or weapons. They knew better than to return all at once; a group of boys eyeing meat racks was far too obvious.

Once back in the village, Jumps Ahead began kicking a bladder ball around with some of the other Magpies. Then all of the Magpies, except for a few with Little Bow, joined in. It looked as though they had just decided to play.

They began their game close to where Cuts Buffalo helped Calling Bird spread choice cuts of meat on the racks for drying. Meanwhile, Little Bow and three others harnessed two large camp dogs to a drag, and after laying Running Hawk on the drag, they covered him with skins.

Jumps Ahead and the other boys drew closer to the meat racks with their game of kickball, while Little Bow and the others eased the dogs toward Cuts Buffalo and Calling Bird, seemingly paying no attention to the two women. Little Bow waved his bow and arrows, pretending to be warding off enemies while moving camp. The bundle on the drag looked every bit like lodge skins being drawn to a new campsite.

When the dogs had positioned the drag almost in front of the meat racks, both of the women stopped their work to watch the boys.

"Where are you going?" Calling Bird asked.

"We are moving camp," Little Bow replied. "Up toward Wind River."

"I see," Calling Bird said with a smile. "Just don't get too near the meat racks."

Then Cuts Buffalo pointed out to Calling Bird that the game of kickball had moved dangerously close behind them. Cuts Buffalo turned to focus her gaze on Jumps Ahead and the others. Little Bow smiled. It was obvious that Cuts Buffalo and Calling Bird saw his group with the drag as decoy and viewed Jumps Ahead and the game-players as the real threat.

"When I poke you, hurry out of the skins," Little Bow whispered to Running Hawk. "I will point you straight to where the racks are. You will have to jump to get ahold of the meat."

Running Hawk mumbled from under the skins. He knew that he needed only one piece of meat in order to get his coup. He must do it just right.

By now Jumps Ahead and two of the Magpies had acquired another bladder ball, making Cuts Buffalo and Calling Bird certain that the threat lay with the small horde of laughing boys behind their meat racks. Now there were actually two games of kickball going, splitting the defense of the two women. Each woman moved just far enough from the racks to defend them and to keep kickball players at a safe distance. They had forgotten completely about Little Bow and the others with the drag.

"Now!" Little Bow hissed, poking Running Hawk. He stood back to give Running Hawk more honor by accomplishing the task on his own.

Little Bow watched while Running Hawk burst out of the robes and moved like a cat on all fours until he reached the closest rack. He jumped up, swinging a hand wildly, and knocked down two pieces of meat. He fell to his knees and clawed the ground frantically until his fingers felt a tongue. Quickly, with a small squeal, he scuttled back under the skins.

Jumps Ahead and the other boys continued to ease ever closer to the meat racks, keeping Cuts Buffalo and Calling Bird's attention. By now a group of real magpies had descended from somewhere in the skies, landing in a nearby cottonwood. Little Bow jumped up and down, waving to the birds as they made their raucous calls. He and the other boys now made an open assault on the racks, while the dogs slowly pulled the drag away. Neither of the women had any idea that Running Hawk had already gained his honors.

"Get away!" Calling Bird yelled. "We know what you're up to! Your attack is spoiled."

The Magpies stopped their game and pretended defeat.

"You boys thought you could pull a trick on us with the game-playing, didn't you?" Calling Bird said as Little Bow and the other boys gathered around her. "We've seen better tricks than the one you tried just now."

"You caught us, that's for sure," Little Bow said. "We'll try again. Maybe we will be lucky next time."

"We'll be waiting," Calling Bird warned. She winked at Cuts Buffalo. "Between the two of us, there is no one who can play tricks on us and get away with it."

Little Bow looked into the cottonwood again and watched the magpies hop among the branches and jabber. He turned back to Calling Bird and Cuts Buffalo, grinning. "Go over to that tree. Those birds will tell you a secret. We will leave and maybe, if you listen to them, you will learn the secret before we return."

"Go on with you!" Calling Bird shooed them away. "Cuts Buffalo and I have lots of work to do."

Still smiling, Little Bow led the boys off to help Running Hawk out of the skins. Running Hawk laughed with glee and held the tongue high above his head. Little Bow and the others placed the boy on their shoulders and ushered him around the village, stopping where the most noted of warriors lived, so that they might see what the Magpies had done.

After their triumphant circle of the village, they carried Running Hawk back to the meat rack, where Calling Bird and Cuts Buffalo greeted them with chuckles.

Calling Bird grinned at Little Bow. "It looks like you *did* have a very good plan. You are all going to be fine warriors one day."

"You will some day be as brave as Jethro," Cuts Buffalo told Little Bow.

"Maybe by that time you and Jethro will have sons for me to train," Little Bow said, and giggled with the other boys.

Cuts Buffalo reached out to yank Little Bow's ear, but he was too quick. Calling Bird then ruffled Running Hawk's hair. "I have never witnessed a braver deed by any boy your age. You do not even need eyes to be a warrior." She handed him two more tongues. "Go with these and feast with your fellow Magpies. When Bull Comes Ahead returns from the hills, I will tell him of your honor."

The boys gathered in front of Little Bow's lodge, where Rosebud prepared a fire for them and placed the tongues in boiling water. Although in the back of her mind she knew that this thievery was really preparation for war, she smiled while she worked. The boys now sounded like the real magpies gathered in the cottonwood at the edge of the village, each lad telling his version of how he had contributed to the success of the plan.

Jumps Ahead, leader of the game-players, received praise for his cunning and his ability to keep the women's attention diverted. Without the skill of the game-players, Running Hawk would not have had a chance to steal the meat. All praised Little Bow for masterminding the whole thing, and for insisting that Running Hawk become a feather-carrier with the rest of them.

"I owe my honor to all of you," Running Hawk said. "It might have been Little Bow and Jumps Ahead who first wanted to give me this day, but in the end, it was all of you who did it."

The boys cheered and formed a tight circle, with Running Hawk seated in the middle. Little Bow retreated into his mother's lodge while Jumps Ahead lit sacred sage and a length of braided sweet grass in a large white trade shell. After Little Bow returned with a small parfleche and took his place in the circle, Jumps Ahead allowed the smoke of the sage and sweet grass to cover himself and then passed the shell to the next boy.

When each boy had smudged himself, Little Bow led them in prayer to First Maker and then opened the parfleche. He took from the bag a long, sleek magpie tail feather and placed it in Running Hawk's outstretched hands.

"This feather is yours," Little Bow said. "You have done a brave deed this day. Wear it proudly."

Bursting with pride, Running Hawk ran his fingers up and down the glossy feather, delighting in every inch of it. Then he deftly placed the feather in the hair on the back of his head, facing it at an angle toward the right.

The boys voiced their approval and once again, this time in turn, began to speak of the day and the events that had led to Running Hawk's honor. They shared the tongues and consumed them slowly, as if enacting a great village feast. Like warriors returning from a successful horse raid, they spent the afternoon and evening congratulating one another and retelling their stories, over and over, until the words became the glue that bound them together.

It was late afternoon, and the Magpies were getting ready to adjourn when Little Bow pointed to a hill above the village.

"Jethro returns from the mountains!"

He rushed from the group to meet Jethro partway up the hill. Breathless, he began the story of how he and the other Magpies had achieved honors in stealing meat from the racks of Cuts Buffalo and Calling Bird. Jethro congratulated him and assured him that he and the others were certainly learning the ways of men. So early in their young lives they were learning what must be known to become successful and influential, to attain the status of great warriors.

Little Bow crossed his arms over his small chest and stood as tall as he could, watching with the other Magpies as the villagers welcomed Jethro's return. Thane and Morning Swan were the first to greet their son. His mother hugged him and ran her fingers through his hair, her smile broad, a hint of moisture in her eyes. Her son had passed a very great test.

High Elk and Cuts Buffalo's twin brothers offered their congratulations. They had been anxiously awaiting his return, so that they might go on their first enemy raid together.

Thane and Morning Swan sent a crier throughout the village to announce a feast in Jethro's honor and to invite all to attend and hear what Jethro might want to tell them. He would be the center of attention, while the warriors of the village would recount deeds of valor and assure Jethro that in time he would surely rank among them, if not above them. He would be given gifts of war articles, except for a shield, which he would soon have to make for himself, under the direction of Bull Comes Ahead.

Jethro had fired his father's rifle and knew that he would be receiving much the same kind of Hawken. But in the fashion of many of the other warriors, he preferred the traditional bow and arrows, and the long lance that meant strength and courage. Rifles were nearly impossible to load on horseback; even afoot, three to four arrows could be loosed in the time it took to reload a rifle.

But he would still welcome the gun from his father, and would give it a name as his father had given his own a name. "Gulliver" had proven very trustworthy over the years, a weapon to be admired and respected. In his father's hands, it had proven to be deadly.

Upon obtaining his weapons and his war shield, Jethro would be ready to start after the Sacred Pipe. How long it would take him to locate Big Owl and Many Berries could not be predicted, but he would search until he brought the good fortunes of the pipe back to his people and appeased the angry spirits.

The celebration of Jethro's return lasted all that night and the next day, and even into the following night. High Elk, still a new warrior himself, remained at Jethro's side a great deal of the time. Other new warriors, including Cuts Buffalo's brothers, listened to the elders reminisce over the old days and tell of how strong, new warriors were coming into honor among the people.

Each warrior in turn spoke of riding with Jethro into battle against the people's enemies and of keeping the Crow lands safe forever. Each could tell that Jethro had learned much upon the mountain and that in time he would become a great warrior. Big Owl and Many Berries would wish they had never decided to steal the Sacred Pipe, for they would soon learn the wrath of a man so powerful that all of the band already looked up to him, even though his life as a warrior was just beginning.

Jethro had come down from the mountain and was ready to fulfill his prophecy.

Little Bow followed his grandmother to the river. He pulled seed heads from grass plants along the pathway, throwing them aside and pulling more as he walked. Morning Swan carried three waterskins but was in no hurry to fill them.

The sun had just risen and the river teemed with life. Elk gathered to drink their fill before settling for the day, and a flock of geese, honking and flapping their wings, swam noisily just upstream.

Little Bow sat down on a driftwood log beside Morning Swan. Across from them, a great blue heron took wing from the shore, gliding downriver into a grove of cottonwoods.

"Grandmother, is it true that the river knows all things?" Little Bow asked.

"The river is as old as time," Morning Swan told her grandson. "The waters have flowed past with the change of each season, and there have been many changes."

A large buck deer had wandered into the open not far away and, ignoring them, was rubbing the last traces of velvet from a rack of horns that towered above its large, floppy ears.

"Would it be so bad for our people if we didn't get the Sacred Pipe back?"

"That is difficult to answer," Morning Swan said. "No one can say for certain what will happen. It would just be best if the pipe could come back."

"Will something bad happen to Grandfather now? Wasn't Bull Comes Ahead supposed to give him the pipe?"

"Yes, Bull Comes Ahead was supposed to give your grandfather the pipe. Maybe he still can in time."

Little Bow watched the buck continue to rub the velvet from its rack of antlers. The buck had its head down and was working feverishly with a hind hoof to scrape the last remnants off into the fallen leaves along the river. Little Bow knew that after the velvet was gone, the buck would rub its antlers against trees and logs until they were sharp and ready for fighting.

"Do you think that Jethro can find the pipe without getting killed?" he asked.

Morning Swan, who had been wondering the same thing, answered, "You ask so many questions that are impossible to answer. That is a very hard question to live with."

"It would be hard for me to live if something happened to Jethro," Little Bow told her. "I would miss him very much."

"We all would," Morning Swan said. "But life is something that cannot be made to happen just the way you would like. You have to take the bad with the good, the unhappiness with the happiness. It will all even out, if you let it."

"What would you do if Jethro died?" Little Bow asked, looking her squarely in the eye.

"I would go on living, Little Bow," she answered honestly. "That is all anyone can do. I know. I lost my first husband, before I met your grandfather. You know that story. And you know that our people have lost husbands and sons and brothers in battle. It is part of life."

"I've heard Jethro say that it doesn't have to be that way," Little Bow said. "He has told me that it is possible to live in peace, without hurting one another."

"That would be nice," Morning Swan said. She leaned over, filled a waterskin and brought it up dripping. "But there are no lands that I know of where the people live like that."

Morning Swan filled her other two waterskins. Little Bow watched the buck amble lazily off into the cover of the trees along the river. The geese were flapping, honking, unsettled. Finally, they took wing and headed south.

"Why is it that Jethro must go to battle against Big Owl when he never wanted that in the first place?" Little Bow asked. "Why must he make war to have peace?"

"There you go again with such a hard question." Morning Swan rose from the log and turned toward the village. "Jethro has been chosen, you know that. Anyone chosen must make harder decisions about life than those who are not chosen. He feels that he is responsible for the Sacred Pipe. I do not believe that he is, but he wouldn't listen to me anyway. He must sort all this out for himself."

Little Bow pulled more seed heads as he followed his grandmother back toward the village. He studied the seeds in his hand; small, hard kernels with life deep inside them, life that would wait through the cold seasons before sprouting. He realized that whether or not Jethro died—or anyone else among the people, for that matter—the seeds would grow into new plants and continue the cycle of life.

"That is how it must be," he said, voicing his thoughts out loud.

"Hmmm? What is it you said?" Morning Swan asked.

"Nothing. I was just talking to myself," he answered, tossing the seeds onto the ground.

FIFTEEN

SEVEN DAYS AFTER BIG OWL BROUGHT THE SACred Pipe of the Kicked-in-Their-Bellies to the Small Robes, one of the greatest warriors in the Blackfeet nation returned to the village, and he was not impressed with Big Owl.

Rising Hawk, at one time the strongest of the war chiefs among the Small Robes, prepared for council with other respected elders to discuss the fate of Big Owl and Many Berries. With the help of his best wife, his Sits-First-Beside-Him wife, he fitted himself into a fine elkskin shirt decorated with dyed porcupine quills and ermine tails. In his hair he placed three large eagle feathers, pointing upward, and three red-tailed hawk feathers, pointing down.

Rising Hawk had risen to power after his father and his father's father before him. All three

227

had been given the honorable name of Rising
Hawk, and all three had brought honor and glory
to the name. The present Rising Hawk owned
nearly half of the horses in the Small Robes'
herd.

He had owned more than that, but he had
given many to the poor and the helpless, bringing himself considerable respect. This third and
most powerful of the warriors named Rising
Hawk would be the last in the family line bearing the name. He had chosen not to pass it down,
for he could never marry the one woman who, in
his mind, would have borne him a son worthy of
the name.

He thought of this woman now as he watched
the elders gather for council outside of his lodge.
This woman, Morning Swan, was the only woman
he had ever known who could bear a male child
endowed with more power than he himself possessed. He had wanted no son of lesser quality.

One night Thane Thompson had sneaked into
the village with the cunning of a wolf and had
stolen Rising Hawk's prize medicine shield. Rising Hawk remembered well the suffering the loss
of the shield had caused him. To this day his eyesight varied from extreme clarity to near blind-
ness—it was never predictable—from having
stared for long hours at the sun until he had
finally learned how to retrieve his shield. He had
that medicine shield now and had vowed never
to make war against the Kicked-in-Their-Bellies
again, lest another misfortune befall him.

A special council should have taken place when
Big Owl had first returned to the village. But that

had not been possible, for Rising Hawk had been absent with two of his wives, visiting their relatives among the Bloods. When word had come to him that Big Owl and Many Berries had reappeared, Big Owl holding a sacred Crow medicine pipe he had stolen from a village to the south along the Yellowstone, Rising Hawk had listened with a rock forming in the pit of his stomach. He had gathered his wives and set out to return before the crier had finished telling him the news.

Rising Hawk knew without asking that the pipe had come from the same village—that of the Kicked-in-Their-Bellies—that was home to one of his oldest and most respected enemies. It had been many winters since he had last seen Thane Thompson—the Bear Man—the one who had married Morning Swan.

Now Big Owl, whom many saw as a bad omen among the people, had returned with honor to the same village where he had nearly lost his life only a few moons before. It puzzled Rising Hawk that Red Calf, who might have died at Big Owl's hands, was so eager to see this crazy man back among them. The people knew of Red Calf's bitter distaste for both Big Owl and Many Berries. But the warrior seemed now to be thinking only of gaining revenge against the Kicked-in-Their-Bellies for the loss of his father six winters ago.

The more Rising Hawk thought about it, the more he realized that Red Calf had nothing on his mind but war. Even if Big Owl had once nearly cost Red Calf his life, the warrior's desire for honors against enemies now convinced him that Big Owl and the Crow pipe would help him

gain those honors. He likely believed that if they
followed Big Owl with the Crow pipe, all of the
warriors, together, would have the power to
overthrow their enemies and drive them from the
lands along the Yellowstone.

Rising Hawk knew better; he was certain that
the pipe would work against them. True, the pipe
would certainly harm the Crow people for having lost it, but it could not be other than a bad
omen for the Small Robes as well. It had not been
made or blessed in sacred ceremony by any of
the Piegan medicine men; therefore it was not an
object that could benefit the people. In fact, the
medicine people in the village, men and women
alike, would not even look upon it—a very bad
sign indeed.

Certainly all of the elders knew this. He could
see no way that any of them could disagree with
him. He wanted to make it clear to everyone that
there was nothing but bad medicine following
Big Owl and Many Berries, and that the bad medicine would only get worse if the two were not
again banished from the village.

"What can you be thinking of?" Rising Hawk
asked Red Calf on the afternoon of his return.
"You must know that Big Owl will lead no one
to victory, but only to loss and sorrow."

"Don't you think the pipe he brought back will
provide power?" Red Calf asked.

"Not in Big Owl's hands," Rising Hawk replied
quickly. "Never. All he can possibly do with that
pipe is to bring destruction to our people."

Red Calf grunted. "If it were your decision to

make, no one would ever go to war. We would all be at home with the women."

"Maybe fewer of us would die, then. Did you ever think of that?"

"What honor is there in dying if not on the field of battle?"

"Tell me, Red Calf," Rising Hawk asked, "do you really believe that we carry our honors over into the spirit world?"

"That is certainly true."

Rising Hawk looked at him sternly. "If that were true, don't you believe there would be just as much pain and sorrow there as here? Don't you think there would have to be mourning in the spirit world if death occurred once again? Can you see the women cutting themselves and taking the joints from their fingers, the way it is done here? That does not sound to me like a happy land. Does it to you?"

"You have grown too old to understand the ways of warriors," Red Calf answered. "But I have respect for you, so I will try to explain."

"You couldn't begin to explain anything to me, Red Calf," Rising Hawk said cortly. "I have seen and accomplished more than you have ever dreamed of. That is why I no longer think the path to war is a wise one. You don't even know what the word warrior *really* means. Too much has changed."

"And that is why you should go to the top of the mountain and give your body to the spirits," Red Calf said. "You would be better off to cross over. You are too old to understand change."

"What do you know of change?" Rising Hawk

asked angrily. "I have witnessed more change than you could begin to imagine. And I know the change now coming is bad."

Red Calf grunted. "Who are you to judge whether change is good or bad? It is coming, and the Powers are the ones who will decide. Now, there are weapons of war I must get together. We will soon be riding against the Crow."

Rising Hawk watched Red Calf charge off toward his lodge. The young warrior was arrogant, but he was right in stating that no one but the Powers could dictate the reason for change or its outcome. Change would come and bring a new focus to life among the Blackfeet people, and it would usher in a new time, one undreamed of by the wise Grandfathers who had gone before.

And the change would be ushered in with warfare of a strange and lasting kind. Conflict of some sort was traditional, but this conflict was deep-rooted and would cover the land with more blood than at any time before.

Although Rising Hawk understood war completely, war no longer held the influence over him that it once had. He had learned too much about struggles for power through his rivalry with Thane Thompson, a rivalry neither of them had really won in the end. It had cost both of them dearly, loss of friends and loved ones had changed Rising Hawk's perspective of life, and he knew that the Long Knife, Thompson, had no wish to see any more battle, either.

Rising Hawk realized that his change of attitude prevented him from even trying to understand the younger warriors. He saw it as foolish that they considered the Sacred Pipe a prize that would bring them power and authority over the Crow. Rising Hawk could not help thinking back on his own attitudes at that age, and how he had wanted as many scalps as he could cut from enemy heads so that his lance and war shield could be lined with blood trophies.

But age and wisdom now enlightened Rising Hawk. He knew that war begets war, and that matters that cannot be settled with the pipe of peace will never be settled otherwise. Issues settled in blood only festered as long as there was more blood to spill.

This desire for a lasting harmony was commonly shared among the elders, whose days of brashness and compulsive behavior had given way to a more peace-loving existence. They no longer cared to hear the drums sounding for war; they preferred the beating of the skins that signified festivity, the rhythmic movement of dance and supplication. Those were the things that brought wisdom and contentment to the soul.

"I long for the days of my Grandfather—" one of the elders had told him, "—even before the coming of the horse, for life was much simpler then. Now the horse has brought us closer to our enemies, and we fight constantly to keep what we call honor."

This ancient elder no longer cared for life. Too much had changed to suit him. He could remember when he and two other young warriors had captured a horse by running it in a circle until it dropped with exhaustion.

"Now," the old man had told Rising Hawk,

"the young men can't even keep up with their horses. They are too lazy and too used to riding them to make themselves strong like we were. Now they believe that just by carrying objects they can be strong and brave. It is a crazy world."

Rising Hawk found it difficult to believe that a man could keep up with a horse, so he dismissed the comparison from his mind. His troubles were centered on the here and now, on what was taking place at this time. Horses had been here for a long time and had brought mobility to the tribes. But now they brought many new people into Blackfeet land, many Long Knife traders. And Crow horses had brought Big Owl and Many Berries back among the Small Robes.

It seemed to Rising Hawk that with the return of Big Owl, anger and anxiety had set in among the people. This could have been predicted, for Big Owl had always been one to keep things stirred, never allowing those around him to settle back into thoughtfulness. Instead, he craved disruption and violence, be it physical or mental.

And Many Berries, the woman whom Big Owl had set out to marry, was the greatest paradox Rising Hawk had ever met. She could at times express the wisdom of the ancients, the openness of heart that belonged only to the yellow breast, the meadowlark. Yet behind this good side of her there seemed to be a dark shadow that would cast itself over her and bind her to a compulsion for power and attention. Then she turned from helping people to taking what she could from them, and causing all manner of pain and suffering.

But Rising Hawk could not blame Big Owl and Many Berries exclusively for the problems that existed among the Blackfeet people. There were many others to blame, including himself, who, as young warriors, had lived solely for war. Then he had thought no distance too far to travel or mountain too high to cross if an enemy could be hunted down and killed.

In those days, Rising Hawk had cautioned himself about putting too much emphasis on the taking of scalps and not enough on the stealing of enemy horses and weapons. The honor in days gone by had been in touching an enemy, not in killing him.

But the times had changed, especially with the coming of the white Long Knives. The Long Knives had trapped most of the beaver from the streams, and now they traded for buffalo robes. They wanted as many robes as they could get. They had brought with them the powerful drink that made the mind crazy and the body cry out for more and more of it. They had established their fort lodges near some of the Piegans' favorite camping sites, so that the people would be drawn to desire the trinkets and the robes and the strong drink.

Not everyone saw that only unhappiness could come from the craving for the Long Knife drink, and from the assimilation of the white man's customs. The Long Knives had brought their medicine men into the mountains. The Blackrobes had been among the people for a number of winters now, and many of the Small Robes believed their medicine to be sacred and had seen its strength in fighting enemies.

The Blackrobes said, though, that their medicine was not for war. They were good men, sacred men of peace; but they wanted the Blackfeet people to give up their customs and ceremonies and worship the Bleeding Chief, the one who had died upon a tree. Although it was true that the Bleeding Chief had been powerful, it did not appear that the Blackrobes themselves understood the man very well.

It seemed to Rising Hawk that some of the ideas brought by the Blackrobes were indeed good, yet not even their own people followed their teachings. The Long Knives lived in ways that went against good medicine.

Although the Blackrobes said that their god did not approve of fighting and anger, there were many Long Knives who lived only to cause trouble. The strong drink they traded for robes brought havoc among their own people as well. It seemed to Rising Hawk that the Long Knives did not believe in their own Blackrobe medicine, although they were anxious to see the Indian people accept it.

Now the Blackrobes were leaving; it was only for a short time, Rising Hawk knew. They would be back. Change had come with them, just as change had followed the Long Knives. The elders said that a dark cloud was coming and that it was a trial the people had to accept. Some pointed out that the Long Knives had brought good items to trade with, items that made their lives easier. Others said that they did not need these items, not if it meant the end of their way of life.

The people argued continuously. Some wanted the new ways, but many did not. A lot of band feuding had resulted, bringing divisions to the Blackfeet people that had not existed before. Rising Hawk could not clear his mind of these troubles as he sat in council with the others.

As it was, arguments about allowing Big Owl and Many Berries back into the village had carved another division in their ranks.

"How easily you forget what trouble this man has caused in the past," Rising Hawk said to one of the elders. "Do you want more of the same?"

"It will not be the same," the elder answered. "Big Owl has brought a pipe from our enemy, the Crow. He will unite our young warriors in battle."

"Big Owl is good only at disjointing, not uniting," Rising Hawk protested. "See how we are divided against one another already?"

Another elder spoke up. "It is my opinion that we should give Big Owl and Many Berries a chance to show that they can be of benefit and not harm. If they prove to be willing to live with us and work for the good of the people, I say they can remain with us."

"They will bring trouble before any good can come," Rising Hawk said. A number of the elders nodded. "I believe that we will see harm come to our people if we do not make him return the Crow pipe to the Kicked-in-Their-Bellies."

"But what if Big Owl is right?" another elder

asked. "What if he can help us conquer the Crow? Then the Yellowstone and the buffalo lands south of there will be ours."

"We can never conquer the Crow," Rising Hawk said. "Not now. Not after losing so many of our people to the spotted sickness. Our warring days should be in the past."

Heated debate followed. Finally, an agreement emerged. An elder said, "I suggest that Big Owl and Many Berries be given the length of one moon to show that they can benefit the people. If during that time there is trouble brought by either one of them, they will be sent away again. Never to return."

"You are making a mistake to allow even that," Rising Hawk warned.

But the majority concurred with the granting of a full moon grace period, and Rising Hawk was pressed into agreement. He knew that the decision had been made so as to provide Big Owl time in which to prove his new powers in battle. Most of the people wanted revenge for loved ones lost in battle to the Crow. Rising Hawk finally shrugged, realizing that the pattern would likely never end.

After the pipe was passed and the council concluded, Rising Hawk left for the hills above the village. He returned at sundown, at the same time a scar-faced Long Knife trader entered the village. The Long Knife rode with his four agents and a contingent of Kainah Blackfeet, known as the Bloods, who had come to visit relatives. Rising Hawk knew the trader as Burned Face.

Even before welcoming their relatives, many

of the people began crowding around the mules that were laden with trade supplies. And before the trader showed them what he had, he broke open two kegs of trade whiskey.

Rising Hawk noticed Red Calf watching from nearby. He hurried over to the young warrior's side. "It would be good if you gathered some of the other warriors and helped me make Burned Face leave the village," Rising Hawk told him. "Bad trouble comes with him, as it did with his uncle."

Red Calf nodded. "I was only a child, but I remember the one called Broken Mouth, the Long Knife with the eyes like a mad wolf."

"This man, Burned Face, is of the same nature," Rising Hawk said. "We don't want trouble among our people."

"For once I agree with you," Red Calf said. "I will talk to some of the others while you gather the elders, who will listen together."

Rising Hawk moved among the elders, protesting the trader's presence. Many did not want to interfere. Those who agreed with him followed him toward the string of mules, where the trader made sign language and passed out whiskey in tin cups.

"I have the best trade items in the mountains," the Long Knife was telling the people in sloppy hand-sign, his mouth running with tobacco juice. "Bring me your finest buffalo robes and you can look at guns and knives and many nice things for the women."

Rising Hawk watched while Big Owl drained a cup of whiskey and demanded another. Many

Berries took him by the arm and tried to pull him away from the kegs, but he jerked free and slapped her. She ran back to their lodge.

"Where is Red Calf?" Rising Hawk asked aloud. "Trouble has already started."

Red Calf finally appeared, but with only a few warriors. "I can't make anybody listen," he told Rising Hawk. "I think I'm going to tell Burned Face to leave myself."

Red Calf started forward, but a warrior who had been drinking heavily stopped him to talk about organizing a war party right away, to go into the Crow lands. Rising Hawk could not believe his ears; no one in a sane condition went to war without great preparation. And nothing could be worse for preparation than the strong drink of the traders.

Rising Hawk tried to help Red Calf talk the warrior out of his foolish idea. Meanwhile, Burned Face had begun trading with the people. Many were laying choice buffalo robes at his feet, while his men handed out small fusil rifles and low-quality goods. Soon two warriors were quarreling over one of the better rifles. Each gripped the stock firmly, pulling against the other in a tug-of-war. They lurched and jerked through the crowd, knocking many to the ground. Big Owl, who by now had managed to secure an entire jug of whiskey for himself, hoisted the vessel to his mouth as the two warriors fell into him.

The jug flew from his grasp and shattered on a pile of camp-fire rocks. Big Owl fell forward, knocking a small child into the sherds of pottery. The child screamed and rolled on the ground. His mother knelt over him and pulled a jagged piece of crockery from his left eye.

Rising Hawk rushed to the whiskey kegs and began pushing people away. Red Calf joined him along with the few younger warriors whom he had managed to make listen to him. The trader protested and began calling for Big Owl.

"This is no way to treat a guest in our village!" Big Owl shouted. Whiskey spouted from his lips. "You, Red Calf, are a fool!"

Red Calf lunged at Big Owl. The two men tumbled to the ground, rolling under the feet of frightened villagers. Burned Face, laughing, yelled encouragement to Big Owl and pushed his agents to start them yelling too. Red Calf and Big Owl pulled their knives and fought for control, neither gaining an advantage.

The contingent of Bloods gathered around the traders, siding with them against Red Calf and any others who might begin fighting on Red Calf's behalf. The atmosphere was tense. No one wanted to fight his own people. The relatives within both factions strove to bring peace, but Red Calf and Big Owl continued the battle. Red Calf had gotten on top of Big Owl and now pinioned his arms, insisting that he give up. Big Owl was spitting at him.

Still laughing, Burned Face tossed a cupful of whiskey into Red Calf's face. Red Calf jerked back, covering his eyes, while Big Owl wriggled up to a sitting position and took a firm grip on his knife. Then, using hard, driving stabs, Big Owl buried the weapon to its hilt in Red Calf's

241

chest. One, two, three times the knife went in and came out. Then four, five.

Rising Hawk finally grabbed Big Owl's arm. Still laughing, Burned Face pulled Rising Hawk backward and off balance, then kicked him in the face before reaching for his knife. One of his men grabbed his arm. Red Calf's mother bent over her dying son and began her mourning song.

"I want that Rising Hawk," the trader said. "He's been agin us from the beginning."

"Forget it, Harlan. We've got to go. Now!"

"You ain't tellin' me—"

"Harlan, if you want your hair, we'll go. Things'll bust loose here if we stay."

The Bloods now stood between the Piegans and the traders. The village had become silent. Many of the Piegans were angry, but Red Calf had jumped Big Owl first. He should not have started the fight.

Big Owl hurried to his lodge to get Many Berries and their belongings. Rising Hawk rose to his feet and walked around Red Calf's mother, who was rocking her son in her arms. His face trembling with rage, he faced Harlan Cutter.

"You have come like a sickness, just as your uncle did. Now you had better leave. If you ever come back, I will see to it myself that you die."

Cutter's eyes blazed with anger. Two of his men restrained him, one of them saying, "We've got to get out of here."

Cutter shook loose and ordered them to gather the robes they had traded for. Big Owl and Many Berries, on Flame and Night Runner, joined the

Bloods and the traders. Cutter mounted his horse and spat a huge wad of tobacco against Rising Hawk's chest, then led his men and the Bloods out of the village.

SIXTEEN

CALLING BIRD AWAITED BULL COMES AHEAD'S return from his morning trip into the hills. She had important news for him, so important that she had postponed her trip to the river for water. She wanted to tell him the moment he arrived in camp.

Life for Calling Bird was nearly back to normal. Although the tendons and muscles that Big Owl had severed with his knife would never be the same, she could now rotate her shoulder and lift items off the ground, feats she had had no way of performing for a long time. Bull Comes Ahead continued to minister to her on a daily basis with formulas of herbs and roots, thus improving her strength against infection.

In many ways, Calling Bird's life had changed dramatically. She had rid herself of much of the deep anger she had harbored for so long, the bitterness at having lost loved ones in war. She could now see how that anger had stifled her life and had brought only harsh feelings at the mere mention of other tribes.

There were further changes. Calling Bird had always been one to like the older people, but now she began to enjoy the children as well, and to laugh with them. After the loss of so many relatives in battle, she had hardened herself against becoming close to the young.

Running Hawk's first coup as a Magpie had taught her once again that with life came fun, as well as sorrow. Since Little Bow and Jumps Ahead had led the Magpies against her meat racks, she had taken a lot of teasing from the village women. She challenged the Magpies to come back and try again. Next time it would not be so easy.

What she now wished for herself and her life could not be acquired in total at this time, though, and she thought about how her wounds had come about and what the ordeal meant to her spiritual growth. There was constant agony in her arm and shoulder, a burden she now considered rightfully hers for having fought Bull Comes Ahead so vehemently when he was striving to heal Big Owl. She felt a profound guilt for having subsequently lost the Sacred Pipe to the Blackfeet warrior and believed that the spirits had punished her—and would continue to punish her—for her lack of understanding.

Calling Bird was willing to pay her debt for her inconsiderateness, but she knew that she would lament the loss of the Sacred Pipe until it was safely back with the Kicked-in-Their-Bellies. This return had to take place, for her own peace as well as for the peace of the people. Although going along on a war party was impossible for her, she saw it as her duty to help get the pipe back in other ways. She saw her role as one of continued support of her husband, and of Jethro, whose life as a warrior now hinged on someday presenting the pipe to Bull Comes Ahead once again.

Today she could contribute more than anyone else had so far. It was only right that it should be this way; Big Owl had taken the pipe from her grasp and had left his knife behind for her to learn from.

She sat near the entrance to the lodge, looking into the hills, waiting for a glimpse of Bull Comes Ahead. In her hand she held the knife that Big Owl had lost in his hurry to escape with the pipe. She studied the blade, as she had done hundreds of times before, and turned it over and over, her eyes scouring every inch of its surface. Ever since beginning her recovery from her wounds, she had worked to make the knife go into her mind so that the thoughts that Big Owl had known when he owned the weapon might come to her.

Calling Bird had often watched Bull Comes Ahead hold a hairball from a buffalo's stomach and close his eyes in an attempt to visualize the path the buffalo might have taken. He commonly told hunters the right direction in which to travel on the hunt—another of the abilities that made him powerful in the eyes of the people.

With Big Owl's knife in her hands, Calling Bird believed that she could find the warrior in the same manner. She could then direct Jethro and the raiding party to Big Owl and Many Berries. That was what she wanted to do, so that the Kicked-in-Their-Bellies might have their Sacred Pipe back forever.

Since beginning her concentration on the knife, Calling Bird had broken through just a small step. It was only a dream, but it was important. Now she awaited Bull Comes Ahead to tell him of her breakthrough, of the dream that would help Jethro and all the people. She had awakened early that morning and had turned eagerly to him, but he had already gone into the hills.

Calling Bird looked once again into the rim of rocks and stands of pine. She could see her husband picking his way down the steep slope, through a fractured segment of the cliffs. She waited patiently, then rose to greet him, her excitement evident.

"You have to make another pipe," she told him as he approached her.

Bull Comes Ahead studied her eyes and looked at the knife she was twisting in her fingers. He nodded and sat down, crossing his legs, and waited for her to take her place beside him.

"You have had that knife under your pillow for a long time," he said. "What did it finally tell you?"

"I will draw the pipe for you," she said, tracing an outline on the dry ground with the point of

247

the blade. "The stripes on this pipe must be yellow and not red, as they are on the real pipe. It must be a shorter pipe, and the bowl must be smaller. You must tie three feathers from the white-headed eagle and three feathers from the golden eagle at the place where the stem fits into the bowl. And you must wrap the stem in sacred tobacco, not to be unwrapped until Big Owl is dead."

"Big Owl must die?"

"He was allowed to live only to provide us with tests to learn from. If we do not learn, he will be impossible to kill."

"And who will kill him?"

"That is not decided. But the pipe I saw in my dream will bring great medicine to Jethro, and then he can find Big Owl."

Bull Comes Ahead nodded. "What is the stem to be made from?"

"Cedar, from a young trunk. A strong and straight branch taken from a young tree."

"Straight branches are hard to find among cedars," Bull Comes Ahead said.

"The sooner you find it, the sooner Jethro can begin to prepare for war against Big Owl," Calling Bird told him. "I have seen all this, but I cannot say when Jethro will get the Sacred Pipe back. I only know that he must carry this pipe into battle and that you must help prepare for battle with the medicine of this pipe."

Bull Comes Ahead looked up. A large formation of geese, honking loudly, passed just over the village and lost themselves in the distance.

"The cold moons will soon be upon us," he

said. "High Elk and three other warriors have gone to scout the winter camp below the Mountains of the Wind. They will return soon and we will have to leave. I must hurry to make the pipe before then. Do you know a song for the pipe?"

Calling Bird nodded. "I will sing it when the pipe is finished. It would be good if you would hurry, for I cannot be certain that the song will have power once the cold moons have come."

Bull Comes Ahead rose and took a deep breath. "I will walk among the hills once again. Perhaps a young cedar with a strong and straight branch will call to me. We must do all we can to help Jethro, for I fear for our people more and more. If Jethro does not bring the Sacred Pipe back soon, all of us may find ourselves standing at the door to the spirit world."

High Elk and the three warriors returned from the upper Bighorn River country with drawn faces. They brought news that the Shoshone had summered there and the grass had been grazed to almost nothing by their horse herds. Camping as the people usually did near the Mountains of the Wind, where the warm waters flowed, was certainly out of the question for the coming season of the cold moons. There was not enough grass left for keeping the horses over until the snow left.

For the first time in many winters, the Kicked-in-Their-Bellies would have to seek a new winter camping spot. The choices were not many, as the other bands and clans among the Crow would be up and down the Yellowstone, as they always were, all the way from Fort Union—at the mouth of the river—on up to Fort Sarpy at the mouth of the Bighorn, and on to the mouth of the Rotten-Sun-Dance-Lodge Creek. There was a shortage of grass everywhere as it was, and the Kicked-in-Their-Bellies' nearly six hundred horses would require a great deal of forage.

After long deliberation, the council decided to move—for the first time—to the area near the Crazy Mountains called Grey Cliffs. None of the bands usually camped that far up for long at any time of the year, because of the proximity to Blackfeet lands and roving Blackfeet raiding parties. But this winter there would be a large village of Flatheads camped not far upriver, where the waters made a sharp turn from the south to the east.

The Flatheads had sent a messenger into camp while Jethro was gone on his vision quest. They wanted to be friendly during the cold moons and keep in close contact, so that the Blackfeet would have trouble if they attacked either village. The Kicked-in-Their-Bellies welcomed the Flatheads and prepared a feast. Jethro heard from High Elk that the peoples had mingled and traded, sharing stories and even a sacred ceremony. The Flatheads had gone back to their lodges confident that should the Blackfeet come, they would be driven away by the two combined encampments.

After the lodges had been erected at Grey Cliffs and the women had caught up with the extra work, Jethro heard some news from his mother: if he cared to talk to a special woman, he should go upriver a short way and wait under the first fishhawk nest he came to. Jethro considered telling his mother that he did not care to speak to Cuts Buffalo, but he decided to go anyway.

The sun had already fallen when Jethro arrived at the large cottonwood that housed the nest. There was a chill in the air, and the leaves were beginning to fall, a few at a time floating down in the breeze to rest atop the slow, shadowy current of the river.

Jethro sat down and watched while fishhawks patrolled the river for one last time before roosting. They skimmed below the tree line, diving like flung rocks at rising fish, then arcing upward again, their prizes flopping in their talons. As one particularly large bird rose with a big trout, Jethro felt a presence at his side.

"Hello," Cuts Buffalo said in a soft voice. "I'm glad you came."

"You knew I would," Jethro said.

Cuts Buffalo laughed softly, "Yes, I guess I did. I have known all along that some day you would start to think of me more often and then begin to see me as I see you."

Jethro watched the river. "I have yet to understand why you want me for a husband so badly. There are young warriors who seek you openly."

"It is you who appeals to me," she said. "I feel foolish telling you this, but I can't help it. I've always known we should be together and raise children."

"Why are you so certain?"

"It is a feeling I have had since I first noticed you," she replied. "I knew that you were special and the only man I could every really love."

Jethro became uneasy. "Even after seeing me with Many Berries, and after all that has happened with the Sacred Pipe, you can still say that I am special enough for you to want me so badly?"

Cuts Buffalo felt no embarrassment. She knew her feelings precisely and had laid them out for viewing.

"There is nothing you could do that would change my mind, Jethro," she said. "I know your heart and what a good man you truly are. No matter the challenges and the changes that lie ahead, you will always be the most special person I know."

Jethro looked into Cuts Buffalo's eyes, a warmness welling up within him. This woman was so open, her love so pure, that he did not know if he deserved it.

Cuts Buffalo leaned closer to him, sensing his feelings. "You will have bad things and good things happen to you," she said. "You will know both dark and light, but you will always be the man I want for a husband. This is all I can say."

She started to rise, but Jethro caught her arm. "Wait. Don't go. Not yet."

She settled back down on her knees. "Do you want to tell me something?"

"I want to tell you that I do care for you. But I feel that it would not be right, even after I am able to marry, to ask your father for you. Not until I have found the Sacred Pipe and returned it to our people."

"Why would that be a reason to hold back from marrying me?"

"I must dedicate most of my time to searching for the pipe," Jethro replied. "That does not leave much time for hunting, or for caring in the right way for a wife. That would not be fair to you. Perhaps you should marry another."

Cuts Buffalo wrapped her arms around Jethro and held him tight. "I don't want another. I will never want another. Take as much time as you need, but don't wish me to marry someone other than you."

Jethro held her tentatively at first, then drew her close. She felt so good in his arms, so sincere and loving. Her words came from her heart. He drew her lips to his, gently. He felt her passion for him, and his desire welled up from within. He pulled her closer, kissing her neck and slipping her dress down over her shoulders to expose the rise of her breasts.

Cuts Buffalo's breath quickened. She stopped him long enough to remove her dress, allowing him to caress her breasts and taste her turgid nipples. He quickly removed his breechclout and pulled her close once more. While he kissed her breasts again, she ran her fingers across his smooth, muscular back, then down along his buttocks, and around to his manhood.

They lay together in fluid motion while the twilight brought crimson to the western sky. Cuts Buffalo lost herself in passion. Jethro was sending feeling so deep inside her that she felt consumed. Gasping, she clutched his powerful shoulders, and they cried out together as the last fishhawk sent a high call into the waning light and disappeared into the shadows of the trees.

* * *

After leaving the Small Robes, the Bloods camped a distance up the Big Muddy, at the mouth of Arrow Creek. Four days had passed since the trouble in the Piegan village, and Many Berries had become increasingly unhappy. She had come to the river early each morning to try to decide what she now wanted to do with her life. She had risen each day before dawn, while Big Owl slept, to gaze toward the south at a high butte that rose from the eastern edge of the High Woods, the small mountains at the southern end of Blackfeet lands.

The butte had always been sacred to her people. It was the place for visions, and from which to see out across the lands when looking for travelers and buffalo. Many Berries had been carried to the butte as an infant so that the Powers would bless her and give her a happy and productive life.

She was now certain that she had offended the Powers. Since meeting Big Owl, her fortunes had turned upside down. He had told her so often that he would become powerful one day and give her all she would ever need. She had believed him and had done many things that were not good, including leaving Jethro.

She knew that she would always pay for that wrong decision. If she could have disregarded power, Jethro would have made her happy. As it stood now, Big Owl would soon drive her into madness. He still had not regained his sexual potency, and this troubled him more and more. He kept saying that gaining war honors would reinvigorate him, that he would then become a man again. He would make her happy and would never hit or harm her in any way.

Many Berries realized that Jethro had been right: Big Owl's manhood had suffered an injury in the fall under his horse. She did not know that he would ever recover. He added to his problems by drinking large amounts of the trade drink supplied by Burned Face and his agents. Under its influence, he grew steadily crazier.

Many Berries wanted no more of Big Owl. He blamed her for his problems, forcing her into sexual acts that did him no good and then claiming that the fault lay with her. He ridiculed her and found reasons to become angry even when none existed. Many Berries knew that the time had come to escape him.

Today Big Owl crawled out of his robes, sick from the strong drink and followed her to the river. "Why have you been coming here without me?" he asked. "Why do you always look at the butte? That place cannot help you."

"You know that I was taken up there as an infant," Many Berries said. "I will take my children up there also. I am only asking the butte for forgiveness for the bad things I have done."

"I think I know what is really wrong," Big Owl said. "I think you miss that Crow dog, Jethro."

Many Berries turned away from him, straining to keep the tears at the corners of her eyes from falling. She would never stop feeling the loss of Jethro in her life; she had loved him so much more than she had thought. Even if Big Owl did gain the honors he continually boasted of, she knew that she could never love him as she could have loved Jethro, the Jethro she could never return to now.

"I have made many mistakes," she said. "Too many."

"Why don't you go back to him, if that's what you want so bad?" Big Owl taunted her from behind. "See if he would even want you. Or see if the women don't cut you into strips for the magpies."

"That might be better than being with you," Many Berries said. "Whom do you plan to kill in this village? And then where will we go?"

"Don't be foolish!" Big Owl shouted. "I had every right to kill Red Calf."

"Do you think you killed him in a brave manner?" Many Berries asked. "Maybe you wouldn't have done it if Burned Face hadn't thrown the strong drink in his face. It is hard to fight when your eyes are burning."

Big Owl raised his hand to strike her.

"Go ahead, mighty warrior," she taunted. "I hope you hit me a lot, so these people will learn about you."

"These people think I am strong medicine," Big Owl said. He lowered his trembling hand. "They know that with the medicine pipe I stole, I can defeat the Crow and drive them from their lands."

Many Berries spoke with the usual edge back in her voice. "You are always talking about all those who are rushing from everywhere to follow you," she said. "I haven't heard any of the warriors asking you to lead them into battle against the Crow."

"They will, in time," Big Owl insisted.

"I don't think so. I wish I had never met you."

"You wanted power and you will have it. What is wrong with you?"

"You talk about power and there is no proof of it. Only a warrior without power would do what you did to Red Calf."

Big Owl ground his teeth. He looked to a small bluff nearby, where a group of children stood, attracted by the commotion. They watched and pointed. If they had not been there, he would have struck Many Berries. Instead, he chose to challenge her again.

"If you are so unhappy, why don't you leave me?"

"Because you would hunt me down and kill me," she replied. "I hear you tell me to go, but in your eyes I see the words: 'You had better stay with me.' "

Big Owl grunted and turned away. "I do not care whether you leave or not."

"I will leave now, then. On the red horse you stole from Jethro."

Many Berries started to walk away and Big Owl quickly grabbed her. She wrenched away from him. "See! What did I tell you? You are obsessed with me. You would never allow me to leave you, no matter what you say."

"I just want you to know that it would be a mistake," Big Owl said, his face pinched with anger. "You need me to protect you."

"I don't need you to protect me! I don't need you for anything!"

"You must stay and let me prove my power to you. The Bloods will believe in me. One or two successful raids and there will be more and more warriors willing to follow me. Soon enough I will have the rest of the Blackfeet nation behind me, and the Small Robes can be sorry."

"What about Burned Face?" she asked. "He gives you whiskey and pretends he is your friend. But in the end, he would kill you for no reason at all. He is bad trouble."

"He hates the big Long Knife, Bear Man, who lives with the Kicked-in-Their-Bellies," Big Owl pointed out. "And he doesn't like Jethro, either. He will want to fight the Crow. And the Bloods like him. Maybe he can do us more good than harm."

Many Berries shook her head. "That is not possible. I trust him even less than I trust you."

Big Owl became angry again, then looked sad. "Give me time to show you that I am a strong warrior," he pleaded. "I promise that before the end of the cold moons, I will have gained many honors. When I have defeated the Crow, I will have my powers back and you will see how much of a man I can really be. If this is not so by the time the ice breaks free from the river, you can leave me and I will not stop you."

Many Berries looked back toward the large butte, rising high and blue in the clear air. She felt trapped. Even if Big Owl achieved honors and regained his sexual potency, she could see no future for herself with this man. And if she left him, she would have to look behind her for the rest of her life, for eventually he would catch up to her and kill her. He had told her many times that she was his and could belong to no one else.

"You will give me until the ice goes out of the river," Big Owl repeated. "Do you agree to this?"

Many Berries realized that she would have to say yes; she had no other choice. "You have until the ice breaks from the river," she said tonelessly.

Many Berries followed Big Owl from the river toward the village, twisting her fingers into knots. She had trapped herself. Despite what she had just told him, she knew that she must get away from him as quickly as possible. She did not want to die, and she surely would if he learned her secret. He would kill her in an instant if he learned about the new life that now grew within her womb.

SEVENTEEN

JETHRO, NAKED EXCEPT FOR HIS KNIFE AND breechclout, braced himself against the cold rain. He carried a large parfleche of wood for a fire, and a small skin bag filled with sage and sweet grass. Bull Comes Ahead—wearing his finest medicine clothes and carrying the new medicine pipe across his heart—led Jethro across the high plain, while the clouds overhead opened up and torrents of water fell.

Jethro could barely see, but the old medicine man walked in front as straight and unconcerned as if it were a bright summer day. They were far from the village, in the area where Jethro had been saved from the stampeding buffalo by the Tree of Life. Bull Comes Ahead had advised he return to this place and secure the hide of a bull buffalo for his war shield.

They walked on while Bull Comes Ahead chanted and raised the pipe to the sky. Jethro wanted to ask how they would find a herd in this weather, but he knew better than to interrupt the ceremony. He had been working feverishly to prepare himself for war against Big Owl before the cold moons came, and there was little time left. He had been given a strong bow by High Elk and a quiver of arrows by Cuts Buffalo's father. Preparing his war shield was the last step before he could go after the Sacred Pipe.

He had declared to the village that he must seek the pipe on his own. He did not feel it would be right to follow another into battle while searching for the lost pipe; and because he had not yet led a party after horses or into battle, none would think his medicine strong enough yet that they would follow him. Once he had the Sacred Pipe back, he could decide how he wanted to pursue the rest of his life as a man.

Jethro gained strength as Bull Comes Ahead continued to lead the way. Although rain streamed from his body, Jethro now felt warm and confident. The power of the old medicine man was indeed strong.

Bull Comes Ahead, still singing, stopped and turned four circles before quitting the chant. "Do you hear them?" he asked. "Do you feel them?"

Jethro turned his face to the west and listened to the low rumble of oncoming buffalo. His muscles tensed.

"Do not worry, they are not alarmed," Bull Comes Ahead reassured him. "They have heard me and are coming.

261

"This is good," Jethro said, relaxing. His face, wet with rain, expanded into a grin. "That is very good."

"Stay where you are," Bull Comes Ahead ordered. "When you see the bull you want, make certain your aim is true."

Jethro nocked an arrow and nodded to Bull Comes Ahead, who raised the pipe and began chanting again. Jethro watched him ease away into the rain until he was finally lost from sight, while the rumbling herd drew closer. He could feel the earth trembling beneath him.

The memory of the stampede returned, and Jethro fought the growing fear, the urge to jump and run, his muscles tense once more as the herd drew ever closer. He could hear the buffalo grunting as they advanced through the storm, but the rain and fog allowed him no clear vision.

"Now is the time," he heard a voice say in his head. "They are close."

Jethro knelt and brought the bow up, ready to loose his arrow. The buffalo appeared, like black ghosts in the rain. They trotted in groups of two and three, passing so close that if he rose and took two steps forward, they would have bumped into him. He studied large bulls, each of them young and in the prime of life, but did not release an arrow. The right one was yet to come.

Then an unusual bull approached through the rain, white, with a dark head and dark feet and tail. The bull was massive, standing well above Jethro's full height at the shoulder, its huge head supporting long, curved horns, polished black and shiny.

Without hesitation, Jethro loosed an arrow as the bull passed, aiming for a point low and just behind the shoulder—aiming for the heart. The bull jerked and grunted, then broke into a run.

Curiously, the others did not panic. Instead, they continued to drift slowly with the storm. Jethro lost the bull in the rain and began to follow, ignoring the others, dismissing the fact that he was in the midst of the herd and would certainly die if it stampeded. He began to trot faster, passing the herd, and in a short time he discovered the fallen bull.

The arrow was buried up to its feathers, the point and shaft having pierced the heart. The bull had lurched onto its stomach, its feet spread forward and behind. Its eyes were glazed in death, its tongue lolling, pools of blood forming in the mud around its mouth.

Jethro heard Bull Comes Ahead singing again, and the old medicine man continued to chant as he came up and circled the fallen bull. Jethro pulled his knife and sliced a large oval of thick neck and shoulder hide, while Bull Comes Ahead stood over the head chanting songs and thrusting the new medicine pipe to the sky, praying in earnest that the Powers would look upon them with favor and allow exceptionally strong medicine to enter the shield.

The herd gathered around them and grazed in the rain without paying them any attention. Soon the storm lessened and the clouds parted, allowing sunshine to touch the muddy grasslands. The herd, an immense sea of brown and black, stretched in all directions farther than the eye could see. Some of the beasts passed close enough that Jethro and Bull Comes Ahead could almost touch them; it was as if the two men and the fallen white bull were nothing more than fixtures. The odor of blood, deadened by the rain, had no effect on the herd.

Jethro said prayers to the sun, then finished cutting the section of hide and staked the piece down to begin drying. Later, in ceremony, it would be dried rapidly over hot stones, thickening it for suitability as a shield. As was the custom, the remainder of the white bull's body was not touched, but left to return to the earth. After a season of cold moons and the return of the warm moons, the skull would be retrieved and used for sacred ceremonies.

When Jethro had finished his work, he turned back to the sun, now falling over the Crazy Mountains. "Come again to give strength to my shield," he prayed. "Bring your power from the Other Side to ward off the thrusts of enemy arrows and lances. Keep the enemy from shooting through my shield, keep him from doing harm to me. I will live the way you want me to. I will need you many times to show me where to walk."

Bull Comes Ahead prayed for half the night, and he and Jethro smoked the pipe and gazed into the flames. Jethro had prayed to the Night Lights and the Sun's Wife in the same manner as he had prayed to the sun, asking for a powerful shield. The buffalo herd, sounding like low thunder, now passed them in a slow, continuous wave. The animals were on the move, migrating to where the grass could feed their vast numbers and there was water to sustain their lives.

It was late when Jethro fell asleep, the sounds of Bull Comes Ahead's chanting still alive in his head, although the words had ceased to come from the medicine man's lips. He drifted rapidly into dream, floating on a sea of water—his own tears—while the lost Sacred Pipe appeared in a huge form just above him, hanging upside down under roiling black clouds. Lines of scarlet paint bled from wounds along the stem, while leaflike pieces of tobacco fell from the bowl into the tear water around him.

Jethro felt that he must reach the Sacred Pipe and turn it right side up; but no matter how hard he tried, he could not lift himself to it. He struggled for some time until finally conceding his helplessness. He could only lie back in the water and watch.

He felt empty inside, empty and lost. Suddenly many of his people—members of his family as well as close friends—began to roll past the giant pipe, held fast within huge pieces of odd-looking white clouds that bounced off of black clouds above them. The clouds seemed to be more solid than normal clouds, and he felt chilled deep within. His breath turned to vapor that spread and froze, then dropped around him like thin shards of ice.

He struggled again to reach up, through the falling ice and the floating tobacco, to help his people, but he failed. He had to watch while they suffered, trapped within the strange, cold white clouds, their bodies tumbling, their mouths opened wide in terror.

Jethro tossed and turned to awaken, but found that he could not, nor could he avert his face from the sight. His tears added to the waters that buoyed him up. The odd clouds thickened and roiled, and he screamed.

When finally the clouds filled with his people had passed, there came a woman bearing the soft down of a cattail with which she wiped the tears from his eyes. He could not see her face clearly, but he could feel her, and he knew the feeling well. Cuts Buffalo. She finished wiping his tears away, her own tears falling and filling the area around them with a warm rain. His breath no longer turned to ice, but mixed with hers in warmth and security.

Then Cuts Buffalo took him by the hand and pulled him up so that he sat crosslegged, facing her. She reached down into the water and brought forth a medicine shield, which she presented to him. Its edges were lined with the thick white hair of the sacred buffalo bull; its center was painted in green and bore the head and curving horns of the bighorn ram.

Lining the shield were four sets of eagle feathers, three in each set, placed close together on opposite sides. From the top there hung the back legs of two rabbits, one taken in winter and one during the warm moons. Attached to the bottom of the shield was the body of a raven, stuffed with sweet grass, its eyes fitted with the shiny blue skystones that came from the ground at the edge of Blackfeet lands, near the headwaters that the Long Knives called the Judith.

Cuts Buffalo held the shield long enough for Jethro to see it clearly, then placed it back in the tear water. He tried to put his hand into the water to retrieve it, but he could not. He leaned over and put his face into the water; he saw only schools of trout and the bottom, lined with blue and white stones. There was no shield.

When he looked back out of the water, Cuts Buffalo was gone. He found himself lying down again, facing the dark clouds above him, watching the upside-down Sacred Pipe bleeding and spilling tobacco out of the bowl, when suddenly a bighorn ram, a zigzagging rabbit, an eagle, and a black-as-night raven ran into the stem of the Sacred Pipe, causing it to spin in a tight circle.

The pipe spun upward. He felt himself rising on wings to follow, held aloft by the Sacred Winds. The pipe turned, leading him over lands he had never seen, toward a place he knew nothing of: grassland and foothill country filled with buffalo and game of all kinds, and mountains where a white light spread out in all directions.

Jethro floated over the secluded peaks, a small group similar to the Crazy Mountains. He followed the pipe as it spun before him toward a large flat-topped butte covered along the north slope with trees, but otherwise open and composed of large rocks.

As he flew over the rocks, Jethro saw that one rock in particular was flat and that a warrior sat crosslegged upon it, his face turned toward the north. The pipe, still spinning, circled the warrior and suddenly dropped into his outstretched hands. Jethro swooped down, narrowly missing the warrior but getting a close look at his face. Big Owl was now holding the Sacred Pipe of the Kicked-in-Their-Bellies to the sky!

Jethro screamed and lurched awake. He sat up in the dawn, breathing heavily in the cool air. A raven was passing overhead, flapping slowly toward the west, cawing in a guttural tone that reached deep into Jethro's mind. The fire was out, and Bull Comes Ahead was on a nearby hill, facing the sun. The buffalo herd was gone and only the carcass of the sacred white bull remained, its back covered with feeding magpies.

After wiping his sweat-drenched face, Jethro pushed himself onto shaky legs and sang a song that came to his lips:

> I see the sky and feel the wind.
> I hear the Sun tell me to be brave.
> Terrible clouds gather, but must part
> when they hear my footsteps, coming
> down from the flat-topped mountain.
> I will find the Sacred Pipe and carry it
> across my heart. I will carry it always,
> and make a pathway for my people.

When the song was finished, Jethro looked to the hill and saw that Bull Comes Ahead had turned toward him. The old medicine man watched him for a moment before he nodded and turned to walk down the hill.

Jethro took a deep breath and picked up the large cut of white hide, then set out to meet Bull

Comes Ahead and walk with him back to the village.

Cuts Buffalo walked from the village toward the river. Although the sun shone directly overhead, her breath was visible in the clean, crisp air.

Back in the village, Jethro prepared his medicine shield. Cuts Buffalo wanted to wait until he had completed his sacred circle of protection before she talked to him again. Only the men could work on their medicine articles, and she did not want to interrupt Jethro and thus possibly cause more bad fortune to befall either him or the people.

Cuts Buffalo knew that it would take some time before he was finished. While Jethro worked, High Elk and her brothers built a fire to heat rocks, so that Bull Comes Ahead could join with Jethro in shrinking the hide to the thickness needed for a strong, durable shield. After prayers, the painting of the shield would follow, the work to be done slowly and precisely. Everything Jethro had learned had to be presented once again in ceremony, so that the Powers would recognize the shield and its bearer. This kind of protection was essential when entering battle. And with Jethro's special mission, the shield would need to have a double power that would see him through great trial.

Cuts Buffalo reached the river and selected a fallen log that stretched into the cold flow of water. She sat down and watched the icy ripples beneath her feet. The days grew ever shorter. Soon the river would be clogged with ice, for the nighttime cold would hold more strength than the daytime warmth. Then the land would be white and the river frozen silent.

Cuts Buffalo did not care now if winter lasted forever; she would have Jethro to snuggle with for as long as she wanted. When the moon changed again, he would become her husband. He had asked her to be his wife and she had gladly accepted. Although it now seemed to her like a dream come true, she saw that it was every bit as real as the air she breathed and the cold, clear water beneath her feet. With the changing of the moon would come the happiest time of her life.

Since his return with the hide for his shield, Cuts Buffalo had walked many times with Jethro, the two of them wrapped together in a courting blanket. He had even tried his hand at playing a love flute for her, one he had taken time and pains to make himself. He should have known when making it that it likely would not sound any better than it looked. When he played it, High Elk and and Cuts Buffalo's brothers plugged their ears, and told him he would scare all the game away. To defend himself, Jethro decided to blame his lack of playing ability on the cold weather; the flute did not like chilly evenings and stayed asleep while he played.

"Just don't wake the flute up," High Elk had told Jethro. "That poor little piece of wood will think it was having bad dreams." Finally, after he received the nickname "Sick Evening Bird," Jethro resigned himself to the fact that his calling was not as a musician. He gave the flute to

Little Bow, who wrapped it in skunk hide and placed it in a badger hole.

Cuts Buffalo laughed to herself as she recalled Jethro's attempts to make beautiful music. He had a lot of abilities, but playing a love flute was not among them. That did not matter to her; she had the best man she could ever find, and she knew it.

As the afternoon wore on, the sun lowered toward the west. Cuts Buffalo remained at the river, thinking of her future with Jethro. She wondered how many children they would have, and if there would be more boys than girls. She wanted to give him a strong son first, a boy who would have a warrior's abilities, yet be as kind and generous as his father. She would work hard to make Jethro the happiest man among all the Crow people.

When darkness pressed near, Calling Bird came to the river. "It is time for you to come," she told Cuts Buffalo. "Jethro's shield is finished. There will be war stories and dancing."

Cuts Buffalo had enjoyed thinking about her life with Jethro as mother to his children. But she knew that she must face the fact that Jethro's mission to regain the Sacred Pipe was foremost in his mind. The dancing and the stories would fortify his resolve to help his people bring their lives back to normal.

In the village, Cuts Buffalo sat back with the women while Jethro displayed his war shield to the circle gathered around the fire. The entire village watched and listened as Bull Comes Ahead prayed and in turn Jethro's father and other warriors of the village recalled war deeds. The men had painted themselves and donned their war shirts, as if preparing for an actual raid. Drums sounded before and after each story, the tales of striking coup honors against enemies bringing cheers from the listeners.

Very late, when the war stories were completed, the men of the Raven Society encircled Jethro and danced to heavy drumming by one of their members. The official induction process would occur once Jethro had attained full warrior status, but this was a clear message that he would be welcomed as an esteemed member just as soon as his honors were gained.

Cuts Buffalo watched and wondered. She recalled the many times that Jethro had spoken with her of his belief that constant fighting had brought bad luck to the tribes of the mountains and plains. But now he seemed to be getting ready for war himself; he seemed set on pursuing the Blackfeet until he brought the pipe safely back to the people.

"You were in a dream," she remembered Jethro telling her. "And after you helped me, I saw the Sacred Pipe, showing me where Big Owl sat upon a high, flat-topped mountain. That is where I will find him and retrieve the pipe."

Cuts Buffalo recalled that after this dream, Jethro had returned with Bull Comes Ahead certain that she should become his wife. For that she was glad; but his intention to fight until the pipe was recovered seemed to her to be overly strong.

"I don't want to lose you, not just after we are married," Cuts Buffalo had told him.

"It will be no good if you worry," she had heard him say. "You must take things as they come."

Cuts Buffalo thought of this conversation as the Ravens continued their drumming and songs. They were followed by the Lumpwoods and the Foxes, and then other societies took their turn in declaring their place within the warrior classes. Finally, it was time for the women to take part.

A drummer began his beat and, beneath a pole covered with enemy scalps, a singer recalled an ancient war song. A line of women proceeded to circle the pole, dancing sideways in a shuffling manner until the circle was closed. At the beginning of the next song, the women began to dance forward, chanting, shouting at the enemy scalps; then they danced backward. They held long sticks with which they struck out at the scalps.

Cuts Buffalo sat by herself and watched. She felt someone touch her shoulder. "Why are you not in the circle of dancers?" Calling Bird asked. "After all, this ceremony is in honor of your future husband."

Calling Bird had become Cuts Buffalo's closest friend. Cuts Buffalo saw Calling Bird as the sister she didn't have and, in fact, she had discussed things with her she had never spoken of to her mother. She knew that Calling Bird would understand her explanation.

"I cannot take place in the dance," she said. "I have to be the balance against the warfare that will come into Jethro's life. I have to be the other half, the half of peace. That is how I feel."

Calling Bird smiled. "Spoken well, very well. I know of no other among our people more worthy of Jethro than you. And no one is more worthy of you than Jethro."

"Are you going to dance?" Cuts Buffalo asked.

"I have been holding the knife Big Owl cut me with," Calling Bird replied. She pointed to the nearby ground, where the knife lay under a piece of skin that had been painted by Bull Comes Ahead with protective medicine designs. "I want to learn more from the knife. That is how I can best help."

Cuts Buffalo nodded. She watched Calling Bird return to her seat and take the knife into her hands. Calling Bird watched the dancers and soon fell into a trance. Cuts Buffalo got up and turned away from the dancing. She was met by Jethro in front of the lodge.

"Are you troubled?" he asked.

"Yes, I am," she answered. "I know that you have spoken against war but that you will soon be going to fight. I cannot understand this."

"It is hard for me to understand it, too," Jethro told her. "But I can see no other way to get the Sacred Pipe back."

"I have been thinking," she said. "Why not have Bull Comes Ahead use the new pipe he made? Why can't that become the Sacred Pipe?"

Jethro shook his head. "That would be good, but it is not possible. The new pipe only screams for the return of the old one, so that the two pipes' power can become one and our people can live in peace and happiness. I must get the Sacred Pipe back or we will see much trouble."

"Perhaps you are right," Cuts Buffalo said. "But my heart is still sad."

"I believe I know your sadness," Jethro said. "But we have to face what comes. And what comes will be worse and worse until I retrieve the pipe."

"Maybe that is true," Cuts Buffalo said. "And maybe we don't yet know what bad is. Maybe we are going to have to face the worst, with or without the Sacred Pipe."

PART THREE

Winter-Spring
1850

EIGHTEEN

WITH THE CHANGE OF THE MOON CAME CUTS Buffalo's happiness. The weather co-operated, bringing sunshine and gentle, warm winds from the southwest. Fitted with a brand-new antelope dress made by Morning Swan and Rosebud, she walked with a crier through the village and waved to the people, who sent her many cheers and wishes for a good life. In the eyes of the people, the union would be good and lasting.

The feast in her and Jethro's honor lasted for two full days, with numerous presents exchanged between the two families. During these days, Little Bow and Jumps Ahead rode double on a four-year-old stallion named Whistle, one of the gifts from Jethro to Strikes-the-Heart. Jethro would have liked to give Flame away also, and he promised the pony to Strikes-the-Heart just as soon as he recovered it from Big Owl.

But Whistle—another pony Thane had given Jethro after the successful buffalo hunt—ran nearly as fast and turned nearly as quickly as Flame. With more training, the pony could become as good in the hunt as Flame was. Little Bow and Jumps Ahead had a lot of fun pretending that the horse liked them better than either Jethro or Strikes-the-Heart, and they wondered if they would eventually have to have something to do with a girl in order to get a good horse of their own.

When the celebration ended, the people gathered on a hill above the village. They were watching an incoming snowstorm. When the storm struck, it remained for twelve full days. After the snow finally stopped, warriors and horse tenders alike searched the river bottom for the many members of the herd that had wandered off.

Whistle was not among the lost, as Strikes-the-Heart had kept the pony tethered to his lodge. He wanted the horse to get used to him before he allowed it to graze with the herd. That way, Whistle would be much easier to catch.

Over the days following the storm, the cold grew stronger and the river closed over with ice. The villagers settled into their lodges around large fires for storytelling sessions that often lasted throughout the night. This year the stories would be offered to First Maker so that the Sacred Pipe might return to the people.

As the cold season progressed, it seemed to the Kicked-in-Their-Bellies that life might never return to normal. Nothing felt right. They were not adjusting to the new camping site near the Grey Cliffs. It was not the same as camping along the juncture of the Wind and the Bighorn rivers, where the waters flowed out of warm pools and the people swam and watched the falling snow turn to steam. The wind blew constantly, as it did in their old camping site, but here it had more bite. The horses ranged farther out from the village, making it harder to watch them, and the hunting proved much more difficult.

The Flatheads came to visit on one occasion when the snow stopped for a time and the weather cleared. The young men of both villages raced their horses and tested one another with various games, while the elders made bets and talked of brave deeds against their common enemy, the Blackfeet. Everyone wondered how long it would be before the Blackfeet showed themselves. Although warm days were better for making war, the Blackfeet could come at any time.

Jethro's shield stood outside the lodge, facing east. Its medicine was whole, with the exception of the two blue stones that must be fitted into the stuffed raven's eyes. He knew that he would have to journey north to get the stones, into the Little Belt Mountains, where the waters of the Judith flowed. It would be difficult to find the stones until after the snow left, and that worried him a great deal.

With the angry talk among both Crow and Flatheads about the Blackfeet, someone would certainly suggest a war party before long. Jethro did not want to face conflict without the blue stones in the raven's eyes, but he knew that he would certainly be asked to go. With the strength of the combined villages and the surprise of an attack during the cold season, the Blackfeet would be hard pressed.

Jethro was right. Soon the young warriors in both villages became anxious to prove themselves. High Elk found Jethro reading from one one of Thane's books, *Gulliver's Travels*, and told him about a plan being circulated in the camps.

"Long Tail, the Flathead war leader, wants to carry the pipe into Blackfeet lands," he told Jethro. "He wants to know who will follow him."

"Are you going?" Jethro asked, a finger between the pages so he would not lose his place.

"Now would be a good time to raid the Small Robes and teach Big Owl a lesson," High Elk replied. "You and I could get our horses back, and the Sacred Pipe as well."

"I don't know," Jethro said. "I don't feel like going."

High Elk looked at the book. "That will still be here when we get back."

"No, there's more to my decision than that. Cuts Buffalo believes she is with child."

"Good!" High Elk said. "Now you can leave her for a while. You've done your job well."

"It's not just that, High Elk," Jethro said. "My medicine shield is not yet complete. I must put two blue stones in the raven's eyes."

"You don't have to fight," High Elk said. "Just go along and take Flame back. I'll find Night Runner and then take the Sacred Pipe back from that wailing child, Big Owl."

"You make it sound easy, High Elk."

"It won't be easy, but it can be done. You will gain honors. We will both gain honors, together. Then when the snow has left, you can get the eyes for your raven and we can go out with another raiding party together and be war brothers, as we have always wanted to be."

"I don't know," Jethro said. "I couldn't even take my shield along, not without full medicine."

"I told you, you don't have to fight," High Elk repeated. "Just take horses."

"What if I am attacked?"

"If you are attacked, you can decide to run or to fight without your shield. No one is going to laugh at you if you do not have your medicine."

"Maybe it is foolish even to go along without my medicine," Jethro suggested.

High Elk shrugged. "You know how much I want your presence. But that is for you to decide. I do know that I am going. There are others who will also go. I know that Fox Caller and Enemy Seeker are going. We will all gain honors and be asked to join warrior societies. If you don't go, you will miss out."

Jethro thumped the book against the side of his leg. "When will you go?" he asked.

"Soon, I am certain. Very soon."

"Let me think about it," Jethro said.

High Elk rose. "I cannot wait for you to make a decision. I for one would certainly like to see Big Owl pay for what he has done to our people. Now is the time to make him do just that."

Jethro watched High Elk disappear into the center of the village, where the warriors were gathering. There would be a council to decide who could join the Flatheads and who should stay behind and guard the village. It was never good to have all of the young men go off and leave the village unattended, especially when so close to Blackfeet lands.

By late in the evening it had been decided that twenty younger men seeking war honors, along with ten experienced warriors, would go on the raiding party with the Flatheads. The rest of the men would remain to defend against attack.

High Elk said nothing to Jethro during the entire evening, but Jethro could feel his friend's annoyance every time their eyes met.

The next morning, when the warriors and young men prepared to travel to the Flathead village to join their raiding party, Jethro approached High Elk.

"I hope you gain honors, High Elk," he said. "I will be the first to congratulate you."

High Elk was tying a blanket and his weapons to the saddle of a pony he had borrowed from his father. He did not turn from his work. "It looks like it will have to be me who gets our Sacred Pipe back," he said, testing a knot. "And if I take Big Owl's scalp, you can touch it. But that is all."

"I cannot see why you are angry with me," Jethro said. "I told you, it would not be right for me to go without my medicine shield."

"You could have come along, just to share the honors," High Elk insisted. "But you really didn't want to go at all."

"If that's what you wish to think, that is fine with me," Jethro said impatiently. "I can see you've become like a stubborn old woman."

High Elk turned around. "You should be talking about old women. You will be here with them while I am gaining glory. You can't read your book all the time. Maybe you should learn how to bead moccasins to pass the time of day."

Jethro turned and walked away. There would be no purpose in returning his friend's anger. He thought it too bad that High Elk could not understand why he had decided to remain behind. He was not supposed to go; he could feel that. But High Elk had never been one to accept another's opinion if it differed from his own.

In a way, High Elk had been right about his being with the women. He would have to listen to their worries about where their husbands and sons were and why they had been so foolish as to go raiding during the worst season of the year. If they returned with horses, and especially with the Sacred Pipe, there would be feasting for

285

many nights. If something went amiss, there would be mourning.

And there was no guarantee of glory against the Blackfeet. Maybe they would get their horses back, along with others from the Small Robes' herd, and maybe they would not. Maybe the Small Robes would see them coming and be waiting for them. In the meantime, what was to keep the Blackfeet from having the same idea and seeking to surprise them in winter camp?

Jethro began to wonder about his friend's common sense. High Elk should realize that the only certainty was the harsh and unpredictable weather. Although it felt good to be outside at present, the winds could change at any time and bring more snow and cold. That worried the people as much as any enemy gun or arrow. Jethro felt that because of the likelihood of deadly storms, all those who returned would be worthy of great honor.

A thin streak of gray broke in the east. High Elk and the others of the Crow and Flathead party donned their war shirts and paint in the darkness. It had been an easy journey to the Two Medicine, where the Small Robes were known to make their winter camp. High Elk anticipated a victory against their enemies, who lay sleeping in their robes just over the hill.

There had been two Piegan watchers, now both dead and scalped; advance scouts for the raiding party had had little trouble in sneaking up on them. It seemed as if the raid were directed from above by the Powers. The village below had no idea of what was coming.

High Elk anxiously awaited the attack. He wanted to get into the camp and find Night Runner and, hopefully, Flame as well. The main Piegan horse herd ranged just a short way from the raiders, and the warriors now discussed who wanted to go down into the village and who wished only to steal horses.

Cuts Buffalo's twin brothers were divided. "Maybe we should just take their horses grazing on the hillside and be gone," Enemy Seeker suggested. "That would be easy."

"But their best ponies are tied down in the village," Fox Caller pointed out. "Besides, Flame and Night Runner are not among the horses on the hillside."

"Maybe Big Owl will ride out from the village on Flame or Night Runner when we drive away the herd," Enemy Seeker said. "We won't have to go into the village after him. He will be with the others wanting to get their horses back. That will make it easy for us. We won't have to worry so much about any of us getting hurt."

"You talk like an old woman," High Elk told him. "How could any one of us be hurt with such easy prey?"

"They won't stay asleep for long," Fox Caller said on his brother's behalf. "If they awaken and get to their weapons, they will fight like wildcats."

Long Tail had been overseeing the discussion. Some of his warriors had also been talking about just taking horses and making a getaway. But many others had come seeking revenge for the loss of fathers and brothers, and insisted on taking scalps.

Long Tail offered a suggestion. "Anyone who wants to stay up here and just steal horses is welcome to do so. No one has to go down into the village to fight."

Discussion again arose. Some of the younger men, who did not feel good about fighting on this day, decided to remain on the hill and chase the horses when the signal to leave was given. Enemy Seeker considered staying with them.

"Tell your brother to be brave," High Elk said to Fox Caller. "It is foolish to travel so far and worry about people who are sleeping."

Fox Caller looked to his brother.

Enemy Seeker stared high into the east. "I see where the camp fires of the Lost Ones are going out," he said. "I do not know which is best for me, but I will go down into the village. I want to learn the ways of a warrior, and I cannot do that by staying back and waiting."

"You have made a good decision," High Elk said, clapping him on the back. "You will make your family proud."

The fighting party mounted and split into three groups. Two groups would attack the village from opposite sides along the river, and the third would come straight down the hill. Long Tail would lead the main force down the hill, and the other two—one led by a Crow warrior and the other by a Flathead—would then converge and force the trap shut.

Those who were not joining in the attack would

begin driving the Piegan horses away during the fighting. Once the Small Robes were on the run, all three forces would unite with those driving the herd and be gone.

The attack had been well planned; all seemed simple enough. But two Piegan watchers from across the river, two Wolves on guard duty who were watching for danger from the other direction, somehow learned of their presence. They made it down into the village and shouted warnings just before the charge. By the time Long Tail led the attack from the hill and the other two factions closed in from both sides along the river, many of the Piegan warriors were armed.

High Elk rode among those charging in from downriver. Piegan women and children were already screaming and warriors had formed a barricade, to allow them to escape toward the river. High Elk and the others quickly broke through the barricade, slaying Piegans with battle axes and arrows. The Piegans fought defiantly, but were not ready for the frenzied Crow and Flathead warriors. High Elk jumped from his horse and took an honor by striking a Piegan across the face with his bow. The Piegan fell backwards and was pinned to the ground when a passing Flathead drove his lance through him from atop his horse.

High Elk watched his pony fall dead as a ball fired from a trade rifle entered the horse's head, just under the right eye. As the Piegan who fired the shot hurriedly reloaded, High Elk loosed an arrow and watched the shaft drive completely through the warrior's neck. After taking the scalp, High Elk began to search through the fighting for Big Owl and Many Berries. Though many Piegan horses were being cut from pickets near the lodges, neither Night Runner or Flame were among them.

High Elk ran toward the center of the village, where some Flathead and Crow warriors herded Piegan horses. Enemy Seeker, a smile on his face, showed a scalp he had taken. High Elk was yelling a victory cry with him when Enemy Seeker groaned and slumped to his knees. An arrow had passed through his body just under his left armpit, its bloody head poking out under his right breast.

Fox Caller ran to them, screaming his brother's name. He caught a horse, and High Elk helped him load Enemy Seeker onto its back. Together they tied a rawhide rope around Enemy Seeker's waist and secured it around the horse's neck. Enemy Seeker's eyes rolled wide and his mouth hung open, his breath sounding like water bubbling in a hole.

Fox Caller then leaped on his pony and led the horse at a run out of the village. High Elk, fighting the shock of what had just happened, began to look for another horse. He noticed a big red stallion tied to a lodge covered with war honors. An older Piegan warrior defended the area, fighting one of the Flatheads hand-to-hand. The Flathead, although much younger, was no match for the accomplished Piegan, who stepped aside from a knife thrust and slammed his war club into the Flathead's face.

The Piegan warrior screamed a war cry and

turned on High Elk, who nocked an arrow to his bow. As the Piegan charged, High Elk loosed the arrow. It zipped just under the warrior's shield and drove deep into his stomach. He doubled over and slumped to his knees, clutching the feathers of the arrow where they protruded just below his navel.

The warrior looked up at High Elk and screamed again. He stood up then and ripped the arrow from his stomach with both hands, pulling out a strip of intestine with it. High Elk stood speechless, amazed and shocked by the performance. The warrior broke the arrow over his knee and pulled his knife. On the ground in front of him lay his shield, painted with the striking image of a red hawk.

"Rising Hawk!" High Elk said to himself. "It is he, the strong enemy of Thane Thompson."

High Elk pulled his knife and lunged forward. Rising Hawk made a bold attempt to fight, but the wound in his stomach robbed him of his strength and he collapsed before High Elk, who quickly put his knife to Rising Hawk's throat.

"Before I kill you, I want to know if Big Owl and Many Berries are in this village," he said.

High Elk's words gave Rising Hawk enough time to free his knife hand. High Elk felt the blade enter his right side, just under his last rib. Only his quick movement prevented the blade from entering his liver.

Rising Hawk thrust again with the knife, but High Elk deflected the blow. The older warrior, even though his abdomen burned with pain, was more than a match for most warriors. High Elk ran his knife deep into Rising Hawk's chest, then across the Piegan's throat. Rising Hawk kicked and thrashed in his death throes. When he finally lay still, High Elk cut a circle with his knife from the hairline along the top of this forehead around to the back of his skull and jerked the scalp loose.

Bleeding from his side, High Elk cut the red stallion free and joined the others in their dash from the village. The Piegans were scattered up and down the riverbank, searching for lost loved ones. The Crow and Flathead raiders, having suffered casualties and injuries they had not expected, were glad for the remaining Piegans' retreat.

A good distance from the Small Robes' village, Long Tail signaled a halt to care for the wounded. Warriors were already mourning lost brothers and friends, and many of the badly wounded sang their death song. Packs of dried yarrow were unwrapped and pressed into wounds to stop the bleeding. High Elk, at Fox Caller's insistence, stuffed yarrow into the jagged cut under his ribs.

High Elk and Fox Caller eased Enemy Seeker down off the horse and onto a blanket laid in the snow. They treated the entrance and exit wounds alongside the arrow to stop the external bleeding. But it was the bleeding inside that bothered them.

"I don't know what to do about the arrow," Fox Caller told High Elk. "I don't think I should try to remove it."

Enemy Seeker smiled. "Don't worry about the arrow, my brother. It is a good day for dying. I no longer have any fear."

"No, you do not have to die, my friend," High Elk said. "You have many journeys yet to make."

"Only to the Other Side," Enemy Seeker said, coughing blood. "My Grandfathers have come. Can you see them?"

"Hold on, my brother," Fox Caller pleaded. "We will be back among our people before long. Then we will have Bull Comes Ahead take care of you."

Enemy Seeker shook his head. "All that Bull Comes Ahead can do is to greet the Grandfathers and Grandmothers."

Enemy Seeker began his death song as High Elk and Fox Caller lifted him back onto the horse. They wrapped the rawhide rope around him and secured it around the pony's middle so that he would not fall off. High Elk offered an extra blanket that he had brought, as Enemy Seeker had lost his horse and all of his belongings. They wrapped the blanket around Enemy Seeker and he smiled again.

"I will be warm when I cross over."

Fox Caller mounted and joined the others who were leading horses carrying the dead or wounded. High Elk groaned as he mounted the red stallion. He nearly fell off but caught a handful of mane and steadied himself. Although the yarrow had stopped the bleeding, he had lost enough blood that he was lightheaded.

Long Tail led the procession onward. Holding his side, High Elk took a look toward the Two Medicine. He wished now that he had listened to Jethro. Had he done so, he certainly would have saved a lot of grief for the Crow people.

NINETEEN

THE MORNING BROKE CLEAR, WITH A WARM WIND that slipped in whispers off the Backbone-of-the-World, as the Blackfeet called the Rocky Mountain chain. But far to the north a bank of clouds, barely visible on the skyline, rolled slowly down toward the Two Medicine.

For a number of days the weather had been balmy, but now the horses raced along the bottoms, kicking up their heels. A change in the weather would come before day's end.

Despite the coming storm, the villagers were in a cheerful mood. A large herd of buffalo had been sighted not far downriver, grazing on grass patches that had been blown free of snow. There would be a hunt, so that an additional supply of meat could be laid away against the remainder of the cold moons.

Many Berries was not among those celebrating. She did not have her mind on food, nor on the securing of food for herself or for Big Owl. Struggling with nausea, she found it impossible to concentrate on his discussion of the hunt. She wished that he would leave the lodge and join the other hunters, so she could hurry out and find someplace to vomit.

Though she had suffered through morning sickness often, she had been able to avoid Big Owl's attention. He paid her little mind. He saw no need to think of her until his sexual appetite returned, which it would do as soon as he gained glory in battle against the Crows.

While Many Berries bent over the moccasins she was beading for him, struggling to control her stomach, Big Owl selected arrows for the upcoming hunt and continued to tell her of how he intended to impress the Bloods.

"When they see how easily I can kill a buffalo, they will want to go to war very soon," he said. "This idea of waiting until the cold releases its grip on the land is crazy. Now is the time to go, while the Crow are trapped in their lodges like scared rabbits."

Finally, Many Berries could contain her nausea no longer. She dropped her sewing and burst from the lodge. She was doubled over when Big Owl came up behind her.

"What is the matter with you? Why are you sick?"

"It is something I ate last night," she said quickly. "I haven't felt good since we went to bed."

"What did you eat that I didn't?" Big Owl asked. "I am having no trouble."

"I must have eaten something you didn't."

"Oh? I can't remember seeing you eating again after we finished the venison and roots."

"Maybe it was a root," Many Berries said. "I don't know what it was."

She brushed past Big Owl and slipped back into the lodge, taking her place next to the fire and picking up her sewing. Big Owl entered and sat down, staring at her.

"Are you sure your stomach is upset because of roots?" he asked, his tone as hard as rock. "Is there some other reason you are sick?"

"What other reason could there be?" Many Berries snapped.

"You know very well what 'other reason' there could be! Are you with child?"

"Of course not! How could that be? You can't even . . ."

As soon as she had spoken, Many Berries realized her mistake. She should have just said no. Now she had insulted Big Owl's abilities as a man.

"I mean," she corrected herself, "that . . . that there could be no way."

"I'm not so certain of that," Big Owl said. "Maybe there is a small Crow dog growing inside of you. Is that it?"

He bent over and asked her again, "Is that it?" His eyes were glowing with rage. Many Berries leaned away from him. He grabbed her roughly by the arm. Then someone yelled from outside.

"Big Owl, are you ready for the hunt?"

Without waiting for an answer, Harlan Cutter stuck his head inside the lodge.

"Burned Face," Big Owl said, "what do you think you are doing, entering my lodge without invitation?"

Cutter leered at Many Berries. "Maybe you ain't quite ready yet," he said to Big Owl. "We ain't got a lot of time to wait, so get on her and get it over with."

Big Owl jumped up and pushed Cutter through the door flap and down into the melting snow. The trader jumped to his feet as Big Owl came out to face him.

"What the hell is the matter with you?"

"You can watch your own men mount their women," Big Owl told Cutter. "You will not enter my lodge and expect that from me. Do you understand?"

Many Berries now stood outside, watching Big Owl glare at Burned Face. The trader wiped mud from the back of his buckskins, returning the intense anger.

"That's not what you said to me the other night, when we shared the jug," Cutter told Big Owl. "You invited me in to watch, and to share, any time I wanted. You'd go back on your word?"

Many Berries stared at Big Owl, who would not turn to face her.

"If such a thing is ever to happen," he told Cutter, "I will pick the time. Not you. Do you understand?"

"Just so you ain't telling me I can't have her some time," Cutter said, his anger easing. He stared at Many Berries and a thin smile broke his lips. "I'd give you some good presents for her. That I would."

Big Owl pointed to the group of gathering hunters. "Join the others and tell them I am coming," he told Cutter. "Don't come back."

Big Owl shoved Many Berries aside and crouched through the door flap. Many Berries heard him inside, gathering his bow and arrows. When he came back out of the lodge, she took him by the arm and stopped him.

"Do you plan to take trade goods from Burned Face, so that I might share his bed?"

"Of what other use are you?" Big Owl asked vehemently. "You will lie down with anyone, so I might as well receive something for it. Don't you think?"

"But you had talked to him about it before, hadn't you?"

"What does it matter when I talked to him? You are worthless."

Big Owl pulled away from her and stormed toward the waiting hunters. Many Berries watched him go, a deep shudder running through her from head to toe. Big Owl had planned for some time to allow Burned Face access to her. Now, with the knowledge that she carried Jethro's child, Big Owl would certainly welcome anyone to have her, especially Cutter. Big Owl would revel in the thought that maybe Burned Face would use her badly.

It was certain now that Big Owl wanted her to die. But he would not kill her himself; he would let Burned Face do it for him, slowly.

* * *

The wind had changed. The snows had melted along the south slopes, leaving the land bare. Here grazing deer and elk, and scattered buffalo, ate their fill before the bad weather came back to drive them to cover.

The returning party of raiders crossed the waters of the Musselshell and turned south along the east face of the Crazy Mountains. They had traveled throughout the previous day and night, and would be back at the Grey Cliffs before nightfall.

Some of the warriors talked about the good number of horses they had taken from the Piegans, and the number of slain enemies they had left behind. But most of them were silent. The raiders had paid dearly for their victory. Long Tail and the Flatheads had lost three warriors, with another five wounded, one seriously. The Crow had lost more—seven warriors killed and eight wounded.

Soon there would be eight Crow warriors dead. Enemy Seeker had stopped singing his death song and would not respond to Fox Caller's questions. Expecting the worst but wanting to deny it, Fox Caller reined his horse and got down to look at his brother. The Piegan horse skittered back and forth at the end of its rope, nostrils flaring. It's right side was coated with Enemy Seeker's blood.

"Can you hear me, brother?" Fox Caller asked.

Enemy Seeker lay slumped over the horse's side, his head hanging. He was atop the horse only by virtue of the ropes that Fox Caller and High Elk had used to tie him to the saddle. The blanket that Fox Caller had placed over him for warmth lay bunched up around his shoulders, the arrow under his arm protruding from underneath.

"Brother? Brother, answer me!" Fox Caller got no response. He held his brother's head up and saw that the eyes were glazed over in death.

The rest of the party had now stopped and was looking back. Holding his injured side, High Elk rode over to where Fox Caller leaned against his dead brother's knee, weeping openly.

High Elk stared. "It is finished for him," he said, his voice barely above a whisper. "And it was I who told him to die as a proud warrior should. I do not feel good, for I do not believe it was his time."

Fox Caller wiped away tears and looked up at High Elk. "My brother and I are one, yet he has crossed over. I feel that I am partly gone with him."

"I had always felt that we four—you and Enemy Seeker, and I and Jethro—would bring much honor to our people," High Elk went on. "Now Enemy Seeker is gone, after his first raid. And it is my fault."

"Do not blame yourself, High Elk," Fox Caller said. "My brother made his choice, and he died a good death. He was fighting."

"He had many more seasons left in him in which to fight," High Elk insisted. "I wish now that he had stayed up with those taking the horses, as Long Tail suggested."

"He will have many horses on the Other Side," Fox Caller said. "He died young, but he will carry honor with him. Let us take him and the others who fell back to our people."

High Elk turned the red stallion and the procession began again. He looked into the north, where the storm had become a white blanket rolling slowly toward them. The icy breeze nipped at his face and cooled his brimming tears. There would be a great deal of mourning when they arrived back at the village. In addition, he had not retrieved the Sacred Pipe, nor did he even know where Big Owl and Many Berries had gone. In all, it been a wasted trip for the Crow people. And all because of him.

The snow began falling, huge flakes twisting through the sky on the light wind that fronted the worst of the storm. Many Berries paced in front of her lodge, anxious to find a way to be gone from this place. With the festivities of the hunt, the Long Knife traders would be passing out the strong drink. It would then be only a matter of time until Big Owl gave her to Burned Face for his use.

She contemplated stealing a pony and making a run for it. But two of Burned Face's traders had remained behind and had been watching her for the entire morning. Even if she managed to escape them, there were enough horse tenders and younger warriors still in the village that she would never get away.

There were always a number of people who kept an eye on her, just as there had been in the Crow village, but no one suspected that she was contemplating leaving. She must not alarm anyone; it would be a mistake to attempt an escape and fail. She did not want to find herself under guard, and she did not want to make Big Owl any angrier. The right time would come, she knew, to make her getaway. Until then, she must somehow maintain patience.

The morning broke into afternoon, and the snowfall increased. The bitter cold still had not moved in, but it would before long. As the hunters returned one by one to announce their kills, Many Berries prepared to join the other women in the butchering of the carcasses. She would go out with them and in that way at least give herself a head start away from the village. Once the storm struck in force, she wanted to be gone. She would take her chances with the Cold Maker; to stay behind with Big Owl would be certain death.

Big Owl then appeared, riding Night Runner recklessly through the village, whipping the horse with a riding quirt he had made. He stopped in front of the lodge and pointed, out away from the village.

"It is time for you to get some butchering done," he said. "I told you I would show the Bloods how to hunt."

Many Berries felt her heart pounding.

"Hurry! The storm is moving in!" Big Owl yelled. "I have two buffalo down. Get on behind me and I will take you to the first one."

Many Berries wrapped herself in a heavy blanket. She held on to a sheathed knife and let Big Owl pull her up behind him onto the back of the pony.

"I am going to get some work out of you before

tonight," he told her. "Then you can work some more, in another way." He laughed and kicked the pony into a run.

They rode at full speed out of the village. The snow fell more heavily as they passed numerous downed buffalo, women already butchering them. Here and there, young warriors reached into the steaming bodies and took the liver to eat raw, signifying that they had made the kill and were now considered good hunters. Most of the animals were four-teeth cows, two-year-olds, with the thinnest hides and the thickest, softest coats of all those in the herd. She knew that the Long Knives treasured these robes over all others.

Big Owl reined Night Runner in next to one of the four-teeth kills. He told her to be careful with the hide. Many Berries had thrown her leg over the pony to get off when Big Owl reached around and pushed her. She fell backwards off the horse and landed heavily on her back in the snow.

"Get up!" he yelled down to her.

Many Berries groaned and rolled to her side. She finally got her breath back and came to her knees.

"Get up, I said!" Big Owl screamed, swinging his riding quirt. "Do I have to get off this horse?"

Many Berries struggled to her feet. Pain shot like a knife through her lower back, but she did not dare go back down to her knees.

"Hurry, get started," Big Owl told her. He pointed to where a group of women were converging on a number of fallen buffalo. "When you

have finished here with this one, go down among
them. Look for my arrows in a young bull." He
whipped Night Runner into a run and disappeared into the storm.

Many Berries waited to be certain he was gone,
then allowed herself to collapse to her knees. She
arched her back and stretched in every direction
to try to rid herself of the pain. When she could
finally rise, she shuffled over to the dead cow buffalo and peered into the animal's face; its eyes
were glazed in death, its tongue lolling out,
bloody froth caked to its nose and mouth.

The cow's body remained warm enough to melt
the falling snow, and the thick hair was dripping
wet. Even if Many Berries back had not been injured, she could not have moved the cow around
by herself. A short distance away, three women
worked together on a kill. They had two ponies
with them and used the horses to strip the massive hide off, turn the buffalo on its back, and
then to spread the hind legs apart for easy access
to the stomach cavity.

Many Berries watched them for a time, thinking that she should go over and take one of the
ponies and be gone. But she feared Big Owl's
early return. Still, she did not want to wait.

Many Berries had started toward the working
women when she heard the sound of a horse's
hooves. She turned to see one of Burned Face's
Long Knife agents approaching her, one of the
two who had remained behind in the village during the hunt. He wore a heavy red capote and
balanced a rifle in the crook of his arm. He dismounted and tied his horse's reins to one of the

fallen buffalo's forelegs and propped his rifle against the animal's head. Then he smiled.

He pointed to the women working nearby. "Did you aim to go help them women over there?"

"No," Many Berries replied quickly.

"Big Owl wanted me to come see how you're getting along," he said. "I think he'd want you to stay here and work on his cow. He says to tell you he'll be back soon."

Even from where the trader stood, Many Berries could smell the strong drink on his breath. He did not seem to mind the snow that blew against his face and melted into his strange, excited expression. He pulled a skin drinking bag from under the heavy capote. As he continued to stare at her, he took a long swallow and laughed.

"If you get cold," he said, "you just tell me. You hear?"

"What is Big Owl doing now?" Many Berries asked.

"He's got business with Harlan. He'll be along soon enough, don't you worry none."

Many Berries knelt down and started to butcher the buffalo, shocked at how deep her anger toward Big Owl had become. He intended to have her watched closely now, so that he could torture her slowly. Her back hurt a great deal, reminding her that she would suffer endlessly from here on with Big Owl. And she would be totally helpless. The Bloods would certainly not interfere; she had no relatives among them, and they did not care about her one way or the other.

As the Long Knife took another drink, Many Berries realized that injured back or not, the time had come to leave. "I would like a drink of that," she said. "May I have some?"

The trader looked surprised. "Big Owl says you never touch this stuff."

"I have wanted to. He just wouldn't give me any."

"Well, now," the man said, a thin smile breaking his lips, "why don't you just let me help you take a swallow."

He opened his capote to let Many Berries in. She edged next to him. When he closed the capote and raised the skin bag toward her lips, she drove her knife deep into his abdomen and sliced sideways. She stepped away quickly as the Long Knife groaned in agony and doubled over, blood gushing down his buckskin pants.

Many Berries sheathed her knife and started around the trader toward the horse. She saw the man reach for his rifle and returned just in time to pull it from his grasp. The effort shot pain through her back and she dropped to her knees.

Clutching his middle, the trader roared in pain and anger. He started for her. Using the rifle, she pushed herself to her feet to meet his charge. She did not know how to fire the weapon, but turned it around and clubbed him over the head with the stock, splintering the wood into pieces. He fell unconscious and lay on his side, bleeding to death as Many Berries climbed onto his horse.

The women who had been butchering nearby stood and stared. Many Berries kicked the horse into a dead run and leaned over its back, clutching handfuls of mane to stay in the saddle. The pain in her back nearly made her black out, and she fought to stay conscious.

The storm became her ally. The wind whipped the snow into sheets of white that would hide her from Big Owl, or anyone else who chose to come after her. They would have no way of tracking her, for the snowfall filled in the pony's tracks almost as soon as they were made.

Many Berries finally allowed the pony to slow to a brisk walk; she had enough head start now to assure herself of escape. Where was she? The storm completely obscured her vision. The world had become a mass of blurred white.

She rode on, maintaining a tight rein on the pony, for it kept trying to turn around and head back toward the Blood village. The blizzard howled, coating her and the horse with ice and snow. Nightfall would come shortly and with it, deadly cold. She realized that she had to find shelter and dry wood quickly. Otherwise, her successful escape would only lead to death.

Many Berries could tell that the pony had taken her down along the river. She hoped to find a cave along the bank, or possibly a war lodge nestled in the bottom somewhere. But the more she thought about it, the more she realized that there would not be a war lodge so close to the main camping areas. The lodges would be farther away, up in the hills and along the smaller watercourses.

Her hands grew numb as she urged the horse ahead. The storm became worse and the cold stronger. She thought about killing the horse, gutting it, and crawling inside. Others had done the same to save themselves from the cold. But what good would it do when the storm passed? She would be afoot in a sea of white and would likely die anyway.

Many Berries saw no answer to her dilemma. She decided to hunt for a bank or an overhang, then hope to secure some wood. But that seemed impossible, as snow covered everything and filled the air.

She had resigned herself to death when she noticed a large mound in the snow just ahead. She urged the horse into a trot. Upon reaching the mound, she dismounted. A wounded buffalo had managed to make it this far from the hunting ground before collapsing. It was a huge bull, an arrow in its shoulder, which had finally fallen forward to die.

Wasting no time, Many Berries sliced through the hide around the hump and began cutting chunks of meat loose. After she had as much meat as she could carry with her on the horse, she removed a rawhide rope from the saddle and secured it around a massive horn. She positioned the pony at one side of the bull in such a manner that the rope would twist the head around and lever the bull's huge body over sideways. With the snow coming down in blinding sheets, she pulled hard on the reins, urging the pony to work with all its might.

After a long struggle, the horse finally managed to tilt the bull over. Many Berries hurriedly cut open the brisket. Her hands warmed with the flow of blood, and the effort to tear out the entrails warmed her enough that she was able to take the horse into a thicket of willow she had spotted. She hobbled its legs so it would not wander back to the village. Now the pony was sheltered and would have the willow tips to eat.

Once back at the buffalo, Many Berries cut the heart and a large piece of liver free of the viscera. She stuffed the meat into the body cavity, and after wrapping herself tightly in her blanket, crawled inside with the meat. She said a prayer of thanks to the buffalo and to the Powers for allowing her to retain life for the time being. She prayed that if she must cross over, it would be with honor.

Outside, the wind howled and piled up snow around the bull, insulating Many Berries from the fierce cold. This shelter would do until the storm passed.

Many Berries fought sleep, concerned lest she die without awakening. Then she remembered a story she had heard long ago from one of the Grandmothers, about a girl caught unprepared in a severe blizzard. Covered by snow, the girl had not frozen. Many Berries realized that snow had already sealed her within the buffalo's body, holding the heat in.

She also realized that once the snow stopped falling, the deep cold would set in. Then there would not be enough heat to keep her alive. She knew that she would know when the deep cold came, for her body would begin to cool and she would immediately awaken from sleep. Then she would have to begin moving again, or face death inside the buffalo.

Exhausted, she allowed her eyes to droop closed. Soon the sound of the wailing wind outside drifted farther and farther away. Finally, all became silent within the body of the giant bull.

TWENTY

THE SNOWFALL BEGAN AS LIGHT, SCATTERED flakes, blowing down from the north. Everyone knew that a massive storm would make its way into the Yellowstone before nightfall.

Jethro stood atop a hill above the village and watched the raiding party return, driving its share of the Piegan horses before it. The Flatheads were not with it. He realized that the Flathead warriors had already taken the horses they laid claim to and now journeyed back to their own village.

Still, a lot of horses moved ahead of the returning party. With that kind of success, Jethro thought that surely the warriors would be painted for a victory celebration before entering the village. But instead, they rode silently, their faces blackened with charcoal. Then he saw those warriors in the rear, leading the ponies that carried the bodies of the fallen.

He looked among those riding in the lead. High Elk rode a red stallion he had no doubt taken during the raid, and he rode slumped slightly to one side. Jethro wondered how seriously he had been wounded. He saw other Crow warriors he knew as well, some injured, others seemingly unhurt. After looking for them a number of times, he realized that he could not find either of Cuts Buffalo's twin brothers.

Finally, when those leading the horses of the fallen neared, Jethro spotted Fox Caller leading a Piegan horse, his brother draped over its back. Enemy Seeker had been killed.

Jethro felt as though he had been struck in the middle with a stone hammer. His breath caught in his throat and his eyes welled with tears. He climbed on his pony and quickly rode down from the hill and back to the village.

Cuts Buffalo stood with her mother and father, snow falling around them, waiting with the others for word of who had fallen. They had heard from a crier that there were dead and wounded, and many of the women, sensing the loss of a loved one, had already begun their mourning song.

Upon seeing Jethro's face, Cuts Buffalo's mother fell to her knees and began to wail. Cuts Buffalo, her eyes filling with tears, stood in front of him.

"Which one has fallen? Please, have they both been killed? Which one?"

"Enemy Seeker is dead," Jethro said solemnly. A gust of wind struck the village, sending snow flying wildly.

Cuts Buffalo fell, sobbing, into Jethro's arms. He held her and talked to Strikes-the-Heart.

"It appears that Fox Caller has not been hurt. He is leading a Piegan horse."

Strikes-the-Heart nodded. "I will see to both of my sons." He disappeared into the storm.

When High Elk and the rest of the raiding party reached the village, they were met by wailing women, who took their fallen sons into their arms and held them for the last time. Had the raiding party returned without so many casualties, there would have been dancing over the scalps, and stories told of the warriors' bravery. But any honor was now overshadowed by the mourners, who walked the snowy riverbank and across the hills, crying out through the oncoming storm. Many did not return by nightfall, and others were sent to find them and bring them back, for a strong wind had begun to sweep in, bringing devastating cold.

That night everyone stayed inside. The dead were wrapped in robes and placed in an unattended lodge, dedicated with the new Sacred Pipe and a ceremonial prayer by Bull Comes Ahead. High Elk told Jethro what had happened and refused medical attention for his knife wound, saying that he must suffer for his poor thinking. Jethro's father seemed saddened at the news that his one-time rival, Rising Hawk, had been killed by High Elk. To him, it represented the end of an era for both the Piegans and the Crows.

The storm lasted through the following day, keeping the mourners inside. After two more days, the sun came out and shone brightly on a land covered with white and bitter cold. The dead were dressed and placed upon scaffolds erected on a hill among the Grey Cliffs. There had never been placement of the dead here before, and Bull Comes Ahead conducted a ceremony to call the Grandmothers and Grandfathers form the Other Side.

Cuts Buffalo and her mother cut their hair short, and both women, together, laid their hands upon a rock. Each, with a sharp knife, took the little finger on her left hand off at the last joint. Many Leaves cut herself in many places along her arms and legs, smearing the blood all over herself. She would remain unwashed until her mourning ended.

Since she was with child, Cuts Buffalo did not inflict any more injury to herself. Her mother could afford to grow weak for a time; she had no extra life within to support. It was enough that Cuts Buffalo had severed a finger, although her torment reached far deeper than any physical pain. She would always wonder what it would have been like to journey through the coming seasons with Enemy Seeker as well as Fox Caller. But the Powers had decided that Enemy Seeker must cross over, along with the other warriors who had so suddenly lost their earthly lives.

As she settled in next to Jethro that night, Cuts Buffalo wondered how many more of their people would die. Holding her abdomen, she began to worry about the new life growing within her.

"It is so hard to watch those you love dying all around you," she said tearfully. "It saddens my heart, for I can now feel the great burden of pain that my mother and father must bear."

Jethro pulled her close. "We do not understand the responsibilities of parenthood until we become parents ourselves. To lose someone close is a terrible pain but when it is a child, the pain cuts that much deeper."

"I remember the time Enemy Seeker chased me so that he could stuff grass down into my new dress," she said. "I wish now I hadn't gotten so mad at him. And there were times as a child that I told him I wished he were dead."

Jethro felt her hot tears against his chest. "This life was never meant to be easy for us," he said. "We both know that. Now we are learning how hard it is to accept that knowledge."

Cuts Buffalo finally fell asleep. Jethro wiped away the last of her tears and leaned over to kiss her. She moaned in her sleep, another tear slipping from the corner of one eye. He lay back and tried to relax. Visions of Big Owl filled his head. No matter how hard he tried, the Piegan warrior remained there, taunting him, waving his hands and arms in fury. Anger welled up from deep within and Jethro felt himself tensing, enacting in his mind what he planned to do when he found the warrior. He envisioned himself attacking Big Owl, throwing him down and demanding that he return the Sacred Pipe.

Jethro felt Cuts Buffalo stirring beside him. He opened his eyes.

315

"What is it, Jethro?" she asked. "Were you dreaming?"

"Yes, I was having a bad dream," he told her. "But I intend to find this bad dream, and then I can finally rest."

Big Owl rode alone through the cold on Jethro's horse, Flame, following the frozen course of the Big Muddy. Many Berries had escaped and everyone in the village now laughed at him. Burned Face was angry that she had killed one of his men. But Big Owl had pointed out that the man was very foolish to have let a woman gut him with a skinning knife.

It angered Big Owl that no one wanted to accompany him on his search for Many Berries, that no one cared that she was gone. She meant nothing to any of the Bloods, except that she was one of the Blackfeet people. She had made her decision to leave, and if she survived, she would be considered strong.

Although the storm had finally ended, it was a bad time to be out traveling. Cold Maker had the land tight, as tight as he ever had before. Everywhere the scene stretched out an endless white, bleak and frozen. Big Owl had wrapped himself heavily in two blankets and a buffalo robe, but his hands and feet were covered only in tight skins. The wind still bit through to his toes and fingers, and found his nose and cheeks. He could not stay out much longer or he would suffer frostbite, and possibly frozen hands and feet.

Despite this, Big Owl intended to save face by finding Many Berries and bringing her back. Either that or find her frozen body and know for certain that she had not survived the storm. But so far he had found no sign of her. The storm had filled in any tracks that might have shown him the way. Yet he knew that she could not have traveled in any other direction without going over steep hills and through draws clogged with snow. She would not have been that foolish.

Big Owl decided to make up a story and return to the village. Then he saw a large flock of magpies just ahead, jostling for position on a frozen buffalo carcass. They scolded and pecked and pushed one another, paying little attention to Big Owl. When he finally reached the buffalo, the birds lifted off the back of the dead beast and sailed into the cold wind, settling along hillsides and atop sagebrush plants poking above the snow line, scolding and jabbering for him to leave.

Big Owl dismounted and tied Flame to a front leg of the buffalo. He could see where Many Berries had sliced through the thick shoulder hide and had hacked out cuts of hump meat to take with her. The liver and heart were also gone. The viscera, frozen harder than stone, lay beside the bull. Magpies had scratched away the snow that had covered the intestines and had pecked ragged holes through the frozen guts.

There were small, jagged holes in all the meat that lay exposed. So far, the magpies had gotten precious little for their efforts. There was no sign that either wolves or coyotes had worked on the remains; the carcass was too frozen. Only magpies would endure where nothing else could make a fit meal.

It appeared to Big Owl that Many Berries had taken refuge inside the body cavity, and had left when the storm had eased, taking her cuts of meat with her. He could see tracks where she had shuffled through the snow to a stand of nearby willow, and the horse tracks that then led out and downriver. The tracks were ever so faint, having been nearly filled in by additional snowfall. But they were certainly real.

Big Owl kicked around, studying the prints, while the magpies settled again on the carcass. He shook his head in wonder. Many Berries had found a way to save herself. He ignored his grudging feeling of respect for her and made himself laugh. He turned and walked back toward the frozen buffalo. The magpies watched him warily, their wings lifted to fly if need be.

"What a poor job of butchering," he told the birds, shaking his head and laughing again. "You do a better job of cutting yourselves food!" His eyes widened and his voice grew high and distorted. "That woman can't be alive! I don't want her alive!"

The magpies rose in a flurry. Big Owl stomped through the snow and waved his arms violently, cursing and screaming. He spun in circles, his twisted face turned upward to the sky. "Many Berries, where are you? Come back here! I want you back here!"

When he had finished, he looked around. Flame stood patiently where he had been tied. The magpies were gone, nowhere to be seen. He called repeatedly to Many Berries. The only answer was the shriek of the cold wind.

The cold remained locked over the land, making wood gathering difficult. The river froze solid and thick. It was necessary to drive the horses up a good distance toward the Flathead camp. A place existed there where warm water spouted in small, steaming springs and ran down onto the ice of the river. Here the horses could drink in turns, alternating with the Flathead herd.

Jethro spent much of his time helping with the horses. He took Little Bow and Jumps Ahead with him on days that were not too cold, and the three of them would hunt for elk or deer, or just sit and watch while the steaming water from the springs spilled out onto the ice, to eventually freeze in new layers over the old, which was already thicker than a man was tall.

There were times when Jethro went alone into the hills to pray and to ask for guidance. He had no idea of when he would be able to search out Big Owl and Many Berries and to recover the Sacred Pipe. But he realized that he would have to go on his own, for he could not allow the further sacrifice of Crow warriors. There would be no luck in war until the pipe came back to the people.

With the passing of another moon, the wind from the southwest came once again, breathing warmth into a land held fast for so long by cold. The people began to go off into the hills on rides or walks, eager to break the monotony of routine camp life. Little Bow and Jumps Ahead spent an entire day hunting and returned with three rabbits. The rabbits carried little fat after the prolonged cold, but they tasted good to the two young hunters who had been sneaky enough to get close and put their arrows to the mark.

Cuts Buffalo and Many Leaves had ended their mourning and returned to their everyday lives, never speaking of Enemy Seeker. He had crossed over and now lived in the world of the spirits. Cuts Buffalo and her mother, along with others who had lost sons in the raid, looked toward the Grey Cliffs on occasion, especially in the evenings. This time of peace was good for praying and for asking that those who would be chosen next to cross over might find their way to the spirit world without trouble.

Life became more bearable as the cold lessened; daytime temperatures often rose above freezing for a time. As patches of ground appeared on the hillsides, Jethro devised a plan to find Big Owl and the Sacred Pipe. His plan seemed important enough for him to bring it before a council meeting.

"I believe that I must take the responsibility for making life for our people better than it now is," he told the listening group. "I feel that everything would be better if we had the Sacred Pipe back." He looked to Bull Comes Ahead and then to his father. "Had the pipe been passed on as it should have been, a lot of misfortune would not have taken place. I want to journey after the pipe on my own."

The council buzzed. Although the quest was a brave and honorable one, such a journey could cost the life of a good warrior and future leader among the people. Loss of the Sacred Pipe had not been good for the Kicked-in-Their-Bellies, but it had not been the seed of every misfortune.

"I believe that our people will enjoy great prosperity once I find the pipe and bring it back," Jethro added.

"Though your words are strong, you cannot know this for certain," Bull Comes Ahead said. "The fortunes of our people are not tied to any one sacred item. There are many such items and many ceremonies within our band. Also, there are outside influences that have been making our lives harder. You should not believe that you have to get the Sacred Pipe back so that we can go on living. It is my feeling that you are taking on too much responsibility."

The other elders agreed. All turned to Thane Thompson, acknowledging silently that his son was indeed a young man of considerable honor. He had courage and strength, and the willingness to do what he felt was right for the good of all. Nothing more could be asked of a tribal member.

"You speak well, my son," Thane told Jethro, "and I give thanks that you know yourself as you do. I would only ask that you think long and hard before risking your life to retrieve the Sacred Pipe. There are many others to consider besides yourself."

"That is why I feel as I do," Jethro said. "I must soon go into the mountains where the blue stones are found and put two of the stones into the eyes of the raven on my shield. I will be very close to Blackfeet lands. I could go and search for a time. If I do not find Big Owl and Many Berries before the coming of the buffalo for the spring hunt, I will return."

Jethro watched the elders talk among themselves. He realized that they considered him an important member of the band and did not like the idea of losing him to death. They could, if they wished, insist that he not go. But he knew that they would not do that.

It was Bull Comes Ahead who finally spoke on behalf of the council. "You are free to make your own decision," he said. "Whatever path you choose, you know that we will be with you. But in deciding, remember that you already have honor among us and need not prove it further. Do as you must, with our blessing."

After passing the pipe, the council members went their separate ways. Jethro walked out into the night with his father and they stood on a bluff above the river. The moon shone nearly full, and the sky held a million camp fires of the Lost Ones.

"You will soon have a family," Thane told Jethro. "Do you really think that finding the Sacred Pipe is worth putting that in jeopardy?"

"It is my feeling that all of our families are in jeopardy," Jethro replied. "I don't believe that I can just go out and find Big Owl right away. It will likely take time. But I let that man live, and he has caused us a lot of grief. I want that to end."

Thane nodded. "But you know what happened to High Elk when he believed that he could find the pipe and make Big Owl and Many Berries pay. As you can see, his side hasn't healed completely yet."

"I know that the raid didn't go the way it was planned," Jethro acknowledged, "but I do not intend to seek a path of glory. I just want our lives back to normal."

"Our lives *are* back to normal, Jethro. It is true that bad things have happened, but good things are happening as well. We have had plenty to eat, and none of the horses died during the cold weather. Don't you think things are evening out?"

"You know what I am speaking of, Father," Jethro said. "Calling Bird, who still sleeps with Big Owl's knife, says that the old pipe must be brought back and joined with the new one. Together, the two of them will make our people whole again."

Thane took a deep breath. "I guess I can't get you to reconsider, then?"

"I need to see if I can't find Big Owl. I *have* to. Something inside is driving me."

"Did you ever consider waiting?" Thane suggested. "Maybe Big Owl will come to us."

"Yes, I have considered that," Jethro replied. "But he certainly won't come alone, and that would put the women and children in danger. I believe it would be safer to try to get the pipe back by myself."

"Why are you so convinced that you can find the pipe?" Thane asked. "There's a whole lot of country out there, too much to wander around in and hope for good luck."

"I understand that," Jethro said. "But I know

where I can find the pipe. When I went out with Bull Comes Ahead to kill the sacred buffalo bull for my medicine shield, I had a dream. I believe that if I can find the big flat-topped butte I saw then, I will find the Sacred Pipe also."

"What flat-topped butte?" Thane asked.

"In my dream, it was somewhere near a small range of mountains that resemble the Crazy Mountains. The pipe led me in my dream to the butte, where Big Owl sat upon a huge rock."

Thane remembered his first year in the mountains. He had ridden up to the top of a large butte with a brigade of fur traders to view the country. It had been from atop this butte that he had first seen Rising Hawk, leading the Small Robes as they moved their village.

"Do you remember the stories I told you when you were a small boy?" Thane asked. "The stories about old Eli Kleinen and how he knew the country out here so well? He took me along with the rest of our brigade, up on a big butte, and I never saw so much country in all my life."

"You know where the butte is?" Jethro asked excitedly.

"If the butte you saw in your dream is next to a smaller, round butte and a little group of mountains, I'll bet it's the same one. It has to be. It's on the edge of Blackfeet country."

"Will you tell me how to get there?"

"If you're set on going, I'll tell you how to get there," Thane promised. "I hope you don't intend to leave until the snow is gone, though. The wind on top of that butte can be fierce."

"I'll know when to go," Jethro said. "I won't leave until the signs tell me it is time."

Jethro watched his father, whose eyes were now turned upward into the night sky. He waited for his father to speak. Instead, Thane just stared into the sky.

"What is it, Father?" Jethro asked. "What are you looking for?"

"I am looking for the right words, Jethro," Thane replied. "It is hard to come to the understanding that things happen in a manner that they're supposed to and that no matter how much you know about what's happening, you just can't change it."

"Do you know something that will happen to me?" Jethro asked.

"I just know that big butte, that's all," Thane said. "And every time I was near it, a lot of things happened that changed my life. I can see now that it won't be any different for you."

TWENTY-ONE

THE SNOWS MELTED ALONG THE LOWER SLOPES and in the valleys. Occasional sprouts of green grass appeared among the old and weathered stalks. It would be at least another moon before the greening became widespread, but the signal that the warm moons were not far off invigorated the people.

Now there were decisions to make. The Crow horses were beginning to suffer, as the slopes had been picked clean for a good distance in all directions from the village. Grazing and browse would have to be found soon, or the horses would not be in fit condition for the spring buffalo hunt. The Flatheads had already moved their village west across the divide, to find more grass for their horses.

In addition, the river remained clogged with

ice. The prolonged severe cold had frozen the channel nearly solid in places, and getting water for daily use was still a major chore. Cracks and small rivulets had opened up, but the women still waited in long lines to fill their skins. And firewood in the area was almost entirely used up. Without a doubt, the village would have to move soon.

Scouts set out to journey along the Yellowstone and up along the drainages from the mountains. They traveled in small groups, ever alert for enemies and watchful for game. The cold had made it necessary for the people to eat more, and the meat and berry stores were nearly gone. The scouts would return soon with news about which areas could provide the people's needs until the warm moons arrived and the spring hunt could take place.

In the meantime, the villagers made the best of things. The women helped each other, thereby making their work go faster as well as cultivating friendships. Everyone helped those with child; and although Cuts Buffalo was not very far along, she rarely had to do much work. Both Morning Swan and Rosebud regularly carried water for her and made certain that her wood supply remained adequate.

As the weather continued to improve, Little Bow and the Magpies grew more active. Little Bow and Jumps Ahead often met with Running Hawk and the other boys. Running Hawk still talked proudly of the day he had taken the tongue from Calling Bird's meat rack. He eagerly awaited the spring hunt, so that new and even more creative raids could be planned.

When the scouts returned to the village, the council met and heard their reports; the elders decided to move camp downriver and then farther south, into the valley of the Stillwater. Because there had been no winter camps made in that valley, there was plenty of dried forage left from the previous year. This would keep the horses until the warm moons brought the green grass in abundance.

The village had moved but a short distance downriver when clouds gathered and dumped huge rains into the valley, making travel impossible. The people erected their lodges as quickly as possible for shelter, remaining inside for the remainder of that day and all of the next while the deluge continued. Jethro and High Elk, along with many of the men, helped the horse tenders keep the herd contained. There was talk of driving the horses on to the Stillwater, but that seemed too dangerous. The herd would be difficult to watch until the camp caught up, and the Blackfeet could come at any time on a revenge raid.

At the end of the third day, the rains lessened. Word passed through the village that the move to the Stillwater would continue at first light.

As Jethro and Cuts Buffalo were setting into their robes, Little Bow came to the door flap and asked to enter. Jethro told him to come in and warm himself. The boy seemed to be very nervous.

"What brings you here so late?" Jethro asked. "Is there something wrong?"

"Running Hawk cried tonight," Little Bow said. "He told Jumps Ahead and me that he feared something would happen to the Magpies. I don't know what he means."

"I don't think that Calling Bird or any of the women are going to war against you," Jethro said, trying to joke.

But Little Bow remained solemn. "I don't feel good about tonight," he said. "Will the Blackfeet come?"

"There are Wolves on watch," Jethro said. "More than usual, in fact. We will know well in advance if there is to be an attack. You had better go back to your lodge and get some sleep."

"Can I stay here with you and Cuts Buffalo?"

"Sure," Jethro said, and then, thinking of Rosebud, added, "Does your mother care?"

"I already asked her. She said I could, if you would let me."

"You've slept over here before," Jethro said. "You know we will welcome you at any time you wish."

Cuts Buffalo arranged some robes for Little Bow on the other side of Jethro, and they settled in to sleep. The rain pattered lightly at first on the outside of the lodge, then grew steadily stronger. Little Bow tossed and turned restlessly until he finally fell asleep. Outside, the rain came stronger yet, and inside, the fire died down to coals.

Running Hawk tried to shake his parents awake. They groaned in their robes, but he persisted.

Finally, his mother raised up on one elbow, irritated.

"What is it?" she asked in the darkness. "It's not time to get up yet."

"We've got to go," he said. "Now! We've got to hurry."

"Are you having a bad dream?" she asked. Heavy rain was pounding against the lodge. "I doubt that we'll be able to move tomorrow anyway. Go back to sleep and tell me about your dream in the morning."

Running Hawk shook his mother again, but she settled back into her robes. He lay down again, but something inside of him would not allow him to be still. He sat up again, more frightened than before. He shook his mother once more and got no response. "I'm leaving," he told her. Still there was no response. He went over to his father's side, but could not awaken him, either.

The desperate need to leave grew like a shouting voice within Running Hawk. He felt for his moccasins and put them on, then gathered up a blanket and wrapped himself tightly in it before going out into the rain.

Running Hawk had always liked the night best, no matter what the weather might be. But tonight he felt disoriented. He found himself stumbling through the village, falling in the mud, then regaining his feet, only to fall again. Finally, he stood very still, unmoving. His panic eased, and he felt a pull in one direction. He started out again and soon realized that he was traveling uphill.

Running Hawk discovered that he had reached the base of a steep, rocky slope. He climbed hard, scratching in the muddy hillside with his fingers and toes, slipping repeatedly but catching himself each time before he slid too far backward. Finally, he reached the top of the slope.

Crawling ahead, Running Hawk felt the trunk of a large pine tree and leaned back against it to catch his breath. Rain poured down his face, mixing with the flow of tears that had begun after he left the lodge. Something bad had started to happen. It would kill many of the Kicked-in-Their-Bellies, and he could do nothing about it.

Over the pounding rain he could hear a low rumble in the distance. His stomach tightened. The rumble grew closer, gradually becoming a roar. He heard sharp bursts of noise, like giant logs crackling in a fire. Running Hawk knew that the loud sound was river ice breaking up and that water now rushed down with the ice from upriver. He had heard floodwaters before, but this sound was menacing and violent. It was as if the force of a hundred rivers had been unleashed upon the village. He turned on his side and covered his ears.

Jethro and Cuts Buffalo awakened to the sound of a low rumble that grew quickly into a roar accompanied by loud popping noises.

"The ice is going out!" Cuts Buffalo screamed.

Little Bow was already up, shouting for them to get out of the lodge. Jethro bolted from his robes, and Cuts Buffalo followed. He grabbed his shield and weapons, then helped Cuts Buffalo to gather a few necessities. Little Bow yelled for them to hurry, then burst from the door flap and churned through the storm toward his mother's lodge.

In the darkness, ponies squealed and tore loose from their tethers, and dogs barked frantically. Men and women who had awakened dragged sleepy children as fast as they could to higher ground. The men who had experienced flooding before grabbed their weapons first. Their would be no time to save the food supplies. Lives were more important, and the waters were roaring down too fast for anyone to even think straight.

Most of the people reached the hillside, but some were caught in the torrent of ice and water and tossed about like grass dolls. Terror spread everywhere as massive chunks of ice crashed into the village, borne like huge white monsters on the rushing flood tide. Villagers clawed their way up the steep slope, the ice and water crashing past just below them. People ran along the higher ground, screaming the names of relatives and friends.

Amid the chaos, Jethro and Cuts Buffalo found Little Bow—who had just led Running Hawk to Rosebud—and both of Jethro's parents. Fox Caller helped to locate the members of Cuts Buffalo's clan but reported that neither Strikes-the-Heart nor Many Leaves could be found. Cuts Buffalo burst into tears, knowing that her feelings were true: her mother and father had joined Enemy Seeker on the Other Side.

Throughout the night, villagers struggled along the hillside in their search for survivors. The rain lessened and the ice flow passed, leaving behind the shadowed remains of the village. Bull Comes Ahead and Calling Bird had managed to escape harm, due to the fact their lodge had not been erected in the center of the camp as usual, but at the upper end; there had not been time in the rain to arrange the lodges in order of owner importance. Bull Comes Ahead had already pledged a sacrifice to First Maker on behalf of his wife and himself.

As daylight approached, Jethro found Little Bow and Running Hawk sitting near Rosebud, discussing the fate of the Magpies. At least half of their number were not yet accounted for. Among the missing were Jumps Ahead and his mother.

"I thought Jumps Ahead would be up here with us," Little Bow said blankly. "But I remember now that he said he was going to run far away."

"Maybe he did run away," Rosebud told him. "You can look in the hills when the sun comes up."

At first light, the survivors broke into groups and began searching along the floodplain for the lost ones. Bodies were hung up in mud and brush, or buried under huge slabs of ice, literally ground into the soil by the massive weight. The mourning cries of the bereaved chorused through the valley, and then farther into the hills beyond the bottom, as mothers and fathers, sisters and brothers, retreated to be alone and to offer their sorrow by cutting off fingers and strips of flesh. There was no one who had not lost at least one close relative.

In some cases, entire families had been wiped out, drowned and crushed in their sleeping robes, thrown about like small sticks, helpless against the huge waves of water and ice that had surged through the village. Running Hawk was the only member of his family to reach the hillside. He would live from now on with Rosebud and Little Bow.

Although some lodges remained, no one wanted to spend that night in them. There was great fear among the people that the river was not finished sending death. The waters had receded back into their banks, but the heavy rain still fell intermittently. If any ice was left, the added torrents of water would eventually upheave the massive slabs, sending more floodwaters cascading into the village.

The people salvaged what they could of their belongings. Occasionally someone would find something that could be cleaned up and saved, but most of their valuables had been swept away or otherwise destroyed, including their stores of food.

Cuts Buffalo and Fox Caller, their family gone now, retreated into the hills to mourn. Jethro's parents and Rosebud helped the grieving and assisted in preparing bodies for burial. After telling Rosebud where they were going, Jethro left with Little Bow to walk the hills in search of Jumps Ahead.

When they were out a good distance, Jethro began to wonder about Little Bow. He was acting strangely. Finally, Jethro asked him what Jumps Ahead had actually said to him.

"I think he told me . . . he had to run," Little Bow stuttered. "I can't remember for sure."

Jethro thought for a moment. "Did you see Jumps Ahead when you were running from the village, before the flood hit?"

Little Bow ignored the question. "I know he went out here to escape," he said. "I wonder where he is. We have to find him. We *have* to."

Jethro wanted to believe that Jumps Ahead had actually said something to Little Bow during the flight from the village. But now he began to suspect that Little Bow had only hoped that his friend might be somewhere in the hills, wandering lost. More likely, Jumps Ahead had not survived the flood and Little Bow had known it all along. He just did not want to face the reality.

"We had better go back to the others," Jethro said.

"No!" Little Bow protested. "I want to find Jumps Ahead first. I promised him I would look for him."

"What if he's back with the people?" Jethro asked. "He would want you there with him, wouldn't he?"

"I believe he is up here," Little Bow argued.

"If we don't find him with the others, we'll come back. How does that sound?"

Little Bow finally agreed. They walked back in silence, but Jethro could hear Little Bow, behind him, stifling sobs.

By the time they reached the hill above the village, many decisions regarding the camp had already been made. Rosebud took Little Bow in her arms as Jethro's parents greeted him.

"Scouts went upriver and returned," Morning Swan told Jethro. "They say there's more ice and that the mountains are filled with rain. The river is rising again. We won't be staying here."

His father told him that the surviving elders had held council and decided that the people would take their dead and journey on toward the Stillwater. Scouts had found a plateau big enough to hold all of the remaining lodge until the rains ceased.

With the rain falling strongly, they started their journey once again. Many turned for a last look as they left the ruined village behind. A number of the dead were still trapped under blocks of ice. The people would return for their bodies when the weather had warmed enough for melting.

They reached the high flat downriver, and the women began erecting lodges while the men gathered to hunt for whatever game they could find. Jethro climbed on his horse and was preparing to join them when Rosebud rushed up to him and grabbed the reins.

"Where is Little Bow?" she asked frantically. "I thought he was riding with you."

Stunned, Jethro shook his head. "No, I haven't seen him since we left."

Rosebud fell to her knees. "Oh, no! Where is he? What has happened to him?"

Jethro looked back upriver and quickly turned his horse. In a few moments he had kicked the pony into a dead run.

Little Bow finally reached the ruined remains of the village. Coyotes and a few wolves scattered at his arrival. The magpies and ravens remained, searching for flesh to feed upon. Little Bow ignored them and sat down on the hillside, breathing heavily to regain his strength. He knew that he had little time in which to find Jumps Ahead; Jethro would be looking for him.

He realized, too, that the additional rainfall meant danger. He must find his best friend before more flooding occurred. Little Bow rose and ran down the hill, back into the village. He looked through piles of debris and found the body of a small baby missed in the search. Then he came to a stop near a huge cake of ice.

A magpie feather was floating in a small pool of water just beside the ice. He lifted the feather, placed it inside his waistband and stepped forward, his mind on Jumps Ahead. Then he saw the mud-stained hand and arm sticking out from under the ice. He fell to his knees and gripped the cold fingers. He began to pull on the arm with all of his strength, struggling against the impossible as hot tears streamed down his face. Then he pushed against the ice with one hand while he pulled the limp arm with the other, but he could budge neither one.

Sobbing, he turned to digging. Blinded by tears, he clawed frantically, screaming Jumps Ahead's name over and over, scratching at the mud until his fingers ached. He did not hear Jethro approach and jump down to tie and hobble his pony, calling for Little Bow to get out of the bottom. He did not see Jethro scramble down the hill toward him, slipping and sliding as fast-as he could come. Nor did he hear the pounding cascade of water, surging down once again toward the ruined village.

Little Bow was still digging when Jethro's powerful hands took him under both arms and swept him up. He kicked and sobbed, yelling, "I want to save Jumps Ahead!"

"It's too late for him," Jethro said, struggling to keep his balance in the mud. "If we don't get out of here, we'll die, too."

Just upriver the crashing sound hammered down, the deafening roar almost upon them. Jethro knew that he would never be able to carry Little Bow up the hill before the flood reached them. Their only hope was large cottonwood a short distance away along the bank.

From among the trees on a hill on the opposite side of the river, three riders watched, dim and ghostlike in the fog and rain. The three bloods had been there since Little Bow had first returned to the ruined village. They had contemplated taking him, so that he might grow up a warrior among their own people. But they could no longer cross the river and get the boy, or try to kill the Crow warrior now helping him.

Convinced that the boy and the warrior would soon be lost in the raging waters, the riders left. They would take the news of the devastated Crow village back to their people and return as members of a strong war party.

The water rushed ever closer as Jethro struggled toward the cottonwoods carrying the limp and sobbing Little Bow, who seemed no longer to care about his own life. Although Jethro's vision was clear, his other senses seemed dimmed by the tremendous fury of the river behind him. He summoned more strength, running as fast as he could, fighting through tangles of debris. To stop to try to make Little Bow run on his own would cost them precious time, and likely their lives.

Finally at the base of the tree, Jethro pushed Little Bow into the lower branches and slapped him hard on the upper leg.

"Pull yourself up! Hurry!"

Little Bow pulled himself up one branch and stopped, still sobbing. The rush of water reached the edge of the village, dislodging much of the debris already settled from the first flood. Now ice and water pounded against the tree as Jethro scrambled to get himself up out of the way of death. An ice-cold blast of spray drenched him and he yelled, scaring Little Bow into a frantic ascent.

The water crested just under their feet as they reached a large limb halfway up the tree. The two of them, nestled together, held fast to the breast of the cottonwood, while just below, waves of ice and water plunged past, carrying lodges and bodies once buried under ice. The new flow appeared to be worse than the first, comprised mainly of water this time. The waves surged furiously, sweeping large trees in their wake, as well as many animal carcasses. Deer and elk and buffalo slammed up against the trunk of the cottonwood, their bodies occasionally catching for a while before being wrenched away to continue with the angry flow. Most of the dead animals, Jethro knew, would have been weakened by the hard winter, unable to muster enough strength to escape the flood.

The roiling flow continued. Jethro and Little Bow held on, their arms and legs aching. Finally, well after dark, the floodwaters receded. The clouds parted and a dark sky filled with the glow of a full moon. Jethro lowered himself slowly and helped Little Bow down. Neither could walk for a time, but sat in the mud at the base of the cottonwood rubbing cramps from sore muscles.

"We have passed the test," Jethro told Little Bow. "Together, we have passed the river's fury. We have both received much strength from this."

Little Bow allowed a smile to cross his puffy face. He rubbed the last tear from a swollen eyelid and stood up. "Now you will have to go to the Little Belt Mountains, won't you?" he asked Jethro. "You are ready to find the eyes for your raven."

Jethro rose and took Little Bow by the hand. "I will find just the right stones to put into the raven's eyes. Then I will find the Sacred Pipe, and the river will forgive me for having lost it."

Jethro and Little Bow started for the slope above the village. When they reached the top of the hill, they saw that Jethro's horse had pulled loose from the tree, but they soon found the pony grazing peacefully in a nearby meadow. Jethro jumped on its back and helped Little Bow up behind him.

"We will hurry and join the others," Jethro said. "They will be worried about us."

Little Bow pulled the magpie's feather from his

waistband, studied it, and placed it against his heart. He took a deep breath and looked up into the starlit sky. Then he took a last look down into the shadowed bottom and whispered, "Goodbye, my good friend."

TWENTY-TWO

MANY BERRIES SAT ON A HILL NEAR THE WAR
lodge she had found. For the first time
in many days, the sky had turned a
deep blue and the birds were chasing one another through the trees. Her gaze swept across
the rolling foothills below, along dark green
sweeps of timber, to the summit of the Little Belt
Mountains. The rains had melted all but the snow
at the very top.

For a time it had seemed as if the storm would
never end. Many Berries had dismantled two ad-
jacent war lodges, each constructed of small aspen trees formed into a tepee cone, to fortify the
lodge she had selected. Then she had caked the
cracks evenly with clay mud, sealing off the inside from the continuous downpour. She had
gathered three deerskins from the lodges she

would not use, and an old elkskin for use as a door flap. Then she had watched the changing winds bring the new season, remaining inside her lodge next to a fire while the streams running down from the high country swelled with water and burst over their banks.

She had been living in the war lodge since escaping Big Owl in the snow. Although it had now been just over two moons, it seemed to her a lifetime that had come and gone. She had made the meat from the bull last a long time, supplementing it with rabbits she caught in a snare. But the buffalo meat had finally been eaten and the rabbits had been few, and she had had to kill the horse. When the weather had finally broken, she had found the old stalks of plants she knew near the creek and had dug under them to pull up their roots.

But in the cold, the food had never been quite enough. She had allotted herself so much a day and had always been hungry. At times she had been forced to suck on the bark of young willows to soothe her enough that she could go to sleep. Although she had thought many times that the place she occupied might not be the best for catching small game in snares, she had never considered moving to a new location; the war lodges sat deep in a secluded draw. Now that the rains were past, she built small fires only at night, and she felt that no one would find her here. Moving would necessarily leave tracks. If Big Owl were out prowling, he might find them and chase her down.

In the beginning, the nights had filled her with

terror. She saw jugs of strong drink bursting, and fire belching out into her face. She saw a huge club, lined with three sharp knives, that she had to keep from entering her stomach. Every night for nearly an entire moon she had awakened screaming, looking for someplace to run to.

Finally, her dreams of Big Owl and Burned Face had subsided, and she had been able to rest better. Her fear of Big Owl's finding her lessened each day, for she realized that if he had not yet located her hideout, he likely would not do so now. She had purposely selected a draw far up from and well off of the main trials. He had no idea of where she had gone, and in such a vast country, he could look forever and never find her.

Since escaping Big Owl, many things had changed for Many Berries, including her outlook on life. Being alone had made her stronger. It had made her face herself and learn who she really was, not who she thought she might be. She had learned things about her true self: how she had thought of others, and how she had lived her life up to now. She swore to herself and to the Powers that if she managed to escape Big Owl for good and have the baby, her life would be different.

Sitting alone on hillsides had taught her about true power. When the weather had begun to change and the warm winds had increased, she had sought out high places from which she could see the country. Invariably, her gaze would shift to the north, where she could see the chain of mountains called the High Woods and a large butte that stood out by itself from a smaller, round butte.

This high butte had always been sacred to her people, a place of visions and power. She knew that she must go up on that butte once her child came into the world. She would know exactly when the time was right, and she would journey there. For whatever reason, the Powers wished that of her. She would obey, for it had been the Powers who had sustained her life after she had left Big Owl. She had decided to dedicate the remainder of her life to following the Powers.

Many Berries now realized that her strength came from within, from opening herself to the Powers and trusting her pathway. She saw that true strength did not come from a warrior whom she thought brave and strong, someone whose attentions would prove her worth to others. When she learned to care about and believe in herself, she would have no reason to wonder whether others thought well of her. It would not matter, for her feelings would be her own, and they would be true.

She saw, too, that the women who received the best treatment were not always the women who demanded it. Those wise enough to accept who they were and to heed their obligations to those around them, especially to their husbands, drew good things their way. These women were the ones given the most freedom by their husbands. Without asking for it, they received the most respect. These things came to them because they cared about others.

During her first few nights in the lodge, Many

Berries had also learned that the face of death could show itself at any time. And that was not a bad thing. Every creature lived for a purpose, and then died with a purpose as well, although only the Powers could know what that purpose was.

Many Berries came to realize that death could occur in the mind as well as in the body, and that an awakening could come about if a person became willing to accept the Great Mystery and the process of life. Her fear of life itself had been broken.

In the cold time, curious wolves had prowled around the lodge at night, sniffing for food. Often the braver ones would stick their heads through the door opening, past the old elkskin, and stare at her with their piercing yellow eyes. She had wondered why the pack did not close in on her and tear her to shreds. The wolves had certainly been hungry enough, roaming around the area with tongues hanging out and ribs showing through their shaggy coats. Then when they had returned late one afternoon with sections from a moose they had killed just upstream, she had realized that they had never intended to make her their prey.

In fact, Many Berries believed they had wanted to share the kill with her, for they had left part of a foreleg near the lodge. All of them had stood in a circle, watching her closely. When she had not approached the leg, the biggest male had come and dragged it away.

Her most severe test had come on the morning she startled a large male grizzly bear at her water hole. Thinking about other things, she had happened over the rise and sat down when the huge bear rose to its hind legs. Her nostrils had flared with the strong musky odor, like old sodden blankets steeped in rancid lard. The bear had come up the hill toward her and she had prepared to die, singing her death song. The huge grizzly, close enough to touch, had merely sniffed her and ambled past into the forest.

That night her dreams had been of snow, and of an old woman wrapped in deerskins, of watching horses file past endlessly. She had awakened with no doubt in her mind that she would not meet death until she had seen many winters. The certainty troubled her, for this meant that she would see great changes and suffer much. But she now knew that she could withstand anything that came to her.

As she watched the sun rise and set, and the fires of the Lost Ones sparkle in the far distant night, she realized that she had no reason to fear death until it called for her. She had already felt it and had already tasted it, and smelled it up close. Yet it had not claimed her.

Many Berries could hardly count the number of times she should have crossed over. She should have died in the cold during her escape, but she had not. She could easily have died from starvation, but she had always found food. Once she had found a large bag of pemmican buried at a stream crossing, placed there by some war party to eat when it was needed.

The pemmican had come at a time when all of the roots had been dug out and no more could be found. All of the rabbits had been caught and she could catch no more. Although elk and deer passed close, there had been no way to take their lives. After many days of weakness and anger, she had finally given up her hunt for any kind of food. She would never have found the pemmican had she not been at peace with the fact that she would starve to death. She had gone to say good-bye to a clan of beaver living in the creek just down from her. She had intended to tell them that she would cross over soon and not visit them again. It was when she sat down to talk to them that she had noticed the parfleche protruding from the bank; the waters had washed just enough of the soil away.

Now her thoughts were on her child. She knew that one of the reasons she had been saved was to give birth. It would not be easy to deliver the baby alone. She had no relatives to turn to anymore, and she did not want to go among the Crow. After what had happened, they would likely kill her and think nothing of it.

This morning, looking at the drenched countryside, she decided to explore an area where she had yet to go. A small stream ran down from a hillside just behind the lodge, then wound back up into the high country. Now that the snow had been melted by the rain, it would be interesting to see what that country looked like.

Many Berries began her journey with a smile. Something told her that the day held a special surprise. The early wild flowers were coming in profusion. Everywhere the small yellow bells poked up from the wet ground, often visible

along the edges of dying snowbanks. And there
were many of the purple open-throats, the cro-
cus, that always popped up among old stalks of
grass when the snows first departed. Brilliant
pink shooting stars burst across the land, covering hills and draws with their beauty.

Farther up the trail, Many Berries thought that
the sun might be playing tricks on her. What kind
of flowers were those not far ahead? Along the
hillside, where the run-off waters had opened a
deep cut in the soil, the ground shimmered a
sparkling blue. She blinked and stared, but the
twinkling continued.

Many Berries eased up the trail to the cut and
with her mouth agape, reached down and picked
up a handful of precious stones. "They are the
sky stones that the Grandmothers talk of," she
said to herself. "I have found the place of the sky
stones."

She sat down among the stones and scooped
them up by the hundreds, letting them fall
through her fingers. She sorted the largest and
most beautiful to keep. Once back in the lodge,
she would place them near the door, where the
morning sun would shine on them.

"I knew this day would be special," she said.
"And now the stones will bring me good fortune."

Jethro hurried Whistler along the main trail that
skirted the bluffs above the river. He had been
traveling since early morning and was nearing
the old campsite, by the Grey Cliffs, where the
flood had destroyed the village. There he would

cross the Yellowstone and turn north, to ride along the east slopes of the Crazy Mountains, the place of his vision quest. Straight north of the Crazies were the Little Belt Mountains, the site of the sky stones. More medicine would come to him there.

The pony seemed as anxious as Jethro to reach the mountains and then return home. After considering it for a long time, Jethro had decided not to search for Big Owl and the Sacred Pipe right away. He would wait until after the spring buffalo hunt. Because the village had lost many lodges and its food supplies in the flood, the hunt was more important than ever. He hoped that once the stones were in the eyes of the raven, his fortune and that of his people would change.

Since the flood, the Kicked-in-Their-Bellies had made several changes. Their village had broken apart for a while. Jethro and his family, with less than half of the Kicked-in-Their-Bellies, now made their camp on the lower Stillwater, while two other groups had moved downriver, one to live with the Sore Lips and one to live with the Whistling Water clan. For many families, much of the upcoming warm season would be devoted to making clothes, weapons, and utensils. Those who joined relatives among other clans could more readily get a fresh start.

For Jethro and Cuts Buffalo and those in their group, the Stillwater had so far been very good. The area had many deer and a large elk herd, and the animals were easy prey. Although the grass had greened considerably, and willow and aspen buds popped out everywhere, the elk and deer were dazed and weak, little more than skeletons with ragged coats of hair stumbling among the blooming wild flowers. The winter range had not provided sufficient forage for them. Jethro found it strange that so many, both among his people and among the animals, had been doomed to death since the first winter storms.

Although the dying deer and elk provided a temporary food supply, their hides were not good enough for lodges. It would be necessary to kill many healthy buffalo in order to make new homes for the victims of the floodwaters. The time would be right when the small fox-tailed grass opened up to make seed, and when the herd had reached prime condition. The buffalos' thick but supple hides could replace the lodges lost in the flood.

As he neared the Grey Cliffs, Jethro noticed that the flow in the Yellowstone was now little more than that of a large mountain stream. The odor in the air told him that just ahead the river was dammed with dead buffalo. He rode higher along the trail, above the bottom, and could see that in the distance a wall of rotting brown carcasses stemmed the flow of water.

It was not an uncommon sight at this time of the year. A large part of a buffalo herd had drowned upriver early in the cold season. The animals had remained locked under ice and snow until the thawing spring winds had released them to wash down with the floodwaters. They were piled high and thick as far upriver as Jethro's eye could see. It would take a great number of predators, and time for decay, as well as the early summer rise of water from snow melt, to gradually wear away the wall of rotting buffalo.

Jethro crossed the shallow river below the wall of carcasses. He noticed Whistler's nose flaring and hurried the pony up and out of the bottom to a nearby slope. Although the stench of death floated thick on the wind, with it came the unmistakable musk of bear.

Whistler pranced nervously as Jethro stopped to view the congregation of grizzlies along one length of the drowned buffalo. The humped brown and yellowish giants were growling and swatting one another with huge paws, setting their territorial rights among the dead. He saw more bears than the count of fingers and toes on three men, and he knew that their numbers would increase as the days passed.

All of the people were aware that anyone who approached a grizzly feeding ground could easily find himself under attack. There were many stories told of how the great bears protected their food supplies with unmatched ferocity. Even though Jethro's father possessed the medicine of the grizzly, under no circumstances would he ever approach one of the bears when it was eating.

Jethro turned the horse up the trail, leaving the bears and the river behind. He would ride along the foothills below the Crazy Mountains, then cross the Musselshell to reach the slopes of the Little Belt Mountains, home of the sky stones. All of the tribes in the area knew of the stones, but few had traveled to see them. The place where the stones sparkled in the ground was sacred and could be visited only by those having a good reason.

Jethro's mother had heard of the place, as had the other women among the Kicked-in-Their-Bellies, but only Calling Bird had ever been there. After she had been taken by the Piegans in the same raid as Morning Swan, she had managed to escape her captors and had wandered through the Little Belts on her way back to the Crow people.

She had crossed a narrow bottom where the Lost Waters flowed and had climbed a steep trail to reach the top. Along the way she had found a hill covered with the sky stones. A thunderstorm had just passed over, and the stones sparkled in the late-afternoon sun. Calling Bird had gathered a handful of them, marveling at their beauty. She believed that she had found something rare, something that would make her special among the Crow woman. But she had lost all of the stones late the following day while running for cover from a Piegan search party.

Calling Bird had eluded the searchers, but she never found any of the stones she had dropped. Still, she credited the stones with her good fortune in escaping the Piegans, and then later in becoming wife to Bull Comes Ahead. She had realized that Jethro had been chosen for special powers when she learned that his raven must have the blue sky stones for eyes.

When Jethro had been ready to leave, Calling Bird had told him something he would always remember. "Be sure you do not make frivolous wishes over the stones," she had said. "Let them make the power for you that they wish to make."

Now Jethro wondered how difficult it would be to find the place where these stones lay on the ground. He had vowed to himself that he would do what he must to find them. With the stones in the raven's eyes, his shield would hold the powers he had seen in his dreams. He would be guided.

Calling Bird had told him: "The sky stones show themselves only to those who really need their powers. And their powers are very unusual."

Jethro wondered if he would be able to handle these unusual powers; for with the sky stones in the raven's eyes, he knew that his power would be strong but his tests would be greater than ever before.

In the Blood village, the talk was of war. Three scouts sent out to find buffalo had returned waving their arms in excitement, bearing news that to the south the rains had caused flooding and a sudden ice breakup along the Yellowstone. The Kicked-in-Their-Bellies had sustained many losses among their people and a great number had been left homeless. The scouts believed that the Kicked-in-Their-Bellies were helpless against enemy attack.

Big Owl had listened with elation. This would be his chance to prove his powers as a warrior. He secured the last wrap of rawhide around his newly made war club and held up the weapon to examine it. This club would bring him many honors.

Three sharp knife blades protruded from the remains of the rifle stock Many Berries had broken over the trader's head. Big Owl had carved holes for the knives, three in a row, near the section where the trigger guard had fit. On the lower section that had once supported the barrel, he had carved out a grip, so that his hand fit nicely around the base of the club.

He had painted the club with red, black, and yellow stripes, three of each, which angled around the stock until the lines of color came together where the knife blades protruded. Grinning, Big Owl stood up and swung the weapon, making a whooshing sound. No one could survive a direct strike; the blades would sink deep and cut through the bone.

The stock had been a lucky find, good medicine for war. On his way back to the village after searching for Many Berries in the cold, he had seen the broken wood protruding from the snow. He had known when he saw it that the stock would become his avenging weapon, the war club with which he would kill both Many Berries and Jethro. This day would begin his rise to power among the Bloods. They would journey to the Yellowstone and he would show them what honor he could bring to the Blackfeet people.

Big Owl drank from one of Cutter's jugs. He stumbled over to where a group of warriors had gathered and showed them the weapon, telling of how he planned to use it to chop the hearts out of the Crow people.

"With their Sacred Pipe and this, I will conquer them all. There will not be one of them left!" He laughed and drank again from the jug.

The warriors grumbled and walked away. Despite his repeated attempts to talk his way toward respect, the Bloods still laughed at him about losing Many Berries. "She must have had a good lover somewhere to have left in the face of Cold Maker," one of them had said. "Or maybe that Crow made her feel so good, she wanted to go back to him," another had told him. "You should have asked him what he had that she wanted so badly."

At one time or another, Big Owl had wanted to kill each and every one of them. But he knew that such a deed would only lead to his own death. Nearly two full moons had passed since his search for Many Berries. Although he had done everything possible to erase her memory, nothing had worked, not even long binges with the strong drink, which only left him sick and helpless the next day. Still, he persisted in the drink, unable to see that the bad spirits that flowed from the jug with the bitter liquid had gained full control over him.

Harlan Cutter had managed to bring many of the Bloods under the influence of liquor. For very little outlay, he now had many fine buffalo robes to take to the company. The law against trading whiskey to the Indians was laughable, and certainly it was not enforced. Cutter and his men diluted their whiskey with water to half its strength or less, and added chewing tobacco and red pepper, or sometimes ginger and molasses, to get a drink with a strong bite and just enough alcohol to dull the senses.

The drink quickly brought addiction to the Indian people who drank it. Eventually their craving for it became unbearable, and then it was easy to trade less and less whiskey for even greater numbers of the finest buffalo robes the Bloods had to offer.

Now that the rains had finally quit, the villagers were thinking again about hunting buffalo. They had traded many of their robes away and had barely enough to sleep on and to keep themselves warm. Although small herds remained scattered nearby throughout the year, the larger herds would be migrating back into the area, looking for the strong spring grass of the north. The moisture made everything grow quickly, and even though the winter had been hard and had taken its toll, soon the buffalo would be fat again. Their meat would be tender and their robes fine for taking and trading.

But that would come after raiding the Crow. The war party would leave before nightfall and travel under cover of darkness to locate the remainder of the Kicked-in-Their-Bellies. Each warrior would take two ponies, for they would have to ride without stopping until they reached the village again. If possible, they would capture many Crow horses. But revenge for the raid against the Piegans was foremost. Old angers would be appeased, and those who had lost loved ones at the hands of the Crow would be able to release the fires of their bitterness.

Big Owl could not contain his enthusiasm. He

would be coleader with an honored warrior named Many Horses. He swung his war club and yelled war cries, while warriors located their best war ponies and assembled their battle gear.

"Now you can see that I have done a powerful thing in taking the Sacred Pipe from the Kicked-in-Their-Bellies," Big Owl told the gathering of warriors. "Even the Powers in the river are against the Crow. And if you don't believe me by now, I will soon show you that I was meant to destroy them, one and all."

TWENTY-THREE

LITTLE BOW SAT UP, BREATHING HEAVILY FROM the bad dream. Running Hawk lay next to him but did not stir. Since Jumps Ahead's death in the flood, Little Bow and Running Hawk had become very close. But even Running Hawk would be unable to understand what Little Bow had just experienced.

Little Bow frowned, recalling the dream. He could still see the strange, three-bladed piece of wood chopping its way through the lodges of his people, the ugly face of the horned badger twisted in evil laughter. He could once again see the colored horses running through the dream. But this time Jethro did not have the Sacred Pipe, and his arms were gone.

The images were similar to the dream that had come to him just before Jethro was attacked by the giant twisting spirit. But Jethro had been whole in the first dream, complete with arms and legs, and had carried the Sacred Pipe. This dream differed from the first one in other ways as well. The woman who had been Many Berries in the first dream had now appeared surrounded not in one color as before, but in two colors, as if she were two people. This puzzled Little Bow. How could one person be two? He did not consider that she might be with child.

Toward the end of the dream, he had seen someone very small carrying an object big and long, like a pipe. The small person had held out the object to Jethro, causing Jethro's arms to grow back. This very small person had to be someone with powerful medicine.

Little Bow suddenly understood that the small person was one of the Little People. He knew that the object he had seen was the new pipe made by Bull Comes Ahead. What he could not understand was how the pipe could travel from the village to Jethro, who had gone to find the sky stones. He realized that if the Little People had wanted to take the new pipe to Jethro, he would not have had the dream. It was up to him to take the pipe to Jethro, so that the Little People could send the power through it to make Jethro whole again.

How could he get the pipe from Bull Comes Ahead? It would be very difficult to sneak into the lodge and take it. Little Bow could see no other way, though. The old medicine man would never allow him to take the pipe to Jethro by himself. It did not seem likely that

Bull Comes Ahead would allow the pipe to be taken anywhere by anyone, no matter what Little Bow had seen in a dream. The first Sacred Pipe had been lost; should something happen to the second, the Crow people might vanish forever.

Little Bow saw no choice. He would take the pipe from Bull Comes Ahead's lodge and go before anyone could stop him. He thought about how to sneak it away without awakening either Bull Comes Ahead or Calling Bird. Then a thought struck him. Was the pipe even in the lodge? Bull Comes Ahead often took it with him into the hills to pray when the moon became full. Sometimes he would return without it, leaving it so that the Powers could make the medicine stronger, and go back into the hills for it on the following morning.

The moon was full now. Something told Little Bow to travel through the darkness into the hills where Bull Comes Ahead had gone to pray the evening before. The feeling was so strong that Little Bow had no worry about getting the pipe.

Careful not to awaken Running Hawk, Little Bow crawled out of his sleeping robes and pushed past the door flap. Although the night was warm, he shivered. He stared into the sky, milky white from the full moon. Out from the rays of moonlight, the Night Lights twinkled brightly. The big light in the north twinkled the brightest.

"That is the one I must follow in order to find Jethro," he told himself. "I will locate a good horse and then go into the hills to get the new pipe."

Suddenly Running Hawk emerged from the lodge, wide awake. He groped through the air until he touched Little Bow. "I heard you moaning in your sleep," he whispered. "Why have you come out here? What is the matter?"

"I have seen Jethro and Big Owl in a dream," Little Bow explained. "I have to find Jethro and give him the new pipe."

"The new pipe?"

"I can't tell you about it now. It would take too long. I have to go before Mother awakens."

"You promised her that you would never ride after Jethro again," Running Hawk reminded him. "You will make her sick with worry."

"I can't help it," Little Bow said. "I have to go."

"How can you find him?" Running Hawk asked. "He is gone into the Little Belt Mountains and you have never been there."

"I will follow the main camp fire of the Lost Ones. I will know the mountains when I reach them. I will find him."

"It's too dangerous."

"There is no other way. If I don't take Jethro the new pipe, he might not have the medicine to get the first Sacred Pipe back."

Running Hawk took a deep breath. "I have already lost one close friend."

Rosebud called from within the lodge, "Little Bow? Running Hawk? What are you two doing up? Come back in here."

"I have to go," Little Bow whispered. He gave

Running Hawk a quick hug. "Tell Mother you got up to look for me but I was already gone."

Running Hawk shrugged and Little Bow disappeared into the shadows. He circled the lodges and found one of Thane Thompson's good horses tethered to a stake. He quickly cut the rope. His grandfather would understand. He led the horse from the village, ignoring the sound of his mother's voice calling after him in the darkness. Then he mounted and rode into the hills.

A main deer trail, one used by Bull Comes Ahead and others who went up to pray, twisted through thick timber and came out into a small meadow where a group of rocks stood alone, jagged dark shadows poking up into the night. Little Bow kicked the pony into a trot. Along one side of the rocks, on a flat surface facing the light of the moon, lay the second Sacred Pipe, wrapped in otterskin.

Little Bow reached down from the pony and took the pipe. Holding it against his heart, he turned the pony toward the bright light in the north.

Cuts Buffalo and Calling Bird did what they could to calm Rosebud. Running Hawk had finally confessed: Little Bow had left to try to find Jethro. Morning Swan stood off by herself, looking into the night sky, wondering what fate had in store for the village now.

"Little Bow promised he would never do that again," Rosebud was saying, pacing in fear and frustration. "He promised me."

"Little Bow always awakens with bad dreams

during Jethro's journeys," Cuts Buffalo said. "Maybe some of the warriors can ride out to find him."

The entire camp had awakened. Even as Cuts Buffalo spoke, High Elk petitioned to lead a party of warriors after Little Bow and determine what had pressed the boy into leaving camp in the middle of the night. Bull Comes Ahead excused himself from the circle and walked out into the darkness. While the council debated, High Elk protested that it was wasting valuable time. But the matter of the warriors lost in the winter raid against the Piegans came up repeatedly, and High Elk could offer no guarantee that another disaster would not take place.

The council had essentially decided against High Elk when Bull Comes Ahead reappeared. "Little Bow has left on a sacred mission," he declared. "He has found and taken the second Sacred Pipe. He could not know where it was without having had a special dream."

High Elk turned to the council. "If you do not allow me to take warriors into the north, I will go alone," he said. "I know that it is important that I help Jethro and Little Bow."

Other warriors pressed the council, declaring their intention to go as well. Despite the casualties in the winter raid against the Piegans the majority of the elders turned in favor of High Elk's proposal. High Elk would take twenty warriors and ride north, to the Little Belt Mountains. Hopefully, they would catch Little Bow before arriving there, although Little Bow had a good head start and would no doubt be riding as fast as the pony could take him.

Cuts Buffalo approached High Elk as he prepared his horse for the journey. "Tell Jethro that his child misses him, and that I also miss him. Tell him to do what he must without worry. I have seen the two Sacred Pipes together. All will be well."

"What of Big Owl and Many Berries?" High Elk asked. "What have you seen concerning them?"

"What I have seen is a lot of flowing red," Cuts Buffalo replied. "And black, flowing toward the red. I can only hope that you find Little Bow and Jethro before the colors run together."

The sun broke through the gray dawn, bringing light to a cloudless sky. Jethro rode his pony through a low pass and looked out upon the eastern slopes of the Little Belt Mountains. Calling Bird had told him that once he left the Lost Waters fork of the Judith River, he should journey through the high mountain country until he crossed over into a large basin. There he should look for sparkling dots of blue in draws that extended down from the treeline. Although he could not yet see any sparkles on the ground, he felt that he had reached the right place; the raven on his shield had turned its head up ever so slightly.

Far out, across the wide gap of grassland to the east, rose the mountains of the Big Snows, deep blue in the clear morning. Just beyond them to the north lay an open grassland basin, a fertile land filled with buffalo. Jethro had heard stories of the two white men named Lewis and Clark. It was they who had named the main river Judith. But most of the stories told about this place had been of war.

The area had been fought over for as long as the Crow people could remember; it was contested ground, fiercely defended by the Blackfeet as their hunting grounds. Still, all of the northern tribes ventured here to hunt, for the herds migrated into these grasslands, the best that could be found anywhere.

As his gaze swept around to the north, Jethro felt a surge of power run through the entire length of his body. Far across the open basin there ran an isolated chain of mountains. On the east end of the chain there rose a small, round butte and a larger, square-topped butte that stood apart on its own. Jethro's eyes widened. This could only be the place called the High Woods, with the large butte of his dream, where he had seen Big Owl raise the Sacred Pipe to the sky.

He considered going directly to the large butte and ascending it. But that could come after he found the sky stones. The raven needed eyes. With the full power of his medicine shield, he would then meet Big Owl and take back the Sacred Pipe.

Jethro eased Whistler through the pass. On a hill above him stood a lone bighorn sheep, a large ram, with horns curled fully one and half times. Jethro smiled. A good sign. His main spirit helper had come to help him on his journey.

Then his eyes caught movement in a draw along a stream across the way. All thoughts of the dream and the butte left him. A woman seemed to be digging roots from the streambank. He watched; she was alone. She moved up and down the creek, among willows and small trees, disappearing from sight and then emerging again.

Jethro studied the surrounding country for some time before he rode across the upper draws, keeping to the timber and brush. He reached a little stream, tied the pony to a willow, and crept carefully downstream. When he was close enough to get a good look at the woman, his mouth dropped open. Many Berries dug roots along the bank not far from him, and she was heavy with child.

He moved closer, careful not to disturb two deer that watched Many Berries for a short time before loping off, wagging their white tails like flags. Confused feelings overwhelmed him. Could the child possibly be his? If so, what could he do for Many Berries? He could not think of repeating the turmoil he had caused the people before. But without Big Owl, things might be different.

Jethro tossed a stone into the stream near Many Berries and watched her start with surprise. "Who is there?" she asked, her voice urgent.

Jethro stepped out of the brush. "What are you doing up here all by yourself?"

Many Berries stared at him. "Jethro? What are *you* doing here?"

He held up his shield. "I have come to finish my medicine."

Many Berries averted her eyes from the shield. She wanted nothing to do with Jethro's medicine, especially after she and Big Owl had betrayed him.

Jethro crossed the creek. Many Berries stood holding a rabbit-skin bag filled with roots, her other hand resting on her stomach.

"It will not be long until your child is born," she said.

"I've been wondering. You are certain it is my child?"

"Surely you remember the day at the spring."

"Yes."

"And you remember that I told you about Big Owl. He has not been able to be a man since he fell under his horse."

"I thought you were telling me that only so I would lie with you."

"I told you that because it was true. And what I just said is also true. This child is yours."

Jethro stepped toward Many Berries. She took his hand and placed it on her stomach. "Are you happy?" she asked.

"I am always happy about new life," he said. "Especially if it is life I have helped to create."

"This is the first time for you, isn't it?"

"Yes, it is. But it is not the only life I have created. Cuts Buffalo is also with child."

Many Berries showed no surprise. A thin smile crossed her lips. "She is now your wife?"

"Yes."

"Cuts Buffalo is a persistent one. She wanted you very much, and now she has you."

"How did you get here?" Jethro asked, his curiosity making him change the subject.

Many Berries told him of her escape from Big Owl and the Bloods, and of the winter in the war lodge. She told him everything, including the way Big Owl had set fire to the grass outside the village and had taken the Sacred Pipe. She told him about Harlan Cutter's continued influence over Big Owl and how they had been forced to leave the Piegans after the fight in which Big Owl had killed Red Calf.

"Big Owl has become attached to the strong drink of the Long Knives," Many Berries said. "The one called Burned Face has given him much of this drink. Now Big Owl stays with the whites who want the robes and trade the strong drink. They are all filled with bad spirits."

"Are Burned Face and Big Owl still with the Bloods?" Jethro asked.

"As far as I know. They spent the cold season talking of war against your people. Now that it is warm they should be getting ready for a raiding party very soon. They might have already started for the Yellowstone."

This possibility had been in the back of Jethro's mind ever since the flooding. Now that the snow had melted, there would be time for war before the spring hunt. And after the joint raid with the Flatheads in the past winter, the chances were good that the Blackfeet people would be looking for revenge.

Jethro told Many Berries about the raiding party against the Piegans in which the Kicked-in-Their-Bellies had lost a number of fine young men, including one of Cuts Buffalo's twin brothers. The fight had cost both sides dearly. It shocked her to hear that Rising Hawk had been killed in the raid, as well as a number of Piegans.

"One day we will wish that we hadn't killed one another off," she told Jethro. "There will come a time when we will be fighting the white man for our lands. Then we will wish we had mended the old wounds between us and joined together."

"I believe you are right," Jethro agreed. "Bull Comes Ahead has said that often, and I believe it to be true. I do not want war any longer, either. But now I must go against my feelings, just until I get the Sacred Pipe back from Big Owl. Our people are suffering greatly, and I have vowed to make the Kicked-in-Their-Bellies whole and strong again."

"After you get the Sacred Pipe back, if you do, there will be other reasons for fighting," Many Berries said. "Do you expect there to be peace after all that has happened?"

"You are a fine one to talk," Jethro said. "You left with Big Owl. You have caused as many hard feelings as he has."

"What about High Elk and your warriors, along with the Flatheads?" she asked quickly. "Don't you think they caused more war?"

"High Elk wanted to find the Sacred Pipe,"

Jethro said. "We all thought that you and Big Owl would be among the Small Robes."

"Why didn't you go with the other warriors?" Many Berries asked.

"My medicine is not yet complete," Jethro explained. He pointed to the raven on his medicine shield. "I must fit eyes into the bird in order to make my power whole. I feel bad that I didn't do this before. Maybe my people would not have suffered so greatly."

Then Jethro told Many Berries about the devastating flood that had destroyed the village and taken many lives. The event had greatly changed the Kicked-in-Their-Bellies, he said, making them wonder about their chances of survival. And, he went on, he could see no way that Many Berries and her baby could survive alone in these mountains.

"What do you intend to do?" he asked her. "You must have some plan."

Many Berries shrugged. "I will live day-to-day with my child."

"If you wished to return with me," Jethro told her, "you could be certain of having the child without worry of harm. Our people are now in need of more women and children."

Many Berries' eyes brightened. "Are you saying that we could raise the child together?"

"No. But you could live with my people anyway. Sooner or later a warrior would take you as his wife."

"No," Many Berries said, "I will not do that. Your people would not stand for it, especially after what has happened."

"But you are with child," Jethro said. "No one would harm you. Big Owl is no longer a part of your life. You could start over with my people."

"I do not wish to live in the same village as you and be separated from you," Many Berries said forcefully. "Can't you understand that?"

"You made your choice," Jethro told her. "Had you not decided to leave with Big Owl, we might have lived as man and wife."

"You would have chosen Cuts Buffalo anyway."

"No, I don't believe I would have," Jethro said. "I loved you from the first day, but you chose to think only of power. I still have feelings for you, especially since you are carrying my child. But now I realize what a special woman Cuts Buffalo is, and I feel very deeply for her. Although I thought I wanted to marry you before, things between you and me could never be the same now."

Many Berries looked away. "I will find a way to live and take care of my child," she said. "You need not worry about me."

"I am going to take you back with me," Jethro insisted. "You can't live alone out here. What would happen if Big Owl found you? He would kill you for certain. And he would kill the child, too. You must come with me."

"You can't make me return with you," Many Berries told him. "I would only find a way to escape from you, as I did from Big Owl."

"You would take chances with yourself and the child?" Jethro asked. "Just because we could not be together, you would stay away and risk death?"

"Yes, that is how I feel. No matter what comes to me, no matter how bad it is, there could be no torture like living near you but without you."

"I don't understand," Jethro said. "You made the choice."

"I made a bad mistake," she told him. "Or maybe I was blinded by power. But the Powers have separated us, and that can never change.

TWENTY-FOUR

MANY BERRIES COVERED HER FACE. TEARS
streamed through her fingers. Jethro
turned from her and walked up the
slope a short way. He sat down and stared into
the distance. The sun shone from directly above
and the air was warm and peaceful. A pair of
golden eagles circled over a high cliff of rocks
nearby.

"You have to understand," she told Jethro,
"that I do not want to go back to your people
and live separately from you. I could never be in
the same village as you and be married to another man. I will make a life for myself and my
child somehow. But not with your people."

"You are right," Jethro said. "It would not be
good if you lived with my people. But who will
you live with?"

"The Powers will direct me," she replied. "I have faith that my pathway will be made clear to me."

"Then I will go," Jethro said, rising. He descended the slope and stopped in front of Many Berries. "First I must find the sky stones to put into the raven's eyes. Then I will be gone."

Many Berries viewed the shield and shuddered. The medicine frightened her. It seemed as if the raven had turned its head to look at her through eyeless sockets.

"What is bothering you?" Jethro asked.

"The bird is speaking to me," Many Berries said, staring at the shield.

"I can't hear it," Jethro said.

"Of course you can't!" Many Berries said. She turned away and started up the draw. "You must come with me."

"What for?" Jethro asked.

"If you will follow me," Many Berries said, "I will show you something."

Jethro climbed the draw along the creek behind Many Berries. He waited outside her lodge until she came out with a handful of dark blue stones.

"Pick from among there," she told him.

"I cannot take those," Jethro said. "I must find them myself."

"No," Many Berries stared at the shield again. "The raven asks that I give you the sacred stones. In saving Big Owl's life that day, you surely saved mine as well. Let this be my gift to you. It is fitting that you pick the sky stones you want."

Jethro took a handful of the stones and studied them. They felt powerful, and two of the larger ones seemed to be calling for him to select them.

"I will accept your offer with gratitude," Jethro said, picking out the two stones. "I am sure that my shield will now have the strong medicine of my dreams."

Jethro ascended the hill behind the lodge and turned to the north, looking across the open grasslands to the large butte at the edge of the High Woods. He voiced prayers as he secured the stones in the raven's eye sockets. He set the shield upright against a rock and continued to pray, calling upon the Powers and thanking them for his good fortune. Many Berries had found just the right stones; Many Berries, the woman who would bear his first child.

Jethro reached to pick up the shield but quickly drew his hand back. At first he thought it might be the wind that had lifted the feathers of the raven. But no wind blew; there was not even a slight breeze. Jethro turned quickly and looked across the slopes of jagged green pine to see a Blackfeet war party, the warriors riding in single file, coming up along the Judith River. Cutter rode Night Runner, his traders behind him. Big Owl rode Flame, next to another warrior at the head of the column.

Jethro picked up the shield and hurried down the hill to Many Berries. He pointed north. "Big Owl and the Bloods are crossing into the mountains. They will be upon us before the sun falls. I will bring the pony."

"I cannot go anywhere on horseback," she told him. "It is almost my time."

"You can't stay here," Jethro said. "You have been living on a war trail. Big Owl and the Bloods will surely come this way."

Many Berries realized that she must take Jethro's advice or die. She entered her lodge and quickly took up her collection of sky stones and a small bag of pemmican. She rustled among her things and found a forked digging stick. The only good thing about leaving was that some of the roots for childbearing grew down on the lower slopes.

When she came out of the lodge, Jethro stood holding the pony's reins. "I will walk with you," he said.

"You will not," Many Berries insisted. "You must hurry back to your people and warn them. You have little time."

"I can't leave you here," Jethro protested.

"I know where I must go, and you know where you must go," Many Berries insisted. She pointed to the north. "My place now is on the big butte. I know you understand that the Powers live there. Now, let me go. Do what you must to save your people."

Many Berries did not tell Jethro that she had once told Big Owl that she wished to take her firstborn child upon the butte, so that the Powers might bless the infant. If Big Owl wished to find her, he would certainly go there. She could only hope hat he remained intent on gaining war honors and would stay with the Bloods to fight. That would give her enough time to have her child and ascend the butte.

"You are certain you will not let me help you?" Jethro asked.

"Go!" Many Berries shouted. "If we are to see one another again, it will come to pass. If not, the Powers have willed it that way."

"I can see that you are just as stubborn as ever," Jethro said, climbing onto the pony. "After you leave the big butte, where will you go? You have no people to live with, and no food."

"You must stop worrying about me and start back to the Yellowstone," Many Berries said. She pointed. "Take the trail that breaks to the west. It will lead you into the Lost Waters more quickly, and slow down the war party. If Big Owl and the others catch you, your people will have no chance for survival.

Jethro turned the pony around and started up a draw that would take him across into the deep canyon, through the heart of the Little Belts. He had to beat the war party to the Stillwater. Leading them down the steep slope into the Lost Waters would certainly delay them.

At the top of the ridge, Jethro stopped Whistler and turned to wave good-bye. But when he looked back, Many Berries had disappeared.

He took the west fork in the trail, which finally led him to the top of a long, timbered ridge above the Lost Waters. From far across the canyon, on a bare knoll, a bighorn ram stared at him. The ram remained there for but a moment before it disappeared into the timber.

Jethro rode a short way into the canyon and then dismounted. The steep trail was hard for one person to travel; an entire war party would be slowed a great deal.

Close to the bottom of the canyon, he remounted. He thought of the bighorn ram, knowing that he must cross the bottom and ascend to the knob. He had to be waiting there before Big Owl and the war party reached the top of the steep trail.

Jethro kicked Whistler into a gallop across the narrow, marshy ground. Just before he reached the other side, a rider appeared at the edge of the timber. It was Little Bow, holding up the second Sacred Pipe.

"What are you doing here?" Jethro asked.

Little Bow held out the pipe. "I had a dream. I was told to bring this pipe to you."

"But only Bull Comes Ahead is to touch this pipe."

"I was told in the dream to bring it to you," Little Bow said again. "You have to take it, Jethro. To save our people."

Jethro took the pipe, feeling immediate power from the sacred object flow through him.

Little Bow pointed back up the trail. "High Elk has been following me with warriors. He is not far behind, but I could not wait for him. I had to get the pipe to you."

"Big Owl with a Blood war party is not far from here either," Jethro said. "You are in great danger."

"You wouldn't send me back alone, would you?"

"I can't do that," Jethro said. "But you must stay a good distance away when the fighting begins."

Jethro believed that the Powers had directed Little Bow. There could be no other explanation for why the boy had found him at this far place in the mountains, and at this very time. He asked Little Bow about his dream and about how he had found the second Sacred Pipe. Little Bow explained that he knew the Little People had given him the power to find the pipe and to bring it so far, to a place he had never been before.

"That is why I am not afraid of being near the battle," he said. "I do not believe I will be in any danger."

"Do not take anything for granted, Little Bow," Jethro warned. "Young boys who become too certain sometimes do not get the opportunity to become warriors."

High Elk and the Crow warriors descended from the open knob above the marshy bottom and joined Jethro and Little Bow. They marveled at Little Bow and his determined ride. No matter how hard they had tried to catch up, Little Bow had remained just ahead of them.

"It was as if our horses could not go any faster," High Elk said. "I believe that you two were supposed to meet for some purpose before we arrived."

"Yes, that is true," Little Bow said. He pointed

to the second Sacred Pipe, which Jethro held across his heart.

"We will need this medicine soon," Jethro said, pointing up the steep hill. "Big Owl and the Bloods are coming this way. The Long Knife traders are with them."

"Good," High Elk said. "We can wipe out a good many enemies, all at once. We should ride up to meet them."

"No," Jethro said. "We will wait here. They must come down the hill to reach us. They will have a hard time."

High Elk nodded. "I understand," he said, staring at Jethro, who now seemed halfway into a trance. "I can see that the pipe is telling you this."

"The pipe is telling me many things," Jethro said. "We will sound the war drums you have brought. The Bloods will not want to wait until another sun rises to come down the hill after us. When they come, they will learn of the medicine, and they will be sorry."

The sun hovered just over the western mountains as Big Owl fastened a loop of buckskin rope to one pole of Many Berries' lodge. He mumbled in anger as he remounted Flame and kicked the pony into a run. The lodge collapsed and the results of Many Berries' hard work scattered over the ground.

Harlan Cutter, partially drunk, laughed and whooped. His men watched blankly, their rifles balanced across the pommels of their saddles. Grasping his war club tightly, Big Owl jumped from Flame and began hacking at the fallen lodge's remains. He chopped until he was spent, then knelt on one knee to catch his breath.

Tall Horse, coleader with Big Owl, looked on with the others. "Get on your horse," he told Big Owl. "We came to destroy many more lodges than just this one."

Big Owl pointed up the hill. "There are fresh moccasin tracks going into the next drainage. Many Berries must have seen us coming. I want to find her and kill her."

"What about these pony tracks?" one of the warriors asked. "Someone else has been here, also. The two did not leave together."

"I don't care about the pony or who was riding it," Big Owl said. "I want Many Berries."

"You decide what you want to do on your own," Tall Horse told him. "There are many Crows who are ready to die. We came to get them, not Many Berries. If you want to prove yourself against one lone woman, you stay behind and do it without the benefit of gaining honors." He turned his horse.

Big Owl watched the others fall in line. Cutter and his men waited for Big Owl. Finally, Cutter spoke. "Why ain't you getting on your horse? Now's your chance to show that pipe medicine you've been bragging about all the time."

Big Owl looked in the direction of the moccasin tracks. "That woman made a fool of me. I don't intend to let her live."

"I'd like to get hold of her myself," Cutter said. "She killed one of my men. But I ain't that worried about her right now. I want Thane Thompson and his half-breed son, if they're still alive after that flood. Those two will die before I come back looking for Many Berries.

Big Owl realized that Many Berries, now likely heavy with child, could not travel fast. The thought made him all the more eager to hunt her down. It made him decide that he wanted her more than he wanted Jethro.

"It won't take me long to get her," Big Owl said. "Then I'll catch up to you."

"I think you're crazy to worry about her right now," Cutter said. "Besides, she got away from you once. She ain't going to be that easy to track."

"I'll get her," Big Owl slurred. "I'll get her and I'll bring her hair to show you."

"Suit yourself," Cutter said. He kicked Night Runner into a gallop toward the moving war party, and his traders followed.

Big Owl watched Cutter and the others join the Bloods as they rode up the ridge and into the timber. His sole obsession now was with Many Berries. As he rode away, he thought of the things he would do to her. Death would come slow. He would tie her to a tree, and his war club would first cut deep into her middle, so that the child would die within her. He would watch her face. He would enjoy her knowing that the baby would never live, would never grow up to look like its father. Maybe he would not finish Many Berries off right away then. It would be better to let her die over a few days' time. It would be good to see her agony.

The tracks were easy to follow, staying on a main trail leading northwest out of the mountains. He knew now where she was going, remembering that she wanted the medicine atop the high butte for her first child. He felt certain that she believed this butte could save her from him. But nothing could save her from him. He would make camp and rest; then, when the sun came again, he would let her climb to the top, where he would end her days in this world.

Harlan Cutter sat on Night Runner, looking across the steep canyon onto an open knob where Jethro stood with the second Sacred Pipe. From the little valley below the steep slope, came the sound of war drums.

Tall Horse, sitting his pony beside Cutter, frowned at what he saw and heard.

"That's him," Cutter said, pointing across to Jethro. "That's Thompson's son."

"I know who he is," Tall Horse said. "And I don't like what I feel. That man has strong medicine."

"Oh, he can't stop us! By the sound of the drums, there can't be all that many warriors with him."

Tall Horse kept his eyes on Jethro. "On this day, he would not need many warriors. His medicine is very strong. He holds the medicine of his ancestors. I, for one, am not going any farther. I am going back to the village. It is not a good day to die."

"You mean that?" Cutter asked. "We come all

this way and you just up and say we're going back?"

Tall Horse stared into Cutter's eyes. "It would be good if you learned to read the signs, Burned Face. If you don't, the Powers will kill you."

"But not them Crows!" Cutter spat. "I aim to finish what I came for."

The warriors were divided. Tall Horse and those Blood warriors who felt the medicine dwelling in the steep canyon below them turned their ponies around and started back. It did not matter how many warriors sounded drums; something very powerful would be fighting with the Crow this day.

"All you who want Crow hair, get ready to ride down that trail with me," Cutter yelled.

Eight warriors remained with Cutter and his traders. Cutter kicked Night Runner into a lope, over the edge of the ridge and down onto the steep trail. Night Runner began taking strong lurches forward to keep his balance.

Cutter's eyes bulged with fright. He tried to rein Night Runner back, but the pony lurched forward ever faster, pounding down through the dense timber. Cutter, yelling, lost his balance and slid down over Night Runner's neck. He dropped his rifle and clung to the pony's mane with both hands, his legs kicking and searching for support as he started to slide under the horse.

Behind Cutter, the Blood warriors and the traders began shouting. One by one their horses fell, tumbling into one another, kicking and squealing. The traders and three warriors were thrown underneath and trampled. The others jumped from their ponies and scrambled away, yelling that something was attacking their horses. They scattered, screaming and clawing their way through the dense timber, now filled with the shadows of evening.

Cutter came to the bottom, still clutching Night Runner. The horse stopped, breathing heavily, and Cutter fell to the ground. He scrambled to his feet and found himself facing the Crow warriors, sitting on their horses in a semicircle, Jethro in the middle. Jethro got down from Whistler and went straight for the trader.

Cutter turned and ran back into the timber, climbing the steep trail as fast as he could. Jethro ran after him. Cutter, looking back at Jethro as he ran, stumbled over a Blood warrior lying in the trail, his leg broken.

"They tore the hearts out of our horses," the warrior said with wide eyes. "We should not have challenged the medicine."

Cutter realized what had happened. He had heard of the Little People, and now he had seen their power. He scrambled to his feet and angled off the trail, Jethro close behind him. He tried to make his way through the dense timber, but Jethro caught up with him easily.

Cutter turned, his knife drawn, and lunged. Jethro blocked the thrust and held the trader's wrist tightly. The two rolled down the slope until they were stopped by a pile of deadfall timber. Jethro slammed backward into a fallen log, losing his breath, forcing him to release his grip on Cutter's wrist. The trader raised the knife and stabbed down viciously. Jethro managed to dodge as the blade sliced past his cheek and sank deep into the log.

Cutter pried and twisted, but the knife held fast. He cursed and jumped off of Jethro to pick up a large, broken limb. He lifted it as a club just as Jethro came to his feet, his breath finally returning. Cutter began swinging the club, first at Jethro's head, then at his body. Jethro dodged the blows until Cutter's last miss smashed the club to pieces against a tree.

Jethro slammed a fist into Cutter's jaw, sending him reeling backward against the fallen timber. Cutter cursed again and tried to rise. Jethro landed a heavy blow to his ribs and another to his face. The trader slumped down, beaten and breathless.

"Where is Big Owl?" Jethro asked.

"You ain't . . . going to kill me, are you?"

"You're not worth killing. Now, where's Big Owl?"

"He's . . . after the woman," Cutter managed.

"Many Berries?"

Cutter nodded, pushing himself to his knees. "What do you aim to do with me?"

Jethro was not listening; he had turned and started for the bottom. Cutter, now on his feet, shook his head. He worked until he had pulled his knife free of the log, then started down after Jethro.

Jethro turned as Cutter came at him, knife raised. There came the whistling whoosh of an arrow and Cutter stopped abruptly. He dropped his knife, clutched at the shaft driven deep into his chest, and fell forward onto his face.

High Elk, his knife drawn, shouldered past Jethro. "He won't be riding my horse ever again," he said, circling the knife blade deep into Cutter's scalp. The hair came loose with a loud, sucking pop.

"I'm asking again," Jethro said to Cutter, "where is Big Owl?"

Cutter looked up at him with glazed eyes and tried to laugh. "He's likely cut her up by now. Wish I was there."

Then the trader began to jerk violently in the throes of death. Jethro left him there and loped down the trail. At the bottom, the Crow warriors were yelling war cries, holding up scalps and displaying enemy weapons taken on the hill in the last light of evening.

"Those warriors had no chance," Little Bow said to Jethro. "Why did they choose to fight?"

"Some will always choose to go against the signs," Jethro replied. "Now you must go back to the village with High Elk and the others. I will travel to the big butte to find Big Owl and get the first Sacred Pipe back."

Little Bow smiled. "I have no fear for you," he said. "Soon I will see you again, when you have the two Sacred Pipes together."

Jethro rode Whistler up the steep trail, past dead Blood warriors and their fallen horses. There were many stories of the Crow medicine brought by the Little People, and this day would take its place among them.

Jethro rode through the darkness, thinking

of the big butte. He passed the remains of Many Berries' lodge. Had Big Owl already found her and ended her life? He refused to dwell on the thought that Many Berries might already be dead. If that were so, Big Owl would have returned to fight with Cutter and the Bloods.

Jethro rode into a high meadow and stopped at a spring to water Whistler. The horse needed time to graze, to replenish its strength. After hobbling it, Jethro sat down with his back against a tree and dipped his fingers into a bag of pemmican. The moon, nearly full, shone directly overhead. He stared out across the top of the Little Belts, into the north. The High Woods were outlined agianst the night sky, jagged shadows bathed in white. The big butte at the far east end stood alone.

Jethro tried to rise, to begin his journey again. But he was too tired. He sat back as a winged shadow crossed the ground beside him. He looked up and glimpsed the broad, silent form of an owl as it passed into the darkness. Death had come to say hello.

Had Many Berries and the child been found by Big Owl? No, the owl had come from behind him, from the canyon of the Lost Waters, where death had found Cutter and the Blood warriors. The owl had been flying north, toward the butte. Death would be there when he arrived.

Jethro could not keep his eyes open. He saw the owl again, its eyes like Cutter's just before he died. He saw the faces of the Blood warriors, frozen with fear in death. One more day, just one more, and he would have the Sacred Pipe. One more meeting with death and it would be over. The terrible passing would be complete.

TWENTY-FIVE

JETHRO AWAKENED TO THE SHARP CAWING OF a raven. He rose and looked toward the butte. His dreams had come and gone, leaving him dazed and ignorant of what lay ahead. He felt as if he had been in many places during the darkness, none of which he could remember, all of which he would now have to face consciously.

The raven cawed again, cruising on broad, black wings across the open canyons toward he rising High Woods in the distance. Jethro watched the bird, its wings a pattern of slow motion against the cloudless deep blue of the morning sky. Way out, the raven turned, only a dark speck now, and veered into nothingness toward the large, flat-topped butte.

"It has entered the spirit world," Jethro

whispered to himself. "And now I must follow."

Jethro rode Whistler down through the timber and across the open grasslands toward the High Woods. The large butte rose in the distance—just past the smaller, round butte—at the opposite end of the mountains. The rising sun colored the slopes a striking dark green against the blue-gray columns of rock.

These mountains that he had heard of but never visited, this big butte that his father had talked about so much, called to him now. Had Many Berries reached the top, as she had planned? Many Berries was a survivor, but he wondered how she could yet be alive if Big Owl had reached her. He worried that his arrival on the butte would be too late, that he would find the remains of Many Berries and his child. It made him sick to think about it. He wished that he had not succumbed to his exhaustion, but had pressed on. He realized that he could not ponder this. Only the Powers knew what was to come; he must be satisfied with that part he could control.

Foremost, he must think of the first Sacred Pipe. Many Berries and the child certainly needed him and he was compelled to save them if he could. By lying with Many Berries, he had entwined his life with hers. But Cuts Buffalo and his people were his true life. They needed the security of their medicine pipe. The pipe he now held across his heart, the second Sacred Pipe, had come to him for strength, but the real pipe had to join with the second one to make the Kicked-in-Their-Bellies whole once more.

Jethro crossed a broad, grassy bench, the western entrance to the Judith Basin, allowing the morning to pass through his head like vapor from a dream. The deer and elk that moved into the timber, the antelope that bolted through the tall grass, the birds that flew past—all of them seemed distant, as if from another world. A small herd of buffalo, grazing peacefully just off the trail, seemed to turn together as he passed, staring at him, their heads slightly lifted.

He could hear their song, a rumbling chorus deep in his mind. It seemed to grow louder. But was it from the buffalo? He looked to the sky, where dark clouds rose up across the summit of the mountains. Midday had come and gone, and an afternoon storm was pushing in. Where had the time gone?

He rode on toward the north end of the High Woods. Again he fought the feeling that his journey had been for nothing, that Harlan Cutter had spoken only death words, nothing that was real. Maybe Big Owl had not even been with the Blood war party. Maybe he had left the Bloods when Many Berries had escaped in the cold.

As the storm built over the mountains, the air changed. The tingling feeling of power surged through the air. Here and there tongues of jagged yellow flashed to the ground. The buffalo continued to watch him, and a small herd of elk, standing in single file along a hilltop, raised their noses to the air and trotted down into a deep coulee to wait out the storm.

As he drew ever closer to the large butte, Jethro came to know again that something very difficult awaited him, a confrontation—most certainly with Big Owl—that would test him past any limits he could imagine. He knew it for certain; in the distance he saw a rider come out of the shadows of the High Woods and kick his horse into a dead run toward the big butte. Jethro could not mistake the movement of the pony. It was Flame.

Many Berries stared down the trail at the nearest rider, Big Owl, who was approaching the base of the butte. Farther out, she saw another rider, who had kicked his pony into a run toward the butte. Although that rider was still too far out for her to see him clearly, she knew it could only be Jethro.

Taking a deep breath, Many Berries carried her newborn child the last steps up the trail, to the summit of the large butte. She had spent the night along the waters called Arrow Creek where she had delivered the baby by herself. She had secured the right roots and herbs with which to keep her strength up and ease the birth process, but the climb to the top had completely worn her down.

Nothing but death could have kept her from climbing the butte. She had know that she must come to this place since well before she had met Big Owl or Jethro. She could not be surprised that Big Owl had come to find her here, for she had told him more than once that this butte was special to her.

Even though Big Owl would soon be coming for her, Many Berries felt relief. She had reached the top with her child, a strong and healthy little girl, whom she had named Morning Wind. Now the child was assured of a long and happy life. Many Berries knew that in the very core of her being.

She stopped to nurse the crying infant, looking back for Jethro and Big Owl. Big Owl had disappeared, no doubt urging Flame up toward the top. Jethro could be seen coming ever closer, yet he was so far behind that he would never catch Big Owl before the warrior reached the top.

It would be a while yet before Big Owl arrived, so there was time to contemplate the world from this place of power. Many Berries looked out across the vastness. Twisting ribbons of blue that were creeks flowed through the broad basin below. Black specks that were buffalo dotted the shimmering green, and small white groups of antelope moved among them. Here and there minute movements, which Many Berries could tell were made by wolves, circled the edges of the herds, seeking out their prey.

It was strange to watch the eagles fly out from beneath the top of the butte, their broad wings turning in wide circles below her. She watched as they, along with the slim-winged hawks that shot among the high rocks, searched for prey in the skies and across the sweeping grasslands below.

Many Berries could not remember beholding a more breathtaking view. She turned in a circle, seeing mountain ranges push up in the far distance in all directions, all but the north, where only small blue humps, called the Little Rockies, were visible. Farther out in the northern distance, in the homeland of the Blackfeet, were the Sweetgrass Hills, obscured now by haze. She remembered them from her childhood and wished that she could see them now. But the haze was growing thicker, the sun losing out to the roiling thunderheads coming over the mountains. From the High Woods there came the rumbling sound of a storm, and jagged light began to streak down from the sky.

Singing a song to the Powers, Many Berries held her child to the sky, asking a long and good life for her daughter. She held the infant to the four directions, then up to Father Sky and down to Mother Earth. The blessings complete, she began to cross the butte, searching for a way down its other side.

But she had waited too long. Behind her, just coming over the edge of the butte, Big Owl rode toward her like a madman, yelling and waving his war club.

Many Berries turned to run but could not. Pain shot through her, drawing her down. She came to her feet, Big Owl almost upon her, and took refuge in a group of young pines growing in thickly along one edge of the butte. She pressed into them, holding the baby against her breast. The trees grew too close together to allow a horse into their midst; at least she might have some chance against Big Owl if he had to come after her on foot.

She pushed herself and her child deeper into the close-growing pines, while around them the storm grew stronger. She could hear Big Owl over the buffeting wind; he was yelling at the edge of the pine thicket, hacking at trees with his war club from atop Flame. Finally, he dismounted and began to push his way into the growth.

Many Berries crouched and held the baby close while thunder rolled and Big Owl hacked his way past young trees toward her. She kept moving onward. Many times Big Owl nearly discovered her, but he never stopped yelling and never maintained enough patience to locate her. Then, when he did stop yelling for a moment, he heard the faintest of sounds under the wind, the sound of a baby crying.

Many Berries had been moving around to a position behind Big Owl. Now nearly at the edge of the butte, she stopped when she heard him laughing. Suddenly he was upon her.

"How long did you think you could hide from me?" he shouted, raising his war club.

Many Berries turned her back and cradled the child away from him. She cringed, expecting the blades to slice into her back. Big Owl laughed and lowered the club.

"You will not die first. Give me that baby," he ordered.

Many Berries remained crouched, holding her child. Big Owl was determined that she witness the child's death before he finished her off. He grabbed Many Berries by the hair and pulled her head back, then yanked her to her feet.

"I said, give me that baby!"

Many Berries fought the pain as he pulled and twisted her hair. He dropped his war club to clutch at the baby. Many Berries struggled to hold on, but Big Owl jerked her off balance and pulled the child from her grasp.

"No, please don't hurt my baby," she pleaded. "Do anything you want to me, but let my child live."

Big Owl slammed his backhand into her mouth, sending her reeling to the ground. She was up in an instant, rushing at him. "Give me my child!" she screamed. "Give me back my baby!"

Big Owl placed a foot against Many Berries' stomach and kicked her backward. She lost her balance again and slid over the edge of the butte, grasping for anything she could take hold of. She clutched at a small tree, but the branch snapped and she felt herself tumbling down.

Many Berries rolled over and over and finally came to a stop, her head against a tree. She tried to raise herself, but everything swirled and she fell back. Overcome by nausea, she turned on her side and vomited. She held her head with both hands, trying to quell the intense pain.

Big Owl peered over the edge, laughing. He held the baby upside down by its legs, thinking of throwing the child over after its mother. But he waited. He could see that Many Berries was stirring. She had not been killed.

Big Owl decided that he would go down

and bring her back up. Then he would go through with his execution of the child before her eyes.

He carried the baby out of the trees to lay it down; instead, he stopped short and brought the child up in front of himself as a shield. Jethro had dismounted and had taken the Sacred Pipe from Flame. He had the other pipe also, and now he stood a short distance away holding both pipes across his chest.

"What are you doing?" Big Owl demanded. He clutched the wailing child tighter and stepped forward. "You can't take that pipe from me."

"Put the baby down," Jethro ordered.

The wind grew stronger and the clouds churned lower over the butte. Rain splattered heavily as Jethro shouted once again, "Put the child down, Big Owl."

"You will not stop what I must do!" Big Owl yelled. He stepped back.

Jethro came forward. "You cannot have the child," he said.

"Stay away from me!" Big Owl warned. "I will throw this child over the edge, as I did Many Berries. You stay away from me!"

Big Owl began to back into the trees, clutching the crying baby in one arm and pushing tree limbs aside with the other. Jethro followed him, holding the two Sacred Pipes, working his way through the thicket. He was torn between rushing ahead at Big Owl and holding back for fear of the child's safety. He could not act impulsively. He had to save the child.

Jethro pushed through another tangle of young

trees and stopped. He was at the edge of the butte. Big Owl had already laid the child down on a rock and now stood over it.

"This will be better than throwing the child over the edge," he told Jethro, laughing. "Now I will finish what I have begun." He raised his war club to strike.

"Hail to Big Owl, hail the mighty warrior!" Jethro shouted. He set down the two pipes and backed away. "Those are for you."

Big Owl stared at Jethro, the wind whipping his hair.

"You have great honor, Big Owl," Jethro continued. "You have killed a woman and now will kill a child. You have great honor, Big Owl, great honor indeed. You may take the pipes, both of them."

Big Owl continued to stare at Jethro. "I will take the pipes," he said. "But first I will kill what is yours. This child is yours. Many Berries is yours. I will destroy anything that belongs to you. Then I will destroy you."

"You are wrong, Big Owl," Jethro corrected him. "I own nothing. Many Berries and the child belong to themselves, not to me. Many Berries left you because you tried to own her. You cannot really own anything." He pointed past the thicket of trees to Flame. "Not even that horse you took belonged to me. The Powers chose to allow me use of the horse for a time. Then you had use of the horse. Everything belongs to the Powers, can't you see that?"

Just to the west of the butte, an odd-colored cloud descended from the layers of thunderheads. The center of the cloud was spinning.

"When I kill this child and you, then I will again have use of the horse," Big Owl said. "It will be *mine* once again, as it should be."

Big Owl, in his attempt to express his wrath, had lowered the war club. He clenched the weapon tightly, shaking it to emphasize his words. "My powers are greater than yours!" he yelled. "How can you hope to stand up to me?"

"I do not claim to have powers of my own," Jethro told him. "I am able to use only the strength the Powers choose to give me. And I have faith that those powers are greater than anything you yourself could ever possess."

The swirling cloud settled over the top of the butte. The wind began to sweep across them, blowing Big Owl's hair into his face. When he reached with his free hand to clear his view, Jethro lunged forward, grabbing the warrior and knocking the war club free. The two rolled and punched and gouged, while the wind suddenly calmed and a long black funnel descended into the trees just beside them.

Jethro felt himself being lifted and thrown as if he were a doll; he landed on his back in the middle of the open. His breath gone, he could only stare upward, his mind dazed as if in a dream. His ears filled with a heavy drone, the horrible sound he had come to know so well a full four seasons past. The sky was gone, obliterated by swirling grass and rocks, pieces of trees whirling just over him, as the Sacred Pipe had whirled overhead in his dream.

When his breath finally returned, he closed his eyes and screamed. When he opened his eyes, the sky was clear.

Jethro pushed himself to a sitting position. His back ached, as did his left knee, the knee that had not been injured previously by the big spirit. Thunder continued to roll in the distance. The odd cloud had risen back up into the storm, pressing out from the butte and over the badlands to the north.

Jethro came to his feet, teetered, and gained his balance. He limped toward the trees. Many of them were gone, torn and uprooted by the giant spirit. He stumbled through the debris left by the funnel, pushing aside broken limbs and shattered pieces of trunk to reach the edge of the butte. There was no sign of the child, nor any sign of Big Owl's war club, nor of either of the Sacred Pipes. Jethro raised his head to the sky and yelled. His voice died in the wind. He yelled again, harder this time, releasing his frustration and anger.

Then, just to his left, he heard moaning and garbled words. He turned to see Big Owl stumbling about aimlessly. His eyes glazed with pain and shock, Big Owl stopped in front of Jethro. The war club had slammed through his upper right arm, the three blades having pierced through flesh and bone, pinning the arm to his side. His free hand grasped a small, uprooted pine that protruded from his stomach and his back. Jethro knew that unexplainable things took place when huge dark spirits descended from the sky, but he could not believe that a soft little pine tree could have been twisted through the body of a man.

"Help me," Big Owl managed. "Get the tree out . . . of me."

Jethro knew better than to touch either the tree or the war club. "It is the work of the Powers," he told Big Owl. "It is not for me to interfere."

Big Owl stumbled sideways. He caught himself against a tree before falling and turned to the edge of the butte. Jethro started to reach out, to stop him, but Big Owl had already lunged forward and over the top. Although he did not make a sound as he fell, Jethro knew when he landed by the sharp sound of snapping tree limbs below.

Jethro looked over the edge. Big Owl's body hung lifeless, halfway up in the branches of a large pine. He lay on his back, his head hanging backward over a limb, his arms crossed over his chest above the small tree that had impaled him. Except for his lolling head, he rested as if placed there by relatives so he might cross over.

Jethro stepped back from the edge. He felt a hand on his shoulder and turned to see Many Berries, her faced caked with blood, her eyes dulled with pain.

"Many Berries! Big Owl told me that he had killed you!"

"Where is my baby?"

"I don't know. What happened to you?"

"Big Owl kicked me over the edge. I hit

403

my head on a tree." She began to weep, her tears mixing with the blood smeared on her face. "I have to find my baby," she wailed. "I have to."

Jethro took her by the hand and they searched the torn tree thicket. The storm had nearly passed; the rain had quit, and the wind had calmed. While Many Berries watched, her tears flowing, Jethro turned over pieces of broken trees and moved dislodged rocks. But there was no sign of the baby.

"She can't be lost," Many Berries sobbed. "She can't be."

"Listen," Jethro said. "Do you hear that?"

From the opposite side of the butte came the unmistakable sound of a baby crying.

They hurried to a large rock at the north edge of the butte, overlooking a sea of badlands below. Naked, immersed in sunshine, Morning Wind lay kicking and crying. Crossed over her tiny chest were the two Sacred Pipes, their junction directly above her heart. She continued to cry out and kick as Jethro lifted the two pipes. Many Berries pulled the baby to her breast, and the child began to nurse.

"You have saved us, Jethro," Many Berries said. "For this, I thank you with all my heart. Go now and live your life in peace. Cuts Buffalo and your people await you."

"What of your injuries?" Jethro asked.

Many Berries turned and looked toward the north. She rocked her baby in her arms while the child nursed. She turned back, and she was smiling.

"I have my child, and the wind is silent," Many Berries said. "I no longer have any problems. When the sun comes again, I will journey into the lands of my ancestors. I know I will find a new life there."

"I wish you good luck," Jethro said. "I will leave the horse, Whistler, for you to ride."

He held out his hand, palm upward. Many Berries placed her hand atop his and squeezed. "I will miss you, Jethro. May your life be happy and safe."

Jethro turned, holding the two pipes across his heart. He walked over to where Flame grazed in the fresh, wet grass. He mounted and took a deep breath; it felt good to be on his own horse again. As he rode across the butte to the trail that led down, he again sang the song he had learned in his dream:

> I see the sky and feel the wind,
> I hear the Sun tell me to be brave.
> Terrible clouds gather, but must part
> when they hear my footsteps, coming
> down from the flat-topped mountain.
> I will find the Sacred Pipe and carry it
> across my heart. I will carry it always,
> and make a pathway for my people.

Before starting down, Jethro turned to wave for the last time to Many Berries. But she was gone. Although he did not see her on top of the butte, he knew that she was there, somewhere. And he knew, too, that she would raise their child well.

Jethro turned again and started Flame down the side of the butte. He wanted to hurry back to the village, to be there when Cuts Buffalo gave birth to their child. He wanted to share in the joy of all when he held up the two Sacred Pipes for them to see. He could not wait to dance all night long to the sounds of drums and singing. His ears longed for the laughter and gaiety of his people. They were whole once again, chosen to live with the sun beside the eternal waters of the river.

THE DRAGON REBORN

Sequel to *The Great Hunt*

Book Three of The Wheel of Time

by

Robert Jordan

Praise for *Eye of the World*

"A powerful vision of good and evil...fascinating people moving through a rich and interesting world."   —Orson Scott Card

"Richly detailed...fully realized, complex adventure."
—*Library Journal*

"A combination of Robin Hood and Stephen King that is hard to resist...Jordan makes the reader care about these characters as though they were old friends."   —*Milwaukee Sentinel*

Praise for *The Great Hunt*

"Jordan can spin as rich a world and as event-filled a tale as [Tolkien]...will not be easy to put down."   —*ALA Booklist*

"Worth re-reading a time or two."   —*Locus*

"This is good stuff...Splendidly characterized and cleverly plotted...The Great Hunt is a good book which will always be a good book. I shall certainly [line up] for the third volume."
—*Interzone*

The Dragon Reborn

coming in hardcover in August, 1991

BESTSELLERS
FROM TOR

☐☐	50570-0	ALL ABOUT WOMEN Andrew M. Greeley	$4.95 Canada $5.95
☐☐	58341-8 58342-6	ANGEL FIRE Andrew M. Greeley	$4.95 Canada $5.95
☐☐	52725-9 52726-7	BLACK WIND F. Paul Wilson	$4.95 Canada $5.95
☐☐	51392-4	LONG RIDE HOME W. Michael Gear	$4.95 Canada $5.95
☐☐	50350-3	OKTOBER Stephen Gallagher	$4.95 Canada $5.95
☐☐	50857-2	THE RANSOM OF BLACK STEALTH One Dean Ing	$5.95 Canada $6.95
☐☐	50088-1	SAND IN THE WIND Kathleen O'Neal Gear	$4.50 Canada $5.50
☐☐	51878-0	SANDMAN Linda Crockett	$4.95 Canada $5.95
☐☐	50214-0 50215-9	THE SCHOLARS OF NIGHT John M. Ford	$4.95 Canada $5.95
☐☐	51826-8	TENDER PREY Julia Grice	$4.95 Canada $5.95
☐☐	52188-4	TIME AND CHANCE Alan Brennert	$4.95 Canada $5.95

Buy them at your local bookstore or use this handy coupon:
Clip and mail this page with your order.

Publishers Book and Audio Mailing Service
P.O. Box 120159, Staten Island, NY 10312-0004

Please send me the book(s) I have checked above. I am enclosing $ _____
(please add $1.25 for the first book, and $.25 for each additional book to cover postage and handling.
Send check or money order only—no CODs).

Name _____
Address _____
City _____ State/Zip _____
Please allow six weeks for delivery. Prices subject to change without notice.

WESTERN ADVENTURE
FROM TOR

☐	58459-7	THE BAREFOOT BRIGADE	$4.50
☐	58460-0	*Douglas Jones*	Canada $5.50
☐	58150-4	BETWEEN THE WORLDS (Snowblind Moon Part I)	$3.95
☐	58151-2	*John Byrne Cooke*	Canada $4.95
☐	58991-2	THE CAPTIVES	$4.50
☐	58992-0	*Don Wright*	Canada $5.50
☐	58548-8	CONFLICT OF INTEREST	$3.95
☐		*Donald McRae*	Canada $4.95
☐	58457-0	ELKHORN TAVERN	$4.50
☐	58458-9	*Douglas Jones*	Canada $5.50
☐	58453-8	GONE THE DREAMS AND DANCING	$3.95
☐	58454-6	*Douglas Jones*	Canada $4.95
☐	58154-7	HOOP OF THE NATION (Snowblind Moon Part III)	$3.95
☐	58155-5	*John Byrne Cooke*	Canada $4.95
☐	58152-0	THE PIPE CARRIERS (Snowblind Moon Part II)	$3.95
☐	58153-9	*John Byrne Cooke*	Canada $4.95
☐	58455-4	ROMAN	$4.95
☐	58456-2	*Douglas Jones*	Canada $5.95
☐	58463-5	WEEDY ROUGH	$4.95
☐	58464-3	*Douglas Jones*	Canada $5.95
☐	58989-0	WOODSMAN	$3.95
☐	58990-4	*Don Wright*	Canada $4.95

Buy them at your local bookstore or use this handy coupon:
Clip and mail this page with your order.

Publishers Book and Audio Mailing Service
P.O. Box 120159, Staten Island, NY 10312-0004

Please send me the book(s) I have checked above. I am enclosing $ _____
(please add $1.25 for the first book, and $.25 for each additional book to cover postage and handling.
Send check or money order only—no CODs).

Name _____
Address _____
City _____ State/Zip _____
Please allow six weeks for delivery. Prices subject to change without notice.